SONS OF ZADOK

**CALUMET
EDITIONS**

SECOND EDITION DECEMBER 2022

ISBN – 978-1-960250-24-7
10 9 8 7 6 5 4 3 2

Cover art and book design by Gary Lindberg

Author's Note

Fact Vs/.Fiction

I owe a considerable debt of gratitude to my longsuffering wife, Gloria, who now claims to recognize me only by the back of my head while I'm seated at the computer working on my novels; and my good friend Eldon Kimball, who provided not only excellent proofreading assistance but was never afraid to express his opinion about problems he saw in my story, opinions that were inevitably right.

Also, many of the intriguing facts and concepts in this story came from other sources that I encountered during my research, so I must acknowledge them here. Helping shape this story were the ideas, theories, calculations, and in some cases anecdotes written or formulated by the following authors, to whom I am deeply indebted: Christopher Knight and Robert Lomas; David Flynn; Chris H. Hardy; Joseph P. Farrell and Scott D. de Hart; Andrew Collins; David Cowan and Chris Arnold. And, of course, the Old Testament patriarch Enoch.

Most importantly, though, I also must acknowledge readers of *The Shekinah Legacy*, the first book in the *Charlotte Ansari Thriller* series. Without my readers, there would be no series. The original book was intended to be a one-off novel. No sequel was planned. But readers insisted on getting more, and after *Legacy* became a bestseller on Amazon, I agreed. Now I don't know how to stop the unfolding story, so there will probably be more Charlotte Ansari thrillers in the future.

Acknowledgements

I owe a considerable debt of gratitude to my longsuffering wife, Gloria, who now claims to recognize me only by the back of my head while I'm seated at the computer working on my novels; and my good friend Eldon Kimball, who provided not only excellent proofreading assistance but was never afraid to express his opinion about problems he saw in my story, opinions that were inevitably right.

Also, many of the intriguing facts and concepts in this story came from other sources that I encountered during my research, so I must acknowledge them here. Helping shape this story were the ideas, theories, calculations, and in some cases anecdotes written or formulated by the following authors, to whom I am deeply indebted: Christopher Knight and Robert Lomas; David Flynn; Chris H. Hardy; Joseph P. Farrell and Scott D. de Hart; Andrew Collins; David Cowan and Chris Arnold. And, of course, the Old Testament patriarch Enoch.

Most importantly, though, I also must acknowledge readers of *The Shekinah Legacy*, the first book in the *Charlotte Ansari Thriller* series. Without my readers, there would be no series. The original book was intended to be a one-off novel. No sequel was planned. But readers insisted on getting more, and after *Legacy* became a bestseller on Amazon, I agreed. Now I don't know how to stop the unfolding story, so there will probably be more Charlotte Ansari thrillers in the future.

Also by Gary Lindberg

FICTION

Sons of Zadok
Deeper and Deeper
Ollie's Cloud

NONFICTION

The Power of Positive Handwriting
Letters from Elvis
Brando On Elvis
The Roots of Elvis

SONS OF ZADOK

GARY LINDBERG

**CALUMET
EDITIONS**
Minneapolis

Prologue

Masada, 73 C.E.

Sarah's head throbs with the incessant beating of the ram on the fortress walls. The blood-chilling shouts and cries from soldiers on the assault ramp frighten and enrage her. These twenty acres of scorched earth atop Masada, now held by the last survivors of the Jewish revolt, is now the only piece of land in all of Judea not under Roman control.

The besieged *Sicarii* are the self-appointed defenders of Judaism. For years they have terrorized the brutal leaders of Rome by covertly assassinating them with a small curved dagger called a *sica*.

Looking back at how these rebels arrived at such a desperate situation, Sarah blames it on the decision to become an organized fighting force—an undefeatable Army of God. But the skilled assassins, accustomed to working alone, never had any real chance of matching centuries of Roman military experience and ingenuity. The Sicarii have been ground down to a few hundred men who finally fled with their families to an isolated desert hill they believe is the perfect sanctuary.

Masada's sheer cliffs defy ascent, rising from the floor of the Judean desert to a flat diamond-shaped mesa 1,500 feet above. A tortuous trail on the eastern side leads to a sumptuous palace compound built by Herod the Great, but is far too steep and narrow for a large-scale assault. At the top, casement walls twenty feet high and twelve feet deep surround the entire mesa.

Within these walls Sarah stands on the battlement of one of the compound's thirty-eight towers. The Dead Sea shimmers in the distance, and columns of smoke from the barricades smudge the brilliant azure sky, but Sarah's gaze is drawn to the Roman camps and fortifications below. A small city has been built around the base of Masada by the Roman Tenth Fretensis Legion. A busy supply road snakes through the desert, disappearing into heat vapors at the horizon. Men scurry like ants below, each busy with the work of preparing a slaughter. Sarah can feel Roman frustration rising like thermals.

The Sicarii, she knows, had seriously underestimated Flavius Silva, the Roman field commander. Over many months, the Roman army under his leadership has moved thousands of tons of earth and stone to construct a monumental ramp that abuts the casement wall on the western approach. Three weeks ago, using formidable siege weapons, the Romans began raking the stronghold's walls with heavy rocks and catapult fire while Roman legionnaires, shielded by a giant iron-plated tower, relentlessly barraged Sicarii fighters with javelins and stones.

This very afternoon Silva had brought up a massive battering ram to administer the coup de grâce, but the Sicarii had cleverly countered by buttressing the casement wall with heavy timbers to absorb the bone-rattling blows. Then, just hours ago, Roman troops had flung torches over the wall, setting ablaze the reinforcing timbers. When these supports collapse, the ram will easily break through the wall and the massacre will begin.

Eleazar ben Ya'ir, Sarah's brother and the Sicarii commander, stands next to her on the tower. "I'm going down to be with the men," he says. "The Romans will be upon us soon. You should be with the women and children."

"I'm frightened. What if they capture us—the women—and instead of killing us …" She looks at her feet, unable to say the word *rape*.

He takes her hand and places in it his precious sica. "Then use this."

Sarah looks up, even more terrified. "Suicide? Eleazar, God will not forgive such a thing!"

"I meant that you should use it on the others."

He sadly kisses her forehead and runs down the stairs.

She takes one last look at the smoke ascending toward heaven like the smoke of a sacrifice and notices something peculiar. The smoke has changed direction. She can feel the wind at her back, stronger than before. Looking down she sees the blazing timbers starting to crumble, and yet the flames and cinders are now blowing back at the Romans, threatening their siege weapons.

The ram's relentless cadence suddenly stops and the Romans grow silent. Teams of legionnaires begin moving back to protect their wooden armaments as a horn blast calls the rest of them back to camp.

Sarah can hear a Sicarii warrior shouting at Eleazar. "Has God delivered us?"

"They will come for us in the morning!" Eleazar shouts back.

Before daybreak, Eleazar awakens everyone, calling them to the fallen timbers, an ironic symbol of their defeated cause. Some of the children are shivering in the morning's first breath. Mothers wrap them in shawls.

Nearly a thousand men, women and children gather near Eleazar as he delivers a message more chilling than the morning air. Very soon, he promises, the enemy will attack with malice in their hearts and swords in their hands.

"They will come to murder, rape, and enslave," he says. "But we can prevent these atrocities."

The crowd presses in around him, wondering what miracle he has conjured.

"Let our wives die before they are abused," he says, "and our children before they have tasted of slavery. And after we have slain our families, let us men bestow that glorious benefit upon one another."

Stunned silence greets him. This is no miracle! Some of the women and children begin to shiver again, though not from the cold. But then heads start nodding. As the full meaning of this gruesome alternative becomes apparent, many tremble and whimper, but only one speaks.

"Eleazar, is this God's will for us?"

The voice is Eleazar's best friend, Matthias, whose mother and daughter are tucked into his broad reach.

Eleazar has heard no voice from God, received no tablets of stone, yet he is convinced of the rightness of this choice. Over the previous dark hours he has agonized over it. Perhaps it is blasphemy to put his words into God's mouth, but it can be persuasive.

"It is God's will," he says.

There is a collective sigh, the unburdening of doubt. Eleazar instructs them to go and be together as families for a few more precious minutes before the final acts of mercy.

Eleazar reaches out for his sister's hand and she nods submissively, expecting to accompany him to the place of her slaying. But he says to her, "We must have some who survive to tell our story."

Sarah looks at her brother grimly. "I will not do what the others cannot!"

"You have a final act to perform," Eleazar explains. "Hear me out. Soon the men will cast lots to select ten who will sacrifice the others. Then one of those will slay the rest. But that last man must not be required to kill himself."

"I see," Sarah says. "So that is my lot? To kill the last man?"

"Listen to me, Sarah, there is more. Your cousin Ruth and her five children are descendants of Judas of Galilee and must be spared. Find them now, and hide them in the large cistern, then return here. Will you do these things?"

Sarah wants only to end her anguish, not prolong it.

"Please, Eleazar, take your knife and…" She raises his hand to her chest, showing where his blade should penetrate.

"I beg you, Sarah! It cannot be God's will that our cause ends here. Now go, gather the six, and trust in God."

✦ ✦ ✦

In the bathhouse where Matthias has made camp, he takes the hands of his mother and eight-year-old daughter, weeping.

"I cannot do this," he confesses. "We must find another way."

His mother drops to her knees and prayerfully lowers her head. To face him now would be to show her fear. His daughter Esther mimics the elderly woman, lowering herself into a prayerful posture.

"Do it quickly, father, so we don't suffer." Esther's thin, quivering voice reaches out to Matthias.

Do it quickly. It is the will of God.

He grasps the sica, steps forward to his daughter and puts his left hand on the back of her neck.

"I love you so," he whispers, then slips the blade between two ribs in the practiced motion of a Sicarii assassin. He listens for Esther's gentle sigh as the blade pushes in. It is nearly painless, he has been told, just the sensation of an icy finger entering the chest, and then a great succumbing to the black waters of sleep.

Matthias's pain is far more intense as he lowers his daughter's body gently to the floor and steps to his mother who is trembling, she who gave him life and now huddles before him as a sheep at the sacrifice.

✦ ✦ ✦

The horizon is blood red as the sun begins to show itself to Eleazar. For a short time there is only silence, interrupted occasionally by sobs and muffled screams.

After thirty minutes Eleazar calls the men back to the fallen timbers where they cast lots to identify ten executioners. Those not chosen form ten columns of about forty warriors, each column facing Eleazar.

In this orderly slaughterhouse, the chosen ten start at the rear and solemnly work their way forward, precisely inserting the curved blade as Sicarii knifecraft dictates. The men fall like dominos, lifelessly crumpling into the waiting arms of their executioners who lower them sadly, tenderly onto the bodies behind. Three men collapse before receiving the knife but are slain in turn. It takes twenty minutes. At last four hundred Sicarii warriors lie in a field of death.

Nine of the living, with Eleazar at the front, form themselves into a single column.

"Sarah!" Eleazar calls.

She appears now from a shadow, horrified by the carnage.

"Prepare yourself, Sarah. It is almost time."

Matthias, the lone executioner, now walks to the rear of the last column. It has become a sacred ritual, a sacrament, this repetitive thrusting of the sica into fellow warriors. It is how Matthias can bear this unbearable duty. When he comes finally to the last of the line, Eleazar, he whispers, "I cannot do this, my friend."

"You must—quickly."

Matthias steps in front of Eleazar, holding out his sica. "Please," he begs, "I have killed my mother, my daughter, fifty of my friends. Is that not enough for God?"

Eleazar touches the man's shoulder and nods. "Yes, it is enough."

Taking the dagger, he turns Matthias around and embraces him. With his right hand, he inserts the sharp blade.

Matthias twitches, as if bitten by an insect, then smiles—*it is not so bad, just very cold*. He is relieved that his mother and daughter had suffered so little.

Eleazar lowers his friend to the ground and turns to Sarah. He holds out the sica, but she has one.

Sarah slowly approaches her brother and he kisses her, then turns, submitting himself to the blade. Placing her flat palm lovingly on his back, she feels the heat of fear, the muscles quaking, his breath quickening.

"When it is finished, join Ruth and the children," Eleazar says.

She nods, though he can't see her. Holding the sica at her chest, point forward, she leans toward her brother, bringing them closer together, pushing the blade in as gently as she can.

The blade nicks a rib.

And that is when Sarah screams, as if the morning's blood and horror and the world's misery had been heaped upon her all at once.

Eleazar collapses and she falls onto his body, the full realization of what she has done suddenly, terrifying clear.

It is finished.

In camp, the legionnaires are confused but joyous. Not a Roman was lost in this great victory! Thinking it a mass suicide, some say it proved the cowardice of the Sicarii. Others say nothing, haunted by a grim spectacle the likes of which had never been witnessed before…

The silent, lifeless army of Sicarii had instantly subdued the bloodlust of the Roman attack force. When two women and five children had been discovered alive in a cistern, no legionnaire could muster the will to kill or abuse them.

On the third day after her capture, Sarah is escorted to a richly appointed tent where she is instructed to await a visitor. Moments later an elderly man with a bejeweled walking stick and stately attire throws back the entrance drape and enters, motioning for Sarah to be seated on a silk cushion.

"Your name is Sarah, I understand."

She nods.

"Your brother was Eleazar, the commander?"

She is not sure she should confirm this.

"Come now," the man says. "You can be honest with me. I am not a Roman. I am something else entirely. Eleazar was your brother?"

"Yes."

"And the other captives are, I would hope, descendants of Judas of Galilee?"

She nods slowly, wondering how this man could know.

"What I am about to tell you, Sarah, you must remember forever. And you must pass it down to the next generation, and ensure that it passes down to the one following, and so on, until there are no more generations. Do you understand?"

"I think so."

"You must *absolutely* understand, Sarah. Do you?"

"Yes."

"Then listen carefully. I will make sure that you and the other six are not harmed. Eventually you will be freed, but your responsibilities will just then be starting. It is your duty to see that Sicarii knowledge and skills are not forgotten. Is that clear?"

"Does that mean you want me to raise the children as Sicarii?"

"Yes. Train them in the Sicarii crafts. And educate them in the ways of God according to the Book of Enoch and Judas of Galilee. There is a purpose for the Sicarii, you see—one that your brother had forgotten, or perhaps had set aside for goals that were petty by comparison. Now here is the important part."

He sits beside her now, leans closer so that he can speak more quietly.

"The Sicarii have a most important role to play in the ultimate outcome of this world. You will become the invisible army and protectors of a council of wise men who shall also remain invisible, even to you, but to whom you must pledge absolute obedience and loyalty. These men, whom I represent, have assumed the most holy responsibility of bringing about the Divine plan."

"But I thought that's what we Sicarii were trying to do."

"You are a small but pivotal part of a great plan that began over three thousand years ago. For this plan to succeed will take even more time. Perhaps thousands of years. If the Sicarii fail to do their part, the plan will suffer a terrible setback. We are all God's agents, you see. But you are the enforcers, helping us to clear the way, shape events, and separate the wheat from the chaff."

"You prize our skill in assassination."

"Of course. You are the tip of God's spear. In this great plan, Sarah, you are the first woman. You are Eve. And among the five children you saved is an infant boy, a direct descendant who was born in the year of the Shekinah, the light and glory of God. This child will become the first Divine Light, the male leader of the Sicarii, and from his line will come the re-unification of the forces necessary for achieving our goals."

"When will this happen?"

"This *coming together*? According to the stars, almost two thousand years from now."

"That's a very long time."

"We are patient. You will see that there is much to do. Over the years you will hear from us, and you must unquestioningly do as we ask. But you must always stay invisible as the wind, which is known only by its actions."

The man rises and heads for the entrance.

"Wait," Sarah says. "What if I say *no*?"

The man smiles. "Then don't tell me. Tell God."

And he is gone.

Chapter 1

Santa Barbara, 2012 C.E.

In the mirror he sees the reflection of a man not yet thirty fastening a stiffly starched Roman collar to his black clerical shirt. The man's face is flushed from exertion, or guilt, or both. His fingers, though well-practiced in this routine, fumble with the metal studs until a woman's slender fingers replace them and delicately, lovingly, complete the fastening.

A woman's voice like wind-chimes softly rings out: "Must I go?"

His eyes make contact with the man in the mirror and suddenly a shiver of recognition overtakes him. He is looking at himself. And then he turns to see the woman—no, just a girl, maybe fourteen—closing her eyes, then nuzzling his neck and purring with contentment.

"Just a few more minutes, please." Wind chimes again.

He cannot look her in the eye, can't utter a word. *Lord Jesus, I am sorry for my sins,* he silently prays, *I renounce Satan and all his works…*

His arms are reaching out now, his hands holding the girl's shoulders, moving her away, turning her toward the closed sacristy door.

"All right, Father." The music in her voice is gone.

The girl is so beautiful, so precious, that he wants to pull her back. With a fierce determination he lets her go. As she opens the door to the sanctuary, he finally speaks.

"Mandy."

She turns hopefully, but the sweetness of her child's face unleashes in him a surge of guilt and he turns his back.

The sound of a door opening and closing. A pathetic, strangled whimper. And then deep sobs like the wailing of the damned.

In the mirror, he sees the reflection of a man who has lost his soul.

✦ ✦ ✦

"Tommy!" Hands shake the convulsing body of Thompson Walker who bolts upright in bed, blinking back tears."

The woman next to him asks, "Mandy again?"

He looks around the room and gathers his wits. "She haunts me. It's my penance."

Thompson stumbles out of bed and staggers into the hotel bathroom. In the mirror he sees the sagging face of a 78-year-old man with patches of white hair sprouting like weeds and eyes red with grief. He turns away in disgust and sees through the open doorway a woman in bed. She reclines on one elbow and stares back at him.

"I'm sorry, Miriam."

"It's all right, Tommy. It's time to get up anyway."

Miriam is the woman he loves—has *always* loved. She's his wife of forty-four years, though only a few of them had been spent together before the day that she had vanished. Not really vanished, just gone away to do God's work, as she explained to him thirty years later. "The mission," she called it.

A cell phone chirps and Miriam—still a fit, beautiful woman at sixty-six—rolls over to fetch it from the night stand. Watching the supple movements of her body gives Thompson enormous pleasure. As she turns back, phone to ear, Miriam sees Thompson's admiring stare and self-consciously waves him off.

He showers and shaves, then walks to the deck overlooking the Pacific Ocean. He loves Santa Barbara and the calmness of the sea. The Mandy nightmare is only a shadow now.

Breakfast arrives and Miriam switches on the TV before sitting down with Thompson for a breakfast of poached eggs, fruit, and tea. She gently pats his hand and smiles at him as CCN—Cambridge Cable News—opens its morning *State of the World* program with a special report on developments in Iran by Senior International Correspondent Charlotte Ansari.

Thompson watches the reporter's commanding performance in detailing yet another assassination of an Iranian nuclear scientist. Her signature long black hair cascades over her shoulders.

"She's wonderful isn't she, our daughter?"

"Always is," Thompson agrees.

"She still won't talk to you?"

"Not since she left me stranded on a road in Delhi five years ago."

"It was all *my* fault, of course. She wouldn't talk to you for thirty years because she thought you were responsible for my sudden disappearance. And then, when she learned you weren't at fault, she blamed you for her son leaving. But there was nothing you could do about that, Tommy."

"Not if I ever wanted to see you again."

"You've always paid the price for others."

"But I still haven't paid the price for myself." The specter of Mandy whisks in and out of his mind.

"I have to leave in an hour, Tommy. Let's leave that poor girl behind."

A sadness overtakes him. He hates what Miriam has become, but when they are together he can forget all that. They can be husband and wife again. For one month every year he has Miriam to himself. That was the bargain he had struck for helping her organization half-a-decade ago. One month out of every twelve he can be a married man again. Better than nothing, he has always told himself. For the past four years, each of those designated months has been perfect, at least in his memory, until the final day.

Today is the separation day of year number five, and he is facing the inevitability that he will be alone for the next eleven months. No wife, no daughter, no grandson. Just alone with his thoughts.

And his sins.

Thompson and Miriam fill their awkward final minutes with talk about trivialities. Thompson knows not to ask about his grandson, Greg, or his wife's role in the Iranian assassination. He has learned there is no point trying to renegotiate the spare terms of his cohabitation agreement with Miriam.

God, how he hates the last day of these annual visits.

She approaches Thompson, wraps her arms around him, and nearly suffocates him with a kiss. "I do love you, Tommy," she says.

"I know."

✦ ✦ ✦

A man seated in the hotel lobby looks up slowly at Miriam, carrying only a purse and a small carry-on bag to the front desk. Miriam is his target. The man has studied this spry woman. He knows that she travels light, except for some personal items. She buys what she needs at each destination and leaves the purchased articles behind, allowing her to pack and leave in a hurry. She also will take public transportation when possible; this makes her conveyance less predictable and harder to monitor.

The man's eyes are partially shaded by the bill of a Greek fisherman's cap and his slouching posture emphasizes a rotund belly that appears to pin him like a paperweight to the sofa. He scratches a bushy gray beard and begins to surreptitiously scan the lobby. Only five others are present, including the front desk clerk and concierge. None appears to have any interest in Miriam, who is now handing over cash to the clerk. Through the hotel's open entrance, the man watches another guest approach a waiting cab only to be steered into a different vehicle.

Miriam's slender figure belies her age. The man in the Greek cap, who could be in his late fifties, could easily mistake her for a much younger woman–younger even than him.

But he knows the truth about Miriam. He knows that she is the matriarch of one of the most feared organizations in the world, one with a history two thousand years old. That despite her gracious and charming demeanor with the hotel clerk, she can be cold and ruthless. That she and her eighteen-year-old grandson determine the life and death of many people of power throughout the world. And that this attractive woman, who is known to her inner circle as Eve, is perhaps the most *wanted* woman in the world. Wanted by intelligence agencies, terrorist organizations, black ops specialists, drug and human traffickers, and weapons dealers. They all want her either on their side… or dead.

And here she is, right in front of him. Smiling at the desk clerk. Fearlessly standing with her back to the hotel entrance.

Eve turns and strides confidently towards the entrance. The man in the Greek cap rocks forward, a motion that awkwardly bunches up his protruding gut even more. Eventually he rises, casually stomps a foot to urge a trouser leg to fall into place, and then follows Miriam out of the hotel.

A lone cab driver standing near the door asks "Where to?" then tilts back his Dodgers baseball cap to air out his scalp.

"Airport."

The driver, who appears in his mid-thirties, opens the rear door for his passenger and slowly walks around to the driver's seat. Miriam climbs into the back with her carry-on. Before she can close the door, the man in the Greek cap leans in and addresses her: "Excuse me, I'm heading to the airport too. Would you mind?"

With a stern look Miriam says, "We split the fare then." She starts to slide over, making room.

"Sorry sir," the cabbie interjects. "Shared rides in the limos only." He gestures to an airport van a few meters ahead. "If you wouldn't mind…" The van driver is just leaving the vehicle to enter the hotel, probably for coffee or a rest room break. The van won't be leaving for a few minutes.

Exasperated, the rotund man slams the door.

As the cabbie releases the parking brake and reaches for the shifter, the front passenger door suddenly opens and the man in the Greek cap slides in beside him.

Startled, the cabbie nervously stammers something unintelligible, but the new passenger interrupts. "I think you probably didn't hear me, son. I'm in a hurry, so I'll be going to the airport in your vehicle here. Drive carefully now."

The cabbie's eyes narrow. His right arm drops. His hand lunges into a paper lunch bag on the seat. But the passenger's left hand is quicker, grabbing the cabbie's wrist and pinning it. The cabbie tries an awkward left-handed swipe at the passenger's face, but his fist is deflected by the chubby man's right arm, which then hammers a vicious blow to the driver's nose. Blood spatters a Rorschach inkblot on the paper bag, which rips open during the skirmish exposing a semi-automatic pistol.

The passenger picks up the gun. "My oh my," he says, stretching out the words to emphasize fake incredulity. "Beretta Model 70, favorite of Mossad. And I was thinking maybe you were an independent contractor."

The passenger turns to view Miriam in the backseat. The woman is holding the barrel of a pistol against the back of the driver's seat as a precaution.

"What—you didn't trust me to handle it?" the passenger asks.

She holds the gun steady. "These guys certainly hold a grudge."

"You killed our chief." The Mossad agent's words are muffled by a bloody shirtsleeve he is using to stanch the flow of blood from his nose. "What do you expect?"

"That was five years ago!" The passenger notices a small blood spatter on his trouser leg. "Will you look at this? Ruined." He looks up and catches the Mossad agent stealing a glance in the side-view mirror as if expecting the cavalry to arrive.

Of course! A Mossad agent certainly would have back-up for a mission designed to abduct the head of a worldwide organization of assassins.

The passenger adjusts the rearview mirror to see behind the taxi.

"So tell me," the passenger says to the driver, "what's your name?"

"Moses."

The passenger doesn't know if this is a joke or not. "I'm Gideon," he says, "the one who killed your chief. He double-crossed us, had it coming. I'm sorry… I actually liked him. But five years ago!"

A blue Nissan with two men in the front seat pulls up behind the taxi. Both men remain motionless. Gideon assumes these are Mossad agents investigating why the taxi hasn't departed.

"Eve, I have a plan." He uses Miriam's title when addressing her.

She leans forward.

A few seconds later, Gideon climbs out of the cab yelling angrily at the driver. The scene is staged for the agents in the blue van, giving Gideon the excuse of a disagreement to abandon the taxi. He trudges over to the airport van parked about two spaces ahead and gets into the front passenger seat. Only a young couple occupies the van, sitting in the middle row. Gideon slides over to the vacant driver's seat.

"Buckle up kids," he says.

Eve's taxi departs, veering around the van. As the Nissan begins to follow, the van thrusts backward, swerving into the drive lane to collide with it. The Nissan's air bags explode into the occupants, immobilizing both Mossad agents.

On cue, Eve's taxi backs up and Gideon calmly steps from the driver's seat of the van and enters the cab. "Drive," he says.

Moses pulls away from the hotel. "So now you kill me?" he asks, glancing at Gideon.

"I don't think so. You guys are clients of ours—from time to time. Why can't we just be friends?"

Gideon looks at Miriam. She nods *no*.

"Bad luck, Moses. I've been overruled. You see, the problem is you tried to kidnap *our* chief—probably with the intent to kill. In retaliation, I suppose. We believe in forgiveness, we really do, except this is kind of personal. You know what I mean."

Gideon directs Moses right on Shoreline Drive, then right again on Castillo Street, then finally left onto a small road that enters Pershing Park. At this time of day the park is almost unoccupied. The cab stops near a softball diamond. Miriam makes a call.

Moses is trembling now. Gideon shoves the man forward, pressing him against the steering wheel.

"This will be painless, I promise you." Gideon produces a small curved dagger—a modern version of the *sica* used in the time of Jesus by Jewish assassins called Sicarii. "Don't be afraid, it will be over soon."

Gideon delicately pushes the sharp blade between two specific ribs in the man's back. To Moses, it feels like an icicle penetrating a lung. Not unpleasant, actually, just cold. So cold…

Gideon arranges the dead man's body to look as if he's asleep against the driver's door. It will be an hour at least before anyone notices that the man has not moved. With no identification or money on him, the police will suspect a robbery-murder. Later they will discover that the man was a Mossad agent. Mossad will have to explain why they were running a covert operation in California without U.S. sanction.

Sweet.

Gideon takes off the Greek fisherman's cap, pulls off a fake beard, and removes a false paunch from underneath his shirt. The man is transformed into an athletic late-forties man with dark hair and alert blue eyes.

"I hate wearing this crap," he says.

"Then you shouldn't have let yourself get photographed in India. Every damn agency in the world has your picture."

Gideon doesn't like to be reminded of his errors. He starts to go through the Mossad agent's pockets and finds a photograph of Miriam.

"Ah, look—a candid. Taken with a telephoto lens in, I would guess, London? Seems that Mossad, at least, knows *your* likeness as well."

He hands Miriam the picture and she sighs, putting it into her purse. "This makes everything a bit more difficult."

"Tell me about it."

Gideon finds a pair of round wire-rimmed glasses in a shirt pocket, fits them to his face and then puts on the cabbie's baseball cap. From another pocket he produces two small dental prostheses. When inserted above his upper molars on both sides, his cheekbones become noticeably more pronounced.

"Does that really work, Gideon?"

"Changes the geometry of the face. Doesn't take much to fool the facial recognition systems."

Miriam just shakes her head.

Less than a minute later, Gideon and Miriam, toting her carry-on, walk through the park, just two friends enjoying a nice walk in the sun. They are picked up on Cliff Drive by a man in a Land Rover. As a precaution they are driven to an alternative airport. It will take two days for them to get home and they can hardly wait.

The Himalayas are beautiful this time of year.

Chapter 2

New York City, 2012

Charlotte Ansari stares at the man with the raised gun. Her heart beats against her rib cage as she recalls a similar scene that occurred five years ago in Kashmir. But she had survived that threat, and she will not let this man take her down.

With a blindingly fast rise of her arms she grasps the 9mm Glock 19 in both hands and rapidly fires five rounds, striking the man in a tight cluster around the neck and upper chest.

She takes a deep breath, but as she lowers her weapon another man from behind grabs her shoulder. She jumps—then laughs at herself.

"Pretty good shooting there," the man says.

Charlotte pulls off her "ears" so she can hear what the man is saying.

"I think that target is dead," the man continues.

"You think? I'm not so sure. Maybe I'll plug him with a few more holes."

She punches a button that moves the target carrier towards the shooter's booth. She stares at the picture of the villainous man pointing a pistol and says, "Yep, he's dead."

"Can I ask you a question, Char?"

"You can ask, sure." She removes the clip from her pistol and installs a trigger lock, showing her finished work to the duty range officer. "But hurry up, Dan. I've gotta go."

Dan looks down at her Glock and nods approval. "I see you here what, maybe three times a week? More than any other chick who comes."

"Chick?" She smiles. "I'm forty-three, Dan. That's almost fifty. Wait, is the duty range officer here allowed to hit on members?"

Dan laughs. He can't be more than thirty, if that. "Just wondering if it's something to do with your work or what. I know you get into some hairy situations, like that Iraq thing, you know? The kidnapping? I guess you want to be able to take care of yourself."

Charlotte places the Glock into a locking case, and puts the case into a larger tote. "Actually, Dan, I work in a very hostile environment. The *world*. But I don't carry when I'm working. It tends to make my interview subjects nervous, not a good way to get them to open up."

"So have you thought about competition—you know, shooting?"

"I get my fill of competition every day, Dan. It's called ratings. And frankly, my ratings really suck lately. The worse things get, the more people don't want to know about it. Gotta go, see you."

Outside the shooting range in mid-town Manhattan, a black Infiniti sedan pulls up to the door. A large Irishman gets out and starts to orbit the vehicle to open the rear passenger door, but Charlotte waves him off.

"Donald, you're embarrassing me. Don't you get tired of babysitting an old woman?"

"Yes, ma'am, I certainly do. But I'm not qualified for anything else."

She knows better. Donald is a first-rate bodyguard doubling as a chauffeur. Cambridge Cable News sees him as an investment in their star international correspondent. His cost comes under "risk abatement" on the CCN books. New York City can be a dangerous place for a woman who is not universally admired by the international rogues she has exposed. And they all have business in New York.

Charlotte's last contract renewal has made her a rich woman—wealthy enough to afford a top floor apartment overlooking Central Park. And yet she's unhappy and alone. After the tragic death of her husband five years earlier, she left her "getaway" in Minnesota and moved here to the nerve center of the world.

She glances at her watch. "Damn New York traffic. I'm going to be late."

"No way. The traffic lets up just ahead."

She wouldn't mind being late for this appointment. The company has insisted that she take a few sessions with their favorite psychiatrist, Dr. Roger Benson. It was that one incident that put her over the edge and made the brass worried about her stability. A little too much travel and exhaustion, that's all, and one night of drinking a tad too much (and maybe a couple of pills—*what were they again?*), and that stupid drunk who came to the wrong door pounding and pounding, scaring the crap out of her, and that one mistake of loading her gun and firing through the door—my God, she was so sure he was trying to attack her! Two weeks of not working was the worst punishment, next to these interminable sessions with Dr. Morose who only wants to exorcise demons that don't exist. And also the humiliation of "treatment" in exchange for keeping it all off the record so the respected correspondent wouldn't lose her credibility and damage the revenue-generating potential of her stardom.

Well, dammit, she'll go to their stupid sessions. But she doesn't have to cooperate!

✦ ✦ ✦

The balding man with thick glasses and sloping shoulders sits motionless in a plush chair opposite Charlotte. His eyes study her, while her eyes evasively wander around the room.

She knows her silence is childish, and that Dr. Benson is smart enough to know that she knows, but still—she is fulfilling the letter of the agreement. She is attending her sessions. She just isn't talking. And Dr. Benson is just sitting there, as he had done for each of the previous three sessions.

Ten minutes to go.

But then Dr. Benson speaks. "It's early," he says, "but you can go if you want to. I can't force help on you. Next time, why don't you bring a book. We both seem to be just living out our sentences here."

Apparently even the esteemed Dr. Benson has a breaking point, and Charlotte has found it. His understated admission of defeat has an unusual effect. As he stands up and dismissively moves toward his desk, Charlotte suddenly feels release from—from *what?* Maybe from obligation. Defiance begins to drain out of her now that there is nothing to defy, no authority to obey, no healer to satisfy by healing.

"Dr. Benson," she says, startling him with sound of her voice, "I was told to come here because I was a woman in trouble who needed help."

The psychiatrist turns to face her. "You shot at a man because you were delusional. The stress and risks of your work overcame you and…"

"*Delusional* –a diagnostic term, isn't it? How much time do we have left?"

"A few minutes."

"I don't need that much time. Sit down and listen."

Dr. Benson reclaims his chair, which squeaks as he lowers himself into it.

"Let me make it easy for you by cataloging my delusions. Number one—my father was a priest who was defrocked for knocking up a fourteen-year-old girl. Number two—my mother abandoned us when I was seven to become the head of an international criminal organization. Delusion three—at the age of thirteen, my son, who has Asperger's Syndrome, was taken from me. He's now the head of that mob of murderers and I haven't seen him since."

She stops and takes a sip of water.

"Delusion four—because of what I know, I've been relentlessly hunted and almost killed by Islamic terrorists, our own CIA, Mossad, the Vatican, even Christian extremists. Delusion five—the only man I've ever loved is an assassin. He's the only reason I'm still alive today."

She stops. Charlotte and Dr. Benson awkwardly stare at each other for a moment, and then the psychiatrist laughs nervously.

"You're making fun of me now, but you have a vivid imagination."

Charlotte continues to stare unblinkingly at the doctor. He shifts in his chair. *It couldn't be true, could it?*

At last Charlotte speaks, filling the void. "Number six—a man pretending to be drunk gained entry to a high-security apartment building and just happened to try to beat down my door by mistake. And this, just after an investigation I was conducting turned up some incriminating information that's, how shall I put it, to die for?"

Charlotte stands up and walks toward the door. She sighs insincerely and adds: "Delusional? You don't know the half of it, Doctor. Thank goodness for doctor-patient confidentiality. Some very bad people would like to know what you know."

On her way out, Charlotte passes three empty chairs in the waiting room. A fourth is occupied by a tall man in a dark suit. The man smiles benignly as she passes.

Something about that smile, though, chills her to the bone.

Delusion seven, she thinks, as she pushes the down button for the elevator. *Maybe I do need help.*

Chapter 3

The Himalayas

The taut muscles of his chest shape the shirt's white fabric as he walks through the meeting hall. The chamber is smaller than it looks, the rock walls nearer than they appear, a clever optical illusion created by some anonymous architect centuries ago. It is enchantingly quiet in here except for the lisping of Gideon's wool trousers and a faint sigh of the wind that rustles his hair.

Three stone passageways open into this meeting hall, each one adorned by an inscription in both Aramaic and English chosen from the apocryphal Book of Enoch. Gideon, like all the other members of the order, knows these words by heart though their full significance eludes him.

The writing over the north passage reads:
I saw the stars of heaven come forth, and I counted the portals out of which they proceed, and wrote down all their numbers

Over the east passage are carved the words:
I drew nigh to a wall which is built of crystals and surrounded by tongues of fire

And above the passageway on the south of the chamber is inscribed:
Purify the earth from all oppression, from all injustice, from all crime, from all impiety

Gideon is drawn toward a shimmering light at the far end of the chamber, a sunlit balcony veiled by opalescent curtains dancing timidly in the mountain breeze. Parting the curtains, Gideon beholds a fantasyland of dark mountain peaks and deep valleys—the Himalayas—his adopted homeland. Drinking in the cool, sweet air washes away the aftertaste of life outside the gompa.

As if defying gravity, the ancient Buddhist fortification juts out precariously from the near-vertical slope of a mountain in the remotest region. Abandoned long-ago by its founders, the crumbling monastery had been secretly resurrected decades ago by Gideon's organization, an almost invisible society of assassins that has been off the charts of history for nearly 2,000 years.

Gideon enters the balcony, placing his hands on the smooth stone balustrade. The sun is like a warm hand caressing his face.

"Are you well rested?" Miriam asks. She is this generation's *Eve*. Her glittering silver robe flutters in the breeze. Standing next to her are a young man and Rachel, Eve's attendant.

Gideon nods. "It's good to be home. The world exhausts me more than it used to. I must be getting old."

Greg, a young man of eighteen, approaches Gideon and gives him a tentative hug and a mechanical double-pat on the back with one hand while holding a cup of tea in the other. "Welcome back, Gideon."

"Thank you, Cain."

Until five years ago, the young man's name was Greg, a name chosen jointly by his mother, Charlotte Ansari, and his grandmother, who stands next to him. But that was long before Greg was identified as the *Divine Light,* the hereditary leader of the Sicarii.

"Would you like any tea?" Rachel offers a tray with a steaming cup. She is perhaps a year or two older than Eve with hair the same shade of dark brown streaked with gray. From the rear you could mistake the two for each other, and Cain had done so a few times to his embarrassment.

"Maybe later," Gideon answers, watching Rachel turn and leave the balcony.

"Rachel has been here since before I came," Gideon remarks. "And yet I don't know anything about her except that she's a true believer."

Eve takes a deep breath before stepping closer to Gideon and speaking in hushed tones. "She's a Jew from Brooklyn with no family. She moved to Israel and became a citizen. At one time, yes, she was fiercely loyal to our cause. But we believe that she has been leaking information about us to Mossad for the last year. For what reason, we don't know."

"Doubt," Gideon suggests. "The great poison of a cause. Do you never experience doubt about what we do?"

Unconvincingly, her eyes averting the piercing gaze of Gideon, Eve shakes her head, then says, "Never."

"Well, if I were you, I would not spend any time alone with her. If she's capable of treason, who knows what else she might be capable of? I just hope you don't ask me to—you know… I'm rather fond of her. I imagine she is under surveillance."

"By me, mainly. Only Cain shares this knowledge about Rachel, and now you. This gompa is a maze of secret passages and hidden observation points unknown to anyone but Cain and me. Just one of the perks of our stations."

Cain impatiently changes the subject. "You should know, Gideon, that we've discovered how the Israelis knew Eve was in Santa Barbara."

"They had a picture of her," Gideon replies.

"Yes, from last year when Eve spent her conjugal visit with Thompson in London."

Eve winces at Cain's tactless choice of terms—*conjugal visit*. Cain often lacks sensitivity. He is intellectually gifted—a savant in some areas—but also emotionally detached and sometimes pathologically frank, evidence to doctors of his Asperger's Syndrome. To the Sicarii, this is a misdiagnosis; instead they see in Cain the heightened objectivity and fearless honesty expected of a Divine Light.

"Who took this picture, and how did Mossad get it?" Gideon is often Eve's assigned protector outside the gompa, and he takes this security breach personally. "I was on watch the entire time she and Thompson were in England."

Eve places a hand on Gideon's arm. "No one can watch every second, Gideon. So don't worry, our estimation of your skills has not diminished. You are still our top operative—next to Caleb, of course. Fortunately, we know how this happened."

"Then tell me, please."

"Not here—inside." Eve takes Gideon by the arm and they enter the meeting hall, veering toward the north passageway.

Gideon has rarely seen the inside of the Center for Intelligence Analysis, or CIA, a name whimsically applied to the operation by Chen Lee, who was already a hacker prodigy at twelve. The Sicarii know that every intelligence agency in the world is trying to intercept their data and find the locations of their facilities. Now twenty-seven, Lee has created a complex network of high-powered computers that is hermetically sealed from the outside world, virtually impervious to third-party "hacking, tracking, and attacking," as he puts it.

Incoming streams of data from nodes in other parts of the world enter the network through one gateway and are carefully scrubbed, filtered, disassembled and reassembled to eliminate threats. No data is allowed to leave the CIA facility. Only two computer stations have access to the Internet through a dizzying maze of connections and encryption services that Chen has said "even I could not decrypt or trace back to us."

Smaller facilities in London, New York, Los Angeles, Mexico City, Rio, Moscow, Tehran, Saudi Arabia, New Delhi, Singapore, Shanghai, Sidney, and Tokyo gather intelligence and perform first-tier analysis before sending it to the Sicarii CIA. In the case of physical intrusion, all data facilities including the CIA can be destroyed in less than two minutes, including complete eradication of data on all resident storage devices. Data back-up is in another location that not even Chen knows, and that facility also can be quickly destroyed.

Standing in front of a large projection screen in the CIA conference room, Chen looks like a teenager in a Dallas Cowboys tee-shirt and dark vest. He glances up at the screen and grins. "This was an easy one," he says.

The screen shows the London photo of Eve. "The background is out of focus, but clearly the location is Piccadilly Circus."

"Yes," Eve interjects, "it was a Tuesday. You can see the lavender shawl I bought earlier in the day."

"From the sun we can tell the time must be approximately two to three o'clock p.m." Chen gestures toward a hard shadow cast by a man walking in the background. "According to London meteorological records, the sun was out only during that timeframe."

"Seems about right," Eve adds.

"Notice that Eve is not looking at the camera. She is glancing to the side, distracted by something. That's when someone took the picture."

"It's hard to recall," Eve says, turning to Gideon, "but I remember you were watching from a distance, making me feel safe as always. And then a man in a raincoat caught your attention. You started heading for him, and I must have glanced over to see what you were going to do. Stupid of me!"

"That's right, the raincoat seemed out of place in the sun, and it wasn't cold enough to need it for warmth, and his hand was in his pocket. Seemed like a possible threat. I wanted to get close so if he had a weapon, I could convince him to uh, well—he pulled out a tissue and blew his nose."

Chen laughs, but stops suddenly when he finds himself laughing alone.

"But who?" Gideon asks. "Who knew that Eve was going to be in London. Who knew what she looked like before snapping the picture?"

"An opportunist," Cain answers, joining the conversation. "Someone with a cell phone camera."

"The image was digital, probably 5MB, cheap wide-angle lens." Chen is staring at the screen. "Most likely an Android phone made by Samsung."

"You're just teasing me now," Gideon says.

"I am, yeah, but there was only one person there who was close enough to take this picture of Eve." Chen pauses for dramatic effect.

Gideon knows there is just one possibility. "Thompson!"

"I'm sure he was just trying to sneak a memento," Eve suggests. "He knows that pictures are forbidden during our—" she glances at Cain "—our *conjugal visits*. He's not supposed to carry a cell phone either, but he did."

"All right, but how did that innocent family photograph end up in the hands of Mossad?" Gideon has started to pace.

A smug look wrinkles Chen's face. "Was pretty easy to hack into Thompson's personal Gmail account. He emailed the photo to his daughter about a month before hooking up with Eve in Santa Barbara. That's nearly a year after the London trip. Why he waited so long we don't know. Maybe he just got lonely. Anyway, here's the message."

Chen clicks a button on a remote. The image changes to a Gmail message from Thompson that reads:

```
Char, I thought you might like to see a recent
picture of your mother I took in London. And
selfishly, I thought that this might get you to
read my message for a change. You haven't an-
swered my emails for a long time…
```

The message degenerates quickly into an emotional outpouring about how difficult it is for Thompson to "share the bliss" with Miriam for only one month a year, and how his daughter's shunning has made him "desperately lonely," and how Charlotte could make life bearable for him if she would only…

"The poor old fellow," Eve says. "He has no idea how much damage he has done."

"At the end of the message, right there—" Gideon's finger-shadow points to the last paragraph of the projected email— "he tells Charlotte he's going to meet Eve in Santa Barbara."

"We think he was trying to entice her into making it a family reunion," Cain says. "A monumentally bad idea, but it's clear he had no malicious intent,"

"And do you make that judgment without prejudice? He is your grandfather." Gideon means this as a gentle challenge. He sometimes prods the young man to see if he can provoke an emotion.

Cain looks at Gideon dispassionately. "Yes, I'm very sure. In a minute you'll see why."

Chen takes a step toward Gideon. "I have to agree with Cain on this one. It appears that Thompson isn't the one who passed the photograph to Mossad."

"Then who did?" Gideon studies the three stern faces that stare back as if waiting for him to reach an all-too-obvious conclusion. "You think *Charlotte*? But why would she do that?"

Eve grows pale and takes a seat. For a moment she seems intent on reading her knees, but finally looks up. "Charlotte's email accounts had no clues. But knowing when she received her father's email allowed us to track her movements in detail over the next 24 hours.

Chen punches the remote and the screen illuminates with a photograph of an attractive, trim American male in his late fifties who is standing next to the former President of the United States. "Six hours after opening her father's message, Charlotte used her phone's calendar to schedule a meeting with this man, William Wyatt."

"Does that name ring a bell, Gideon?" Eve asks.

Gideon shakes his head in disgust. "William Wyatt, former director of the American CIA. Five years ago he ordered me killed. And then I almost killed him. Probably should have."

Gideon stares grimly at the face on screen. "He's now an executive with Blackwatch, the so-called security firm that rents out mercenaries around the world. But Charlotte hates this guy as much as I do. He put her on the Agency's dead-or-alive list. Their last meeting was extremely unpleasant. Why would she want to meet him?"

"Because my mother wants to destroy us." Cain's blunt words bring the conversation to a temporary halt.

Eve stands. "Charlotte is a special case, as you know, Gideon. She's my daughter, and Thompson's. She's Cain's mother. You and she developed a special bond—"

Gideon objects. "I was her assigned bodyguard, that's all."

"She called you her *Guardian Angel*," Cain reminds him.

With a wave of his hand, Gideon dismisses this.

"We're quite sure that Charlotte wants to expose our organization," Eve continues. She is trying to be matter-of-fact, but accusing her daughter of personal betrayal is not easy. "She is obviously willing to sacrifice her family—and you, Gideon—to take us down. Looking at it from her point-of-view, it's understandable. We did keep her in the dark about her son's true lineage until he was thirteen. And we killed her husband, who betrayed us. And we separated Cain—Greg, that is—from his mother with no contact since, which must feel to her like he was abducted into a cult. So she's probably pretty angry with us, don't you think? All that, plus she has what you might call serious *moral objections* to our line of work."

"Keep in mind that she's CCN's star international news correspondent and has deep connections around the world," Cain adds. "So she's not without resources. And her celebrity can win her a lot of new friends."

Chen pokes his remote again. The screen begins to display a series of documents. "So let me cut to the chase. Over the last year—after a tip-off from an associate in the NSA—we've been tracking Charlotte's electronic communications, and the photos on her cell phone. She likes pictures of children and dogs. She's also fond of taking pictures of documents, I suppose so she can transcribe them later. She's had a number of conversations with law enforcement and intelligence personnel and others who aren't a logical part of any CCN story."

Gideon watches the sequence of email subject lines, highlighted comments, and photo attachments showing crime scenes.

"So what exactly am I looking at? What does it add up to?"

"She's been conducting an investigation," Cain says. "Most of this research has to do with contracts we've fulfilled. At least a third of them by you, Gideon.

She's trying to tie us to high-profile assassinations. And she's enlisting help from some very capable resources."

Gideon turns to Eve. He doesn't need to ask the question that's on his mind.

Eve avoids Gideon's eyes as she speaks. "It's a very bad time for this to be happening," she says. "This year is pivotal for us. We can't allow anything to disrupt our work, particularly now. Cain, please… make it clear for him…"

Cain looks Gideon in the eye. "Charlotte must be eliminated."

"She's your mother," Gideon says, baffled by the boy's callous tone.

"She's a threat." Cain's terse reply seems practiced, like the snap of a bullwhip.

Gideon turns to Eve. "She's your daughter. Are you sure about this?"

Eve can't muster the same kind of whiplash response. She pauses first, as if gathering her resolve—who could blame her?—and says, "Do you know the story of Abraham and Isaac?"

Gideon nods. Of course he does.

"Did Abraham refuse to perform the sacrifice just because Isaac was his son?" She pauses briefly, staring fiercely at Gideon. "This is *our* test—mine and Cain's."

"God spared Isaac at the last minute. What if God doesn't spare Charlotte?"

"That's entirely up to God, isn't it?"

Gideon fidgets. Eve senses him struggling to accept this.

"Do I have to remind you of the story of Sarah?" Eve asks. "It was the will of God that she slay her own brother on Masada. I don't think that was easy for her, do you?"

Gideon looks away.

"And God did not stay her hand, did He?"

Cain is uncomfortable with the direction of this conversation. He steps forward. "Gideon, we've decided you should be the messenger."

Flung like a fistful of grit.

Gideon knows that Cain means *messenger of death*. Suddenly he wants to take a deep breath, to let out a long sigh, but his lungs won't cooperate. His breath is caught in his throat. Feelings surface—emotions he had never acknowledged, that even now he tries to bury. Hadn't he once, maybe a few times, dreamt of a normal life, maybe as a stockbroker or a high school football coach, with a wife and children and a home in the country. And wasn't it always Charlotte in these fantasies?

Cain peers into Gideon's eyes. He seems to be searching them for some sign of doubt or weakness.

Unblinkingly, Gideon stares back, though his eyes still burn from the grit. He is not allowed to have feelings for Charlotte. She was just an assignment. He did his job. It's over. Sicarii do not have girl friends or wives; they are married to the mission. Sicarii do not have homes away from the order; the order is their home.

Sicarii assassins must remain unknown, unattached, unrepentant, undefeated.

The order is all he needs. All he will ever need.

It is his family.

"Do you accept our decision?" Cain asks.

It is both terrible and magnificent, Gideon thinks, *that this man-child can rise above emotion, if any exists within him, for the good of the Order.*

"Of course I accept."

"Good. It must be done soon."

Eve turns away so the others won't see the mother's pain in her eyes. She believes that Abraham's and Sarah's eyes must have betrayed their pain, too, just before picking up the knife.

Cain stays in the room after the others leave, his mind oddly fixated on the memory of seeing his mother's stretch marks for the first time, scars that he had caused but nature had ordained. In a rare moment of emotional clarity, he doubts just a little the great plan.

That evening, in the coolness of his bed, with the moon throwing shards of light against the wall and his mind caught in the blurred border between the land of the living and the realm of the dead, Gideon dreams of Charlotte.

Chapter 4

Thompson Walker leans against an ancient olive tree overlooking Jerusalem. With its fat, gnarled trunk and arthritic limbs, the sprawling tree may have witnessed the days of Jesus. It's easy to imagine this secluded vale a few hundred yards from the "official" Gethsemane as the original Garden in which Judas betrayed Jesus. The tree connects Thompson, the author, with the old traditions that are the subject of a potential religious best-seller to follow his immensely popular *The World's Great Wisdom Traditions*.

There is no adequate penance for the harm he inflicted on an innocent girl many years ago, but he has spent most of his life trying to redeem himself by helping others find a path to an omniscient being he hopes is a forgiving God. He has had some notable moral lapses over the years, primarily ones of selfishness and deceit, but on the whole he is pleased with the outcome of his efforts. That his daughter shuns him for past transgressions is but part of his continuing punishment, and he wears that pain like a spiked metal cilice around his thigh to purify himself.

He marvels at how much his bent and swollen fingers, which are trying to manifest his thoughts into written words on a yellow tablet, look like the contorted branches of the olive tree. It makes him laugh.

"Beautiful day."

The disembodied words startle him.

"Sorry, I didn't mean to frighten you. But it is beautiful, isn't it?"

The words come from a thin woman with sandy hair, a white blouse, and khaki pants. Her sandals kick up the marl as she approaches.

"At my age," Thompson says, "every day is a beautiful day."

The woman laughs, showing perfect teeth. She is about thirty with an athletic build and a firm, almost masculine handshake.

"I'm Iris—from Cleveland."

"Thompson Walker."

"Nice to meet you, Thompson. My first time to Jerusalem. Had to get away from the crowd. But I'm interrupting your privacy, so sorry."

"No, really, I don't mind."

"Thompson Walker—I have a book by a Thompson Walker. Great Religions, something…"

"The World's Great Wisdom Traditions. I'm the author."

He smiles humbly.

"No kidding! You're famous. I'm so impressed. I can't wait to tell my sister. Are you working on another book?" She motions to his legal pad.

"I am at that. I hope you'll buy it when it comes out. I need the money."

She laughs, and the sound cheers him. He starts to stand up.

"No, don't bother. I'll come down to you."

Still smiling, Iris crouches.

"Can I show you something amazing?"

"Of course you can."

Thompson is enjoying himself. This young woman reminds him so much of Charlotte. For just a minute he can imagine that he and his daughter are…

The cold barrel of a pistol pushes into his cheek. He sucks in his breath.

"Amazing, isn't it? I'm showing you this gun so that you will remember something very important. Do you know what it is?"

Thompson slowly shakes his head *no*. The barrel moves with his cheek.

"You must never take pictures when you are with your wife. In London you photographed her, and that was very against the rules. If you were not married to Eve, you would be dead right now. So listen, you only get this one do-over. Can you remember that?"

He slowly nods *yes*.

"Good, because this time you almost got Eve killed. Your little memento wound up with some very bad people, and now we have a lot of trouble. So I'm counting on you to behave from now on. Agreed?"

Thompson closes his eyes and nods *yes*. The gun barrel pulls away and he can hear sandals skidding over the marl as Iris walks away.

"Have a nice day now," she says, already in the distance.

He breathes out.

"You too."

Chapter 5

From an Art Deco chair near the concierge desk in the Waldorf Astoria lobby, a young woman stares in the direction of the ornately carved bronze clock that dominates the space. The clock is set on an octagonal base of marble and mahogany and topped with a miniature Statue of Liberty. Like the clock in Grand Central Station, this one also has become a classic meeting place.

The time is 5:20 p.m., but the woman is not looking at the clock. She is studying Charlotte Ansari, who stands near the clock's base visiting with three Indian men in expensive business suits. Charlotte is moving her hands dramatically, trying to make a point that seems to ricochet. With a look of undisguised exasperation, she makes a small shrug of surrender, having lost whatever battle she was waging, and politely shakes hands with all three men, who leave Charlotte to consider her losses.

The young woman stands, straightens her dark blue skirt, tugs down the matching jacket, and purposely strides toward the CCN correspondent. Charlotte, unfortunately, takes off in the opposite direction, clearly aiming for the door.

Quickening her stride, the young woman tries to close the distance without calling undue attention to herself. She is only seconds behind Charlotte as they exit the hotel and Charlotte motions for the first of three waiting taxis. Coming up closely behind Charlotte, the woman reaches into her purse just as another guest attempts to pass in front of Charlotte, making the reporter step backward into the young woman, who drops her purse.

Turning, Charlotte sees an attractive woman of about eighteen, with long raven hair, crouching to pick up her purse and spilled belongings.

"I'm so sorry," Charlotte says, bending to help pick things up. "Let me help."

The woman sweeps her things back into the purse and stands quickly. "No, really, it's all right, Miss Ansari."

"You know me?"

The woman glances away shyly, then returns her gaze to Charlotte. "Everyone knows you. You're famous."

Charlotte smiles demurely. "Not everyone. You'd be surprised how many people have no idea. About anything, actually."

A taxi has pulled up to Charlotte and the driver opens the back door.

Miss Ansari, Could I show you something important?"

Charlotte glances at the cab driver, turns back at the shy young woman and relents. "But it must be quick, okay?"

The woman reaches into her purse, pulls out a business card and hands it to Charlotte.

"What's this?" Charlotte asks, but a quick glance answers her question. "This is the card of my boss, Daniel Hudson. The big boss at CCN."

"He's my guardian. He said that he had talked to you about me? My name is Rebecca Sinkler. Sorry, I should have introduced myself earlier."

"Of course! Dan suggested that we talk about you becoming an assistant."

"A personal assistant."

"Right, personal assistant."

Charlotte turns to the cab driver, hands him a ten dollar bill, and waves him off with a "Sorry, change of plans."

Taking Rebecca by the arm, Charlotte escorts the young woman back into the hotel. "Let's talk about this inside. Are you old enough to drink?"

✦ ✦ ✦

The discrete lounge called Peacock Ally is quiet this time of day. A waitress brings a glass of tonic water to Rebecca. For Charlotte she presents a Paul Hobbs Chardonnay 2008.

"I'm partial to the Sonoma Chardonnays," Charlotte confesses, sipping the white wine and nodding. "So you say that Daniel is your guardian?"

"Since before I can remember. My parents were killed in an accident when I was young. I was raised by a long list of foster parents, but Dan stepped in at some point and became my legal guardian. Of course, I'm of age now, so he no longer makes decisions for me, but he's the closest thing to a real father I've ever had. He has a really big heart."

Charlotte raises her eyebrows slightly. Rebecca's account of Daniel Hudson, the untamed lion of CCN, doesn't quite square with his business reputation or Charlotte's direct experience.

"Everyone has his soft spot, I guess." Charlotte says, inadvertently completing her thought out loud.

"What do you mean?" Rebecca looks confused.

"I'm so happy that you've had a person of… of *stability* in your life, Rebecca. You're very fortunate to have Daniel."

"Thank you. He said that any decision to allow me to be your assistant was entirely yours. So—is this an interview?"

Charlotte takes a larger than usual sip of Chardonnay, rolls the glass between her palms as if contemplating the wine, then looks up at Rebecca. "Here's the thing, Rebecca. I actually don't need a personal assistant."

The sudden disappointment on Rebecca's face provokes a better explanation.

"I have never had a personal assistant. Not sure I'd know how to use one. Surely there are many other correspondents in the company who would be lining up to get a personal assistant like you. But I'm—I'm just not one of them. Too much of a lone wolf, I guess."

These words do nothing to relieve Rebecca's letdown. She can't mask it. But she courteously doesn't push the issue.

"I see," she says. "I'm was hoping, of course… I'm such an admirer. But if it wouldn't work for you, well—"

"I'm sorry, Rebecca."

"It's okay, I'm not really that surprised. I thought I was better prepared for, you know, rejection, but I guess not. Pretty immature, huh?"

Charlotte smiles encouragingly at the young woman, but her mind is made up.

"I still hoped," Rebecca continues, "even after Greg told me that my chances were zilch."

Greg! A name with the power to knot Charlotte's stomach.

"Did you say Greg?" Charlotte asks, knowing the answer. "My *son* Greg?"

Rebecca nods, her eyes penetrating Charlotte's.

"Do you know my son?"

Rebecca nods again before saying words that change everything.

"I speak to him all the time."

Chapter 6

Across the street from Central Park, the apartment building has standard security features. As in most buildings, they are easily defeated. Key card access through the foyer's inner door is bypassed by anyone patient enough to wait for another person to enter or leave.

It is only a matter of seconds before an Italian woman exits with her lively Pomeranian. The open door allows entry by an expensively attired businessman with a neatly trimmed beard and horn-rimmed Cary Grant glasses. Aware that at least five surveillance cameras are recording his movements, the man enters the lobby with a slim brief case and walks to an open elevator that had just delivered the departing woman. He pushes the button for the top floor.

Thirty-two seconds later, the man exits the elevator, turns left, and approaches a door secured by a key card access system. To make sure the apartment is empty, the man pushes the doorbell and waits.

No answer.

He tries again.

Certain now that no one is home, he looks at the card reader next to the door. Cracking open his brief case, he removes a small wooden box. Inside he finds a two-inch metallic cube. This object is a grade N45 neodynium magnet.

He removes the cube and holds it against the key card reader. The powerful neodynium magnet immediately disrupts the magnetic field inside the combination chamber, causing the door's bolt to withdraw. He steps into the apartment, closes the door, and places the cube back into his brief case.

As he looks into the apartment, he sees a spacious living room and large kitchen to his right, just as the floor plan had promised. The view of Central Park is magnificent. To his left is the master bedroom. He walks straight ahead past a half-bath and discovers a guest bedroom that has been turned into an office.

Not just an office—but a research center.

Two large-screen monitors connect to a tower computer that whirs almost silently beneath a desk. Stacks of papers and books, piles of notes, and other detritus of the technology age fill up the room. But what catches the man's attention are the walls.

He cannot actually see the walls because they are entirely covered with pictures and Post-It notes. Lengths of colored string fan out from some of the notes to various images, creating the illusion of overlapping spider webs. One wall focuses on photos of people, another one on company logos and buildings. A third wall has become an enormous world map studded with pushpins. And the last wall is a kind of handwritten genealogical chart scrawled onto butcher's paper.

The man sits down at the desk. A spilled stack of unopened mail encroaches on the computer keyboard. He lifts the top envelope and notes the addressee: Charlotte Ansari.

He wiggles the computer mouse. Both monitors come to life. Charlotte's email account is still open. The man clicks through some incoming messages, studying them carefully. Then he opens the Sent folder and inspects the latest messages. Next he scrolls Charlotte's contact list.

Leaning back in the chair and swiveling slowly, he studies more carefully the collage of images pasted to the walls. The photographs of people, mostly men, are particularly interesting. Some of these people, all deceased, he knows intimately. You cannot be more intimate with someone than to kill him.

The man taps his fingers on the desktop and sighs. Reaches inside his suit coat. Pulls out a 9mm Glock. Obsessively checks the magazine.

Finally, Gideon takes off the horn-rimmed glasses and puts them in a shirt pocket. He scratches his false beard, then decides to simply pull it off.

So much better!

Now—what to do until Charlotte comes home.

Chapter 7

Happy Hour has multiplied Peacock Alley's customers into a flash mob. Charlotte lifts her wine glass but finds it empty. She could use another dose right now. Catching the eye of a waitress, she makes the standard hand signals for another round.

Charlotte had intended to make a quick exit from this conversation after letting Rebecca down gently. But now she is mystified by this young woman. She needs to learn more.

"So Rebecca, you say that you know my son."

"Greg—yes I do."

"I'm asking because, well, you see—I haven't spoken to him for a while now." By *for a while* Charlotte means *for about five years since he was taken from me*. "How is he doing?"

"Oh, he's fine, really. Working hard."

Rebecca seems reluctant to give Charlotte more than she asks for.

Charlotte lifts her glass again, finds it still empty. She could really use some alcohol right now. "You see, I'm curious about why he talks to you, but... why he... how is it... Rebecca, he—Greg—hasn't spoken to me in a long time."

"Yes, he told me that."

"He did?" Charlotte finds some comfort in knowing that Greg has thought about her. "What did he tell you?"

"You mean about *you*?"

Charlotte nods.

"He just told me that he loved you, but had a hard time letting you know. And to keep you safe, he couldn't contact you. Not sure what he meant."

Charlotte looks away. The words thrum her emotions until she summons the well-worn armor of distrust.

A waitress sets two glasses of wine on the table.

"Rebecca, was Greg here in the States?"

"Oh no. He hasn't been back here for years."

Confused, Charlotte takes a long sip of wine. "But then how did you meet? How do you communicate? Did you go to… to his home… overseas?"

"No, but I'd like to. He tells me it's beautiful. He loves it there."

Charlotte isn't getting the answers she wants. Rebecca senses this and turns away with a look of desperation, as if she wants to satisfy Charlotte but can't figure out what the woman wants.

Charlotte reaches out and grasps Rebecca's warm hand. My God! It's been a very long time since she has touched someone so intimately. This simple act, the sudden spark of human contact, makes her aware of how lonely she has been. What a shame that her gesture is just a ploy meant to disarm the young woman.

"Sweetheart—Rebecca—can you tell me how you communicate with my son? Does he have a phone number?"

Rebecca's eyes flicker with exasperation. "I feel like I'm being interrogated here, Charlotte."

Charlotte squeezes the young woman's hand. "Sorry, just the reporter in me coming out," she says, her voice cunningly soft. Her instincts tell her the woman is a fraud. But then, how does Rebecca know about Greg?

"It's just that—I'd like so much to speak to my son, to hear his voice. And I… I kind of envy you for being able to talk to him… when I can't…when I don't even know if he's dead or alive."

"He's alive, that much I'm certain of. I talked to him just last week."

"Did he call *you*?"

"It's not like that. We don't talk that way."

"Then *how*, Rebecca? How do you talk?"

"We talk—on the grid."

The Happy Hour crowd has grown more raucous. Charlotte moves her chair nearer to Rebecca's and leans closer.

"Rebecca, honey, what do you mean *on the grid*? You mean, like the electrical grid? I don't understand."

You'll think I'm a whack job. Everyone does, except for Daniel."

"Listen to me Rebecca, I won't think you're a whack job. I promise. Just please—please explain to me what this means."

Rebecca sniffs and wipes her nose with a napkin.

"I'm what some people—do I have to do this?"

Charlotte blots a tear in the corner of Rebecca's eye. "No, not if you really don't want to. But sometimes it helps to let someone you trust in on your secrets."

Charlotte has never been able to take this advice, but it sounds good.

Rebecca looks at Charlotte and cocks her head, as if determining if this woman will keep her word.

"I'm what some people call an Indigo Child." Rebecca defensively stares at Charlotte as if expecting instant mockery.

Charlotte knows about Indigo Children. She did a story, what?—maybe eight, nine years ago? Seemed like some kind of New Age absurdity then, a belief that a wave of children was being born into the world, and these children possessed special and sometimes supernatural abilities. Distinguished by an indigo-colored aura, they were said to be highly empathetic, curious, strong-willed, intelligent and intuitive. While they often resisted authority, they were innately spiritual and many were natural "peacemakers." It was hoped that these Indigo Children would create new, more mature paradigms of behavior and social interaction to help the world advance to a higher level.

Charlotte had dismissed these notions back then. Even now her body stiffens with suspicion. Maybe this woman is a kook after all. Or maybe someone had convinced Rebecca that she was an Indigo to explain away some personality or attention deficits.

Rebecca pulls her hand away and looks down at the table. "I'm nuts, right?"

Charlotte can't solve this puzzle, and that disturbs her. She continues to probe, looking for some inconsistency in this bizarre tale.

"And Greg—is he also…"

"An Indigo? Of course he is. He found me, you know. On the grid. I can't really explain what that is. It's like a kind of… I don't know… a place, but not a real place. It's like a place in our heads where we can… talk, sort of. Communicate. We can understand each other. When we're there, it's like being in a big, warm, flowing world. Greg sought me out on the grid—that's what everyone there calls it—because Daniel was my guardian, and he knew that Daniel was your boss and could get us together. I think Greg wants to communicate to you through me."

Charlotte gulps the rest of the wine in her glass. "You can understand, can't you, that this is a lot for me to process?"

Rebecca nods. "This is why I wanted to be your personal assistant. Why I asked Daniel if he could help. I never intended to just blurt this all out like some kind of deranged person. I'm so sorry. I'd certainly understand if you wanted to bolt out of here right now and never see me again."

Charlotte's innate skepticism, honed by years of deceit by high-level charlatans of every stripe, keeps her from accepting Rebecca's outrageous claims.

Rebecca seems to sense this. She stands and self-consciously straightens her skirt. "No, I should be the one to go. Sorry I took up your time with this nonsense. But I did promise Greg that I would give you a message if we ever met."

Charlotte looks up at the young woman, who can't bring herself to look Charlotte in the eye.

"Greg says it's time to forgive your father," Rebecca says. "You're going to need each other in the coming days."

If this woman is a con, or a Trojan horse, she's good! And even if she is, Charlotte kind of likes her.

But then she reminds herself, that's how cons work.

Chapter 8

Charlotte slides the security card through the glide path of the reader. With a metallic thud, the door unlocks and she pulls it open.

The apartment building lobby is deserted. She passes through it like a ghost, pushes the elevator UP button, and leans backwards against the cool marble wall waiting for the comforting chime of the door.

Which comes within seconds.

A hot bath and a nap. Time to untangle her brain. Listen to some Beethoven. Order in some Szechuan from that little place down the street.

She baits herself with enticements to stay awake, keep moving. The elevator doors open and she stumbles into the corridor, walks slowly to her apartment door and swishes the card through the reader. Once inside, she drops her purse and closes the door.

But something is not right.

A faint noise startles her. It comes from the living room. And there is the faint odor of something burning.

Charlotte's fatigue is instantly replaced with fear. Someone is in her apartment. Her instincts shift into high gear.

Kicking off her noisy shoes, which sound like hammers on the bare wood floor, she silently slides into the master bedroom and finds her 9mm Glock in a nightstand drawer. She ticks off the safety and begins surreptitiously stalking the source of the sound. She passes the front door and rounds a corner that reveals the entire living room and the kitchen beyond.

The kitchen lights are on. A man in a white shirt, sleeves rolled up, is standing by the stove with his back to her. Quietly she approaches, the pistol held forward in both hands, her eyes nervously searching the corners of the darker living room for other intruders.

At last she steps into the kitchen, keeping a distance between her and the man. He is preparing food.

"Put your hands in the air!" she yells.

Startled, the man raises his arms.

"I have a gun. Now turn around slowly. No sudden movements or I swear to God I'll shoot you dead."

The man turns slowly. He is smiling.

"Gideon?"

"Nice to see you, too," Gideon says. "Hope you're in the mood for spaghetti and meatballs. You don't keep much in the pantry."

"I don't eat here much. What the hell are *you* doing here?"

"Mind putting down the gun? You know most accidents occur in the home."

Charlotte can't shake her suspicions all at once.

"C'mon," Gideon says, "the meatballs are gonna burn and the noodles'll turn to jello. Just thought you might be hungry when you got home."

Charlotte lowers the pistol. "It's only been five years."

"And two months, eleven days, thirteen hours since we saw each other last. Get the plates, will you? Food's ready."

Charlotte shakes her head. This is just too surreal. The professional assassin, who strangely was assigned to protect her from numerous shadowy forces years ago, is now standing in her kitchen making spaghetti. Good thing for him that he's the only man she has ever been able to trust completely.

She sets the gun down on the center island, and then stares at it for a moment.

"Hey," Gideon says. "If I was going to kill you, you'd be dead already. Just looking for a nice quiet supper for two. Really."

She leaves the gun on the island and rattles around in a cupboard, finally producing two plates. In an obscure drawer two steps to her left she finds silverware.

"Who taught you to organize a kitchen?"

"Never was the domestic type. If you don't like where I put things, be my guest. Mi casa es su casa."

Gideon drains the noodles and pours them into a serving dish, then scoops the meatballs and sauce into a large bowl, setting it all next to a loaf of bread on the kitchen table.

"By the way, where do you keep the wine glasses? I found a bottle of Chardonnay hidden away."

Dinner conversation is a lot like two old war buddies revisiting past skirmishes. Charlotte loosens up after several glasses of wine and even manages a laugh now and then. But mostly she finds herself imagining a life like this—dinners at home, perhaps someone to love, and be loved by…

Too much wine today.

Even as a little girl, Charlotte hadn't fantasized about love and marriage. How could she? Her father was a priest defrocked for sleeping with a teenage girl, her mother a criminal who abandoned her daughter. With these two as role models, how could Charlotte have failed to turn out cynical, distrustful and selfish. Her own reckless pursuit of fame had made her an incompetent mother and destroyed any chance of a relationship with her emotionally-challenged Asperger's son.

No, a romantic relationship is too late for her.

But for a few minutes maybe she can pretend...

Her cell phone chirps. She finds it in the kitchen and answers. "Okay, I'll take a look and send it back."

On her way to her home office, Charlotte glances at Gideon. "Just have to check an email and reply. Work stuff. Don't go away."

Her heart is beating fast, like a school girl's with a mad crush on a boy. *Get over it*, she tells herself.

In the office she sits down at the dual monitors and wiggles the computer mouse. Just that fast her whole world changes.

The Archive folder is open in Outlook. Someone has been snooping.
Gideon!

She looks around the cluttered office. My God! Everything she has been investigating is out in the open.

And in that horrifying instant she knows why Gideon is here.

The problem is, her gun is still in the kitchen.

Her head is pounding now. Her mouth is suddenly dry. Blood rushes to her face. She may have just shared her Last Supper with her assassin. Breathing deeply to steady her nerves, she heads for the kitchen, knowing that Gideon will see her anxiety. She will need a story to explain her appearance, her behavior.

Gideon is carving off a slice of crusty bread with a sharp knife as she enters the kitchen.

"Charlotte, are you all right?"

"That was some bad news. A friend was in an accident."

Gideon squints his eyes. "I thought it was a work call."

Charlotte flounders. "Yes—it's... it's someone I work with. I was, uh, going to be traveling with him tomorrow to London."

"I'm sorry to hear that. Because I understood your next trip wasn't until a week from tomorrow."

"How would you—?" Charlotte stares at Gideon, understanding in a flash how he would know her schedule. It's all on the computer.

"Sorry, Charlotte. I was hoping we could have a little more time together before getting down to business."

Charlotte looks down at the knife in Gideon's hand.

She makes a snap decision and lunges for the gun a few feet away. Oddly, Gideon makes no motion to stop her. He merely stands up.

She points the Glock at him with both hands, her feet planted solidly—the classic target shooting stance.

"Funny thing." Her face is wracked with disappointment. "I actually cared for you. You bastard—I should have known."

Gideon steps to his right so the table is no longer between them.

"I said don't move!"

He takes a step toward her.

She shakes the barrel of the gun menacingly. "I swear to God, I will shoot."

"You will not kill me, Charlotte. Not today."

"I'm not afraid to pull this trigger!"

"I know you're not. You've been training for moments like this."

He takes another step.

She fires. *Click.*

Again! *Click. Click.* No shots.

The barrel is now pushing into Gideon's chest. As he opens a hand and shows her the gun's cartridges, she starts to sob.

"Guns don't kill people," he says. "Bullets do."

Eve has not slept all night, so when her cell phone rings early in the morning it doesn't wake her. She thumbs the screen and puts the phone to her ear.

She hears Gideon say, "It is finished. She will not be found."

God did not intervene, she thinks, and then chokes back tears. No one must see her weakness.

Chapter 9

Rebecca feels vulnerable standing on the east side of Central Park West and looking up at Charlotte's building. She knows the apartment number, and Daniel told her that it overlooked the park, but she can't tell which windows are Charlotte's.

It doesn't really matter.

She has been standing here for about five minutes, and during this time she has noticed two peculiarities. Number one: a man with dark hair, a neck big as a man's thigh, and a tan jacket has walked past the building three times. Number two: a Land Rover is parked just outside the building with two men in the front seat.

Rebecca spots a new person, a chubby man in a running suit who is walking briskly down the sidewalk. When the man turns toward the building's entrance, Rebecca follows him, dodging a taxi as she crosses the street. As the man slides his security card through the reader's slot and opens the lobby door, Rebecca is right behind him.

"Beautiful evening," she says.

"Very."

The man holds the door for Rebecca as she enters the lobby. "Are you a resident here?" he asks, following her into an elevator.

"Temporary… staying with Ms. Ansari for a few days."

"Ah! The famous correspondent. Don't see her much."

Rebecca smiles and nods. The man exits seven floors later.

"Give my regards," he says.

Again Rebecca smiles and nods. At the top floor the doors open and she sees a sign directing her left to Charlotte's apartment number.

Suddenly she's nervous and considers abandoning her mission. Reminding herself that she only needs to leave an envelope at the door, she forces herself to move forward. It would be better to speak to Charlotte, of course, to more sincerely apologize for her brusque departure at Peacock Alley. But then again, leaving a handwritten note may less confrontational.

As she stoops to deposit the envelope on the floor, the door cracks open. Startled, Rebecca straightens and stares into the eyes of a bearded man with Cary Grant glasses. The man is as as startled as she.

"Who are you?" the man barks.

"I'm, uh—I'm Rebecca. I thought this was Charlotte Ansari's apartment.

"Who?"

"Ansari. You know, the CCN reporter?"

The man looks down the corridor one way, then the other. Suddenly his hand pulls her through the doorway, closing the door behind her.

"Rebecca, you've come at a very bad time," the man says.

"I'm very sorry—I was just, I wanted to leave something, this note, at the door."

The man takes the note, puts it into the inside breast pocket of his suit coat.

"The trouble is, Rebecca—now that you're here, I can't just let you go."

"What?"

"It was complicated before. Now it's even more complicated."

He pulls out a pistol. Rebecca sucks in her breath.

"I'm so sorry," he says.

And his eyes almost make her believe that he is.

The thick-necked man is walking past the apartment building's entrance again, but then turns abruptly and heads for the Land Rover.

"How long?" he asks.

"All night if we need to," the vehicle's passenger says. He's an older man with thick silver hair and a bit of a paunch beneath his light jacket.

"What if he doesn't come tonight?"

"Then tomorrow, or maybe tomorrow night he'll come. Or she'll go to him."

"All right, I'm going to switch sides of the street, maybe look at the park."

"Whatever, just stay close."

The thick-necked man crosses the street as the man with the silver hair looks down at a Nikon digital camera. An LCD screen displays the last picture taken— Rebecca crossing the street moments ago.

Gideon's grip on Rebecca's arm hurts. He suspiciously drags her into the master bedroom and pushes her into a seated position on the bed.

"Rebecca!" A woman's voice.

Rebecca turns and sees Charlotte standing in the bathroom doorway.

"What are you doing here?" Charlotte asks.

"You keep her calm," Gideon urges Charlotte. "We leave in one minute."

"What's happening?" Rebecca pleads. "Are those men downstairs looking for you?"

These words grab Gideon's attention. "You saw men downstairs?" he asks.

"Three men milling around the building. Actually, one man walking back and forth, and two men in a Land Rover parked on the street."

"Probably nothing," Charlotte suggests.

"The men were there when I arrived," Gideon says. "I was just going down to see if they'd left. So here's the plan—one minute and we head out. The girl comes with us. Because if they saw her, they probably have pictures. She won't be safe here."

"Who are they?"

"My guess, Mossad. Those guys don't stop. They're after *me* I would guess, but since they're here we can't assume they're not after you, Charlotte. You made 'em look foolish in India."

"Five years ago."

"These guys think in terms of *thousands* of years. One minute, be ready.."

Gideon races past the guest bathroom where a pile of ashes—the smoldering remnants of the research collages stripped from the office walls—lies in the middle of the ceramic floor. A rattling fan sucks the smoke out of the bathroom.

In the office, Gideon glances at a gray pop-up window on the left monitor. It confirms that all data on the hard drive has been deleted.

This is not good enough. On his knees, Gideon pops off the side panel of the computer case, exposing the drive. He places the cubic neodynium magnet next to the drive and counts to ten. The powerful magnet should erase whatever the disk scrubbing utility failed to eliminate.

At the door to the hallway, Gideon finds Charlotte with one arm around a very frightened Rebecca, the other holding a loaded 9mm Glock. At her feet is an overnight bag of belongings.

"Listen to me, both of you. There's an emergency exit into an alley on the north side of the main floor."

"How do you know that?" Charlotte asks.

"This is the battlefield—it's my job to know it. Here's the thing—the bad guys may have someone watching that exit, but it's our best chance. Hopefully they won't know we're tipped off and will still be thinking we'll come waltzing out the front door."

The elevator lowers them to the second floor, where Gideon guides them down one flight of stairs to a corridor that leads to a back exit. Beyond this door is a dark, trash-filled space between the apartment building and the adjacent structure. To the right is a latched gate that prevents druggies and prostitutes from using the space as their personal storefront. Gideon leads the women to the gate, which can be unlatched from the inside for emergency reasons.

"I'm going to neutralize those guys out front so we don't have to worry about them," Gideon says. "Stay inside this gate until I come for you."

He steps out of the gate and turns right toward Central Park, stopping at the corner of the apartment building. Peering around the corner he spots the Land Rover with two men in the front seat.

Where is the third man that Rebecca mentioned?

He carefully surveys the landscape. A young couple is walking on the east side of the street in Gideon's direction. A male dog walker is further down, crossing the street. And then Gideon spots a stationary man across the street flicking a cigarette butt onto the sidewalk.

Gideon wonders if these men will recognize him in his beard and glasses. There is one way to find out. He crosses to the lone man's side of the street and turns south toward the thick-necked man. As he approaches the man's position, he holds up an arm and waves.

"Excuse me," he says in a fake German accent. He loves accents. "Do you have a light, by any chance?"

The man looks at Gideon, irritated. He glances at the Land Rover—his friends are focused on their cell phones. Nervously licking his lips, he reaches into a pants pocket for a lighter. When the man's hand is least available, Gideon delivers a crushing blow to the underside of his chin, smashing the lower jaw, severing the tongue and crashing the brain into the top of the skull, instantly causing a blackout.

The distracted men in the Land Rover have seen none of this, but they can't ignore the concerned citizen with a beard who is approaching them.

"Excuse me," Gideon says to the driver. "Did you see what might have happened to that fellow?" He gestures to the unconscious agent.

The silver-haired man leaps from the car and rushes to the thick-necked man. He crouches by the crumpled body, then rolls it over to reveal a river of blood. Shouting an obscenity, he turns toward the Land Rover but is blinded by Xenon headlights. He doesn't see his partner lying in the street. And he is still rising to his feet when a fender clips his leg, shattering the knee.

Gears growl as Gideon shifts into reverse. He means to back up and head north to the side street where he can retrieve Charlotte and Rebecca. But another car, an Escalade SUV with one occupant, is bearing down on him from the south.

Damn! A fourth man.

Gideon points the Land Rover north, pulls his gun out, and shifts into reverse again. The Escalade screeches to a halt, almost running into his rear. The driver had expected Gideon to pull away. During that brief moment of confusion, Gideon stomps the gas pedal. Tires screech. The Land Rover lunges backward into the Escalade's grill, activating the air bags in both vehicles.

Gideon fires his Glock at the air bag that's nearly suffocating him, accelerating deflation. Then he leaps from his vehicle and marches toward his adversary. The Escalade driver's air bag is slower to collapse. He is just now positioning his gun outside the driver's window to fire a left-handed shot.

Gideon lobs the powerful neodynium magnet at the driver's hand. It smashes into the gun and sticks to it with such magnetic force that the man can't shake it off. Gideon high-kicks it out of the driver's hand and jackhammers a fist into the man's left temple, leaving him unconscious.

The faint shriek of sirens warns that someone has called the police. Gideon quickly recovers the driver's gun from the street. With a twisting motion he removes the magnetic cube and then races back to the side street.

Concealed by the corner of the building, Charlotte has seen everything. Rebecca huddles next to her looking shell-shocked.

"Not exactly a covert operation," Charlotte remarks.

The sirens grow louder. Flashing lights can be seen several blocks south.

"You can grade me later. Right now, we're going out for a little walk."

He wraps his arm around Charlotte—amazing how much this comforts her—then takes Rebecca by the hand. He guides them north on the Parkway, mimicking the stroll of the unconcerned.

They are only twenty paces down the street when the sirens stop. The young couple he saw earlier is talking to the police and pointing at Gideon.

"Stop! You there—stop!" a policeman shouts before leaping into his vehicle.

Gideon pulls his companions into a full gallop toward subway stairs a full block away. The squad car is rapidly gaining on them.

Chapter 10

At street level, a green iron railing guards the subway stairs. Gideon and the women descend into New York's enormous subterranean world. As they race past the first landing, the squad car squeals to a stop above. Car doors slam. Voices shout for them to halt.

Charlotte and Rebecca are agile runners. They keep up with Gideon, who leads them down more stairs and onto a subway platform where three tired commuters wait for the next train.

For Charlotte, the only way out seems to be by subway or going back up the stairs into the arms of the police.

Without warning Gideon leaps from the platform. The women follow impulsively. Gideon heads into the south tunnel, pointing out the tracks and other obstacles at their feet. The police, having arrived on the platform, use their flashlights to probe the tunnel but show no interest in giving chase. Gideon hears them call for support, presumably to intercept them at the next station.

The fugitives silently push forward for another block or two—it's hard to judge distance down here. Illumination from lights near the station don't reach very far into the graffiti-covered tunnel. Darkness engulfs them.

"And if a train suddenly appears ahead?" Charlotte asks, the first words spoken since they became prey.

Instead of answering, Gideon pulls a small flashlight from his pocket and turns it on. Another click switches to an ultraviolet beam. In the eerie purple light, something flashes on the right wall about twenty yards ahead.

Gideon grunts with relief. "Thank God we didn't pass it!" He steadies the beam on a glowing graffiti scribble.

"What is that?" Rebecca asks.

"A sign," Gideon explains, approaching it. "Says *exit*."

"What—in Vulcan?"

"Aramaic."

"Aramaic?" Rebecca says skeptically. "You're kidding, right? Didn't Jesus speak Aramaic?"

Gideon nods as he kneels. The word is spray painted on a sheet of metal affixed to the wall by a large bolt halfway across the top edge.

"That's an ancient language," Rebecca says, "so what's it doing on a wall in a subway tunnel?"

"Showing us an escape route," Gideon says.

He grasps the metal plate on both sides and turns it clockwise. The plate pivots on the retaining bolt revealing a hole in the wall large enough for a person to crawl through. Flicking the flashlight to bright beam, Gideon looks inside. The hole opens onto a vertical shaft with a ladder leading downward. A faint light glows at the bottom.

"In you go," he tells Rebecca."

"What—down there?"

"Go!" Gideon's voice leaves no room for argument. Rebecca climbs through the hole and begins moving down the ladder.

"Now you," Gideon says, glowering at Charlotte.

She follows Rebecca into the shaft. Gideon climbs in after her and maneuvers the metal plate back into position, covering the hold.

It's very dark in the shaft.

Something rattles below, spooking Rebecca. "What the hell was that?"

"Probably just a rat," Gideon says. "Keep going."

At the bottom of the shaft, Rebecca steps into a large room illuminated only by a light at the far end of another tunnel. Charlotte and Gideon are right behind.

"Where are we?" Charlotte asks.

"An old subway station abandoned back in the thirties. The city has maybe a dozen of these, most of 'em forgotten. And scores of old train tunnels that have been sealed off and put out of mind. Ladies, you are now in the great catacombs of New York City."

The flashlight beam travels across baseball size chunks of concrete and railway debris, mounds of packed earth and garbage, and hundreds—maybe thousands—of old shoes.

A loud scraping sound comes from a dark corner of the dim station. Gideon steps between the women and the noise. Staring into the shadows he says, "Sorry if we're bothering you."

"Just keep it down, will ya?" The words are more a croak than human speech.

With eyes finally adjusting to the darkness, the women see the dark shape of a man emerge from the blackness. Filthy and ragged, he holds a wine bottle in his right hand and staggers forward, obviously drunk.

"Who invited you?" the man growls.

"We're just about to leave. Didn't know anyone was home," Gideon says. Glancing at the women he adds, "One of the *mole people.* They live down here. Drunks, druggies, homeless—I guess the rent's cheap."

The wino stumbles forward aggressively. Gideon beams his flashlight into the man's eyes. The man shields them with a hand and retreats.

Switched to ultraviolet light again, Gideon's flashlight sweeps the walls of the old station platform. Graffiti grows like mildew on the moldering walls. The purple light finds two more glowing marks.

"Directions," Gideon explains. "This one with the arrow says *North*. Good to know—easy to get turned around down here. The one over there says *Sword*. Meaning weapons… and other supplies we might need. That's what we want."

Gideon heads into the darker tunnel going south. The women scramble to catch up to him. They march through the rubble for about thirty minutes, kicking their way through nests of rats and piles of litter. Occasionally they see shafts of streetlight streaming into their underground world from grates high above. Continuing on, the tunnel finally opens into another abandoned station, this one smaller.

Gideon's ultraviolet light finds another glowing squiggle.

"Sword," Gideon declares. "We're there." The mark is on a steel door that is tightly shut with no handle or latch.

Gideon holds the magnetic cube to the door and Charlotte can hear a faint *thwack* as something, probably a metal crossbar, binds to it through the wood. As Gideon moves the magnet to the right, the bar moves with it. A hefty shove opens the door into a cramped but tidy space containing shelves stacked with various items, crates, two cots, a table and four chairs, and lots of weapons.

"Are we in the middle of a war? Or is this hell?" Rebecca asks.

Gideon switches on a battery-operated light. Taking a seat, he clasps his hands behind his head and says, "So let me explain."

Chapter 11

Jeremy Pitts, at twenty-five a former college track star and Iraq veteran, opens the passenger door as the silver Mercedes sedan comes to a rolling stop. He dashes across the dark street as the car drives off. His objective: a weathered wooden door sandwiched between a tired apartment building and a rundown bodega. No one ever notices this door. It has no handle and no lock. The door pushes to open but is solidly barred from inside against forced entry.

Jeremy is part of a Sicarii mobile team that travels a prescribed path through New York City each day. When the alarm went off three minutes go, he was the nearest agent to the intrusion site.

Using a magnetic cube, Jeremy slides the hidden bar that locks the door. He enters a dark, narrow stairway, slams the door shut, resets the metal bar and checks the pistol hidden beneath his light jacket. He turns off his cell phone to conserve the battery—there's no reception where he's going. In a blur, he flies down a long flight of dusty stairs, almost slamming into a wall. At the bottom a dim corridor travels left or right. He chooses to go right, running hard, imagining he's in the 800 meter. By his calculation, with the usual obstacles, he is four minutes from arriving at his destination.

Sometimes he goes weeks without excitement, so today is special.

The dog walker outside Charlotte's apartment building sits on a bench outside the low stone wall that surrounds Central Park. His German shepherd lies quietly at his feet, interested in everything that moves.

The man is Indian, or perhaps Pakistani, but blends in with the multinational mash-up that is New York. He pushes the END button on a cell phone, exasperated.

His dog perks up, sensing a small animal behind the wall, but is calmed by the gentle stroke of a hand.

"Be patient," he says. "As soon as our call goes through, we can go home."

He makes the call again and waits for a connection, his face brightening when a voice greets him.

"Hello," the voice says.

"Cain?"

"Yes, this is Cain."

"It's Arnav. I have bad news."

"Gideon failed?"

"Worse. He turned. I saw him fleeing with Charlotte and someone else."

The man hears a deep sigh, senses great disappointment on the other end.

"My orders said to surveil, not to intervene," Arnav says, "or else I would have attempted…"

"You did the right thing, Arnav. Now notify the team. No one is to assist Gideon, is that clear? He must be stopped at all costs."

"And the women?"

"*Women?* The third person is female?"

"A *young* woman—maybe late teens."

There is a long pause. The man pets his dog and awkwardly looks up and down the street, wondering if he has lost the connection.

"Whatever it takes, but don't harm the young woman," Cain says at last. "How long ago did this happen?"

"About a half-hour ago. Couldn't get the call through to you."

"Okay, now call the team."

Arnav calls another number.

"This is Arnav. We have a rogue agent. High alert—wanted dead."

"Really!" The female voice replies. "That's a first. Who is it?"

"Gideon."

"You're kidding, the guy's a legend. Are you sure?"

"Directly from Cain."

"Mmmm, we don't really have a protocol for this, a chain of command thing for taking out Brothers." I think we need something more."

"I said it's directly from Cain."

"That's what you say, but you're not a Brother."

"Not yet. But I'm on the track."

"I need something more."

"Look, just tell me if anything unusual is happening. Have there been any breaches?"

"Okay, we've had an alarm at Sword 14. Sent Jeremy over to check."

"All right, have him contact me with any news."

"He's underground right now. No phone coverage until he's back on top."

"Can you have his driver meet me at the nearest access point?"

"I suppose I can do that."

"Which is where, by the way?"

✦ ✦ ✦

Cain hangs up and finds himself vibrating.

He stiffens himself against it.

Some might call it a shudder, but Cain knows better. As he leans against the balustrade and surveys the peaks and valleys of his mountainous homeland, he can feel the oscillating sweep of telluric currents tuning themselves to the measure of this moment. He is no more than a needle on an acupuncture point, a finger pressing a meridian of history, as much *influenced by* as *influencer of* unfolding events.

Arvam's call has stirred up competing emotions—outrage at Gideon's clear betrayal but relief that his mother is still alive. This cannot be! Instantly he tries to tame his feelings—seldom a problem for this emotionally-challenged young man—and to understand them. Intellectually he knows his duty. He knows that he must scour away all bias of personal relationships, every scrap of sentiment and selfishness, to carry out his demanding role. He fears that subconsciously, despite the rightness of his actions, he wants his mother to survive. And that could spell his doom, particularly on a day when the Twelve have summoned him to the Inner Chamber.

Synchronicity would dictate that the unprecedented second Congress of Souls, to convene in a few minutes, will occur at this particularly difficult time through sheer coincidence. But he does not believe in synchronicity. He believes that the Congress knows, as it always does, the hearts and minds of its servants, and when to intervene.

There is one best answer to the dilemma posed by Charlotte, only one person who can outmatch Gideon. Cain lifts his phone and punches in a long series of digits. After several rings, he leaves a message on a secure memory device. "Caleb, this is Cain. I have an assignment for you. *Irrevocable.*"

He takes a deep breath, then gives the instructions, noticing that he is vibrating again. After finishing the call, he gives in to the gentle buffeting, discovering in it some spiritual comfort by imagining the breath of God vibrating a leaf in harmony with many others to produce the choral song of the wind.

It is time to prepare himself for the Council.

✦ ✦ ✦

Rebecca stares at Gideon. "So who the hell are you? And this better be good after what you've put me through. You kidnapped me!"

Charlotte puts her hands on Rebecca's shoulders and forces the young woman to sit down. "More like *saved* you."

"I just need to know what's going on."

"Gideon is… well, an old friend, kind of. This is going to sound a bit strange but—he was assigned to keep me safe during a mission I was on five years ago. Without my knowledge, I might add. Normally, though—" she glances at Gideon self-consciously— "normally he kills people for a living."

Gideon rolls his eyes. This isn't the way he would have explained it.

Rebecca stares at Gideon. "So you're a professional killer?"

"Assassin." Gideon uses his preferred terminology. "Of bad guys."

"Well that kind of makes sense, the way you went all Chuck Norris on those guys at the apartment. Who do you work for?"

"You're pretty direct, aren't you—for a kidnap victim?"

Charlotte intervenes. "Rebecca, it's time for introductions. Please meet Gideon. No last name. Gideon, this is Rebecca Sinkler." She motions for them to shake hands.

They do, unenthusiastically.

"Now then, Gideon works for a secret order called the Sicarii. They originated back in the time of Jesus and…"

Rebecca interrupts. "And grew out of the Essene brotherhood who left us the Dead Sea scrolls, yes I know. Cain told me that much. But you're saying the Sicarii are assassins, not an order of ascetics?"

Gideon stands up. "Hold on. How do you know Cain?"

"He said he used to be called Greg, Charlotte's son. He speaks to me on the grid," Rebecca explains. But Charlotte has to fill in the details to a highly skeptical Gideon.

"So tell me, Gideon," Rebecca says. "Why are we running from, it seems, *everyone*?"

Gideon exchanges a glance with Charlotte, who leans forward.

"We may be in a hurry, so I'm going to give you the short version. My organization instructed me to…" he hesitates, sheepishly looking at Charlotte, "I was directed to assassinate Charlotte."

Rebecca turns to Charlotte, confused.

"But you're still alive," she says. And then to Gideon: "Are you not very good at your job?"

"Charlotte, being the nosy investigative journalist that she is, was investigating our organization and apparently getting too close to something. They felt threatened. Seems that this year something big is going to happen, something important, and they couldn't afford any interference."

Rebecca turns to Charlotte. "Investigating—*why?*"

"They took everything from me. My whole family. Don't you think I have a right to be a little pissed off?"

"My head is swimming here," Rebecca says. "So you wanted to, what? Expose them, like in some sort of *60 Minutes* thing? And if you succeeded, then what? They'd go away? And what about your mother? And Greg? What would happen to them?"

Charlotte doesn't like these questions so she turns away.

Rebecca has another thought. "But if Greg and your mother are now the head of—of this Sicarii thing—and the organization ordered you killed, then your son and your mother... they must have—"

"Given the order." Charlotte completes the statement. It's the first time that she has admitted out loud that her own son and mother want her assassinated.

"I just can't believe Greg would do this," Rebecca says.

There is a pause in the conversation.

"On the other hand," Rebecca says at last, "you kind of picked the fight, didn't you, with your investigation?"

"So you're taking *their* side?"

"Hey, I'm in the middle here. I just came to your apartment to leave an apologetic message so maybe you'd, you know, reconsider me as your assistant."

Rebecca stands and walks around the small room, looking at shelves stacked with cell phones, ammunition, canned food, and other survivalist supplies. In an open crate she sees a number of automatic firearms.

"Okay, it's clear to me now," Rebecca says. "This is hell."

Chapter 12

To enter the Inner Chamber, Eve and Cain walk down a fifty-foot promenade, a tunnel roughly hacked out of stone. Not until this year had Cain fathomed the significance of the unusual features of this path. Ahead lies the door to the chamber, but the path leads them between two polished standing stones, each shaved flat at the top to hold an enormous cluster of white quartz crystals. These crystals guard a circle of smaller upright stones that surround the door, a kind of miniature Stonehenge.

The Inner Chamber is smaller than Cain had envisioned before his first annual Congress of Souls. At the front of the chamber is a dais containing a long wooden table with five chairs facing Eve and Cain. Another table is situated on the floor below with another seven chairs facing the guests. All of the chairs are occupied by men in black business suits.

At the high table, the center man, perhaps just shy of sixty, is European with hazel eyes that seem to turn blue in certain light. His scarlet tie stands out like a tongue of fire. To his left is a darker skinned man, perhaps Semitic, in a purple tie. To the left is a man who easily could be Italian in a blue tie.

Behind the chair of the man in the scarlet tie, a column rises, providing the resting place for a black stone about a foot long, maybe eight inches wide and less than a half-foot thick. The glistening flecked stone seems to hover above the man, who finally gestures for Eve and Cain to take a seat at a small table facing the Twelve.

"Thank you Michael," Eve says.

"As you probably know," Michael replies in perfect English, "this meeting breaks tradition. Never before have we had two sessions in one year."

"We are honored," Eve says.

Michael looks to his right, then his left, as if gathering his thoughts.

"Ever since Sarah accepted the mantle of Eve nearly two thousand years ago, your Order has performed without failure each of the missions this council has assigned. Not that some didn't present challenges. I would like to acknowledge the role that you and Cain have played in continuing this important tradition."

Michael stands and begins to applaud. Following his cue, the others stand and their applause echoes in the small stone chamber. Eve and Cain slowly nod their heads in acknowledgement.

But then, after the men in black take their seats, a tomblike silence engulfs them all.

Michael's smile disappears. He speaks quietly, but his eyes are suddenly blazing. "Do you know why we have called a second Congress, Eve? Do you, Cain?"

Shaken by Michael's suddenly somber tone, Eve cowers, her eyes searching the table for an answer.

Cain boldly speaks up. "This is the year of the Merging," he says.

"And do you know what that means?"

Cain looks at his grandmother and replies, "We do."

"No, I'm afraid you do not," Michael says. "You may superficially understand your new mission, but you cannot possibly comprehend the consequences of failure… or of success, for that matter."

Cain doesn't know if he is being chastised or prepared for a briefing, so he simply nods his head.

"If you don't complete this most important mission," Michael continues, "it will be as though the past three thousand years never happened. We are here out of concern."

Cain sees where this is leading. He decides to take the initiative.

"Excuse me, if I may make a comment?"

Michael nods approval.

"I believe you are concerned about our family matter."

Michael calls upon the gentleman to his right. "Gabriel?"

Gabriel adjusts his purple tie and says, "*Family matter* is a benign way of describing a threat." He hesitates, as if for dramatic effect. "Charlotte is your daughter, Eve. And your mother, Cain. A woman of high capability who has embarked on a personal mission to expose us. She is perhaps our greatest risk, next to her father, of course. Both of them have had the opportunity to learn, however inadvertently, useful information about the Order. Sariel?"

Gabriel turns to the man in the blue tie, who speaks with a French accent without looking at either guest. "It would be natural for either of you to have some misgivings about taking the necessary actions to resolve this situation. So we would like to be very clear—Charlotte Ansari and her father, Thompson Walker, are major liabilities. They must be eliminated soon. We understand you have ordered this action." He looks up at Eve and Cain for the first time. "Is that correct?"

"We directed Gideon to carry out the actions," Eve responds.

Cain feels the heat of twelve pairs of eyes.

"Cain, do we have any news about this mission?" Michael asks.

"Gideon has betrayed us," Cain replies boldly. *They probably already know*. Eve looks at Cain, clearly shaken, but with a flicker of—what? Hope?

"So Charlotte is still alive and now under the protection of Gideon." Michael forms a pyramid with his fingers, thinking deeply. "Then all three must be eliminated. Now the question that is before us is, do you have any hesitation?"

Eve stoically looks at Cain who replies with a simple "No."

"When assembled in this room," Michael says, "the Twelve have the God-given power to discern the truth, so be careful how you answer. Lying to the Council is treason."

Sariel ominously leans forward in his chair. "Because of the extraordinary conflicts of interest here, we have no choice but to undertake the unprecedented act of judging a sitting Eve and Cain. If either of you are found to be wanting, you will be removed from your position. *Permanently*."

Eve and Cain both understand the meaning of *permanently*. It means death.

"If both of you are found wanting, then you must decide who will continue to lead the Sicarii—under strict supervision of course. Or, as an alternative, one of you can simply eliminate the other. We cannot lose you both at a time like this. If you understand, please rise."

Eve and Cain slowly rise. Cain is not one to experience flights of emotion, but the thought of losing his grandmother is terrifying. He has seen the look of despair on her face when discussing Charlotte's fate. She had agreed with the termination order, but she is certainly clever enough to attempt a clandestine rescue if she were bluffing.

As his mind ticks off concerns about his grandmother, it suddenly detours into even more frightening territory. He starts to wonder about the repressed doubts he'd had when imposing a death sentence on his mother. Does he still harbor uncertainties? Even the phone call from Arnav—the one giving "bad news" about Charlotte and Gideon on the run—gave him a shiver of pleasure. Will the Twelve find him wanting as well?

"Eve," Sariel says, "Do you have any misgiving about the fate of your daughter?"

Eve sullenly shakes her head and says, "No."

"And are you prepared to do your utmost to see that this mission is accomplished quickly?"

"Of course I am."

Cain senses the emotional battle that Eve is going through despite her cold and definitive responses. Will the Twelve sense this as well?

Sariel continues. "Cain, are you completely free of any reservations about the decision to execute your mother, and do you pledge to direct this effort without doubt and remorse to the best of your ability?"

Cain stares straight at Sariel and replies, "Yes, absolutely."

"As for the Twelve," Michael says, addressing the Council, "when each of you has reached a verdict in both cases, please raise your hand."

Immediately nine hands are thrust into the air, including Michael's. Within a few more seconds all hands are up.

"You may lower your hands," Michael says. "Now then, if you believe that Eve has failed to honestly testify to the truth, please stand."

For a moment, Cain feels hope. No one rises. But then, one by one, with a groaning of chairs and shuffling of feet, each of the men in black solemnly stands.

Only Cain can hear Eve's terrified gasp.

"You may all be seated except for Cain," Michael says.

Eve slumps into her chair, reeling from the sudden turn of events. Her legs would not have supported her for another minute.

"And now, in the matter of Cain," Michael continues, "if you believe that he has shown a lack of truthfulness and that his commitment to the mission must be questioned, then please stand."

One man in the front row rises hurriedly, followed by two more. Within seconds all but one is standing.

"Raphael," Michael says, directing his gaze to the lone seated man, the oldest in the room. "Do you have any questions, my friend, or are you resolute in your verdict?"

Raphael looks up at Michael. "I cannot make a determination. I'm so sorry."

"Then we have a unanimous decision of the remaining eleven. Cain, you may be seated."

Cain sits down next to his grandmother.

"Since both of you have been found wanting, you have six hours to resolve the matter among yourselves. We care not which method you use. You may both be excused."

Eve and Cain rise and walk out of the Inner Chamber together.

In the promenade, Cain says, "Maybe this is just a test."

Eve stops suddenly and Cain turns to stare into the old woman's moist eyes.

"This is no test," she says, whispering. "They *know*. They *always* know. It is not enough to do. We must also believe in what we do."

A cresting wave of dread crashes over Greg. He feels as if he is drowning in emotion. Never before have his feelings cascaded so uncontrollably. The sheer weight of the surge takes away his breath and his words.

Visibly trembling, Eve sums up their predicament. "It seems neither of us wants to lose our entire family."

"I don't want to lose *you*," Greg clarifies. He had never imagined a time without Eve, without *any* family at all. Thinking about it is like falling into an abyss. *Where are these feelings coming from?*

Eve gathers herself and starts to walk. "So there it is, the outcome of the totality of causes. Nothing to be done about what's done. I suppose we'll have to prepare for battle. Which of us do you suppose is on the side of good?"

The question staggers her grandson. But then a brightly sonorous voice, either remembered or imagined, slashes like a comet through the storm in his brain.

The voice says, "Are we in the middle of a war? Or is this hell?"

"If this is hell," Cain says out loud, answering the imagined question, "it's one of our own making."

"Then it's time to make something else."

Chapter 13

At this time of night, Arnav quickly catches a cab, arriving at the anonymous gray door within a few minutes. He pays the driver extra for transporting a canine and begins his pretend routine of dog walking. Within a minute, a Mercedes sedan pulls up beside him.

"Arnav," the driver says.

"Danny, how's it going?"

"Okay. Jeremy's down below. Alarm went off."

"I know, could be trouble. I'm his back-up."

"Need a cube?"

Arnav shakes his head. He has a magnet. "Just something besides this 9mm."

Danny pops the trunk open and Arnav steps around, takes out an automatic rifle with a red dot laser scope. "This should do."

This could be his ticket to becoming a full-fledged Brother.

"Around the world," Gideon explains to his captive audience, "the Sicarii have mapped out and utilized the existing subterranean worlds beneath many major cities. Here in New York, in London, Paris, Rome, Moscow, Seoul, and many other places. It's an ideal world for a clandestine organization. In New York, did you know there are over a thousand subway lines with over seven thousand miles of track? And that's just the operating lines. Many more are abandoned, closed off, hidden—forgotten. Including entire train stations, like the two you've seen. And there are nearly fifteen hundred miles of sewer lines large enough to walk through. Twelve transport tunnels under rivers. Abandoned floodways. Bootlegger chambers and gang hideouts, even seventeenth century forts. All underground. And we know them all."

Rebecca is stunned by this. "I mean, for how long have you…"

"For thousands of years. A few decades after the crucifixion, the Sicarii were chased onto the top of Masada in Israel where they committed mass suicide. But a mother and several children survived. They taught other Jews about the immense catacombs beneath the Temple of Jerusalem, and they used these underground chambers to launch attacks. They also hid weapons, supplies, and great treasures in those caves and tunnels. So you see, the Sicarii have been mole people for two thousand years."

"And the signs?" Charlotte asks.

"The ancient Essenes spoke and read Aramaic, which is quite different than Arabic. Today we use it as a code language, kind of like how the U.S. Army used the Navajo language as an unbreakable code during World War II. Not many people today know Aramaic. But all Sicarii do."

Gideon glances at his watch.

We don't have much time left. They'll be here soon."

"Who?" Charlotte asks, concerned.

Gideon ignores her, instead finding small backpacks on a shelf. He tosses one to each of the women. From a crate in the corner of the room he removes a hard-shelled box the size of a large brief case. Using his neodynium magnet, he slides a metal bar inside the lid, which allows it to open. Inside are stacks of U.S. currency in one hundred dollar denominations. He starts handing out bundles of the bills to Rebecca and Charlotte.

"There should be a couple hundred thousand here."

They stuff the money into their backpacks. Gideon's pack is larger, allowing him to add numerous loaded 9mm clips and a Dell notebook he finds on a shelf.

He rustles through some other boxes and finds one that is locked. It opens easily with the magnetic cube. Inside he finds several items that please him greatly. He removes them, sits down on a chair, racks his Glock, and faces the door.

"Any minute now," he says. "Here, put these on."

Jeremy weaves through the dark entrails of subterranean New York, his headlamp beaming like a great Cyclops eye. By his calculation he is within thirty seconds of Sword 14, the secured supply room. There've been no Level 3 warnings so he's not too worried about enemy intrusion. Still, as he was trained to do, he switches off his lamp before making the final turn to the station platform.

Dusty streaks of light finger through grates and vents carving out objects in the darkness. Slowly now Jeremy leaps from the twisted track onto the platform, inching his way toward the featureless door he has visited countless times during his rounds.

The door is shut tight. If someone had entered, they have either left or locked themselves in. There is no visible damage to the door, which means that whoever set off the alarm had a legal means of entry—a neodynium magnet. That would usually indicate a member of the Sicarii.

Even so, Jeremy's heart begins a mad dance as he approaches the door and listens, hearing nothing. Next step, he must enter the room. Placing his cube against the door produces the distinctive *thump* of the metal bar. The problem with this step is that if someone is inside, they have now been alerted. He slides the bar to the right.

Step three for interrogating the room is to push the door open and stand back, weapon ready for action.

He pushes.

He stands back.

The room is dark and silent. Maybe the visitors have left.

Perhaps not.

Step four is to toss in a canister of "smoke," a special mixture of chemical agents that humans can't tolerate for more than a few seconds. Unfortunately, Jeremy left the canisters in the car. He'd never needed them before. He had never gotten to this step. On two occasions he has been greeted by fellow Sicarii seeking a safe harbor. Once a Brother was simply needing to restock supplies for a mission.

Step five is to secure any non-Sicarii occupants. Well, there is only one way to do that. Enter the room prepared for confrontation.

Never has he entered a dark Sword chamber, so he steps forward slowly, tentatively, as if stealth is able to cast a cloak of protection around him.

One step, then another.

One more step—

Flying!

Striking the floor now. Not sure how.

The wind knocked out of him.

Light in his eyes.

"Jeremy!" A familiar voice.

The room lights switch on, the door slams shut, the metal bar *thumps* and *thwacks*!

The young man is pulled by his shirt to a seating position.

"Gideon?" he says.

Gideon and the women pull off their gas masks.

"Where's the smoke?" Gideon is distressed. "Didn't I teach you anything? Good God, man, you're going to get yourself killed."

"Sorry, I—I left it upstairs. Didn't seem like a big deal down here."

"Everything is a big deal, that's how we stay alive."

Gideon hauls the young man to his feet, pulls his face close. Jeremy can feel Gideon's hot breath as he hears: "I should kill you right here."

Jeremy is thrown into a chair. He looks up, humiliated, then glances at Charlotte. He cocks his head, trying to place that familiar face. "CCN, right?"

Charlotte just stares back.

Jeremy turns to Rebecca. "Daughter?" he asks.

"Kidnap victim." Rebecca says.

Jeremy doesn't hear her. His eyes are feasting on Rebecca's beauty.

"Listen to me, Jeremy." Gideon guides Jeremy's eyes away from Rebecca. "What have you heard up above? Anything we should be concerned about? Is anyone looking for us?"

"I haven't heard anything," Jeremy replies, his eyes uncontrollably drifting back to Rebecca. "Honest, nothing. Course I've been down here for a while now."

Gideon nods. "Jeremy, we need you to take us upstairs by the shortest route, okay?"

"No problem. But what's up?"

"Listen to me now, you know me, Jeremy. I recruited you, trained you. And now you must trust me completely, no matter what anyone says. I can't explain right now, but some very complicated things are happening. Some of our own are trying to assassinate me."

This snaps Jeremy out of his Rebecca reverie. "That's not possible!"

"It is, Jeremy. Now can I count on you to help us get out of here? Do you trust me?"

Jeremy's brain is moving at light-speed.

"Yes, sure—of course."

"Trust me and we'll all be fine."

"So let's do it."

Silently, they all pack up their supplies. Gideon leads them to the door. He has to assume that the scene at the apartment building has given away his traitorous actions to the ever-vigilant Order. It's possible that Sicarii agents have already reached Sword 14 and are waiting outside. But they can't stay here.

He turns out the light. "Sixty seconds for your eyes to adjust," he says.

A minute later he slides the metal bar to the left and pulls the door open.

Crouching, he slips through the opening. Only a few objects—mainly stacked boxes and fallen rocks—litter the station platform. Thin shards of light leave most of the space in darkness. With his eyes mostly useless, Gideon focuses on listening—and wishing the supply team had thought to stock the room with night vision goggles.

He can hear his own heart. Some drops of water ahead. The faint rumble of a train somewhere overhead, then gone.

He steps forward slowly, hears the crackle of something underfoot. Damn! In this echo chamber, that mistake could be his last.

But nothing happens.

Slowly feeling for other noisy objects with his foot, he takes another step. And then he feels Rebecca's hand touching him on the shoulder, making sure he's within reach. He knows that Charlotte is behind Rebecca, and Jeremy at the rear.

Something here makes him nervous, but he's not sure what.

He takes two more steps, appreciating the unpracticed stealth of those behind him. His sense of hearing is stretching out now, compensating for lack of sight.

A rat scurries across the platform floor, and the sound of it seems magnified. Rebecca's frightened hand on his shoulder squeezes tightly.

Another step, and then yes! Now he understands.

He hears it. The soft panting of a dog.

He turns his eyes in that direction. The panting grows louder.

Gideon strips off his suit coat, wrapping it around his left forearm.

"Down! Now!" he shouts.

His companions drop to the floor as Gideon ducks behind a large box.

A disembodied voice says, "Gideon, I don't care about the others. Just you."

"Sorry, we're a set," Gideon says. "All or none."

"Then—sorry, Brother."

The sound of paws scrambling over concrete. A fierce growl. And then the dog is on Gideon, fangs tearing at his padded forearm. The dog is strong and mad, knocking Gideon onto his back, working its muzzle toward his throat.

"Bella, here girl!"

Jeremy's voice, impossibly cheerful, echoes in the darkness.

Confused, the dog releases Gideon's forearm and turns its head.

"C'mere girl."

Suddenly the dog jumps up and trots over to Jeremy.

Gideon hears munching sounds. The young man is giving the dog treats!

Sitting up, Gideon sees a red laser beam penetrating the dusty air, the end of it painting Jeremy's body, trying to avoid the dog.

Gideon points his Glock at the source of the red beam and fires once. Twice. Then again and again.

The red beam slants toward the floor, then disappears. With his flashlight on, Gideon races to the spot where the assassin must have been standing.

A man in night vision goggles lies there. Gideon pulls off the dead man's goggles then turns away. It's not easy killing a friend.

"Sorry, Arnav."

Jeremy, Charlotte and Rebecca rush toward the light, not wanting to be too far from Gideon. Bella, the German shepherd, looks down at Arnav, whimpering and licking the dead man's face while Jeremy strokes the dog's head.

"Here, take these," Gideon says, handing the night vision goggles to Jeremy.

He has killed a Sicarii agent.

There is no turning back.

Ever.

Chapter 14

"Three men down?" William Wyatt can't believe what he's been told. "This guy has made absolute fools of us."

Allison, who possesses an oversize intellect in an oversize body, nods sympathetically. "As he has in the past."

"Who assigned the three stooges to this mission anyway?"

"You did, sir."

"Well I didn't know enough about them. And you would think that *three* would be able to handle it. Anyway, does the client know about this bungle?"

"Not yet."

"Not ever! Understand?"

Wyatt leans back in a plush executive chair. The leather squeaks annoyingly. With a popping sound he nervously puffs air out of his mouth.

Until three years ago Wyatt had been the Director of the U.S. Central Intelligence Agency, the best intelligence job in the world. But then his party lost the big election. He won a sizeable pay raise, though, when he landed an SVP job at Blackwatch, the world's largest private military and security provider. He brought his loyal assistant Allison with him and she was able to trade up from a tiny shared Georgetown apartment to a large home in northern Virginia. The big contractors refer to this public-to-private migration as *chutes and ladders*.

"You have a two o'clock conference call with Moshe this afternoon for an update on the mission. I can postpone."

"No—may as well get it over with."

Ever since his predecessor was assassinated by the Sicarii, Moshe Gavish, the current head of Kidon—the department for assassinations and kidnappings inside Mossad—has been a lucrative Blackwatch client. In the old days, like the CIA, Kidon had outsourced its most difficult and dangerous assignments to the Sicarii because of their stellar reputation. The Sicarii motto could be *We Never Fail*. This reputation remains unblemished, but when the previous Kidon director, David Weiss, and a highly valued agent were assassinated by Gideon five years ago, an implacable grudge was born. No matter that Weiss had betrayed the Sicarii first.

And now, just days ago, another Kidon agent was slain by Gideon in Santa Barbara. This man's killing occurred during a failed attempt to abduct Eve, the Sicarii's matriarch, heightening Kidon's humiliation. The man's corpse, when found near a softball diamond and identified by American authorities as a Kidon operative, incited a very unpleasant behind-the-scenes skirmish between U.S. and Israeli diplomats over the acceptable limits of Israeli operation on American soil.

Moshe wants Gideon killed. And after that he wants the Sicarii organization defanged. It has ceased to be a reliable ally. The problem is that Moshe, like William Wyatt and the heads of many other military and intelligence organizations, personally fears the Sicarii. For two thousand years Sicarii have successfully remained hidden to all but those who have needed their professional services. They operate like ghosts and have proven their ability to penetrate hardened defenses without detection. For centuries the Sicarii have altered the course of history by pruning back the sprouts of leadership that give life and hope to their enemies.

But no one knows the Sicarii agenda. When it coincides with that of a client, the Sicarii agree to take an assignment—for a high price. Many believe it is these staggering fees that financially support the clandestine organization. But no one knows for sure. The only certainty is that the Sicarii will always fulfill a mission. Unless crossed. And in the world of intelligence, everyone crosses someone sometime. This makes Sicarii clients nervous, because this shadowy group of lethal operatives appears to have no reservations about retaliating in a very personal way.

Just ask David Weiss.

"Might I suggest, sir, that we tell Moshe we have Gideon under surveillance and are waiting for the best time to fulfill the contract?"

"Do we have him under surveillance?"

"If we want to continue building a profitable relationship with Moshe—then, yes we do. Or will."

"You know, this *Gideon* is a real pain in the ass."

"Will you authorize all necessary resources to resolve that pain?"

"I was just thinking, this is the kind of job that we should contract out to the Sicarii. They could handle it."

Allison smiles faintly, understanding the irony in this.

Wyatt continues: "The cost of seeing this through now that Gideon's slipped the net could be more than we're being paid."

"True, but then, you know Gideon will soon find out that *you* ordered those three agents to Charlotte's apartment. Things could get personal, like they did in New Delhi."

"I survived that."

"He let you go, sir. I wouldn't count on him doing that again."

"This is what happens, I guess, when you make a pact with the devil."

"Is *he* the devil, sir?"

That he has to think about the answer does not make William Wyatt any more comfortable.

Chapter 15

"This is very bad," Jeremy says, looking down on the slain Arnav. "They'll wonder why him and not me. They'll want to know what I saw, who did it, where you were going."

Gideon nods. He knows that Jeremy will not survive the Sicarii interrogation.

"Maybe you knocked me unconscious?" Jeremy says, desperate. "Gideon, just rough me up a bit. If I was out cold, I didn't see anything, and maybe…"

"Forget it!" Gideon starts searching Arnav's body. "It'll never work. You're coming with us."

He finds Arnav's cell phone, puts it into his shirt pocket.

"So what am I going to do then?" Jeremy asks.

"Same as Rebecca—stay alive for a while. Unless that doesn't interest you."

Jeremy is still searching for a way out. "Hey—I'm sure I can explain this in a way that…"

"Think, dammit! They sent you down here to check out the alarm. Then they sent Arnav here to get me. They just don't know the outcome yet. But they do know you were my recruit. My trainee. They know the kind of bond that can form. They will never believe that you didn't help me out. Believe me, if you go back, you're toast."

Jeremy jams his hands into his pockets. "So what's going on here, Gideon? You gone rogue?"

"They ordered me to do something I couldn't do."

Jeremy turns to Charlotte, studies her for a moment. "It involves *her*, doesn't it? They wanted you to kill her, but…"

"Yes! Now we've got to move out." He takes a step.

Jeremy doesn't budge. He says, "So now I'm on the run because you fell for a woman. What about the oath you taught me? The undying loyalty you said linked us all together?" He is looking betrayed.

Gideon's eyes drill holes into Jeremy. "Make a decision. Come with us—or stay." He waits a few seconds, then turns toward the tunnel and starts walking.

Charlotte and Rebecca scramble to follow.

With a sigh and a glance at Bella lying beside Arvan, Jeremy reluctantly brings up the rear.

✦ ✦ ✦

An hour later, four grimy people push through a door in the sub-basement of an office building in midtown Manhattan. Jeremy leads the group to a freight elevator that takes them to the seventeenth floor.

At the far end of a dimly lit corridor, he taps out a number on an electronic keypad next to a sign that reads AMOS GARMENT CO. A door unlatches. Inside are racks of clothing and shelves of other articles for Brothers on the run.

"Two minutes," Gideon says. "Find something that fits and put it on. We've just alerted the command center that someone's entered the dressing room. Let's do it!"

In a flurry they change clothes and flee toward the freight elevator. Which is on the move.

"They're here already," Gideon says. "They'll have people on the elevators and coming up the stairs. Just follow me."

Gideon leads them to a stairwell and down two flights of stairs. Ducking into the fifteenth floor corridor, he motions for the others to back up against the wall while he listens for footsteps. When the sound of shuffling feet is past, Gideon silently opens the door. He waits for the sound of a door opening and closing above, signaling that no one is still in the stairwell.

He leads the other three down the stairs to the first floor but pauses before opening the door to the lobby.

"They will have left someone down here. Jeremy, they don't know that you're on our side. Go out and disable whoever's there. Can you do that?"

Jeremy looks at Rebecca, who stares back hopefully.

He nods.

In the lobby Jeremy finds a beefy, blonde man with an automatic weapon. The man is alone and surprised as Jeremy approaches.

"Jeremy, how'd *you* get here?"

Jeremy notices that the main elevator is now in motion. Someone is coming back down.

"No time," Jeremy says. "They've just flushed Gideon from the dressing room. He's coming down the elevator."

The blonde man turns toward the elevator. Lights on a panel show a rapid descent. He takes a nervous step toward the lift, and that's when Jeremy puts a foot into the back of his leg, sending him painfully to the floor. A hard kick to the chin knocks him out. Jeremy picks up the man's weapon, a compact Heckler & Koch MP5K.

Gideon leads the women out of the stairwell and through the lobby.

"The elevator's on the way down," Jeremy warns Gideon.

But there is a vehicle in front of the building with its lights on. Probably a Sicarii driver.

"I got this," Jeremy says. He exits the building and races toward the black Acura SUV, waving his arms. The driver pops the door locks for his "associate" and welcomes Jeremy into the front seat.

Gideon turns to the elevator. The panel shows it is now at floor five. He turns back to the SUV just in time to see an unconscious driver being shoved into the street.

Grabbing Charlotte's hand, Gideon rushes the women into the back seat of the SUV. Turning, he sees three Sicarii agents kneeling by their fallen comrade in the illuminated lobby. Suddenly the men stand and look in Gideon's direction.

Gideon leaps into the front seat just as the frantic Sicarii team bursts through the door. The SUV lunges forward and a single shot strikes the right rear taillight.

"I always wondered what it would be like to be on the wrong side of us," Jeremy says. "Now I know."

"No you don't," Gideon says while inspecting Arnav's phone. "Not yet."

Jeremy adjusts the rearview mirror and catches a glimpse of Rebecca shyly meeting his gaze.

Chapter 16

The cavernous living room/office sits between two large bedrooms in the Waldorf Astoria suite.

Gaining access without leaving electronic breadcrumbs to the suite was difficult. A large sum of cash and one of Gideon's false passports, in the name of George Stinson of Milwaukee, had eliminated the need for a credit card, which could be traced. The fake document had not been provided by the Sicarii; instead, it was evidence of Gideon's foresight. He had long considered the possible future need to separate himself from an Order that no one is ever allowed to leave. A longtime friend in New Delhi, now deceased, had prepared the counterfeit passport and some other documents in exchange for professional services provided by Gideon "off the books." These materials have been hidden in secure locations known only by the assassin himself.

Gideon is hunched over the notebook computer taken from Sword 14. He is hacking the software to make the computer untraceable on the Internet, a skill he acquired recently as a barter with an British geek called "Wonderboy" who was co-founder of a global hacking consortium known as Sentient. This skill defines the limits of Gideon's geeky capabilities. To make the hack work, files need to be deleted from the hard drive, and several new files must be downloaded and installed from a complicated, password-protected URL that Gideon has memorized.

Charlotte is trying unsuccessfully to nap on one of two plush sofas while Rebecca, lounging on a matching unit, fiddles with the remote that controls a large flat panel TV. She impatiently flips from one news channel to another.

"All this action tonight, and nothing about it on TV," Rebecca complains.

"Pretty early for the media to get the scent," Gideon says. "That's good for us. Sometime tomorrow—" he glances at his watch—"today, that is—they'll figure out that Charlotte is missing because she won't show up for something important. Then it will take a while to try tracking her down before they realize that she's actually disappeared. That's all the time we have before they call in the authorities to investigate. Then everything gets more difficult for us, especially here in New York."

Frustrated, Rebecca switches the TV off. "It occurs to me that, actually, no one at all will notice me missing. Maybe ever."

Charlotte hears sadness in Rebecca's voice. She starts to sit up to—*what*? She clearly is missing the mother gene. And lacking the instincts to comfort and nurture. That's why she was the *worst mother ever* when it came to Greg. That's what made him become Cain—what flushed him from her nest into the clutches of her own mother, the co-architect with her husband of the world's most dysfunctional family. With Miriam—Eve—as her role model during her impressionable first seven years, what chance did Charlotte have to learn how to be a good mother?

What she learned was how to abandon a family, as Miriam did, leaving unannounced to take the hereditary reins of the Sicarii. Like her mom, Charlotte had become expert at abandonment; she had abandoned her son through obsessive work, selfish dreams of fame, constant travel, and most of all an inability to communicate with her Asperger's son. Charlotte, the professional communicator, didn't know how to talk to her own son. Whether from guilt or shame or frustration, she could never share her feelings with Greg. So he remained cut off, without a lifeline.

And here is a young woman, Rebecca, alone like Greg and terrified of what's happening, desperate for comforting, but unfortunately hooked up with a professional assassin who has few if any nurturing skills and a failed mother who can't even communicate with her own shrink.

Charlotte has just finished sitting up when a knock on the door startles everyone. Gideon grabs his Glock from the desktop and motions for everyone else to sit tight as he approaches the door. The knocking—two quick raps, a pause, then three more quick raps—was the signal Jeremy was instructed to use if it was safe for Gideon to open the door.

But you never know for sure.

Gideon looks out the peep hole and sees Jeremy's face. He cracks open the door and stands back, pointing his weapon directly at the young man who enters.

Jeremy thrusts his right arm into the air in surrender but continues to hold a paper bag with the left. "Hey, it's me, man."

Gideon quickly closes the door and fastens the night latch, stuffing the Glock into his waistband.

Jeremy sets the bag onto a polished cherry coffee table. "I brought food. I'm starving, guys, how about you?"

Apparently everyone is famished. They cluster around the bag as Jeremy pulls out Chinese take-out, egg rolls and candy bars.

"Ohhh, man—they forgot the hot mustard!" Jeremy looks crushed.

"But they remembered plasticware and napkins," Rebecca says helpfully.

As the others divvy up the food, Gideon asks, "Jeremy—the SUV?"

"In a No Parking zone about five blocks away," Jeremy smiles mischievously. "They'll have to pay the fine. Like you said, I left Arnav's cell phone on the front seat, switched on."

✦ ✦ ✦

Eve stands on the balcony looking out over the dark mountains. How many years of service now? Too many, all unappreciated. Hadn't she given up her family, proven her loyalty countless times, performed every responsibility without fail? It doesn't matter.

And Greg—just a boy when he came here. He learned so fast, became so dedicated. The Sicarii had become his life.

And now grandmother and grandson must work out a solution. One of them must die so the other can continue to lead the organization. What a sadistic choice.

"Grandma, they'll be coming soon. Are you sure?"

"Very," Eve says.

Rachel has been waiting inside the chamber to be called. Eve used to wonder at what could have made Rachel, a woman even older than Eve, betray her Order, but that question has been answered. When one's organization turns against you despite your steadfast allegiance and courageous leadership, all loyalty drains away. Thoughts of revenge rise up. Righteous indignation begins to rule.

But in the end, for Eve it all comes down to her grandson. There is only one acceptable solution.

Eve turns and motions for Rachel to join them on the balcony. Both women wear the traditional gray robe. "Rachel, do you understand the decision that we have made?"

"I do."

Eve looks over the balcony at the rocks hundreds of feet below. If only she could just fly away! The thought of a body smashing into those boulders makes her shudder.

"I'm not sure I have the courage to do this by myself," Eve says. "Cain must be the one to push me, do you understand?"

"There must be another way," Rachel says.

"This is the *only* way. Now come closer and help me with the ritual."

✦ ✦ ✦

The Twelve have agreed to accept the decision of Eve and Cain on the grand balcony. As they march out of the North passage, beneath the words of Enoch and into the meeting hall, a piercing scream echoes throughout the chamber. Their pace quickens until they are all standing on the balcony facing Cain.

"It is done," Cain says. Then he turns to the balustrade and looks into the abyss. "You will find her body down there."

Chapter 17

The food is gone. Even the candy bars.

"It's 4:30 in the morning," Gideon says. "Time for some shut-eye. A lot to do today. Jeremy, you and I have the west bedroom. Wake-up call in five hours."

"Not until I get some answers," Charlotte interjects.

Gideon's shoulders slump. He knew this was coming. He stares into Charlotte's bloodshot eyes, which are half-hidden by droopy lids. "Where do you want me to start?"

Rebecca and Jeremy, half-dozing until now, stir with the promise of some resolution to their perplexity.

"Just help me understand why you're helping me," Charlotte says.

Gideon stands up and walks to the mini-bar. He bypasses the bottles of expensive alcohol and grabs a plastic bottle of designer water.

"It's simple," he says, taking a long gulp before sitting down again. "You screwed up, Charlotte. You started investigating the Order. I don't know why, but you should have known they'd find out. They've had access to pictures on your cell phone, call logs, meeting dates, emails, even some of your conversations. Never underestimate Sicarii resources."

Charlotte fidgets. Her eyes dart from face to face. She is feeling stupid right now. Responsible for getting everyone into this mess. "It's my job to expose international corruption and political crimes," she says in her defense. "Your Order assassinates people for hire. I think that fits the definition."

"But this was personal, wasn't it?" Gideon fires back. "Charlotte, the Sicarii know you were working on this outside of CCN. This was not a job. This was revenge. As hurt as you are by the actions of your mother—and your son—they were personally cut to the bone by your vengeance."

Charlotte turns away, her face flushed. "Their feelings are hurt? I say *good*! They couldn't possibly hurt more than I do. So how do you feel about it, Gideon? Were you hurt that I've been trying to bring down your precious Order?"

Gideon taps his fingers on an end table and breathes deeply.

"Two things you should know," he says calmly. "One, it should be clear to you that it's no longer *my* Order. This evening I committed an act of high treason. They will hunt me until I am dead. And two, there is no chance in hell of bringing down that organization."

Rebecca and Jeremy are wide awake now, watching the jibes bounce back and forth like a tennis match.

"All right then," Charlotte says. "Two things you should explain. One, why did you turn your back on the Order and save me this evening? In fact, why save me at all? And two, I've been investigating for over two years. You saw my walls, my computer files. Why'd they decide to have me killed now?"

"Obviously they believe you're a threat. Maybe you were getting too close. I know that this year is something special for the Order, but I don't know what. They really didn't want anything to get in the way of whatever is going to happen this year."

"Well, there are only a few days left in the year. "Charlotte leans closer to him. "How about point number one? Why risk your life to save me?"

Gideon looks down at his knees, makes a steeple with his fingers, searching for words.

"I believe you're worth saving," he says without looking her in the eye. "For the last three years I've had my own doubts about the Order. About some of my missions. For years I never questioned the ultimate wisdom of our—*their*—council. But I started to see things differently. I wasn't so much investigating, like you, as observing. And thinking. And I discovered I couldn't make sense of it anymore. So I thought, well now, are you really going to jump ship? But of course, once a Brother, always a Brother, *'til death do us part.*"

He looks at Jeremy, who is now in the same difficult position. Jeremy, who he persuaded to join the Order. Whose loyalty he nurtured. Who, in all likelihood, he misled.

"I started planning," Gideon continues, "for the eventuality that I might one day betray my oath. The questions loomed bigger than ever. Once my eyes were opened, the whole business seemed—just wrong. A week ago I killed a man who tried to abduct your mother, and afterward I wondered if I shouldn't have just let him do it."

He turns his gaze to Rebecca, who is clinging to his every word.

"Rebecca," he says gently, "like you, I had no parents. I was adrift. The Order became my home—and they were generous to me, loving. No one had ever loved me before. They became my family. How could they do wrong? They were so wise, and they had all the answers and reasons for everything. They deeply loved God, and so I came to love God as well."

He turns now to Charlotte, who stares at him with misty, uncertain eyes.

"But eventually I figured out that the God I loved was not the same God they followed. And then they told me that I had been chosen to assassinate you, Charlotte. It was a great honor, because you were a great threat. But you see, I had already gotten to know you in India. I protected you there. I was prepared to die to keep you safe. I came to believe in you."

He wants to say more about his feelings, about how he has dreamed about Charlotte for five years, of being with her, having a life—foolish as such dreams are for a condemned man. But he can't say these things because he knows a Sicarii assassin is not allowed a life like others, but must live with the knowledge that every moment is his death.

He is not allowed to dream.

The room is dead quiet until Gideon thinks of one more thing to say.

"Tonight was not a rash decision."

Chapter 18

Still groggy from the twelve-hour El Al flight from Jerusalem, Thompson Walker retrieves a weathered suitcase from customs and staggers through the tedious process of entering the United States. It's now 6:15 a.m. and his body craves caffeine.

The suitcase is his lone travel companion. One of its wheels is stuck, the telescoping handle is loose, the sides are bruised and beaten, but if he retired this old friend he'd be truly alone.

Walking gets the blood flowing to his legs and feet. He is coming alive now. The aroma of coffee lures him down the JFK concourse to a small coffee shop with a mercifully short line. He orders a medium light roast, room for cream.

This New York Congress of Bible Scholars has come at just the right time. Since that rude Sicarii scolding in Jerusalem he has been on edge. Tomorrow afternoon he will speak on *The Paradox of a Warring God and a Peaceful Messiah*, one of the main themes of his new book, *The Meaning of Religion*. Colleagues will congratulate him on his latest work, though sales are a fraction of what his earlier landmark tome yielded six months after publication. But he knew that *The World's Great Wisdom Traditions* was what he would be remembered for—his life's work, his redemption. Everything else would be a footnote.

The heavyset barista hands a scalding cup of coffee to Thompson who finds a jug of half & half and begins to pour a thick stream into his brew. Despite the humid steam billowing upwards, he feels a sudden chill. He's learned to trust his body's signals, and this one usually means danger. Something he has seen or heard or felt, maybe some pattern of signals, has triggered a subconscious tripwire.

He lifts the cup. The hot coffee stings his lips and tongue. Cautiously his eyes scan left and right, looking for some camouflaged threat. Hundreds of people march past, stand in ticket lines, wait for coffee, sit in uncomfortable seats for their flights. Still holding the cup, he begins wheeling his suitcase toward the exit. With a brief glance he notices a tall man step out of the coffee line to follow him.

It is always the same, this prescient tingle of nerves, the perpetual threat of surveillance, the peril of being Eve's husband. For countless operatives he is either the bait or a beacon. As lonely as he is, it seems he is never truly alone.

Almost no one is waiting for a taxi at this time of the morning. Most arriving parties are being picked up by friends or family. But Thompson, of course, has no loved ones to greet him. He is ushered to a cab where a driver flings his battered suitcase into the trunk and motions Thompson into the back seat. Before he climbs in, Thompson looks around one last time.

The tall man from the coffee line is hugging a woman next to a silver Nissan.

For Thompson, the chill persists.

"Waldorf Astoria," he tells the driver.

Allison intercepts a call at Blackwatch headquarters and passes it on to William Wyatt.

"Walker arrived just as scheduled," a voice says.

"And where did he go?"

"The Waldorf. Checking in now."

"All right, just stay with him. At some point he'll contact his daughter. I'm hoping she'll have a change in heart and agree to meet the old guy. When they do, let me know. If we find Charlotte, we find Gideon."

"Yes sir.

"One more thing. You are authorized to kill the Sicarii."

"Roger that. Will be in contact."

After wolfing down room-service brunch, the casually-attired "George Stinson" family takes the elevator to the lobby. To the public, they could be a family on vacation ready for a day of sight-seeing.

Mrs. Stinson's long black hair has been cropped short and spiky by Rebecca. Wearing a pair of oversized-glasses, bought in the gift shop this morning by Jeremy, she looks almost nothing like the Mrs. Stinson who checked in last night.

Each of the four "family" members carries a backpack, which they now refer to as their *battle essentials*. In other words, the pack contains everything they brought to the hotel. As the family passes the concierge desk, a throaty voice reaches out and grabs the attention of Mrs. Stinson.

"Charlotte?"

Charlotte's carefree facade shatters. She turns to an elderly man in a beige chair and their eyes meet coldly.

"What are you doing here?" she asks,

"At present, sitting down. I wasn't sure it was you—your *hair*…" Thompson turns to the man standing next to his daughter. "Gideon, how good to see you. I understand we just missed each other in Santa Barbara."

Charlotte takes a chair next to Thompson's. Rebecca and Jeremy crowd around. "Really now, how did you find me?" Charlotte asks in a near-whisper.

"Accident," Thompson answers. "I'm here for a speaking engagement, all expenses paid—otherwise I wouldn't be staying in a palace like this." He looks around and continues: "Just waiting to be picked up and taken to lunch."

Rebecca stares at the old man, who notices and turns back to Charlotte.

"This is, what, your replacement family?" Thompson's words cut. Immediately he glances away, ashamed.

Charlotte shows the pain. She replies curtly, "We need to talk, all right? But not here, not now." She looks at Gideon for approval as she says, "This evening, say seven o'clock, in your room. Which is?"

"Nine-fourteen." Thompson turns again to Rebecca, who is still staring. "Pleased to make your acquaintance," he says, holding out a hand. As Rebecca shakes it, he adds: "I'm Thompson Walker, Charlotte's father. Pleased to make your acquaintance…"

His tone makes it clear he is expecting her name.

"Oh, yes, I'm Rebecca. Nice to meet you too."

Jeremy offers his hand. "And Jeremy. Looking forward to this evening, sir."

"Well then, you all seem to be in a hurry to get somewhere, so off with you now." Thompson is playing the role of understanding father even though the sight of his estranged daughter makes his heart quiver. It has been five years since he has seen Charlotte.

She's aged, he thinks. *Life has been hard for us all.*

The "Stinsons" commandeer a taxi and Gideon quickly negotiates a generous four-hour fee. In Soho they visit a bland apartment above a string of shops. Gideon thumbs over a wad of bills to an "artisan" named Uncle Bill who takes photos and pledges to have counterfeit passports, visas, and American drivers licenses for Anne Butler, Christine Krippler, and William Dossey by morning. The names were gleaned from a database of usable identities matched by age, sex, and ethnicity. Even Gideon doesn't know where the actual forgeries are made, but it doesn't matter. False travel documents keep government agents from spying on their movements.

Across town Gideon stops to see "Hightower" at the Cell Shack, which does a considerable backroom business in unlocked world phones with pre-paid minutes and swappable SIM chips for every country. Every phone is stripped of GPS and customized with anti-cloning technology. Locations and calls are untraceable. All this for cash, no questions asked.

Hightower is a nonstop Mobius strip of information, often repeating, sometimes digressing, always coming back to the spirituality of wireless communication.

During a breath in the incessant flow of barely intelligible data, Gideon squeezes in a question.

"And for controlling a remote phone?"

"Oh, well, yes—you called about that, and you're in luck because I have information about fourteen known unpatched bugs in WebKit, do you know what that is?—an essential browser component used by just about every mobile operating system, and so you can exploit those bugs to gain full "root" access to the phone and use it to install a remote access tool, which means from your own phone you can activate someone else's microphone even when they're not on a call, or relay that person's phone calls or text messages to you, or track that other phone on a map..."

Finally a breath.

Gideon interjects, "So how do I use it?"

"Two grand gets you the information but you need a top-level geek to turn it into an app."

"Got just the person in mind. You sure it works?"

"Depends on the geek."

"Email me the information."

Gideon provides a complicated email address from an offshore ISP, then settles up and takes a corrugated box full of phones—tools of his trade—back to the taxi.

Travel purchases are next on the shopping list. Personal hygiene items, a few beauty aids for the ladies, walking shoes and socks, three changes of clothing and one hard-shelled suitcase with heavy-duty wheels per person. Nothing more. Just enough for living on the run.

One more stop. Gideon picks up a supply of theatrical make-up items—the ingredients for disguises.

On the way back to the Waldorf, Gideon fiddles with one of the new world phones, setting up an email account. Then he forwards the WebKit bug information to Sentient master-geek Wonderboy. He adds a specific request and promises to forward money, as much as needed, to a neutral bank account to which Wonderboy has access.

+ + +

Back at the Waldorf, the "Stinsons" march through the lobby with shopping bags, boxes and backpacks in tow, just another family of tourists returning from a shopping spree. They take an elevator to the eighth floor.

"I'll enter first," Gideon instructs as he removes the DO NOT DISTURB placard and opens the door to their room. More than once he's been surprised by unexpected guests.

The suite appears undisturbed. The beds are still unmade, meaning the cleaning staff has stayed out as directed. Gideon inspects the upper drawer of the nightstand beside his bed. As a simple intrusion detection measure, he often leaves a drawer pulled out about an inch. A clandestine intruder will usually close the drawer completely after searching it.

He notices that the drawer is now fully closed. "Someone's been in the room," he announces. "Our location is compromised."

"That's not possible," Charlotte says. "How could anyone have found us?"

"Someone followed your father," Jeremy answers, earning a respectful look from Gideon. "And as they were watching the old guy sitting in the lobby, we waltzed right over to him and had a nice visit. Then we told him we'd be back this evening."

"Well, they found nothing here," Gideon says. "Everything was on our backs. But they're probably watching us now. And Charlotte, your father is now in real danger as well."

Charlotte shakes her head. "We're like the walking plague. Everyone we touch is…"

"Even worse," Gideon interjects, "with all our stuff, when we move together it's like a major troop movement. Hard not to attract attention. Jeremy, what should we do?"

Jeremy straightens, sensing that this is a test. "We should get Charlotte's father and then split up and meet someplace else."

"Like where? We can't use any of the Sicarii safe houses. We need to go completely off the grid."

"My place then."

"Remember your training, Jeremy. Any place that has a connection to a known member of the group is not off the grid. If someone has identified you, like—I don't know, maybe your Sicarii brethren?—they'd sure as hell stake out your place. And Rebecca's."

"Then where?"

"First things first." Gideon picks up the phone and calls Thompson's room. After a few seconds he hangs up. "He's not back yet. No matter, we're going to Thompson's room now."

"How'll we get in?" Rebecca asks.

Gideon holds up the neodynium magnet.

Chapter 19

A few minutes before seven o'clock, Thompson enters his one-bedroom suite and immediately sees a room full of people.

"Sorry I'm late," he says sarcastically.

"Afraid we hit up the mini-bar," Charlotte replies.

"No problem. All expenses paid, they said. "But something tells me I won't be enjoying this wonderful suite for very long. Char, what's going on?"

Charlotte provides her father with a short-hand version of recent events, culminating with their compromised suite.

"And now *they*, whoever they are, know where we're all staying," Thompson summarizes. "And all this because you, Charlotte, were poking your nose into Sicarii business?"

Charlotte huffs. She finds this pompous old man insufferable. "We're here to keep you safe," she says coldly.

"Seems like the further away I am from you, the safer I am."

Gideon rises from a sofa, arching his spine backwards to work out the kinks of sitting. "Be smart, Thompson. You think you're safe because you're married to Eve, but don't be a fool. She gave the order to assassinate her own daughter—your daughter. And now they're likely to believe you're in league with us—why else would you be meeting us here?"

"To see my daughter," Thompson offers.

"Yeah, like they'll believe that," Charlotte snorts.

"Here is what they already know for sure," Gideon says. "You came to New York and met your daughter, who is their biggest threat—and me, a traitor. They also know from past experience that the three of us together make a potent force. In a word, my friend, you are *toast*."

"Miriam wouldn't do that to me," Thompson looks a bit deflated as he slumps into the last overstuffed chair. The group lets his hopeful denial linger in silence. Four sets of downwardly cast eyes tell Thompson that no one is buying it.

He finds himself starting to doubt his own words, so he changes the subject.

"Charlotte, here's what I don't understand—trying to attack the Sicarii by yourself. How you could you do that—go against your own flesh and blood?"

"I guess I learned it from Mom," Charlotte shoots back. "Her own flesh and blood means nothing to *her*." She pauses thoughtfully. "Sorry, I meant to say *blood* means *everything* to her. Murder. Assassination. Endless killing. Her insanity has infected her own grandson."

Thompson clears his throat and looks into Charlotte's angry eyes. "You want me to help you, that's why you're really here, isn't it?"

Charlotte looks away. She can't humiliate herself by asking for his help.

"Well I won't do it!" Thompson says. "I won't help you. Not if it means Miriam will end up dead, which is what would happen."

Charlotte's body has clenched into a tight ball. Tears sprout from her eyes. "I knew you'd choose her and not me," she says. "Fine. So why don't you just join her then? Why live apart like you do?"

Thompson leans forward aggressively. "Because I don't—I can't—Dammit, I don't condone what she does. I can't be part of it." He slouches back into the soft chair. "But I can't live without her."

"You can't be part of the killing but you can just ignore it? Pretend it's not happening? My God, what do you do when you're with her? Do you ever talk about the people they've killed? Do you laugh it off before dinner?"

"I won't do it!" Thompson defiantly leaps from his chair and marches across the room, then realizes there is no place to go. He has been pushed over the edge of his festering guilt. "I will not betray my wife," he says, turning back.

"She's not your wife." Charlotte's words are chosen to inflict maximum pain. "That woman is the bride of Satan. You can both go to hell for all I care."

Thompson turns his back on her. His hand is trembling, his face is flushed. Finally he says, "You have a son in this as well. You want to discard him too?"

Now it is Charlotte's turn to feel the edge of the knife. "He's got too much blood on his hands. Can't be saved now."

Tears stream down her face. She wonders if her mother had felt this much agony when ordering her daughter's assassination. Probably not.

Thompson turns again to face his daughter. "I'm sorry, Char—I just can't help you."

As Charlotte sullenly stares at her father, Gideon turns to Rebecca and says, "I think you should tell Thompson what you know, what you told us a few minutes ago." He glances at the old man standing rigidly across the room. "Thompson, you should sit down."

Exhausted by his outburst, Thompson returns to his chair.

Rebecca clears her throat. "Your wife has been executed," she says. Then, realizing how tactless her statement was, adds: "I'm so sorry."

Thompson looks at Rebecca, confused. "You're saying that Miriam is dead?"

"Yes, the Order believed she was a liability because of her, well, the family stuff and conflicts of interest and…"

"How could you possibly know this?" Thompson demands. It makes no sense that this newcomer, this interloper, could know such a thing. Lies, probably.

"I've been in contact with Greg."

"How is that possible?" Thompson leans forward again, postponing grief by challenging the messenger's credibility, searching for a loophole.

Jeremy intervenes. "She has an unusual ability to communicate long-distance with people without, uh, without any technology."

Thompson's ruddy face suddenly pales. "Yes, I see. A few times Miriam told me about some of their people, mainly the leaders, who had the ability to—"

"I'm very sorry to be the one to bring you such terrible news," Rebecca says.

"I knew that Miriam had this ability. We were so close. Sometimes she would just know things even when she hadn't talked to anyone." Thompson is fighting back tears, hoping that by talking he can stall the inevitable.

"Your wife wanted you to know that she will always be with you," Rebecca says, "and that you will be together again. That's what she told Greg before he…"

She stops talking because Thompson has put his hands over his face and his body is convulsing in sobs. Rebecca instinctively moves over to put her arms around the old man.

Charlotte watches her father dispassionately. She has her own internal conflicts in resolving the death of her mother with the death of a mass murderer. Miriam—Eve—was an evil woman, so why, Charlotte wonders, is she fighting back tears? She had been prepared to lead a charge that almost certainly would have resulted in her mother's death. So why is she feeling this stabbing pain?

Before she breaks down like her father, she gathers herself, focuses on a point of confusion. If she can stay focused, perhaps she can remove this sadness.

"Rebecca, you were just about to say something about Greg—that Miriam told him something before he… *what*? You didn't tell us this part before."

"To prove his loyalty, Greg was the one who…"

"My God!" Thompson interrupts. "My grandson killed my wife?" He stiffens and draws in a long, shuddering breath. "The news just keeps getting better, doesn't it?"

"He didn't want to do it," Rebecca offers.

Thompson pats Rebecca's comforting hand and stands. He walks to a desk, finds a tissue, blows his nose, and then looks around the room. Everyone is watching.

Turning to Charlotte, he straightens his back and says, "All right, let's take the bastards down. Is there a plan?"

"Yes," Gideon answers. "To do it before they kill us."

Chapter 20

Shortly before sunset, Cain leads the Twelve, who have all extended their stay for the solemn burial ceremony, through the Sicarii catacombs, a labyrinth of tunnels carved into the heart of the mountain christened long-ago as the new Carmel, the "Mountain of the Lord." By tradition, only torches are allowed to illumine the passageway. Eight resident guards, carrying Eve's body on a wooden platform, lead another sixty Brothers and staff members toward the Matriarch's final destination.

The fall from the balcony had damaged Eve's body so severely that it cannot be viewed. After it was retrieved, the shattered corpse had been wrapped in a white burial shroud and made ready for entombment. In many cases, the revered corpses interred in these catacombs had been obtained with great subterfuge in the countries where the individuals had died or were intended to be buried.

Greg leads the procession to a fork in the tunnel. To the right, untouched by torchlight, is the Hall of Martyrs containing the remains of assassins who perished in the line of duty; one hundred thirty-five bodies lie there.

The Hall of Respect, containing even older ossuaries, is located beyond the Hall of Martyrs. For centuries, a dedicated team of Sicarii tomb raiders has tracked down and relocated in this hall the remains of historic figures of importance to the Order. A handful of Old Testament prophets, two of King Solomon's High Priests, and various other more recent individuals—including Judas of Galilee, the founder of the Sicarii Order—had been discovered and identified with varying degrees of confidence.

Greg guides the procession past these chambers, following the left fork through the Council Chamber, which is the resting place for past members of the Twelve; the coffins of over two hundred of these influential personages, all men, are lined up here in neat rows on rock-hewn shelves.

At last the procession arrives at the final dimly-lit Shekinah Chamber. Here are interred the bodies of twenty-three Divine Lights and thirty-three Eves; Miriam now becomes the thirty-fourth. As Cain surveys the fifty-six stone coffins, he realizes that one day this will be his home.

An open stone sarcophagus receives the linen-wrapped body of his grandmother. The guards seal the stone box and place on the lid a lit candle symbolizing Eve's life spirit. Michael, the apparent leader of the Twelve, motions Cain forward for his part in the rite.

Cain first snuffs out the candle, signifying the end of his grandmother's earthly life, and then begins reading the grand mission of the Sicarii as described in the Book of Enoch. "Purify the earth from all oppression, from all injustice, from all crime, from all impiety, and from all the pollution which is committed upon it. Exterminate them from the earth." This sacred dictate adorns the entrance to the north passageway.

Michael follows, reading Enoch's description of the purpose: "Then shall all the children of men be righteous, and all nations shall pay me divine honors, and bless me; and all shall adore me."

Cain speaks the next verse. "The earth shall be cleansed from all corruption, from every crime, from all punishment, and from all suffering; neither will I again send a deluge upon it from generation to generation forever."

"In those days I will open the treasures of blessing which are in heaven," Michael says, "that I may cause them to descend upon earth, and upon all the works and labor of man."

Greg has learned that there can be no mention of Eve in the brief ceremony, or of her accomplishments, because the works of the Order are not for personal glory; God knows her merit, and nothing else matters.

For a moment he watches the smoke of the doused wick rising toward heaven. Then he relights it with a small torch, symbolizing the arrival of Eve's soul in heaven.

Wordlessly, respectfully, the procession begins to filter out of the chamber. Only the Twelve and Cain know the cloud that hovers over his grandmother's legacy, and Cain appreciates the secret kept.

Michael sees Cain lingering by Eve's sarcophagus and approaches him. "You can stay a while if you'd like," he says.

"Yes, just a while."

"It would be easy to be angry at us."

Michael pinches off the candle's flame, silently indicating his disdain for Eve's weaknesses.

And perhaps, Cain thinks, to provoke a response.

"I'm not angry," Cain replies, purposely ignoring Michael's insolent gesture. "To be a leader here I must accept your decisions."

Michael studies Cain for a moment, as if trying to penetrate his mind, explore his thoughts, but finds no witness to interrogate.

"You are sometimes difficult to understand, and that makes some of us uneasy," Michael confesses. "And yet you are the last one standing. Given the circumstances, that makes most of us confident."

"In the chamber, during my test," Cain asks, "did you find me wanting? Or were you all bluffing?"

Michael laughs. "You are not afraid to speak your mind, are you?" Cain remains silent. "As you said, to be a leader here, you must accept our decisions. That is what matters—not how we reach them."

Michael smiles and grasps Cain's arm gently—*affectionately?* Cain wonders—and then follows the procession out of the chamber.

Still holding the small torch, Cain leans over the sarcophagus and re-ignites the candle. The snap and sizzle of the flaming wick cheers him.

In the deathly silence of this foreboding tomb, it sounds like resurrection.

Chapter 21

Jeremy removes the remnants of room service dinners to the corridor and rejoins the group huddled in Thompson's front room. Charlotte, the news junkie, has turned on CCN. A barrage of commercials creates the soundtrack for a continuing discussion about where they go from here.

Jeremy takes a seat on the sofa as Thompson says, "Here's my concern. If Rebecca really can communicate with Greg…"

"*Cain.*" Rebecca reminds him.

"Sorry, my dear, but my grandson's given name is Greg. And if you can truly communicate with him, then unfortunately you may be a security risk for us. After all, you could inadvertently give him strategic information about our plans."

"Or *advertently*," Gideon adds. "The truth is, Rebecca, we don't know very much about you. Except that you claim to be plugged into Greg's brain somehow. Thompson's right, that makes me nervous too."

"I'm not even sure she can do that communication thing," Charlotte remarks. "This isn't the Magic Kingdom."

"Truth is, the Sicarii believe it," Gideon replies. "Always have. The leaders use it to consult on decisions, and some say to eavesdrop on us underlings. But apparently not everyone has the capacity."

"And you believe it?"

Gideon nods. "I've witnessed it—not that I have the capacity. But one time when I met with the Twelve—it was frightening, to be honest, how they knew my thinking."

"Could be parlor tricks, you know," Charlotte suggests, "to keep the masses in check. You saw the wizard, but not what was behind the curtain."

"I believe it too," Jeremy adds. "During my training I saw it demonstrated. I couldn't do it, couldn't tap into it, but it was clear that Eve could. And so, since Cain is her grandson, seems natural to me…"

"This is hard for me to grasp, guys." Charlotte leans back in her chair, exhausted by unfolding events and revelations. "When Rebecca told me about this ability, I thought, okay, maybe… But the more I think about it, I don't know. She says she's an Indigo Child. But then, if Greg has this ability too, maybe she's a gifted Sicarii agent."

To Rebecca, this sounds like an accusation. She stands up nervously. "It feels like everyone's turning on me."

Jeremy comes to her defense. "That's not true."

"Well I'd just like to remind everyone that it was not my choice to be here with you on this merry little adventure of yours. If you're thinking that I'm a mole or something…"

"No, no, my dear," Thompson says, mustering his kindest grandfatherly tone. "We don't think anything of the kind. We're just concerned about—well, about *leaks*. Could it happen accidentally?"

Rebecca sits back down. "Cain's told me that some of them have the ability to penetrate through mental defenses, like, you know, trying hard not to think about something. But I don't think Cain can do that. Sometimes he gets a little angry when I don't answer his questions, so I think I need to consciously send him information, kind of like when you speak to someone. If you don't speak, they can't get the message."

"So you *talk* to Greg?" Charlotte asks, confused.

"I can't explain it. I kind of have an image of him when we're on the grid, but not really. More like a mirage. And we don't speak to each other with words exactly—it's so hard to explain. I have to *think as if I'm speaking* before he can hear me. Wish I could be clearer."

"So do I," Charlotte says abruptly. She is feeling a touch of jealousy, perhaps, over Rebecca's conversations with Greg.

"During our one-month holiday each year," Thompson interjects, getting back to the main point, "Miriam—I prefer her real name, not Eve—would sometimes announce to me out of the blue that she had to contact headquarters about some specific thing or another. And I always wondered how she knew. It was kind of like…"

Rebecca completes his thought: "…she was on the grid."

"Have you even had contact with Eve?" Thompson asks.

Rebecca shakes her head. "Never." But then her eyes dance evasively to an empty spot in the room.

Charlotte catches Rebecca's nervous dodge. "Never? Are you sure? Eve never even tried to communicate with you?"

"There was maybe once that I can remember. We didn't communicate, actually, but she was… I thought I saw Eve standing next to Cain when he and I were communicating, almost like she was listening in. But like I said, these mirages are not clear, they're just kind of watery images, so it's hard to be sure."

Her hands fly to her face, trying to hide a rush of emotion. "Since we've been together, he's come for me more often. I'm trying not to speak with him, honest I am. But he keeps coming."

Suddenly Rebecca shoots upright from her chair. She stands there rigidly, her face growing ashen. "Like right now—he's trying to communicate with me now. I can see him, in and out." Her eyes are staring straight ahead, focused on nothing. "What should I do?" She sounds frightened.

Gideon reaches into a pocket and finds his neodymium cube. He rises and walks to Rebecca, then hands her the powerful magnet.

She gasps! "I can see him clearly." She shakes her head. "He wants to know where we are so he can help us."

"No!" Charlotte screams. "It's a ruse. Don't tell him anything." She has become a believer.

"He's insisting," Rebecca says. "I can't keep my mind closed to him."

Gideon wrenches the neodymium cube away from Rebecca and walks it into Thompson's bedroom, tossing it into the closet.

"The image of him…" Rebecca says, it just sort of wiggled and faded away. "And now he's gone. We're not together on the grid any longer."

She slumps into her chair.

Thompson arches his brows and says, "Eve had a magnet like that one. Always kept it near her. I thought it might be a talisman of some kind, but maybe it amplifies a person's capacity."

"Which was why assassins were instructed to always have it on us," Gideon says. "I thought it was just a tool of the trade—for opening magnetically encoded locks, that sort of thing. But I've been thinking lately that there must be some other purpose for it. I think we've found it. Somehow it helps them know what we're thinking."

"But you haven't been on this grid," Charlotte reminds him.

"Not that I know of anyway," Gideon concedes. "Then again, maybe I'm just not sensitive enough to see it."

Thompson walks over to Rebecca's chair. "It's clear Rebecca is extra sensitive, and the magnet boosted that sensitivity, which is why she's been in contact with Greg more often since she's been near it. It would be a good idea to keep that little cube away from her, don't you think?"

Rebecca nods more aggressively than the others.

"Am I the only one here who's wondering what our next move is?" Jeremy asks.

"To get out of the hotel alive and in a way that we can't be followed," Gideon answers. "We can be sure that powerful forces will do everything they can to prevent that from happening."

"To be honest," Thompson says, "solving the mysteries of our Indigo child seems simpler than finding a way out of this place."

"Do you have a plan?" Rebecca asks.

"Yes." Gideon looks around the room. "I've stayed here before, so I've studied the building. There is a sub-basement entrance to the tunnels beneath the city."

"Which will be guarded by Sicarii," Jeremy suggests.

"That's right. And we'll never escape out the main entrances. So we're going up, not down. Charlotte, it's time to use your contacts. I've got to reach Uncle Bill and figure out how to get our documentation."

Chapter 22

A few minutes past four in the morning, Jeremy is sent into the corridor to check out the stairwell. A pistol is tucked into the back of his pants. He finds no obstacles up to the top floor, meaning the enemy forces are focused on the building's exit points, a logical strategy. He returns to the room and waves the other four to follow him. Carrying all their needed possessions, the group quietly ascends the stairs to the rooftop exit. Normally locked, the door is now propped open.

"They have men on the roof," Gideon whispers to Jeremy before racking the breech of his Glock. "Remember your training?"

Jeremy nods.

"You go right," Gideon instructs, then motions for the others to stay behind.

Slowly he pushes the door open and they step through. It's likely that a guard has been posted to watch the door, so Gideon and Jeremy stay low, walking in a low crouch, their feet barely scuffing the stones on the roof.

The door is unguarded. They have emerged on the roof above the Peacock Alley section of the building. In opposite directions, Gideon and Jeremy search around the huge rotating heat exchange fans. Standing near a buttress overlooking Park Avenue, Gideon finds a black-clad sniper. Using his silenced Glock, he strikes the man in the leg, which sends him down and spins him around to meet a shoe in the face. With a plastic tie he secures both hands of the unconscious sniper to a metal railing, then stuffs one of the man's socks into his mouth and secures it with the man's own belt. This one, at least, is not a Sicarii operative.

Jeremy has searched the remainder of the perimeter of this section and motions to Gideon to move toward the Waldorf Towers section. Checking his watch, Gideon notes that they have only five minutes to complete their search-and-destroy mission. The next rooftop is a confused maze of large utility boxes, fans, and other obstacles.

Suddenly Gideon hears shouting, and the words, "I've got one." Peeking around a fan enclosure, he can see one dark figure holding a pistol at the head of Jeremy. The entire operation is now jeopardized.

Gideon hears footsteps racing to Jeremy's position. Another sniper has responded to the call, a big mistake. Now two snipers are collected into one small targeted space. As the second man begins to fan out in search of other targets, Gideon stands and fires two shots. The second sniper tumbles to the ground, struck in a hip and shoulder. The other one, still holding a gun to Jeremy's head, reflexively points his pistol toward Gideon—another mistake. With the threat to Jeremy diminished, Gideon fires and the man crumples.

"Sorry," Jeremy says. "Didn't see him." Suddenly he crouches to retrieve his dropped pistol. In one fluid motion he lifts the gun, points, and fires three quick shots in the direction of Gideon.

A yelp is followed by the crunching sound of a man falling onto the rooftop.

Gideon wheels and sees the fifth sniper lying just ten paces behind him. "Thanks," Gideon says. "Didn't see him."

"How'd they get so many guys up here?"

"Must've checked in, like us."

Gideon spots the lights of a helicopter approaching from the east. This is their ride. No time left to secure the landing zone.

Gideon and Jeremy run back to the stairwell and motion the others onto the rooftop. A Bell 214ST helicopter prominently marked with the CCN trademark zooms toward them and then stops, descending slowly and whipping the air into an eye-stinging storm of dust. It hovers inches above the roof, which cannot support its weight.

With Gideon guarding the rear, Jeremy leads Rebecca into the helicopter, then Charlotte. Gideon spots another two men beginning to emerge through the stairwell door. He fires shots that back them off as Jeremy pulls Thompson into the aircraft.

Knowing that the men will have a clear shot at him when he turns to clamber into the chopper, he approaches Jeremy. Above the roar of the rotors he says, "Take them up for thirty seconds, then come back for me."

Jeremy gives the thumbs up. The young man climbs aboard as Gideon fires two more shots into the open doorway to intimidate the gunmen. He quickly takes cover behind one of the huge fan enclosures. As the chopper's roar announces the start of its ascent, another man bursts through the doorway, his pistol positioned to fire at Gideon or the escaping helicopter. Gideon takes him down before he can fire.

In the seconds before the chopper descends again, Gideon rushes to the door, searches the stairwell for more gunmen and finds none. He pulls the downed man from the doorway, slams the door shut, then positions the body to keep the door from opening.

The Bell 214ST is waiting for him. He jumps into the helicopter and turns back toward the doorway just in time to hear three gunshots from close range.

Charlotte has fired her Glock at a man who has pushed the stairwell door open. The man falls to his knees holding his right arm.

"They just keep coming," Charlotte says.

"That was close," Gideon answers. "But we're out of range now."

The pilot turns toward Gideon and grins. "Just like old times, huh?"

Gideon smiles at Herb Rossi, the white-haired pilot with skin like parchment and tobacco-stained teeth like rotting fence posts. "Nah... nothing like Delhi. Those were the good ol' days," he says. "I heard that Charlotte got you a contract with CCN. This old bird's still flying, I see."

"Got more years in her than I do," Herb Rossi replies. "Hang on now. Gotta drop you guys off for your next leg, then go face the music about my flight pattern. Gotta say, though, someone pulled some strings on getting permission to fly into the City like this without getting shot down. New York airspace is a fortress."

"Thanks to my boss at CCN, who is also Rebecca's guardian," Charlotte says. "The power of the media can be a wonderful thing."

William Wyatt barks angrily into the phone. "Eight of you against two Sicarii, two women and an old man. And I left the Agency for this outfit."

"We're better on foreign soil, sir." The voice on the other end crackles with wounded pride.

"With this current administration in power, you are on foreign soil, son. How many men down?"

"Six, sir. One dead, five wounded—one critically."

"Okay, you know the drill. Get it cleaned up fast. We can't be found there, do you understand?"

"I do, sir."

"I'm sending an ambulance that's under our control to pick up the deceased... who had a *heart attack*, got that? *Heart attack*."

"Yes."

"You figure out the others. It's still the middle of the night. Just get everyone out of there."

Wyatt terminates. If this mess isn't cleaned up there will be hell to pay. If they're caught carrying out a mission on American soil without government sanction, it could jeopardize Blackwatch's many other U.S. contracts. Wyatt fears that his personal vendetta against Gideon and Charlotte, going back five years to his humiliating defeat at their hands in Delhi and Kashmir, has led him over the edge on this one.

The phone rings again and he angrily picks up, switching on the speaker so his assistant Allison can hear. "What is it now?"

"It seems that Charlotte already alerted the local papers and TV stations to the, uh, kerfuffle at the Waldorf."

"*Kerfuffle*? Is that what you called it?"

"This could be bad, sir."

At times like this, Wyatt wishes he could swear, but his evangelical faith discourages that, so he just yells.

"Unbelievable!"

He turns to Allison, who whispers, "No IDs on them, right?"

"Harry, make sure none of them have IDs. Are the live ones trustworthy? I mean, will they keep their mouths shut until our lawyers get involved?"

"Depends, sir."

"On what?"

"On whether we're hanging them out to dry. They'll know."

"Okay, so if anyone's just hanging on, you know? If they're not likely to make it…"

"I understand. The dead can't talk. But they're ours, sir—are you sure?"

"Part of the mission, soldier. And you, Harry, disappear into the crowd. I need you to hang around and see what the reporters and police figure out. I can't stress enough that we need absolute deniability on this."

He hangs up and looks Allison in the eye.

"We have a domestic counterterrorism contract. When this comes back to bite us, maybe we can clothe it in the old *national security* rags and get by without making a statement. Could be there was a terrorist attack or something."

"And we didn't notify the city with the biggest counterterrorism force in the world?"

"Allison, work with me here, will you,?"

Chapter 23

At 4:47 a.m., Charlotte watches bulldozers and tall cranes loom larger and larger as the Bell 214ST drops down on a Long Island construction site. She and the other exhausted passengers slowly disembark. Herb Rossi urges them to hurry up.

"I was never here, so shoo!" he shouts.

As the chopper lifts off, Charlotte leads the small band through the gloom towards the flashing headlights of a green van. The side door opens and a husky chauffeur motions them inside.

The driver whispers to Charlotte, "He's already at the office. Coffee's on."

Exhausted and shell-shocked, the passengers are silent during the fifteen minute drive to the world headquarters of Ambienz QS Inc., one of the most successful high-tech business start-ups of the past several years. Its revolutionary breakthrough in quantum computing has opened the floodgates of acquisition offers even though the company's first products have not yet been released.

Charlotte is the first to exit the van in front of an inconspicuous building on the fringe of a vintage 1990's business park. There is no sign announcing the building's occupant and at this time of day only three cars are in the front parking spaces. Charlotte follows the driver toward an unmarked front door. He punches a series of numbers into a keypad and submits to iris scanning. This is the only clue that something special may lie inside.

The door locks with a substantial thwack behind the last guest. Looking around, Charlotte is astonished by the sleek, modern furnishings, dramatic low-key lighting and abundance of surveillance cameras.

In the momentary silence, the slap of sandals on carpet makes her turn around. From the far end of a corridor Meysam Madani approaches with a big grin and his eyes fixed on Charlotte. He is thirty-four but looks much younger in his grungy tee, slouchy jeans and bedhead hair, a look that more adequately matches his American nickname "Mason." No one, except close acquaintances, would imagine this handsome, publicity-shy techno-mogul to be one of the most successful businessmen of the past seven years.

After anonymously steering a social media company into the stratosphere, Mason suddenly had cashed out, leaving his founding partner to flounder on the rocky shoals of intensifying competition. With his fortune intact, Mason had financed a host of start-ups he considered to be more meaningful than "shepherding millions of Internet dolts into a series of shallow and time-sucking interactions" with each other, an unfortunate statement he had made to Fortune magazine three years ago. Out of his five new ventures, one had failed quickly and two had struggled until finding only modest success. For a time the business media had beaten Mason to a pulp for his failure to instantly achieve another mega-triumph. Eccentric but sensitive, Mason had despaired at the personal attacks and had grown even more reclusive.

It was at this time that Charlotte had gained an interview with Mason, not because of his reclusiveness and *geekitude*, but for his personal story and inside views on one of America's fiercest adversaries. Mason had been born in Tehran to a Muslim father, who was a computer scientist serving as Minister of Science, Research and Technology, and a mother who was a member of the Bahá'í Faith, a religion born in Iran but considered heretical by the radical Islamic regime.

For a time, Mason's father had been able to protect his Bahá'í wife from the intense persecution suffered by many fellow believers, but eventually the entire family had been forced to flee for their lives, first to London and then to America. Despite Iran's persecution and killing of Bahá'ís, Mason had remained a Muslim, though he no longer actively practices the Faith. Like his parents, he blames the extremist clerics in Iran, not Islam, for that country's human rights violations and has maintained close contact with many Muslim friends in his homeland.

At first, Charlotte had been intrigued by the incredible success of a young Persian immigrant. But there had been a more personal impetus for the CCN interview. Charlotte had been married to a Persian Jew, Mihad Ansari, who turned out to have had a despicable motive for marrying Charlotte. Eventually Mihad was assassinated for betraying the Sicarii organization that had put him up to it.

When broadcast, the interview had helped humanize the reclusive geek and he regained much of the respect he had unfairly lost. Mason's gratitude to Charlotte had helped foster a relationship of trust.

Since the Ansari interview, one of Mason's other start-ups, a medical device company, had made it big and had been bought out by a much larger company. Mason's fifth new venture—actually the first one he had started— is Ambienz, which has a new breakthrough technology, this year's prize acquisition bait.

"Charlotte!" Mason shouts, rushing down the hall to wrap his arms around her. To the others he says, "This woman is like my favorite aunt." He kisses Charlotte on the cheeks and then backs away. "It's so good to see you!"

"Sorry it's so early," Charlotte remarks, then quickly introduces the others.

Mason's eyes spark when he is introduced to Rebecca.

Jeremy bristles slightly as she smiles back. Charlotte detects a hint of jealousy.

"So what kind of a host am I?" Mason says. "I've set up a conference room for you—very secure. When you're hungry, just let us know. We can bring in anything you want."

He hesitates slightly, and his face takes on the look of a child caught in an embarrassing situation. "It's not necessary," he continues, "but of course I'm hoping that you will tell me what is going on. I love adventure, as you know."

He takes Charlotte by the arm, ushering her down the corridor to the conference room. "It would be hard to find a more secure location than Ambienz," he says. "The threat of industrial espionage is very high, and we've had a few physical threats as well. You'll find us well protected here, personally and digitally."

"Give us a chance to catch our breath, Mason, then we'll share our story."

Mason opens the door to the "conference room," a wholly inadequate term to describe the high-tech theater they encounter. An oval table contains laptop computers for each of the fifteen seats. Broadband Internet access and satellite communication, all encrypted beyond military specifications, is available on demand. Enormous flat-panel monitors surround the table receiving input from any source in the room, and many sources beyond. A filled coffee pot stands ready by each of six chairs, meaning that Mason intends to join the five guests for at least part of their stay.

"I'll return in, say, half-an hour?"

"Perfect," Charlotte replies.

When the group is finally alone, Rebecca speaks up, her star-struck countenance glowing.

"He's really *hot*."

Chapter 24

William Wyatt steps into the Cohen Deli and searches the tables for Moshe Gavish, head of Kidon. He finds the man's dour face along the back wall. It's never pleasant when a client demands a face-to-face meeting after a blown assignment. There was a time when Wyatt, for six years Director of the CIA, would have sat in the power chair at such a meeting. Now he feels like a grade school student being sent to the principal's office for bullying.

When he had stepped into his position as second in command at Blackwatch, he had not known how skewed the organization's skill set was. Its heavy-handed paramilitary tactics usually worked well in less developed and more corrupt societies. But on home turf, Blackwatch lacked the required subtlety and finesse. There were just too many aggressive news gathering organizations and multi-layered, state-of-the-art law enforcement agencies on high alert. In Baghdad you could storm a few homes looking for a bad guy and the event might not even be noted in the newspapers. But in New York, a single operative caught jaywalking could be all over the cable news channels for days.

"Quite a dust-up over at the Waldorf last night," Moshe says as Wyatt takes a seat. "Woke me up."

"You stay at the Waldorf?"

"Not usually. But last night, yes. Thought I'd catch the fireworks."

"So you knew."

"Well of course. Just because you were hired to perform a mission doesn't mean that we are not observing. We just had a man follow one of your men to the Waldorf, where he met up with more of your men. Unfortunately I didn't stay awake for the fireworks. Slept like a baby, though, knowing that if things went bad, it would be on your head, not mine. Worth every penny. But I don't think we'll be needing your services anymore."

"Have you ordered? I recommend the pastrami on rye." Wyatt maintains an air of calm though inside he is seething.

"Any idea, William, where the targets went?"

"None."

"I'll bet the authorities reamed you a new one though, am I right? Generally they don't like open-air shootouts on the roofs of their famous New York buildings."

"We did a good job cleaning up." Wyatt would like to tear this idiot's head off, but he doesn't need another *kerfuffle* right now.

"Not good enough. I understand you were called in this morning to explain things. Couldn't have been pleasant for you."

A waiter approaches the table.

"Since you're no longer a client, Moshe, I suggest we go Dutch on this one."

Moshe looks up at the waiter and orders. "We'll both have the pastrami on rye. And black coffee."

The waiter scribbles on a small pad and leaves without speaking.

"So William, in the spirit of friendship, I want to leave you with a bit of good news. Interested?"

Wyatt silently cocks his head, ready for another barb.

"This is good news, *really*." Moshe leans forward confidentially. "We have an informer inside the Sicarii organization."

"Impossible!" Wyatt thinks Moshe is making this up to further humiliate him.

"It's true. She's been there for years. Unfortunately even she doesn't know where their headquarters is—just that it's somewhere in the Himalayas."

"That's your good news, that you don't know where they office?"

"No—we just learned from our source that the organization has assigned one of their operatives to settle the score for us."

"You're not making any sense, Moshe. Gideon is their top operative. He knows all their tricks, their secrets. How could another agent best him?"

"They've brought back Caleb."

William Wyatt leans back in his chair, astonished. "Caleb? Are you sure?"

"As we can be."

"If it's true, this is good news indeed!"

Wyatt considers the possibilities. In the closed circles of clandestine operatives, Caleb had earned the position as all-time MVP. To say Caleb's reputation is legendary is to seriously underestimate it. His reputation alone had inspired three movies; in two of them his character was portrayed as a hero, in one as an evil mastermind.

For thirty years, Caleb had accomplished the most difficult assignments in the most treacherous environments, all without anyone learning anything about him—not his background, his appearance, his voice, where he lived. Nothing at all, except his code-name. Only the top of the Sicarii chain of command, Eve and Cain, know Caleb's identity and how to reach him. So valuable had he become that he is now used only for the most important engagements, which means he is allowed to live in semi-retirement. His last assignment had been three years ago—the assassination of a foreign head-of-state. Since then there had been many rumors of his death. All false, apparently.

"Even Gideon is no match for Caleb," Wyatt mutters.

"And that is why we no longer need your services. Given time, Gideon and Charlotte Ansari will be gone. Caleb has never failed."

"Then grant me just one thing," Wyatt says. "Today, lunch is on me. I insist."

The thorn in his side is about to be removed.

Chapter 25

Surrounded by the aromatic remnants of a Szechuan lunch, the group leans back in their chairs. They are exhausted by the info dump they had relentlessly piled onto Mason Madani, a barrage interrupted only by Mason's obsessive retrieval and dismissal of business text messages. The man is a master multitasker. Still projected on the large screens are images of research photos and documents from Charlotte's computer, the ones copied to the cloud by Gideon.

For a few seconds there is complete silence in the conference room.

Finally Mason speaks. "Now that you've told me these things, I'm not sure I should know them. You're in the middle of a very dangerous situation."

"Honestly, Mason, I didn't want to endanger you in any way." Charlotte looks at him warmly. "I just thought that, since you offered us refuge, you had a right to know *from what*."

Gideon stands and stretches. "It would be best if we regrouped and left," he says to Mason. "Every minute we're here, we're putting you at risk."

Thompson is next to stand. "It does seem that every time we stop for a minute, we endanger someone new. I agree we should go… I'm just not sure where."

Agreeing to this line of reasoning, Charlotte, Rebecca and Jeremy stand as if preparing to leave. Only Mason remains seated.

"Hold on for a minute," Mason says, leaning forward and rubbing his temples. "Please, sit down—there's no hurry to leave. Let's think this through."

His guests take their seats.

"I suggest that you spend the night, at least. I can arrange a safe place to stay. You need time to plan, to figure things out. For example, what's your goal? Certainly it's more than just staying alive."

Charlotte looks at Gideon, then her father, then back at Mason. "We'll be chased until we're killed, unless…" She hesitates.

"Unless what, Charlotte? Unless you see your investigation through and disrupt the operations of the Sicarii?" Mason turns to Gideon. "Unless you somehow make peace with Kidon and this Blackwatch group that Wyatt is running?"

"I know Gideon can keep us safe for a while," Charlotte replies. "But not forever. He's the best operative the Sicarii have, but he's only one person."

"Sometimes the best defense is a good offense," Mason says.

"We've been on the run so long we haven't had time to think," Rebecca offers. "I'm just dizzy from it all right now. The fog of war, I guess."

"And I'd like to remind everyone that we have more than one Sicarii operative in the group," Jeremy says. "*Operative-in-training*, to be accurate, but here I am. And I'd like to point out I had something to do with our escape."

"As did Charlotte," Thompson interjects, looking at his daughter. "Nice shooting."

Moving his attention to Mason, he adds, "Last night I told everyone I was ready to take these bastards down, or die trying. After our rooftop adventure this morning, I'm even more determined."

A woman opens the door and addresses Mason. "They're here, sir. I put them in the Fishbowl."

Mason nods then addresses the group. "This is a good place to start laying out your plans. I have another meeting now, but I'll check in with you in a couple of hours. Remember where the rest rooms are?"

✦ ✦ ✦

Gideon is feeling his age. The scrapes and bruises sustained over the past couple of days remind him that his physical powers are diminishing. Somehow he will have to make up for his gradual decline by improving his mental alertness. Everything is a balance. Mental agility can be a more effective countermeasure than strength and endurance. Analytical ability combined with creativity is more important than combat skills. Staying out of trouble is a better strategy that getting out of trouble.

"I'm still not sure we should have told him so much," Gideon says, watching the door close behind Mason.

"He helped save us," Charlotte replies. "We owed him an explanation. Anyway, I trust him."

"But you understand that he has become our responsibility now."

A PA announcement interrupts: "Mr. Stinson, please come to the reception desk. You have a guest."

Gideon enters the corridor and marches toward the front desk.

"Uncle Bill, good to see you," he says to the Passport counterfeiter.

Uncle Bill turns with a grunt and holds out a package. "Any idea what a cab costs to the Island and back?"

Gideon takes the package and hands an envelope to the grumpy man, who peeks inside at a bundle of one hundred dollar bills.

"I appreciate it," Gideon says, guiding the Uncle Bill out the door. "As agreed, this should cover your time and expenses. Nobody followed you?"

"Who the hell would want to come to Long Island?"

Caleb sits in a 2005 Prius watching the unmarked Ambienz front door. And thinking.

Every assassin, even the top ones like Caleb, need a little luck now and then. This time luck had paid a visit. Knowing that Gideon would be needing forged documents for his associates, the obvious play had been to pick one of the three most reliable sources—Caleb and Gideon know the same sources—and then observe the chosen one. In this case, bingo! Guessed right. When Uncle Bill climbed into a taxi with a package, it seemed a sure bet that he was delivering the goods to Gideon. Slapping a magnetic GPS transmitter onto the cab had made it easy to track.

Caleb doesn't relish assassinating another Sicarii agent. Though they have never met, Caleb knows Gideon by his impressive reputation. The man has earned his rank as *number two*, which is why it was so surprising for Caleb to receive an irrevocable assassination order: kill Gideon and everyone he is protecting—except the girl.

In Sicarii procedure, an *irrevocable* order cannot be rescinded by anyone, or under any circumstances, except by Eve. It is a failsafe directive used to ensure that a mission is completed even if the issuer is forced under duress to cancel the order. Once started, an irrevocable order cannot be stopped, except by Eve in exceptional circumstances, unless the assigned operative is killed. And Eve is dead.

Caleb knows something that most others do not. It is often less difficult to kill another Sicarii assassin than the average target. This is because Sicarii operatives know how other Sicarii agents think and behave. Despite their training to adopt anonymity and avoid establishing patterns of behavior, in truth this is impossible. The anonymous, patternless life of an assassin is itself a pattern that requires predictable behaviors to achieve—such as reliance on counterfeit documents. And if Gideon needs fake passports in a hurry, it probably means the group is planning to flee the country.

Already Caleb has had two opportunities to kill Gideon with a sica. The first occasion had been while standing next to Gideon in a Waldorf elevator surrounded by his companions. Caleb could have escaped undetected before Gideon collapsed from his wound; such is the value of the sica. The second opportunity had occurred while watching the amusing Blackwatch rooftop amateur show through the scope of a high-powered sniper rifle. The escape had been entertaining but all too predictable. Caleb had rooted for Gideon.

For Caleb, the thrill of an engagement is no longer the kill itself, but rather the challenge it poses. So far there has not been much challenge on this mission, so Caleb has upped the ante by tipping off Gideon about the looming threat. If Gideon hasn't discovered the message yet, he will soon.

There is another reason why Gideon has been spared so far: intense curiosity. Never in Caleb's tenure has the Sicarii organization ordered the termination of an active assassin. What had Gideon done to deserve this? Why is this mission irrevocable? And why is the girl off-limits? For Caleb, who is interminably bored by life, the mysteries raised by this man's eventual death are tantalizing.

Caleb watches Uncle Bill exit the building and climb into his waiting taxi.

Another pawn moving across the board.

Chapter 26

Carrying the package with the fake documents, Gideon walks down the length of the hall past the conference room and makes a hard right toward the rest rooms. He walks past the Fishbowl, a glass-enclosed conference room that is short on confidentiality but long on a view of the office park's outdoor patio, now closed for the season. Inside the room, Mason is shaking hands with six other individuals, all of them stern-looking businessmen.

Just past the glass wall, Gideon stops. Something in the room had disturbed him, but he can't quite put his finger on it. Only a sense of dread remains.

Slowly he turns, takes three steps back to the glass wall and cautiously peers into the room, studying each of the men as they take seats at a marble conference table.

He recognizes one of the men. Dressed in a dark suit, crisp white shirt and scarlet tie, the center man facing the glass wall had led a very memorable meeting attended by Gideon three years ago.

The meeting had been at Sicarii headquarters.

The man's name is Michael, and he is the head of the Council of Twelve.

This is what cell phone cameras were made for.

Thompson is pouring a cup of coffee as Gideon re-enters the conference room. The assassin seems wired, his eyes studying each of the ceiling-mounted surveillance cameras. Thompson senses that something is wrong.

Gideon finds his backpack leaning against a perimeter wall and surreptitiously removes a Glock 9mm pistol, racking the breech with his back to the cameras.

Thompson's heart begins to thump. Something bad is about to happen!

Gideon motions the others to a corner of the room, away from the microphones on the conference table. "We have a problem," he whispers. "I saw a member of the Sicarii Council meeting with Mason down the hall."

"What?" Charlotte is so stunned she almost shouts.

"Be quiet," Gideon continues. "Everything we say and do in this room may be under surveillance." He glances up at the nearest video camera.

"Of course it is," Charlotte says defensively. "He told us this is a secure facility. Industrial espionage is a real threat."

"And the Sicarii down the hall? This guy is not an operative—he's the head of the damn Council!"

"Are you sure?" Thompson inquires.

"I met him three years ago. The others called him Michael."

"Popular name," Thompson says thoughtfully. Do you remember the names of any others?"

"I'm an assassin, but these guys scared me. There was Michael, and next to him was Gabriel, and a man called Sariel…"

"Hmmm," Thompson grunts. "The names of Angels. And were any of these men wearing robes? A scarlet robe, for instance?"

"No, just dark business suits. But Michael—he was wearing a bright red tie. Wearing it today, in fact."

"Scarlet."

"Yes, scarlet"

"Do you remember if Gabriel was wearing a purple tie—and Sariel a blue one?"

"It was three years ago, but it could be." He closes his eyes. "These guys all had gray faces and dark suits. The ties were just about the only color… Yes, there was a purple tie there."

"Where are you going with this?" Charlotte demands.

"Stay with me here." Thompson begins a gentle rocking motion as he struggles to dredge up some arcane information from his vast store of religious knowledge.

"Maybe something here can help us understand what the Sicarii are up to," Thompson continues. "We know, for example, that the Sicarii grew out of the Essenes, who were an extreme Jewish sect that lived at Qumran. They hid the Dead Sea Scrolls that were eventually discovered. We know that in the Essene vows of initiation, they promised to preserve the names of the angels. And in the Book of Enoch—which is not in our Bible, even though Jesus quoted from it—we were given a hierarchy of angels. At the top of this hierarchy were Michael, Gabriel, and Sariel—in that order."

Gideon's eyes widen. "The Book of Enoch is our most sacred scripture. Holier than any other book. Verses from Enoch were carved in stone above the passageways in our gompa."

"Okay, so let me think this through. Most scholars agree that one of the main missions of the Essenes was to preserve the bloodlines of the priests that served under King David. The high priests were descendants of the original high priest named Zadok. The Essenes wanted to bring the pure priestly bloodline, which had been lost or corrupted, back to power in the Jerusalem temple of their day. Particularly the Zadokite priests, because they were the high priests."

Jeremy has been tinkering with the microphones. "I'm not much for history lessons," he says, "but I can hear you guys from over here, so don't think others aren't picking you up. Fortunately, I've figured out how to turn off the mics, so you can come back to the table."

The group joins Jeremy, but Thompson continues to speak as if there has been no interruption. "This is all relating to little snatches of conversations I remember Miriam having on the phone, things I never fully understood but which made me wonder."

"So you're saying that this man down the hall in the scarlet tie—" Rebecca says, "—you think he's really a Zadokite priest?"

"I wasn't saying that, but I wonder... Here is what I know. The Essenes maintained the hierarchy of temple priests in their commune. The person who assumed the role of the high priest was called Michael. When not performing priestly duties, the various priests wore colored garments appropriate to their station. Michael wore scarlet, Gabriel purple, and Sariel blue."

"The colors of the ties," Gideon says.

"This way, even outside the temple, people who understood the color codes knew these men were Zadokite priests. Of course, by the time of the Essenes, no one was absolutely sure that the high priests were actual descendants of Zadok, but the Essenes believed they had preserved the bloodline. There was a lot of dispute, though."

"Isn't there always?" Gideon says.

"Hey, this is interesting and all," Jeremy remarks, "but I don't get how any of it's gonna save our asses."

"I'm not sure either," Thompson replies. "But there's something important here. We just need to figure it out."

"We only know one thing for sure." Gideon fingers the pistol tucked into his belt. "The leader of the Council of Twelve is sitting in a room right now, not fifty yards from us. He wants us dead. And I want to know why he's meeting with our billionaire host."

His phone buzzes. Looking at the screen makes him smile.

"All right," he says, shaking a clenched fist. "The phone patch from Wonderboy just landed."

"So what now?" Thompson asks.

"Charlotte, what's Mason's cell phone number? Time to text him."
He enters the number, then adds a cryptic message:

Big prob. Need you bk here. Gideon.

The message transmits to Mason's phone. Gideon stares at the screen, sips some cold coffee and grimaces in disgust. He continues staring, as if willing Mason to pick up the text message during his meeting, as all obsessive texters do.

He literally jumps in his chair when the screen flashes to a menu with three buttons: LISTEN, which turns on Mason's phone mic so Gideon can hear dialogue in the room; CAPTURE, which sends Mason's phone calls and messages to Gideon's phone; and MAP, which shows the phone's location.

He presses LISTEN.

It's too late to hear anything important. Mason is excusing himself from the meeting, which clearly was winding down anyway.

The sound of a door opening and closing suggests that Mason is on his way to the conference room.

Chapter 27

Mason Madani grimly enters the conference room, closing the door behind him. "So what's the big problem?"

Out of habit he takes the seat at the head of the table. There is no response, only silent stares. Suddenly he feels uncomfortable. He turns toward Charlotte, making a gesture that begs her to answer.

Instead, Gideon speaks. "There was a man in the Fishbowl named Michael. We need to know why he was there."

Mason is confused. He mentally ticks off the names of the men he just met with, but none of them are named Michael. "I think you're misinformed," he says, leaning towards Gideon in a show of executive power. "And why is it any of your business?"

Gideon smiles and places his Glock on the table. "Let's just say it's important to us."

Mason instinctively retreats from the Glock. He knows that Gideon is an assassin, and this deadly combination of profession and gun strips away any desire for argument. He looks to Charlotte for reassurance, but her eyes are cast downward.

"Fair enough," Mason says meekly. "But you'll have to give me more. There was no Michael in my meeting."

Thompson touches the assassin's arm and half-whispers, "He probably wouldn't use his Zadokite name in business."

With an icy gaze, Gideon turns to Mason. His eyes are cold. "The man in the scarlet tie, facing the corridor. Who was he?"

Mason tries to reconstruct the seating arrangement in his mind, remembering one man in a red tie. "William Sinclair," he reports.

"What was his business with you?"

Glancing down at the Glock, Mason replies, "He represents a private equity group that invested a small sum of money in our start-up. They're interested in expanding their stake." The shock of seeing the gun on the table has worn off now. Mason feels a bit bolder. "You must know him, otherwise why would you ask?"

"We're both involved in another venture."

"Small world. But then, I'm sure Sinclair is involved in scores of ventures. This was the first time I met the man myself. Usually just his surrogates."

Charlotte's eyes narrow. Clearly she is struggling with something. "Tell me, Mason—why would you take money from an equity group at such an early stage? You have enough money to fund this company on your own, I'm sure."

"Of course I do," Mason responds. "But in my world, you never know how long a venture will take to get off its feet, or how expensive it will be." He nods toward the gun. "I wonder if we could put that thing away now."

Gideon ignores the suggestion. "It's quite a coincidence, isn't it, that Sinclair is here on the same day that we show up?"

"Yes, it must be a coincidence. The Sinclair meeting has been on the calendar for over two weeks. And until a few hours ago, I didn't even know that your *predicament* would lead you here. Believe me, if there was anything sinister in having Sinclair here at Ambienz, I never would have put him in the Fishbowl for all to see."

"That's true, Gideon," Thompson says.

Mason watches Gideon struggle with the logic of his defense, but suspects that the man Charlotte has called her *Guardian Angel* relies on instinct as much as reason.

"Look, I know this is troubling you all," Mason says. "But I don't know what other connections there might be. Maybe something about my company? What we've developed? All I can tell you is that I'm not part of any plot involving Sinclair and you." He hesitates for a moment, then adds, "At least not knowingly. I wouldn't do anything to hurt Charlotte, believe me."

"So tell us about your company," Charlotte replies. "What is it that you have that so many people want?"

Mason loves talking about his breakthrough. "It's a technology we call *quantum computing*. We've made a breakthrough in using quantum mechanics to process information."

"So you're a start-up Intel?" Charlotte suggests.

"Actually, we are the replacement for Intel and other makers of traditional processors that power computers."

"I've heard about quantum computing." Charlotte says. "CCN did a story on it last year, but it seemed like science fiction to me. I thought a couple of big universities funded by big companies were doing this research. How did you get the jump on them?"

"It's what I do, Charlotte. I have enough money to do it myself, and to do it the right way, which is without the bloated bureaucracies and petty politics that slow down most scientific research. We just chase down results, and never have to worry about where funding will come from, or whose feet we're trampling. It's a very simple model."

"It takes some guts, I expect," Thompson says.

"That's why I usually bring in a minority investor like Sinclair's group. When other people have some skin in the game, it gives me extra incentive to keep going. I have this *thing* about letting people down who invested in me."

"What was your big breakthrough, or is it a trade secret?" Charlotte asks. Her investigative reporting instincts are getting the best of her.

"Well, not to bore you to death with science, but the big barrier in quantum computing has always been a thing called decoherence, a kind of *quantum bug* that destroys the fundamental properties that quantum computers rely on. We figured out how to use high magnetic fields to reduce the level of noise in the surroundings, which in turn reduces decoherence by a thousand times."

The phrase *magnetic field* prompts Gideon to take out his magnetic cube and set it on the table. The Glock immediately slides across the tabletop and slams into the magnet.

"A neodynium magnetic," Mason says. "Kind of a magic cube you've got there. Amazingly powerful. We learned a lot about magnetic fields from that."

Rebecca has become engaged in the conversation. "This quantum computing is faster or more powerful than what we have today?"

"Let me put it this way," Mason answers, more professorial than before. "It's a game changer. Traditional computing encodes information into traditional *bits*. A bit is either a one or a zero, but can't be both. Quantum computing, on the other hand, uses quantum bits called *qubits*. Qubits can exist in multiple states at the same time, which is seemingly impossible. Qubits can be both a one and a zero simultaneously. We call this *superposition*, and it skyrockets computer power by allowing the simultaneous processing of many calculations at once. Today we're using crystalline molecular magnets to build qubits out of multiple quantum particles, instead of from a single quantum object. So we can really scale things up."

The group is staring blankly at Mason. He fears that his science homily has overloaded them with too much geek speak.

"Using magnets and crystals, we've built a profoundly more powerful computer." he summarizes, hoping to get them back. "Think of what this could mean. Quantum cryptography for super-secure cloud computing, accurate weather modeling..."

Rebecca interrupts, "I suppose your network security here is based on..."

"Quantum cryptography." Mason loves talking about his baby.

"Maybe your quantum computer could find the connection between Sinclair and our group," Gideon says in jest.

"I wouldn't doubt it—if we had the time." Mason is dead serious. "And if we were at our research facility in London. That's where the big iron lives."

With a twisting motion, Gideon separates the Glock from the magnetic cube. "Sorry about the gun," he says. "But it does seem to speed up getting answers."

"Well, you might want to keep that handy. Just before I came in here my head of security said our cameras picked up an occupied vehicle sitting in the parking lot. Been there most of the day. Maybe someone followed you here."

"I'll check it out," Gideon says.

He stands, racks the breech of the Glock and tucks it into his belt. As he walks toward the door, Mason says, "You've got something sticking out of your back pocket."

Gideon reaches around and pulls out a scrap of note paper folded once. He unfolds it and finds a scrawled message:

Looking forward to meeting you at last.

Caleb.

Gideon doesn't frighten easily, but this message scares him. At some point Caleb had been near enough to stuff the message into his back pocket. Close enough to assassinate him. *That close.*

Yet Gideon had not recognized the master assassin.

The parking lot just got a lot more interesting.

Chapter 28

Gideon is impressed with the security command center. Twenty-three cameras surveil the building's exterior and interior. On a monitor, Gideon and Mason watch CAMERA 6 zoom in on a Prius in the front parking area.

There are two rows of parked vehicles separated by a sixty-foot wide stretch of pavement. In the first row, parked cars are nosed up to the building. The Prius is backed into the second row facing the building, ready to pull out immediately. Gideon can make out a person in the driver's seat of the Prius, but a hard shadow conceals the face.

"He hasn't moved since I noticed the vehicle." Whitney, the Chief of Security, aims CAMERA 7 at the Prius, but it's too far away to show any meaningful detail. "Maybe just a guy sleeping."

"I'm going out to take a look," Gideon says, pulling out his pistol.

Mason looks worried. "I can't afford to have any PR mishaps, if you know what I mean. This is a sensitive time for the company."

"I'll take care of things," Gideon says.

Mason isn't so sure. "No police reports, okay?"

Gideon nods, but clearly his mind is elsewhere.

Whitney guides Gideon to a side door that exits around a corner from the suspicious vehicle. Gideon walks outside and surveys the terrain. He will need to cross the narrow parking lot, then duck behind the parked cars in the second row and make his way around the corner to the Prius. He should be able to stay concealed by vehicles if he's careful.

Crouching, he crosses the lot and slowly moves closer to the target. It seems unlikely that Caleb would be so stupid as to park in one place for more than an hour, especially since the surveillance cameras were installed in highly visible locations to discourage criminal activity.

Slowly he maneuvers to an old '99 Ford pick-up that is parked next to the Prius. Moving behind the target means that he will appear in the rear- and side-view mirrors of the Prius, so he opts for the direct approach. Grasping the Glock steadily in both hands, he points it ahead and moves forward. As he passes the front of the pick-up, the shadowy figure of the driver, still as a statue, looms in front of him.

Something is wrong. He knows it. Quickly he scans the terrain to each side, then behind, suspecting an ambush. But no one is there.

He slowly moves forward. Still the driver does not move.

That's when Gideon suddenly understands. His heart sinks—not the reaction of a professional assassin, but of someone who has left that ruthless career behind. Without seeing the face, he knows who the driver is. Yanking open the door confirms it.

Uncle Bill.

A dried river of blood streaks downward from a bullet hole in the head. There is no blood spatter, though, and no blood on the seat from the wound, so the unfortunate counterfeiter must have been shot somewhere else and moved to this vehicle. On the dashboard is the Prius' fob—necessary for starting the vehicle—and on the seat beside the body is a hand-written note. Gideon doesn't have to read it to know the author, but he glances at it anyway.

Found your friend dead.

Notified the police for you.

Caleb

Damn!

The police could be just minutes—or seconds—away from the building. Gideon has to move fast. If the authorities find a murdered man here, everything will get more difficult. And Mason doesn't deserve this.

He races back to the side door, scanning the other cars for signs of Caleb. Something tells him that the master assassin is nearby, probably watching. And gloating.

From the north he can hear sirens approaching. This is no bluff—Caleb means to make life miserable for Gideon before killing him.

Standing inside the doorway, Gideon shouts at Mason. "Get Jeremy to the Prius now!" His tone is motivating. "And everyone else here to the command center. Whitney, is there a garage where you park the van at night?"

"Huh-uh," the security chief says, looking confused. "But there's a bay around the other side of the building where trucks can pull in and unload."

"Good, now listen carefully. I'm going to move the Prius to that bay, so make sure the door is open. The police are going to be here any minute, and we don't want them to see that car, do you understand?"

The security chief nods with little conviction.

"Whitney, do what I tell you now, or you'll make me very angry. And you don't want to do that."

Whitney notices the sounds of sirens. He nods more aggressively.

Gideon returns to the Prius and pushes Uncle Bill's body into the passenger seat. He inserts the fob into the dashboard slot, steps on the brake to enable starting, and pushes the power button. But nothing happens.

Of course.

Caleb!

He leaps from the vehicle and circles around, pulling open the passenger door. With a mighty heave he hoists the body of Uncle Bill onto his shoulder and walks to the back of the pick-up truck. The bed is filled with scraps of wood, machine parts, and an old tarp. He flings the body into the bed of the truck, conceals it beneath the debris and starts pulling the tarp over it as Jeremy arrives.

"Start the truck!" Gideon yells.

"Got keys?"

All he gets from Gideon is exasperation.

There are no keys in the pick-up's ignition, which is not a problem for Jeremy. Hot-wiring was covered in Gideon's basic training class. The loud wail of sirens is unnerving, but in less than a minute Jeremy has the Ford running.

Gideon shouts at him, "Drive it away now, a couple of miles. Wait for a call. Shoo!"

The car rooster-tails toward the parking lot entrance. Jeremy turns east onto a road about thirty seconds before a squad car arrives at the same entrance. The siren stops and the car slows down as it drives through the front parking lot, obviously looking for the reported 2005 Prius.

And finding it.

The squad stops. One of the officers stays in the car while the other approaches the Prius, cautiously peering through the windows, then opening the driver's door. At last he looks back at his partner. "Car looks clean," he says, then notices a man walking toward him.

"So'd you catch him?" Gideon asks, taking on a blue-collar persona.

"Catch who?"

"The guy I chased out of the car. Saw him sitting there for a couple of hours at least, drunk probably. I came over to see if there was a problem. Guy's face was sorta bloody, like he'd been in a fight or something."

"Was he alive?"

"Hell yes, when I knocked on the window he jumped up like a scared cat and just bolted outta here. I figured the car was stolen."

"Someone reported a dead body in the car."

"Well, it sure looked like one at first." He chuckles and says, "Dead body, huh? That would be a story to tell, wouldn't it?"

The second officer gets out of the squad car and calls out to his partner. "Just ran the plates, car's stolen."

"Guess I was right," Gideon says. "Need a description or something?"

Chapter 29

Gideon is just hanging up a call to Jeremy as Whitney lets him into the command center. Everyone but Jeremy has been watching the saga unfold on the multiple video monitors.

"What'd you tell the police?" Mason asks.

"They're off looking for a car thief." Gideon reaches into a wallet and pulls out three hundred dollar bills. "Jeremy will be back with the pick-up in a bit. Give this to whoever owns the rig."

He hands the bills to Mason.

"For what?"

"Jeremy's renting a fishing boat. Our friend is going to be the anchor, with the aid of a few heavy objects from the back of the truck."

"My God!" Mason, stunned, slumps into a chair.

"Everything's being taken care of," Gideon says. "There's no connection to you or the company—except for the car in your parking lot. No one's looking for a body right now. Jeremy even lifted a couple of license plates for the truck and damaged the Vehicle Identification Number so it can't be traced back to the owner. As soon as he's back, we'll be out of your hair. Sorry for the inconvenience."

"Inconvenience, hell… I've never had this much excitement. But I've gotta admit, you guys are magnets for trouble."

Charlotte steps closer to Gideon. "Mason wants to help us out. He offered up his corporate jet."

Mason shrugs his shoulders. "Non-stop Long Island to London, no problem."

"London?" Gideon looks confused. Obviously a lot has been discussed since he left the group in the conference room.

"Thompson has a theory. We have to visit a colleague of his from Oxford."

"We're going to London to investigate a hunch?" Gideon looks displeased with this plan.

"It's certainly safer there than New York right now," Rebecca says. "At least it could buy us some time."

Thompson clears his throat to get everyone's attention. "Forgive me, Gideon, but *everything* is just a theory right now."

"Agreed. But not all theories are equal. Who do you need to meet?"

"An old friend of mine—with an emphasis on old—has been working on a project for years, probing into the genealogy of the Cohens."

Despite the stress of the last few minutes, Gideon laughs. "Cohens? As in the Jewish Cohens?"

"Your powers of perception are really quite amazing, you know," Thompson replies sarcastically.

Still chuckling, Gideon says, "Well sure, why not take some time out from saving our lives to do a little ancestral research. Anyone here named Cohen?"

Charlotte doesn't see the humor. "Can we get back to business? Mason's jet could be the most clandestine way for us to leave the country. Unless you'd prefer the secrecy of a major international airport. As you said, Gideon, we can't stay here now that we've been tracked unless we want to end up like Uncle Bill. And by the way, who the hell killed him?"

Gideon hadn't wanted to get into this right now. After a period of indecision he answers directly. "Caleb."

There is a long pause, then Charlotte asks, "Who?"

In a few choice words, Gideon tells the group about Caleb. It is not his description, however, that frightens them, but rather Gideon's countenance as he speaks. Charlotte has never seen even the subtlest signs of fear on Gideon's face. Until now.

After Gideon has succeeded in quieting his audience with the tale of Caleb's awesomeness, Charlotte speaks up. "Why did he kill Uncle Bill?"

"To send a message."

"What message is that?" Thompson asks.

"That he can strike us at any place—at a time of his choosing. He's being cocky. Playing with me."

"Playing with *us*," Rebecca reminds him. "Maybe Mason's jet is the best way to ditch him."

"Let me be clear about this," Gideon says. No one likes the tone of his voice. "The corporate jet may help us evade detection from others who are trying to get us, but not Caleb. He already knows our connection to Mason... knows he owns a jet... probably means to pick us off one at a time just to humble me."

"But we've got something Caleb doesn't have."

Gideon turns to Charlotte, squinting with uncertainty. He can't think of anything. He cocks his head, encouraging her to fill in the blank.

"We've got *you*," she says.

✦ ✦ ✦

Caleb hasn't had this much fun in years.

Caleb had counted on Mason's fondness for Charlotte to help her escape from the staged fear-inducing events. The pawns had reacted exactly as Caleb had predicted.

Get out of Dodge.

A phone call confirms that the Ambienz Astra-Gulfstream 1125 corporate jet has been ordered for prep. Scheduled take-off time is 11:00 p.m. Now that the group has been herded onto a private airplane, the execution of Caleb's mission is much easier. An airplane explosion terminates all the targets at once. No tedious sequential eliminations of five different targets. No engaging in a dramatic but unpredictable Blackwatch-style gun battle.

Fortunately for Caleb, several of the world's best explosives experts live in the New York area, and for the right price, all are available for special assignments. By any definition, a bombing is contrary to the Sicarii principle of inflicting minimum damage through surgical strikes, but these principles usually apply only to individual assassinations. The operational plan created by Caleb is a group event, and under the terms of an irrevocable order, anything goes.

In other words, just get the damn thing done.

The beauty of a plan is that the planner can be proactive, while the target is by definition reactive. In this case, the explosives were being installed proactively while Gideon was busy with the Uncle Bill affair. Even if Gideon were to arrive at the airport early to supervise flight preparations, a "maintenance team" already will have done its work.

It surprises Caleb, though, that Gideon had apparently let the herd instinct overtake his leadership. This is the one nagging concern—*is he up to something Caleb doesn't expect?* Time will tell. The biggest concern is making sure that the plane takes off without Rebecca. Caleb is responsible for her protection.

No matter what, this is fun. A direct battle of wits and wills between the top two Sicarii assassins.

And what more fitting location? Republic Airport on Long Island lies next to eight cemeteries: St. Charles Cemetery, Cemetery of the Resurrection, New Montefiore Cemetery, St. John's Catholic Cemetery, Beth Moses Cemetery, Wellwood Cemetery, Pinelawn Cemetery, and Long Island National Cemetery.

Even before taking off, the targets are surrounded by death.

Chapter 30

The Ambienz van driven by security chief Whitney deposits the five travelers and Mason inside the hangar at about 10:00 p.m. The plane is already fueled. Pilot and co-pilot are methodically going through the pre-flight inspection.

Gideon is nervous. During his career there have been many times when his adrenaline has skyrocketed and his senses have been on high alert, but seldom in recent memory has he experienced true anxiety. He knows what has pushed him over the edge: trying to protect four people by himself.

And Caleb, of course.

Wearing a light jacket, Gideon ushers the passengers onto the jet so if an attack occurs, they won't have to run a gauntlet to board and make a fast take-off. He checks his watch. It is 10:05, which means his contractors are late.

This boosts his anxiety.

The pilot is relaxed and friendly, obviously ignorant of the dangers present.

Gideon tries his best to act nonchalant but his usual detachment has abandoned him. He can't muster the façade—this is too personal. He smiles weakly at a bad joke and finds himself staring out the hangar door for—

There it is, a Toyota SUV with a driver and one passenger. It pulls up next to Gideon, who breathes out for what seems to be the first time all evening.

"This the bird?" the driver asks through an open window.

"Obviously! And we're running late," Gideon answers. "But don't short-change the inspection."

The explosive-detection experts hustle out of the SUV with their equipment packages. One begins inspecting the exterior of the aircraft and the other focuses on the interior. Gideon knows these guys are good, but he's also aware that a top-flight technician can plant an explosive that only a formal tear-down could find. It doesn't seem like there's been enough time for such a maneuver, but no one can be sure.

✦ ✦ ✦

Thirty-five minutes into the inspection, Caleb lifts binoculars in time to see the inside inspector emerge from the aircraft door holding a small device. This is the bomb that had been placed in a ventilation duct. It blocked some of the air flow, which is how it was finally detected.

This is the first device, the one installed to be easy to find and give everyone a false sense of security.

The inspector high-fives his teammate and Gideon, then inexplicably spends the next five minutes pointing out some of the highlights of the device, presumably to demonstrate his knowledge.

Finally the threesome seems to grow bored analyzing the found device and the two inspectors go back to work, but with a diminished sense of urgency. Caleb guesses they will half-heartedly inspect for another ten to fifteen minutes, then declare the aircraft explosive-free.

That is, if Caleb's experts have done their job.

No matter what, at 11:00 PM a surprise guest will make a dramatic entrance and Gideon's escape plan will go up in smoke.

✦ ✦ ✦

"Almost eleven o'clock guys, how're we doing?" Gideon inquires.

"Found nothing out here," the exterior man says.

"Nothing more in here," the interior expert says.

Gideon looks at both men, who are now silent. "So are we good or what?"

"Unless we do a real tear-down, not much more we can do. Looks clean as a whistle now that we defused that one. FBI will tell us more about it."

"Huh-uh, no FBI," Gideon says, handing each of the men another thousand dollars. "Like I said, this is a private engagement. Matters of corporate trade secrets and all that. Industrial espionage."

"Using bombs? What's that about?" the exterior man asks.

"High stakes, guys. Just leave the device, and thank you very much."

The experts shrug and drive off. The pilot and co-pilot climb the stairs into the aircraft. Mason starts up the stairs.

"Where are you going?" Gideon asks him.

"With you—to London. It is my airplane, you know."

"Are you crazy? We're like a lightning rod. Stay away from us."

"And miss the action? Not on your life."

Gideon detects motion on his left and turns, astonished at the sight of a female U.S. Marshall approaching him.

"Excuse me, sir," the Marshall says, walking closer and flashing her badge. U.S. Marshall Evans. Are you the owner of this aircraft?"

She is looking at Gideon, but Mason answers, "I am, yes. Is there a problem? We've filed a flight plan."

"Sir, do you have any passengers on board?"

Gideon's senses go into high alert. He's certain that Caleb has something to do with this intrusion. He instinctively reaches behind to make sure his Glock is still tucked into his belt beneath his jacket.

"We have, let's see, four business associates on board, yes, and my partner here." Mason gestures toward Gideon, who has just received a promotion. Probably with no salary increase.

The Marshall shuffles through some papers. "Is this young woman, Rebecca Sinkler, on board?" She hands the papers to Mason. On top is a photograph of Rebecca.

"Yes, she's on board. What's the problem?"

"Could you ask her to exit the aircraft, please?"

"I must insist that you tell me what this is all about."

The Marshall takes a step backward and positions her hand over a holstered pistol. "Please sir, I won't ask again. Ask Miss Sinkler to exit the aircraft."

Rebecca is standing in the aircraft doorway. "What is it you want?"

"Come here, young lady," the Marshall says. "We don't want any problems."

Gideon is trying to figure out what is going on. Rebecca descends the stairs and walks over to the Marshall.

"Miss Sinkler, I have a warrant for your arrest. Please turn around the put your hands behind you."

Shocked and dismayed, Rebecca complies. As the Marshall handcuffs the young woman, Mason and Gideon protest vehemently.

"Miss Sinkler has been identified in a security photograph implicating her in a shooting at the Waldorf Astoria in New York City," the Marshall explains. "The rest of you are free to go, but Miss Sinkler must come with me. If this is a mistake, I'm sure it will be all worked out in due time."

The Marshall grabs Rebecca by the cuffs and begins to walk out of the hangar. Gideon looks up at the aircraft door and spots Charlotte staring at him, horrified. Gideon doesn't want to tangle with a U.S. Marshall, which could make Mason and his company the target of a federal probe, but he can't just abandon Rebecca.

Something is wrong here. Why was Rebecca identified, and no one else? Why is the Marshall here without tactical support? It doesn't add up.

The Marshall and Rebecca are almost out of the hangar.

"Excuse me," Gideon says. "Can I see the arrest warrant?"

The Marshall stops, hesitates just a little too long before speaking. "Of course," she says finally. But as she turns, Gideon sees the flash of metal in her hand. A gun!

Rebecca is too close to the Marshall to risk firing a shot, but he shoves Mason to the concrete floor just as the Marshall shoots, narrowly missing the tycoon.

Rebecca crumples to the ground, making it impossible for the Marshall to continue pulling her backward.

Hearing the shot, Jeremy leaps from the aircraft door onto the paved floor, pistol in hand. He rolls under the plane, providing another angle of fire at the Marshall, who makes a snap decision to abandon Rebecca and flee.

Gideon provides covering as Jeremy races to Rebecca and pulls her to her feet. They run toward Gideon, who steers them into the aircraft, then pushes Mason up the stairs. Inside, Gideon orders everyone to buckle up and barks at the pilot to fire up the engines.

The Gulfstream rolls easily out of the hangar and onto the runway. With clearance from the tower, the jet roars into the air, climbing swiftly.

Safe at last.

Caleb, frustrated and angry, watches the jet disappear through the clouds. Holding a cell phone, Caleb knows that making a call will detonate the second bomb, causing the plane to disappear in a fireball. Caleb enters the phone number, desperate for immediate revenge. Unfortunately, Rebecca's on board.

A thumb hovers over the CALL button.

To hell with it.

The thumb taps the button.

Chapter 31

The second explosive device had been made to look like a terrorist bomb so that inspection of the wreckage would deflect attention away from the actual perpetrators. The sophisticated bomb is located in the toner cartridge of a laser printer. Don't all corporate jets have a built-in office? The cartridge is loaded with 400 grams of odorless military grade PETN—pentaerythritol tetranitrate—a white powder that is one of the most powerful known explosives. This amount could level a house.

Cell phone circuitry, minus the case, had been wired into the mechanism. An incoming call triggers a flow of electrical current from the phone battery, heating up a thin wire filament located inside a plastic medical syringe. The syringe contains about 5 grams of lead azide, a powerful chemical initiator that ignites when the filament becomes hot enough, detonating the PETN.

Failing reception of a call, there is a failsafe. Any attempt to switch on the printer will set off the bomb.

As the jet rises over the patchwork of cemeteries below, Charlotte hands the dismantled toner cartridge to her strapped-in seatmate, Gideon.

"Here, just holding it makes me nervous. You're sure it's dead?"

"As can be. Unless there's a third one on board."

Gideon's tease makes Charlotte squirm.

"If I was Caleb, I wouldn't rely on just one of these bad boys," Gideon says, touching her arm reassuringly. "But I don't think they had enough time to make and hide three of them."

"You don't *think* there was time?"

"I'll let you know for sure when we're down safe."

Charlotte doesn't look convinced.

"Look," Gideon says, "my guys are experienced in detection, and they only get paid if we arrive safely. And paid well, I might add. Howard actually worked a case where toner cartridge bombs were shipped to Jewish organizations in Chicago. It's an old ploy, which means Caleb's team scrambled to cook this up. No time to innovate."

"Caleb's *team*? No wonder I feel like we're on The Amazing Race."

"I'm disappointed though."

"Disappointed? That we were saved?"

"I'm disappointed in Caleb. Bombs—not very artful. "

"Maybe it was someone else?"

"I doubt it."

"Then your old employer is really desperate to get us. That's when art goes out the window."

Charlotte notices that Gideon's hand is still on her arm. His touch, not his words, comfort her. For just a few seconds her guard slips and she wonders if some day, if they ever get out of this…

In frustration, Caleb taps the CALL button repeatedly, almost putting a thumb through the touchscreen, but the jet simply glides into the clouds.

Damn Gideon! His team must have discovered the second bomb.

Confidence has now become a liability for Caleb. The entire group had been in hand, but they had slipped away in full force. Not even one had been killed. For all the effort, Caleb had been dealt a setback. Seconds ago, the target's exact location had been known. Now only a general destination is known— London—and that destination probably will change now that Caleb has revealed her knowledge of the flight.

This is an inconvenience, at least.

Perhaps Caleb had been too cocky, too sure of the plan to conceal redundant bombs, too certain of the U.S. Marshall deception. Caleb's frustration will be taken out on the explosive concealment team later. Right now, though, the chess match between Gideon and Caleb has become more challenging. What Caleb had thought to be checkmate had only placed Gideon in check, but he had found a way out.

The phone in Caleb's hand vibrates.

An incoming message. Cain wants an immediate call-back.

No way. The kill order is irrevocable. There is no good news to report. Caleb needs no outside intelligence to track down the targets. Any conversation with a superior would only distract from the mission.

Time to book a flight. Caleb knows exactly how to intercept the targets again. This time it will be a true checkmate.

Jeremy holds Rebecca's hand and can feel the trembling. She is almost cata-
tonic, just staring at her knees, as she has done since Jeremy buckled her into the
seat.

"You've been through a lot," Jeremy says, trying to coax her out of her
stupor.

With moist eyes she turns toward Jeremy. "Thank you… for saving me. I'm
sure you must think I'm such a baby."

"You're safe now, up here."

"There could be another bomb."

"Gideon says no. He's never wrong about these things."

"And when we land? They could be waiting for us."

"One thing at a time, okay? You've got two expert bodyguards. Who else
can say that?"

Her hand is soft and warm. She squeezes his, a way of acknowledging his
feeble attempt at encouragement. And maybe something more. When she puts her
other hand on top of his, it seems almost… intimate. Maybe this plane ride can last
forever.

After a long, tender silence, Rebecca whispers, "I'm very confused."

"Aren't we all?"

"No, not about all this—this spy stuff. It's just that… I wasn't supposed to
be here. It's all kind of, like, bad timing, you know?"

"I do, same goes for me. I'm out of a job and being hunted by the people I
used to work for. And they're very good hunters."

As these words slip from his mouth, Jeremy wishes he could take them back.

Rebecca's hands tighten around his. Her eyes suddenly flare with fear.

"Sorry about that," Jeremy says, knowing an apology can't remove her distress. "Just remember, Gideon's the best."

"Except for Caleb, right?"

"No—that's just a myth. Caleb's gotten old. Probably out of practice. In my
book, Gideon's the best. We made it out of the airport, right? We're alive."

Rebecca sighs and nods. "I'm confused about something else, too."

Her lashes are impossibly long, her green eyes vulnerable, her satin cheeks
flushed. Jeremy hopes that he doesn't have to say anything right now, because he
is mesmerized into muteness by this astounding creature. His mind pulls him back,
tells him that relationships are forbidden for Sicarii assassins.

But then he realizes he is no longer bound by those rules.

What was Rebecca saying again? *I'm so confused about something else.*
Jeremy wonders what that could be.

Oh.

Suddenly his entire body seems filled with light.

Chapter 32

Within thirty minutes of take-off, all passengers but Gideon and Mason are asleep. Two hours later, everyone stirs as the craft is buffeted by temporary turbulence. After the choppy air smooths out, Mason helps his passengers arrange their seats to face each other. He has had numerous meetings on the Gulfstream, but had never imagined his jet would become a war room.

Gideon sees the fogged-over eyes of the group and wonders if they'll all be able to keep up. Things are not likely to get any easier. He motions for Mason to speak.

"While you were all sleeping, Gideon asked that we divert our destination from Heathrow to a different airport." Mason's voice is hoarse from exhaustion. "I think you know why. We've selected Luton Airport, which is about thirty miles from central London. We haven't changed our flight plan, because that could give away our intention to the wrong people if they're well-connected. Instead, we'll claim aircraft problems and get permission to set down at Luton."

"That's where we get off the bus," Gideon says. "I have a small flat in the middle of London the Order doesn't know about—my own little safe house, in case I ever found myself in this kind of position." He looks at Jeremy with a sly grin. "Remember your training, Jeremy? Sometimes contingency plans pay off."

Gideon refocuses on the group. "We can bunk at my flat until we get organized. This all begs the question, of course, *why London*? I'm wondering myself, so I'll let the esteemed author and strategist Thompson Walker explain, as this was his suggestion." Gideon's final remark is tinged with sarcasm.

All heads swivel to look at Thompson, whose red eyes reveal an old man seriously in need of an energy transplant.

Thompson clears his throat and begins. "As I said—" he checks his watch, finds it is nearly 2:00 a.m. New York time, "—was it only yesterday? Seems like a year ago. Anyway, we're going to trace the Cohen family tree."

"I thought you were joking about that," Charlotte says. "I had a Jewish friend in high school, Al Cohen. Really cute. Big family. Sometimes I wonder how life would have been different if I had married Al instead of... well, you know—"

Charlotte's mind slips carelessly into painful terrain, remembering in a white-hot flash her husband, Mahid Ansari, a Persian Jew who also was a purebred Sicarii. Under orders from Charlotte's now-deceased mother, Mahid had drugged Charlotte during their courtship, then raped the unconscious woman. Thinking the baby inside her was the product of an alcohol-induced indiscretion, Charlotte had married Mike to camouflage her recklessness. Her son, a child of the pure Sicarii bloodline, was destined to become the Divine Light of the Order, the new Cain. After betraying the Order, Charlotte's doubly devious husband had been assassinated by Gideon. Charlotte had never shed a tear over her husband's death. And she had never expected to be in love with his killer.

No, she is not in love. There is no time for that now. Perhaps never.

Charlotte notices the others staring at her. She is embarrassed for having slipped into this emotional quagmire. "So tell me, *father…*" she says, hoping to divert attention from herself, "…why this obsession with the Cohens?"

"Ahhh," Thompson sighs. "Let me tell you about the Cohens. This name, and its many derivatives, goes all the way back to the name Kohath. Anyone care to tell us who Kohath was? Don't raise your hands all at once now." He smiles smugly, sure that none of these historical illiterates knows the answer.

Rebecca's hand shoots up before she realizes that Thompson was jesting. "In the Old Testament," she says, self-consciously lowering her hand, "Kohath was a patriarch, a son of Levi. I think Moses and his brother Aaron descended from him?"

"I'm impressed, Rebecca. You know your Bible."

"I've always loved Old Testament stories. They all seemed to be more in touch with God. And the people lived a long time, which is nice."

"Well, let me summarize." Thompson lapses into his professorial demeanor. "As some of you may recall, Aaron was installed as the first high priest of Israel, a most noble calling, as only the high priest could enter the Holiest of the Holies, the most secret and sacred chamber in the Tabernacle, to perform his priestly duties. That was where the Ark of the Covenant was kept.

"Through his firstborn son, Aaron's male descendants—and *only* those descendants—inherited the right to be high priests. Any legitimate claim to the priesthood must come from that bloodline. Such individuals became known as *Kohathites*, or *Kohanim*. In more modern times they were called *Cohens*."

"Do you remember Al Cohen?" Charlotte asks her father. "Definitely not high priest material."

"Today, of course, there are thousands of lines of Cohens and other common variants like Katz. Most are way out of the priestly line, as you might expect. The ones we are interested in would be descended from David's and Solomon's priests. Their names were Zadok, after David's first high priest, who was twelfth generation from Aaron himself. From that point on, the high priests were referred to as Sons of Zadok. Some of my colleagues call them the Zadokite priests."

All but Thompson begin nodding. They know that Mason's hopeful investor is the leader of the Sicarii Council of Twelve. And if Thompson's belief is correct, that the Council is made up of Zadokite priests, then investigating the family tree could reveal important clues.

"You want to sift through thousands of years." Mason shakes his head considering the magnitude of the task. "Millions of possible descendants."

"A staggering challenge, yes," Thompson replies. "That's why I hope to get us some help from an old friend at Oxford. He may have done some of the work for us already."

"What is it you want to know?" Mason leans back in his seat.

"After being scattered across the globe, how is it that a group of Zadokite priests remains intact?" Thompson asks. "Or that they managed to reassemble?"

"And with its own intelligence and assassination arm," Gideon adds.

Charlotte nods. "And what the hell do they want?"

Chapter 33

Michael brushes a few white flakes from the shoulder of his thousand-dollar navy blue blazer, which magnificently frames a crisp white button-down shirt and the obligatory scarlet tie that identifies his eminent station. Traditional camel trousers round out the ensemble. It's smart and casual with just a hint of military severity in the sharply tailored lines.

When meeting subordinates who are skeptical of outsiders and used to commanding large forces with absolute authority, it's important to project professionalism and even greater authority. Michael, who uses the name William Sinclair in business, has found that the correct clothing can provide a beneficial boost to both attributes. Even though he enjoys sartorial splendor, however, he knows it is just packaging.

He could dominate most other men stark naked.

Standing outside the chauffeured limo he takes a deep breath and surveys the secure Virginia compound of Blackwatch situated on 400 acres of impressively varied terrain that is ideal for training. A very attractive woman approaches him from the log-and-cinder-block corporate headquarters. Apparently the executives believe that luxurious digs are inconsistent with fostering an attitude of discipline and self-control in the mercenaries they employ.

Clearly an exception to the luxury rule has been made for the female help. The woman who introduces herself in a breathy voice as Cherry, and who caresses Sinclair's arm as she seductively guides him toward the HQ entrance, is supermodel-worthy. The packaging is flawless. Her walk is a metaphoric lap dance. But Sinclair smiles at the lack of subtlety in the company's presentation, knowing that Cherry, like all the others here, is a mercenary.

Appreciating the reputation of Blackwatch, Sinclair suspects that Cherry is probably trained in martial arts, too. He doesn't intend to find out.

The lobby is one step above a standard US Army HQ, the chief upgrade being an art collection of dramatic action paintings featuring military vehicles, aircraft, and weapons. Inspiring in a way.

Cherry ushers him directly into a knotty pine conference room outfitted with a wall of video monitors—all switched off for the meeting—and other high-tech communications equipment.

"Coffee or tea?" Cherry inquires, pulling out a chair for Sinclair.

"Nothing right now."

"Maybe later?" Cherry temptingly proposes, and then swishes out of the room before Sinclair can respond.

In a clever bit of well-timed stagecraft, her boss immediately enters. "Don't get up, please. I'm William Wyatt."

He offers a hand, which Sinclair firmly shakes.

"Mr. Sinclair, it's a pleasure to meet our new owner." Wyatt struggles to sound sincere.

"My pleasure, indeed," Sinclair replies. "I followed your career in public service with a great deal of admiration. Was the transition back to civilian life a difficult one after your tremendous responsibility at the CIA?"

"Well, to be honest, Blackwatch is kind of like a halfway house. Not exactly a civilian type of operation we have here."

"I was sorry to hear about John Weinert's tax problems. Was he a good friend?"

"Still is. He built this firm from the ground up. It was his vision. And he was the reason I came here as second-in-command after the CIA. I don't know how he got in so deep financially, but you know the government. When you owe the IRS a lot of money—as he did, apparently—they don't offer terms."

"Terrible thing. But like he said, he thought his financial team was taking care of the financial end for him. At any rate, his need for cash became our opportunity, so here we are."

For just a fleeting moment, Sinclair flashes on the months of intelligence gathering his financial team had spent pulling together evidence of Weinert's blatant tax evasion, the consequence no doubt of his extreme Libertarian views.

And I want to begin by saying that we hope you stay on with us. We'd like you to step up to full command of the firm, since Weinert is gone and we have no interest in placing someone else in that role."

"I appreciate that," Wyatt says guardedly.

"With a commensurate increase in compensation, naturally. And we'll identify some other perks I'm sure."

Wyatt nods appreciatively.

"You'll find we are not micro-managers, but over time we'll likely make suggestions on the overall mission of the firm. You may find it expanding in some areas, contracting in others."

"I'm not sure I follow. Contracting in what ways?"

"Well, for example, we'd like to see less activity in… let's call it domestic special ops. You know, like the rooftop scuffle at the Waldorf. A bit overdone, wouldn't you say? Not your specialty, really."

The blood instantly drains from Wyatt's face. Sinclair sees that Wyatt is stunned by his knowledge of that failed operation.

"The risks in this country are just too high," Sinclair continues. "What works outside the country doesn't always work here. So we'd suggest more emphasis on helping the U.S. militarily and with intelligence operations, and other nations and governments with their struggles in their own lands. Over time I expect we'll be able to deliver some lucrative new contracts in that regard. The fact is, we have other resources to competently satisfy client needs here at home. No need to overlap services."

Sinclair pauses to revel in Wyatt's attempt to camouflage his perplexity.

"Your military experience prior to the directorship of the CIA makes you an ideal leader for Blackwatch," Sinclair adds. "As I recall, one of your CIA predecessors became president. It could be that your role here at Blackwatch could prove to be even more important. But that's for another day. I know this is all rather sudden, but I sense you're a decisive man. Are you prepared to accept our offer and become CEO of Blackwatch?"

Wyatt stares at his guest the way a poker player searches his opponent for a tell. Sinclair is sure that he has revealed exactly what he intended and betrayed nothing else. He seldom loses in either poker or business.

The mysterious new owner of Blackwatch had intended a bit of *shock and awe*, baiting Wyatt's curiosity while strafing him with high-powered intelligence and domination. He's having fun. If Wyatt declines, he's expendable.

Wyatt's nervous drumming of fingers on the tabletop gives away his indecision. He remains silent.

Should Sinclair give the poor man one last little nudge? Oh, why not?

"I appreciate it's a big decision," Sinclair says, relieving the tension. "So take the rest of the day to think about it." He stands, signaling that the meeting is ending.

Wyatt stands up too, replying, "I will. Would you like a tour of the compound before returning to the hotel?"

"Oh, I already know all about the facility here. Very impressive, by the way. Before I leave, though, I'd like to give you something to commemorate our meeting—the first of many I hope."

Sinclair reaches into his blazer's breast pocket, removes an envelope, and hands it to Wyatt. "Please… open it," he says.

Wyatt notices the heft of the envelope. He smiles awkwardly at Sinclair then opens the package, removing an object that sends shivers through his body.

A bronzed sica.

Wyatt knows it symbolizes assassination.

"Just a small token from your new sister organization," Sinclair explains. "I hope you'll stay with the firm, William. It would be our honor to ensure your prosperity and safety. Don't worry about reciprocating. I have everything I could ever want, assuming that Cherry is available to escort me back to the limo. Delightful young woman."

Chapter 34

Charlotte's eyes snap open. Someone has opened a window.

Charlotte looks around the room, finds nothing familiar. Totally disoriented, she sits up, heart pounding, breath catching in her throat. Where is she?

"Good afternoon." Gideon's gentle voice calms her, smooths her re-entry into wakefulness. This must be Gideon's flat, though she has no recollection of traveling here from… from the airport. They must have landed, she assumes. A pale memory of walking away from the plane emerges… of Gideon negotiating something with—with *whom*?—a customs agent perhaps… a bribe most likely… then carrying their things to a vehicle.

But nothing after that.

"You slept all the way here." Gideon is smiling, like her father used to smile at her when she was little. "I carried you in. You're cute when you're asleep."

He probably means this affectionately, but her reflex is to respond angrily—she is no child, after all, and certainly no bimbo to be wooed with baby-talk. His sincere expression, though, and the way he almost timidly glanced away is just too endearing. In the London light streaking through the window, this man looks much younger than his age, no more than a schoolboy. His winning half-smile, as he pretends to look out the window at Holland Park instead of admiring Charlotte—which his hungry eyes seem to crave—lends him an innocence that temporarily erases the fact that this man is a professional killer.

The light paints him with golden brushstrokes. The hopeful songs of birds from the park float on gentle breezes through the window, a peaceful serenade. This instant may be the only truly romantic moment Charlotte has ever experienced—perfect except for the annoying, persistent sputter and drone of…

Thompson's snoring.

And Jeremy's nasal accompaniment.

She laughs. It feels good to exercise those unused muscles. Gideon laughs too, and the sound of their amusement wakes up the others, who rise slowly, wondering what is going on.

Mason's head pops up from a heap of towels on the floor. "Worst night's sleep of my life," he mumbles. "Reminds me of college."

"What time is it?" Thompson croaks while he searches for his glasses.

"Almost five in the afternoon," Gideon replies.

"What day? How long have we been asleep?"

"Same day we arrived. Three hours."

"God, I need another ten," Rebecca complains, rolling over and pulling a thin blanket over her head.

Through his brain fog, Thompson is trying to make sense of this. And finally does as he consults his watch. In a move that would be a leap in a younger man, Thompson awkwardly makes it to a standing position, eyes wide open. "Good God, we have to meet my friend at the British Museum in an hour!"

Jeremy has only one thing on his mind. "Man, we need to get some food."

Charlotte glances at Gideon who is still standing by the window. A cloud has blotted out the magical sunlight, and with it the mirage of an innocent man. Before her now stands a warrior confronting his next mission, eyes fierce and focused, body poised for action, mind already ahead of everyone else by thirty-three steps—the sequence of actions required to get them all fed and transported safely to the Museum.

The romantic moment has passed. Charlotte wonders if it will ever come again.

+ + +

Thompson enjoys leading the small band into the sprawling maze of underground trains knowing that, with the possible exception of Gideon, they are reliant on his expertise in navigating the "Tube". Fifteen minutes later they emerge from the Tottenham Court station and, as swiftly as Thompson's creaky legs allow, march down Great Russell Street to the British Museum.

"Hurry up," he mocks, "we're late already. He'll be near the *Mitoraj*."

Which means nothing to Charlotte or Gideon.

Arriving finally at the mammoth Museum building, Thompson spots a stiff, frail man inspecting his watch next to a large sculpture of a woman's face by Igor Mitoraj—a huge, floating black mask containing only eyes, nose and lips.

"There he is." Huffing from exertion, Thompson hurries over to the man, extending his arms outward in anticipation of an embrace.

The men hug each other, pat each other on the back, then hold each other at arm's length to inspect the erosion of age since their last encounter.

"You look terrible," Thompson jokes.

Bertram Doering is likely ten years older than Thompson. Mainly cartilage and bones held together by thin, wrinkled skin, Bertram looks on the verge of death, but the sight of Thompson seems to animate him.

"You look worse," Bertram says. His laugh turns into a wheeze, then a cough. "You're late. I may have only minutes left to live, you know."

"Nonsense. You'll outlive us all." His unintended meaning seems to prophesy imminent doom for the group. Thompson changes the subject by introducing his companions by their assumed names. For Mason he supplies the false name Fred Khan.

"I may be an old man, Tommy." Bertram's bony hand takes Charlotte's. "But I know this young woman is your daughter, the famous Charlotte Ansari."

Charlotte smiles demurely and nods.

"And so I suppose the others all have real names as well?" Bertram turns to Thompson, proud of his deductive reasoning."

"Yes, they do."

When Thompson doesn't offer to supply those names, Bertram sighs and suggests, "It's probably best I don't know them, I suppose. But it's a pity, I've always wanted to shake hands with the famous entrepreneurial *savant*, Meysam Madani."

"If he were here," Thompson responds, "I'm sure he'd want to shake your hand as well. But since he's not, perhaps Mr. Khan could be a suitable substitute."

Bertram exuberantly shakes Mason's hand.

"We need to speak privately, Bert," Thompson whispers. "Do you still have a place inside?"

"Until they pry the key from my cold dead hands."

Bertram guides them into the British Library, which occupies a full city block of the vast museum. The main room, referred to as the Manuscripts Saloon, adjoins the Kings Library and rises three stories high. Leather-bound, hand-written volumes fill the floor-to-rafters shelves. Long ladders and catwalks make the upper shelves accessible to researchers. Floor-level glass cases house a breathtaking collection of many of the world's greatest and most historic documents—the Magna Carta; the original score of Handel's Messiah; the oldest manuscript of the Holy Scriptures called the Codex Sinaitica; the only extant manuscript of Aristotle on the Constitution of Athens; the prayer book used by Lady Jane Grey on the scaffold. And so much more.

Oxford Professors in history, languages, and archaeology are assigned Museum study closets with access to Library resources. In these carrels they can work privately or with small numbers of students. Bertram leads his guests to the carrel that he has used for nearly forty years. Even though he is now Professor Emeritus, the Museum has granted him permission to use his old space until… well, until he is no longer able to use it.

Some serious refurbishment has been going on in the corridor. The group passes opened walls, a couple of saw horses, and assorted tools and supplies on the way to the carrel. Gideon is interested in a circular saw and the shiny 8-inch metal-cutting blades housed in their colorful safety-guard packages.

"So you like bright objects," Charlotte teases. "Were you a carpenter in an earlier life?"

"Tools can be put to many uses," Gideon replies cryptically.

Bertram opens a creaking door to reveal a dim room barely large enough for the six of them. Three will have to stand, as only three chairs are present. The professor snaps on a green-shaded study lamp, then places his briefcase on a wooden surface that serves as a desk. Tall stacks of papers stand on this surface like a row of skyscrapers. Some minor refurbishing is underway here, too, and Bertram blows away a coating of construction dust.

From inside his briefcase Bertram retrieves a notebook computer and expertly connects it to an Ethernet cable and electrical outlet finally switching it on and entering a long password. Clearly he is security-conscious.

The carrel contains a locked strongbox large enough to contain perhaps a dozen large books and assorted files. Bertram unlocks the strongbox and removes one of two notebooks, placing them on the table before sitting down at the computer.

"Nowadays only a few of the carrels are enclosed," he explains, motioning for Mason to close the door. "We only got high-speed Internet access several years ago. But it's a bit different than what you may be used to." He is addressing Mason.

"How is that?" Mason asks, the perfect straight-man.

"The IP addresses are all in Roman numerals."

Bertram chuckles at his own joke. Out of courtesy, the others laugh with him.

"If I don't come in at least once a quarter, they will revoke my privileges," Bertram continues. "This room is a second home to me."

"We're so happy you were willing to meet with us," Thompson says. "As I mentioned, the topic we wish to address is of the utmost urgency."

"And secrecy," Bertram adds. His rheumy eyes begin to glisten. "My dear friends—at my age, a little intrigue is a welcome thing. Now Tommy, you said it had to do with the Zadokite priests, or am I remembering incorrectly?"

"You've never remembered *anything* incorrectly, Bertram. But before we tell you more, perhaps you could share with us all the nature of your project."

"Of course," Bertram replies, smiling. "For over twenty years now I've been mapping the pure lineage of the Zadokite priests, separating it from all the other strands of Cohens. Would you like to know why?"

Chapter 35

In the Manuscripts Saloon, Caleb intently studies one of only four exemplifications of the Magna Carta. The landmark document, drafted in 1215 CE, required King John of England to proclaim certain liberties for the general population. It was the first document ever forced upon a sitting king by his subjects. More evidence, Caleb concludes, that man's authority is temporal, and only God's is absolute.

It is God's authority that grants Caleb the right to terminate a life for the fulfillment of His cause. God's sovereignty transcends all mortal laws including the charters of international leagues, the legislation of nations, previous religious decrees, even the bonds and rules of families. But since the days of David and his son Solomon, only a few individuals—including the Temple's High Priests—have had direct access to God's specific pronouncements. Since the Romans destroyed the Temple in 70 CE, three years before the fateful annihilation of the Sicarii on Masada, there has been no Temple. No Holy of Holies. In its place has been substituted something even more powerful, something that will not only restore the Temple, but transform the world in the most brilliant, magnificent way under the benevolent mentorship of...

A tourist bumps into Caleb and apologizes.

It's time for Caleb to move forward with the plan, which now focuses on picking off each member of the group one by one. Tedious and deliberate.

Caleb's phone vibrates. Chen has analyzed the image of the elderly gentleman photographed by Caleb outside the museum. He is Bertram H. Doering, Ph.D., Professor Emeritus in History and Linguistics at Oxford, last lectured thirteen years ago. He is a holocaust survivor, son of a Rabbi, and author of eleven scholarly books. Presently he is the titular head of the Zadok Project, a loosely-knit group of volunteer researchers exploring Jewish genealogy.

Caleb approaches the Library's main desk. "Can you tell me if Dr. Doering has a carrel in the facility?"

"Bertram? For decades now, yes. Getting up in years, don't see him as often."

"Can you point me toward his carrel?"

"Yes, down the corridor to the left, but you'll have to go through security."

"Thank you. I'll just wait out here. There's a lot to see."

Bertram's fingers are surprisingly agile. They dance over the keyboard, calling up a series of images on the computer monitor.

"Without computers," he explains, "this project would be impossible. We are compiling and collating hundreds of thousands of information fragments from disparate sources all over the world. For nearly fifteen years we have been pleading with Jews and others, wherever they may be, to send us any information they have about their ancestors."

He taps a key and images of handwritten notes display. "We get copies of personal notes on scraps of paper, hand-drawn family trees created from memory from the elderly. Photographs with annotations. As you might expect, scores of languages. This kind of information helps fill in the more recent generations, although we have big gaps during the holocaust."

"I was wondering about that," Charlotte says. "How can you possibly plug those holes?"

"We'll never plug them all, but God seems to have watched over his chosen Ones, who have always been very resourceful."

The old man's bony fingers continue to tap keys and display images, the next ones of old rags and shoe soles on which crude scrawls appear.

"During the holocaust, Jews cleverly kept alive their traditions and Scriptures—even their family histories—by writing them down and hiding them in secret places. With chunks of charcoal from fires built by the guards, they would write on the insides of their prison uniforms, in their ruined shoes, on their flea-ridden blankets, on found scraps of paper, even the back sides of bricks and stones pulled from the walls. They'd hide their prized messages in crevices and behind rocks. They'd cling with their lives to their precious rags. The guards would occasionally find some of these messages. But not understanding Hebrew, they usually considered them to be merely childish scribbling."

Jeremy is mesmerized by this tale. "It's almost like they knew that someday people would find their messages."

"And we did find many of them," Bertram replies. A key tap displays a short Hebrew message on a stained and tattered piece of paper.

"Twenty-four years ago, I returned to Auschwitz where my entire family was murdered—except for me, of course." Bertram suddenly cannot look into the eyes of his guests. Instead he focuses on the picture. "I found a small brick that I had loosened in a wall while I was confined there. Behind that brick, after all these years, I found a note I had hidden."

Charlotte's eyes are wide and moist. "What did you write?" she asks.

"A record of my family, back to my great-grandparents. I was so afraid that I would be forgotten, that my family would disappear from history. It was a way to hold onto my identity despite the harsh conditions."

Bertram's eyes blink, fighting back emotion. "This little scrap of paper is my family tree. In a way, it's my *family*."

Mason leans closer to the monitor, staring.

"This is quite a story," he says, then steps back. "But there are thousands of years of genealogy to fill in before this time. And I would guess that record-keeping was, well, incomplete. How can you possibly trace back through all those years, when even the recorded history in the Old Testament is incomplete and inaccurate?"

"A very good question, Mr. Madani—excuse me, I mean Mr. Kahn." He smiles wryly. "The fact is, Jews kept remarkable genealogical records, particularly pertaining to the priests, because lineage was so important to establishing the priestly stations. You may not know this, but when excavations were made by the Knights Templar beneath the Temple Mount in Jerusalem—the Templars were searching for treasure—guess what they discovered. Chamber after chamber contained walls written over with genealogical records and other messages! Up to the year 70 CE or so, when the Temple was destroyed, we have excellent records."

"A huge job you've undertaken, Bertram." Thompson touches the old man's shoulder. "But what about after 70 CE?"

"The people of Qumram," Bertram replies, "a group we call *Essenes*, believed that the priesthood lineage had been corrupted."

Mention of the Essenes, the group from which the Sicarii originated, perks Gideon's attention.

"Certainly the Romans may have forced the installation of non-hereditary priests. And the Essenes may have suspected other shenanigans in the past. Some scholars think that may be why the Essenes separated from mainstream Judaism—they wanted to purify the priestly line. Anyway, there is some confusion in the records over that time. The more radical Zealots, who gave rise to the Sicarii assassins, were probably followers of a man called Judas of Galilee. Personally, there is a case to be made for Judas being of pure Zadokite lineage."

"The historical continuum is daunting," Thompson remarks. "I'm just wondering how you could track records in the Middle Ages."

"Well, I can give you an example. We've located additions and updates to the record in thirteenth-century Germany. But during periods of great massacres or epidemics—like the Great Plague—data integrity sinks to an all-time low. A lot of Jews were scapegoated for that plague and forced to flee, losing track of their roots."

"And of course, all the historical records you find are in the King's English, I'd imagine," Thompson offers in jest.

"Afraid not, and that's one of the great drains on our time. We are up to snuff on the usual languages—Hebrew, Greek, and some Aramaic. But there are a host of ancient languages, even lost ones like Judaized Syriac or barbarized Roman Latin."

"Where do you get your funding for this kind of project?"

"Several Jewish foundations, hundreds of small individual donors, the Millennium Broadcast Network…"

"Hold on," Gideon interjects. "Millennium is an Evangelical Christian network. Are they a large donor?"

"Yes, I think so. Maybe the largest. I'm not much involved in fund-raising anymore. I seem to recall a brief decline in their support about five years ago, however, after their founder was murdered in his car. Tragic."

Charlotte's eyes scroll knowingly to Gideon. She had always suspected that he had assassinated the popular TV evangelist Pastor Crate, probably for betraying the Order, an unpardonable sin. She recalls an operation five years ago in which Crate had hired the Sicarii to further his goal of building a new Temple in Jerusalem. The sect's oddball theory was that Biblical prophecy prevented Christ from returning until after a new Temple was built on the site of the old one. But a new temple could not be built without a hereditary high priest to officiate.

"Excellent summary, Bertram," Thompson glances at the assemblage. "Now perhaps it's time for me to explain why this priestly family tree business matters very much to us."

Thompson gives Bertram the equivalent of a survey course in their predicament, emphasizing the likely Zadok connection to the Council of Twelve and skimming over the most terrifying events of the past couple of days.

"I am convinced that if we can learn more about the current Zadokite priests," Thompson concludes, "we will discover clues to their agenda, and possibly to a counter-strategy."

Throughout Thompson's animated synopsis, Bertram's eyes have continually landed on the chiseled face of Gideon.

"We all thought the Sicarii were long gone," Bertram explains to Gideon, "so please forgive my foolish staring. For an old historian, encountering a modern-day Sicarii is a bit like a zoologist discovering that the abominable snowman is real."

"No offense taken."

Bertram takes the notebook that has been lying next to the keyboard and hands it to Thompson. "Please take this, Tommy. I've compiled some notes you may find helpful."

Bertram hands the strongbox key to his friend. "There may be some other items of use in the strongbox. We're not supposed to, but I made a duplicate key."

"How long will it take to build out the entire genealogy chart?" Mason asks.

"We have too little staff, and our computers are slow. Maybe ten years, possibly fifteen." He takes a deep breath, a sign of exhaustion. "Now, which of you has the better memory?"

Nobody raises a hand.

"Then all of you should commit my username and password to memory—please don't write it down. Log in and you will have master access to all the data we have. Username—mwdoering1897. This is my father's initials and last name combined with the year of his birth. My way of keeping his memory alive. Password—auschwitz198556. My prisoner identification number. A way of keeping your memory of me alive. Do you need me to repeat it?"

Charlotte immediately speaks. "I'll remember it, and you, forever."

Chapter 36

Caleb finds the British Library fascinating. This feast of history relieves the tedium of waiting for the next step of the mission to unfold. She makes a mental note: *come back again and spend the day.*

Caleb is lost in her study of original manuscripts written by Charles Dickens and JRR Tolkien. When her professional career is over, Caleb may take up writing. Political thrillers would be a good bet. Certainly not a memoir.

Her vibrating cell phone interrupts. An encrypted text message changes her mission. It has been determined that the ancient Oxford professor Bertram Doering poses a threat and must be eliminated. This has been prioritized over assassinating the others. But don't cause a big scene in a public place, etc.

Caleb knows the drill. This means going old school.

Besides her 9mm pistol, concealed on Caleb's body is a carbonized plastic sica. Like the Sicarii assassins in Old Jerusalem, Caleb will maneuver close to the unsuspecting victim and at just the right moment plunge the blade between two particular ribs. At first, the victim will feel just a minor pain—most think it is a gas pain or a heart attack. The bleeding is almost entirely internal. The blade itself is often wiped clean upon removal by the victim's garment. Within a few seconds the victim will feel weak, then stagger and collapse. It will probably take a few minutes or more for anyone to suspect foul play, particularly when the victim is a frail 89-year-old man. By the time Doering is dead, Caleb will be long gone.

Caleb is already anticipating Gideon's humiliation at losing Doering in such an understated and elegant manner, one in which Gideon is also well-schooled.

A group of manuscripts by John Lennon catches Caleb's eye.

She still mourns his death.

✦ ✦ ✦

As the discussion about the Sons of Zadok unfolds in Bertram's carrel, Gideon grows oddly impatient. No, not impatient—*anxious*. He knows of no imminent threat, but he knows that if Thompson's theory is correct, Bertram's knowledge and activities may also pose a threat to the Sicarii.

He has learned never to underestimate the Order or its mysterious overlords.

And then there is Caleb. It seems impossible that Caleb could have tracked down Gideon in the short period since the escape from the Long Island airport, but so far Caleb has not missed a beat.

While the others confer, Gideon goes back over all the details of the past day, right up to the U.S. Marshall scam and the attempted abduction of Rebecca.

This is the part that he doesn't understand. Gideon had made a mistake in using a document forger that the Order had also relied upon in the past. A sharp operative easily could have anticipated the need for travel documents and staked out the likely suspects, then followed Uncle Bill to Long Island. No magic there, just agile thinking.

Caleb also could have known that Ambienz had a corporate jet and anticipated that Gideon would opt for avoiding a major airport when fleeing New York. Checking with local airports would have revealed the location of the Ambienz Gulf Stream and uncovered its flight plan. So Caleb certainly would have known that the group was bound for the United Kingdom. The diversion to Luton airport would have been just a minor annoyance.

Then there is the matter of the U.S. Marshall charade at the airport, which is so odd. Gideon had expected Caleb either to target Gideon—the leader—or the entire group. By having Rebecca removed from the jet, Caleb seems to have signaled that the young woman was to be spared. But why?

He searches his memory of the airport events for any clue as to how Caleb might be able to track them in the U.K. Even assuming that the assassin discovered the Gulf Stream at Luton Airport, Gideon is absolutely certain that his safe house in London is unknown to anyone else.

Maybe Gideon is worrying too much. Given time, Caleb will find a way to locate them unless they move around. But in the few hours since they had left Long Island, it seems impossible that they could have been found.

Still, he combs through the details of that strange confrontation with the fake Marshall. The handcuffing... walking away... placing her arm protectively around the young woman...

Suddenly Gideon knows they are not safe. If he were Caleb, he would have...

"Are you still with us?" Bertram addresses Gideon, who seems distracted.

"Yes, of course." Gideon lies unconvincingly.

He has a pretty good idea of how Caleb might attempt an assassination in public. The Sicarii have been doing this for millennia. Gideon suspects that he will be the chief target, but with Caleb you never know.

If something happens to him, Gideon wonders, will Jeremy be up to the task?
"Excuse me a minute," he says. "Bathroom break."
Time to change into Superman.

✦ ✦ ✦

Being this close to the true touchstones of history is thrilling. Caleb can remember other documents that would rank with these, some of them secret documents authored or signed by victims of the sica and destroyed before the force of their words could collide with the Plan of God. Caleb could fill a large display case in the British Museum with personal artifacts that had changed the course of history—weapons used in famous assassinations, disguises, stolen files, damning financial records of public figures, photographic evidence of...

Caleb is accidentally bumped by a woman. She hears an insincere apology and turns to see a much larger mass of people than were present even a few minutes ago. Several groups have entered. This is good news. A sparsely populated library would make her job that much harder to do.

Peering down the corridor that leads to Bertram's carrel, Caleb sees the newest target wobbling toward the Manuscripts Saloon surrounded by Gideon and his growing band of Merry Men and Women. Time to let the crowd work its magic.

✦ ✦ ✦

Gideon has positioned the group members strategically. Jeremy and Mason lead, with Rebecca and Charlotte immediately behind. Bertram and Thompson, the most vulnerable because of their frailty, follow closely behind the women. Gideon brings up the rear. The object is to prevent anyone from penetrating their ranks and plunging a sica into someone's back.

Seeing the throng ahead, Gideon knows the peril has grown. He encourages his group to maintain discipline, but Bertram's backward glance indicates he's not taking this maneuver seriously.

The group enters the immense Manuscripts Saloon and Jeremy heads directly for the main exit. As Gideon had feared, they must pass through a large tour group. Gideon decides this may actually give them some cover.

Jeremy looks back and is urged to keep going. He leads the group into a knot of sightseers.

Suddenly a painful howl echoes in the great hall. Near the group, a woman falls to the floor. The mass of visitors predictably reacts with mild panic and confusion. People begin elbowing and bumping each other.

"I was tripped!" a woman shouts.

Bertram instinctively turns to his left, rubbernecking to see the complaining woman and unwisely exposing his back to the mob. Gideon is jostled aside just enough to lose control of the situation, but he can hear a loud grunt. Between bodies he sees Bertram leaning forward, grimacing, then falling to his knees and gasping for breath.

Gideon knows the man has been stabbed.

This is a disaster. Gideon glances around for the assassin, standing on his tip-toes to see over crowd. He spots a woman in a gray blouse and black slacks who is oddly walking away just as everyone else seems magnetically drawn to the commotion.

First task, check Bertram. Gideon feels the man's back, finds a hole in the tweed jacket where a well-placed sica had penetrated the fabric. He pulls away bloody fingers.

Bertram crumples to the floor.

Gideon rolls him over. Sees death in the man's eyes. Motions for Jeremy to pull the others away and follow him.

He marches out the exit, hoping to spot the woman in the gray blouse.

She has vanished.

But then, in a flash, she reappears from behind a column.

Faces him with a silenced Glock.

Fires! Three times rapidly. A tight cluster in the chest.

So quiet. No one seems to notice.

The rounds slam Gideon backwards. Tear holes in his shirt.

Jeremy appears and the woman flees. He leans over Gideon. Lowers his head. Checks, listens. Looks up in shock.

The others standing there stunned. Horrified.

So much has happened.

So fast!

The woman is gone. Jeremy motions the others to follow him, but Charlotte is stuck in place. Can't move. Just stands there. Staring. Choking back tears.

Her Guardian Angel.

Jeremy shouts. "Charlotte, he's gone!"

A security guard rushes over.

Police sirens wail.

Jeremy pulls Charlotte away. Stumbling, looking back.

Disbelieving.

Who knew that Guardian Angels needed back-ups?

Chapter 37

Caleb didn't have time for the classic hit—two taps to the chest, one to the head. Instead she put three rounds into his heart. All the shots were true, though the third was just a bit high—probably because Gideon was falling backwards at that point.

No man could live with three jacketed soft point 9mm rounds mushrooming through his heart.

All in all, a good day's work. A twofer. How fitting that both Bertram and Gideon had become history at the museum. As it turns out, Gideon was a disappointing adversary. So often Caleb's targets, no matter how experienced, have underestimated a woman.

Caleb dials a phone number and it starts ringing.

At fifty, Caleb is still a knockout. Hard training, even during her extensive "off" times, has helped her maintain a stunning figure. She can take on a man twice her size and twist him into a pretzel. Spin and fire her Glock at a target twenty paces away—and hit bull's-eyes. Her 34-inch vertical jump could outperform most NBA players, and she has walked a high wire for a hundred meters without a pole—not by choice, of course. But these physical attributes are not what makes Caleb, in the view of the Sicarii, the best assassin in the business. She has an agile mind that possesses both high creativity and superb analytical powers. She also has the temperament of a Zen Master. Her pulse barely ticks upwards even when she is threatened. Her dangerous work produces no adrenalin rush. In fact, these days she views each assignment as spiritual development. She is doing God's work, and each completed mission brings her closer to perfection, and the world that much closer to its destiny.

Caleb had never expected to be performing such important duties at her ripe old age. How does she keep doing it? Constant training. A zealous belief in the mission of her Order. And a strict vegetarian diet, which she believes will prolong her life—which is ironic in her case, because she literally does not care if she dies performing her job. She'd rather live, of course. She is no suicide bomber. But she has no fear of pain or death.

Caleb is not her name. It is an accident of phonetics. Her birth name, chosen by her parents, was Katherine Loeb. For reasons since forgotten, most people called her K. Loeb. When she was recruited by the Sicarii, Eve was amused at how her name sounded like *Caleb*, the warrior whom Moses had sent to spy on the land of Canaan. And so K. Loeb, the female assassin extraordinaire, was given a man's name, and she has always worn it with pride.

Her outgoing phone call is picked up. A voice on the other end says, "Yes?"

"This is Caleb. Bertram Doering is dead. Gideon as well. The others will be soon."

There is silence on the line. Finally, Cain says, "And the girl?"

"She will not be harmed."

Caleb reflects on her decision to detonate the bomb on the corporate jet with Rebecca on board. This conversation with Cain would be much different if Gideon had not found the explosive in time. In that case, Caleb might have been the next one to be the subject of an irrevocable termination order.

But who would be sent to accomplish such a task?

With Gideon out of the way, the assassin who will move up in rank is a capable ex-intelligence officer recruited out of the U.K. He is highly skilled with broad scientific and technical knowledge—a plus for today's world—but is not in the same class as Gideon or Caleb. As for Jeremy, now the bodyguard for Charlotte's little troupe of amateurs… thinking about the remaining targets makes her laugh. Jeremy, the screw-up junior Sicarii. A woman journalist. A rich geek. And an octogenarian. Not exactly your A-Team.

"Caleb," Cain says, "get the girl and you've accomplished enough."

"The order is irrevocable. At the very least, Charlotte and Thompson are still on my list."

"I repeat—not necessary," Cain affirms.

Caleb can hear a quiver of indecision in Cain's voice. This is not the authoritative tone she is used to. Clearly something has changed. This is why irrevocable orders are *irrevocable*.

"Sorry," Caleb replies. "If I terminate the directive, it would be treason."

There is nowhere positive that this conversation can go. With a flick of a finger she terminates the call. Nothing like hanging up on your boss to enhance your career prospects. Oh, that's right—she doesn't care about career anymore. Her next move is not up, but out.

Her decision. Made just now.

Retirement after this mission.

Killing one of her own has left Caleb with a sour aftertaste and unsettling questions. Why, for example, had Gideon turned from the most trusted, loyal exemplar of his class to a traitor racing toward perdition? Love perhaps. Could be that woman, Charlotte. A woman is often the downfall of a man. But Caleb cannot imagine Gideon the stalwart, the true believer, throwing everything away for a woman. There must have been something else, something that caused him to lose his faith.

Something is gnawing at her.

Not full-fledged doubt, really—more like a tiny splinter of it.

Sometimes a woman, even one as independent as Caleb, just needs to talk to another woman. Caleb calls Eve, listens to the phone ringing. Eve has always been straight with her. This is a way to triangulate the messages she has been getting.

A masculine voice answers.

"Cain?" Caleb says, startled.

"Caleb? We must have been disconnected."

"Right—sorry," she lies. "But why are you answering Eve's number?"

Caleb can hear a long intake of breath on the other end.

After a long pause, Cain bluntly says, "Eve is dead."

"Impossible! Your grandmother's too stubborn to die."

"She's gone, Caleb."

Now it's Caleb's turn to take a deep breath. "How? An accident?"

"No. It's a long story. Not on the phone."

"Was she dead before you gave me the order?"

"After."

"My God—in the field?"

"No, here."

Caleb recalls that Cain had ordered the assassination of his own mother and grandfather. Tentatively she asks, "By *your* order?"

Again there is a long pause, then Cain softly says, "No. But by her choice."

"I have to go now," Caleb says, quickly disconnecting before her throat swells and her eyes clench. This flood of emotion is unfamiliar to her. "It's certainly unbecoming to a cold-blooded assassin. She thinks it must be grief, but it's been a long time since she's felt that so she can't be sure.

Eve had been like an older sister, a true confidante, a mentor—not in the craft of assassination, but in the profound spiritual purpose of their mission. A mother, almost.

This news puts a lock on Caleb's decision. After this mission, which she will complete with all haste, she is leaving the Order. Permanent retirement. Eve had given her the okay to choose her time—a special privilege from a beloved friend. Maybe she'll open a bed and breakfast in the Hamptons, or a restaurant in the Caribbean. Make friends. Be a real person.

She's done enough to bring about the will of God. Now, just one more job.

Chapter 38

Alone, Cain sits in the Inner Chamber chair that had been occupied by Michael during that fateful Council meeting just two days ago. In the past year he has found more than solace in this room. He has found a source of power and focus, as if the crystals that guard the Chamber entrance and decorate the wall behind the raised dais lend some kind of force to his mental energy.

Now, though, he needs more than his preternatural Asperger's gift, that rare ability to block out everything else and weave the strings of unraveled reality back into its normal state so it can be understood. Unfortunately the gift has vanished, and in its absence frustration seizes him like a fist. More than his bloodline, it had been his startling ability to perceive the imperceptible and make sense of the senseless that earned him the position of Divine Light at the tender age of thirteen. And yet now, while facing his greatest test, two great puzzles defy him.

The first is the Lost Secret of the Sicarii, the fundamental mystery at the heart of the Order. The prophecies cannot be fulfilled unless the Secret is uncovered, and there is little time left. According to tradition the Secret was known to the first Eve, handed down to her by an elder of an ancient line of Enochian guardians whose sole purpose had been to make sure it was not lost or shared with adversaries.

To ensure this purpose, only four individuals in any generation would have the privilege of knowing the Secret: the current Eve, the Divine Light, the Michael, and the guardian. Such restrictions had practically guaranteed that the Secret eventually would be lost, and indeed, sometime in the Fourth Century CE, a perfect storm of untimely deaths had wiped out almost all knowledge of the Secret. A few fragments had survived, though. Cain knows that the Secret is a place—the location to which the patriarch Enoch had been taken by the Watchers to be shown the great plan of the universe. The Book of Enoch, known to many of the Old Testament prophets and quoted by Jesus himself in the New Testament, described this journey and this secret place. It is at this place that the prophecies must be fulfilled at a time calculated to be the winter solstice of 2012. It is the great purpose of the Sicarii to find this place and set into motion the events foretold in the writings.

This is Cain's assignment.

Not only is he the one expected to solve the greatest riddle of all time. He is also the pivotal figure of the prophecies, the protagonist who must step onto the vast stage of history and usher in a new era.

But it all hinges on uncovering the Lost Secret.

A second puzzle muddles the first. Identifying the place is meaningless without knowledge of what must be done there to fulfill the prophecies. Cain suspects that Michael knows this secret. He believes that Michael's orders of protection for the girl named Rebecca reveal that somehow she is the key.

Rebecca, like Cain, moves easily on and off the *grid*, a fifth-dimensional morphogenetic matrix that powers a psychic link-up. Aware of this phenomenon, many New Agers had invented a ludicrous explanation involving new generations of Indigo and Violet children—gifted souls with advanced psychic and healing abilities—whose goal is to serve as guides for a world going through a paradigm shift. Cain knows the truth, however; that such gifted souls are not a new generation but have been around for millennia, Enoch being one of the first. And that the earth itself, as a creation of God, has provided the grid—though its matrix has shifted over time and its power has diminished.

For a year now, Cain has been communicating on this grid with Rebecca, hoping that she will share something that will help him solve the second puzzle. He likes this girl, considers her a friend. Perhaps his only friend, now that Eve is gone.

During the year that Cain and Rebecca have been communicating, Cain has noticed that their psychic link-up is stronger when he is in the Inner Chamber, as if the room serves as an antenna. Probably the crystals, he surmises. In the early days of radio, primitive "crystal sets" combined the rectifying property of crystals with a thin "cat's whisker" wire that was used as a point-contact diode to detect radio signals. The sets needed no external power source, running exclusively on power received from radio waves by a long antenna. Cain had discovered an old crystal set in the attic of his mother's Minnesota home. The box had been labelled "Thompson." Cain had never understood why his mother had kept any of her despised father's things, but after some fiddling and some Internet research, he had actually gotten the thing to work.

Cain imagines that focusing his mind is like tuning in that old crystal set to receive signals from a radio station. He focuses on Rebecca's name, feels layers of his mind peel away, rocks slightly in his chair as space seems to distort around him. Thoughts—no, *voices*—no, *thoughts*—begin to fly past him. A great, noisy rush. He resists the temptation to reach out with his mind and seize them, to eavesdrop on the fears and passions of others on the grid.

The cat's whisker of his mind keeps tuning past the interference of unwanted signals, searching for Rebecca's.

This time the signals are not just sounds, but visuals as well. The Inner Chamber seems to tilt and go out of focus. Watery images quiver and dance—the indistinct shapes of people.

He struggles to bring them into focus. He reaches out, but there is no one there. Searches past the fleeting ghosts. Feels himself falling. Grabs the chair. Looks up to steady himself. And then Rebecca is there.

I'm afraid for you, he says.

Me too, she says.

Let me help you.

You can't—it's too late.

I have the power to save you.

You have no power alone, she says.

Rebecca—the shimmering image of her—violently spasms. Her voice crackles and fades. A cacophony of voices deafens him. He has lost her.

Then she is back.

Who do I need, then?

You need me, she answers.

This is what he has been looking for. She is not just the key. She is the solution itself. In his Asperger's mind, in a white-hot flash of insight, everything suddenly skids into place. The two of them. Fulfilling each other.

Yes, I need you.

I don't know if I can, she says.

I can help you—tell me how.

It's up to me now, she says.

Confusion. Sadness. Not only her thoughts are bombarding him now, but her emotions. Anger and shame.

You don't know, do you? she asks.

There are many things I don't know.

You speak like an angel, but you're not, she says.

No I'm not.

Then stop telling me your powers, she says.

All right, he says. *Maybe you are the angel. Maybe you can save all of us.*

Maybe, she says. Except your mother.

Another visual spasm.

A fierce rattling of sounds.

She is gone.

Chapter 39

Some violent force jars her shoulders and shakes her head. The flickering image of Cain vibrates erratically. Then is gone.

Rebecca looks up at Thompson's red face. His strong hands are still grasping her shoulders as she sits on a lumpy sofa in Gideon's safe house. It's unusual for her to enter the grid so completely, to lose contact with her surroundings.

"Where were you?" Thompson asks.

"What?" She is disoriented.

"Just now. With Greg?"

She nods. "Sorry—he needs me."

"Whatever that means, I hope you said no."

She isn't sure what it means.

"So this matrix stuff..." Thompson says.

"You mean the grid...?"

"It's for real?"

"Or else I'm completely psycho."

Looking around, trying to bring her mind back to London, Rebecca notices Jeremy tearing through her backpack. She leaps to her feet and yells. "Hey, what are you doing?"

"Nothing here," Jeremy says, exasperated. "There's got to be something somewhere."

Thompson turns to Rebecca, explaining. "Jeremy thinks that one of us is transporting a beacon that Caleb tracked to find out where we were."

"One last place." Jeremy approaches Rebecca and pats her down, checking every inch of her garments.

She thinks he's enjoying this too much. "You go to TSA School or what?"

Finally he reaches into her jeans pockets and pulls out a handful of coins. "When did you have time to get a British fifty pence coin?" he asks.

She frowns, confused.

Jeremy fiddles with the coin, first staring at it, then holding it edgewise with the fingers of both hands and turning in opposite directions. Several twists unscrew the top face from the bottom, revealing a miniaturized tracking device packed inside.

"Clever," Jeremy says. "Caleb obviously stuffed this into your pocket while escorting you away from the corporate jet. Must have figured that even if you exchanged some currency when you got to London, there'd be no point in trading in a British coin."

Rebecca angrily grabs the coin and flings it onto the floor, preparing to stomp the shit out of it.

Jeremy shoves her backwards. "No!" he shouts. "That little device can be our own double agent."

"Yeah, but we've still got to figure out how to get out of here," Mason says. "Sure bet Caleb's watching."

Conversation stops as they all consider the dilemma.

Thompson spots his daughter slumped in a chair across the room and walks over to her. "Sorry about Gideon. Real tough, losing someone you care about."

Charlotte looks up sadly, sensing sincerity. She barely has the energy to acknowledge his remark. "And I'm sorry about mom," she whispers, her throat tight with grief.

Thompson sighs. "Now that we've both lost someone we loved... how about we kick some butt to honor them?"

This brings a smile to Charlotte, about all she can muster. For Thompson, a smile from his daughter seems to be enough.

"Jeremy," Mason says, "get us away from here. I've got a safe place to go."

"Already working on it," Jeremy exclaims, desperately seeking Rebecca's attention. "Caleb will expect us to leave together. She knows that a Sicarii would not want any of his protectees out of his sight. So we're gonna split up and then rendezvous later at some designated spot. At the very least this will confuse Caleb. You know, which one of us to follow. I think she'll follow *me*, to eliminate the last skilled party. Not that you guys don't have skills, just that as a Sicarii..."

"We get it," Mason says.

Charlotte stands. To Rebecca, it looks like Char has decided to take charge. "Splitting up is good. But I'm absolutely certain Caleb will follow *me*. Not that you guys aren't important... just that I'm the one she's after."

Mason's hands indicate a disagreement. "What if she follows you until we all meet up?"

"Actually, I'm counting on that," Charlotte replies. "I'm just hoping that Caleb's not in sniper mode. Would hate to get nailed stepping out the front door."

"From what I can tell," Thompson offers, "this Caleb character is a bit of a show-off. Speaking as a male version, I think she'll want more than just Charlotte. She'll want the whole group, so she'll follow Char, not pick her off outside the flat. But it's high stakes poker."

Rebecca stares at Charlotte. "How do you not lead them to the rest of us?" Immediately she feels selfish.

"One way is we don't meet up later," Char answers. "You guys just split off and go live your lives. Period."

Rebecca starts to ask the less selfish question. "And how do you—?"

"Save myself? Doesn't matter really. Maybe I do, maybe not. In this scenario, the less you know, the better."

"Well, then I'd like to make one little suggestion," Thompson says, "to make this plan agreeable to the rest of us."

Chapter 40

Caleb is used to long vigils. Her life is comprised of long stretches of tedium punctuated by short bursts of sheer terror and exhilaration. She is also used to long hours and has devised ways to stay awake. Only a few of them involve chemicals.

The beacon is still sending out its location, which means the odds are 60/40 that her prey has not yet discovered it. Good news. Caleb expects her prey to depart during daylight using heavy traffic as an obstacle to tailing. For this reason, within five seconds of her reach is a Honda Silverwing scooter ready to follow Charlotte anywhere she could go. The smooth ride makes shooting from the saddle, if necessary, a real pleasure. Caleb will be disappointed if she doesn't have the chance to try it.

If Charlotte and the others leave separately, or split up, Caleb is committed to Charlotte. Amateurs usually plan to regroup at a later time. The nosy correspondent will lead Caleb to the others. If not, Charlotte will simply be assassinated and Caleb will hunt down and safely retrieve Rebecca. The others? Well, if it's convenient, they'll be killed with Charlotte. And if not, they'll be killed later. Caleb is patient.

It has now been five hours since Gideon was eliminated. Traffic outside the flat has peaked. As expected, Charlotte and her companions are planning to depart separately. Caleb knows this because one of London's classic black taxis pulls up in front of the safe house. It is followed by another. Within two minutes, five black taxis have pulled out of the flow of traffic to park outside the flat.

The game is on.

In obvious disguises, all five of Caleb's targets charge out of the front door at once. Charlotte is easy to spot in a cheap blonde wig and Nike running suit. She enters the first taxi. Rebecca wears a drab scarf and oversized sunglasses—not much camouflage. The men have barely attempted to disguise themselves. With one occupant each, the cabs take off, turning in different directions at the first intersection.

On her Silverwing, Caleb confidently follows taxi number one. The vehicle takes a purposely circuitous route, ending up at Piccadilly Circus, a busy square in London's West End. As the taxi slows to a crawl, Charlotte leaps from the back seat, scattering pigeons as she marches across the square.

Caleb maneuvers her Silverwing out of traffic, abandoning it to thieves.

Charlotte stops at the corner of Piccadilly Circus and The Haymarket. Caleb is confused. She had been sure that Charlotte would weave her way into Soho, Chinatown, or some other nearby destination, making it harder for a tail to stick with her. But instead, Charlotte sits down on a stone ring encircling the four bronze horses of Helios, the centerpiece of a magnificent fountain.

Caleb lifts a pocket camera. Through its zoom lens she watches Charlotte smile at passersby, glance left and right, then reach both hands up to her head. Caleb watches her target remove a blonde wig and shake her head, revealing short-cropped brown hair. Reaching into a zipped-up jacket, the target removes two pads—*falsies,* they used to call them—casually dropping them into the gurgling water of the fountain.

Caleb curses. Such a simple trick!

The female impersonator begins walking away with a naturally masculine gait. There is no point in following this stooge, so Caleb stuffs the camera back into her pocket and pulls out a smartphone. The screen cheerfully displays the location of Rebecca's beacon. Studying the display to determine the tracking beacon's route, she watches the flashing symbol move in a most unappealing direction…

Her heart sinks.

The beacon stops at Piccadilly Circus.

Return to sender.

Someone has just dropped it off practically at her feet.

She has to laugh. This was an unexpectedly clever trick, but just a minor inconvenience. Her pride is hurt more than her mission, because there is only one logical place for her targets to go. And Caleb will be right behind.

Chapter 41

As planned, Jeremy is the first to disembark the Stena Adventurer in Dublin at 5:48 a.m. Coincidence had placed Thompson on the same three-hour ferry ride from Holyhead, though neither of them had acknowledged the other. After exiting, Thompson had walked a half-mile to Molly's, an independent coffee establishment. Jeremy had strolled to a Starbuck's across the street where he could maintain eye contact with Thompson through the front window.

Stuffed with local pastries and caffeinated to the hilt, Jeremy leaves his high-table perch at 11:10 and makes his way back to the ferry landing to watch the 11:35 arrival of the superferry Stena Nordica. Thompson follows a good forty paces behind. As planned, Charlotte, Rebecca and Mason are all on the Nordica, disembarking separately.

Jeremy watches Mason raise a cell phone to his ear, speak briefly, then put the phone back into his pocket. Two minutes later a tan Toyota van maneuvers through a clutch of arriving passenger rides and pulls up near Mason, who climbs in. Charlotte and Rebecca each find the van.

Jeremy verifies there is no tail. With a sigh, he walks over to a silver Ford Focus and enters through the left rear door. He points straight ahead at Thompson, who is now slowly walking back toward Molly's. The Focus pulls alongside and Thompson gets into the front seat. All accounted for.

Sean, the boyish-looking driver, extends a surprisingly meaty hand and Thompson is surprised at his exuberant handshake. "God be with you," Sean says, looking into the rearview mirror to include Jeremy in the back seat.

"Dia dhuit," Thompson replies in perfect Gaelic. It comes out sounding like *Jee-uh Gwitch* and means *God to you*.

"You speak Gaelic, then?"

"Lived in a monastery near Cork for eighteen months," Thompson explains. "Glad to see the language being resurrected in the Universities."

"Name's Sean."

"I'm Thompson, and in the rear is Jeremy."

Thompson turns stiffly to catch Jeremy out of the corner of his eye. "I'm glad to be able to finally break our vow of silence."

Jeremy nods. "I won't ask how you knew a drag queen in London."

"An *entertainer*, son. And no less a spiritual seeker than most others. As he proves, you can't judge a book by its cover."

"You weren't concerned about his safety?"

"One thing I learned by being married to…" he glances at Sean, reconsiders his comment—"to *you-know-who* was that any public act of violence carries a risk, so you don't do it needlessly. Caleb had nothing to gain by harming Jack. Enough now. I suggest we both rest."

The Focus skirts the northern edge of Dublin then heads north through the bucolic green spaces of Irish countryside. To the slumbering passengers it seems like only minutes before they approach a single story building near Gardners Hill on the fringe of Balbriggan, a beautiful village on the Irish Sea. The building is unique for its total lack of windows, a single featureless door, and complete absence of signage.

As the vehicle approaches, garage doors open on the building's south end. The Focus pulls in alongside the van. As Thompson and Jeremy extract their stiff bodies from the automobile, their fellow exiles race over and greet them with warm embraces. Somehow they have all survived the departure from London.

"Have you heard anything from Jack?" Charlotte shoots a look of concern at her father.

"I called him and he's fine. Caleb never said boo."

Rebecca slyly glances at Charlotte. "Man, he had your movements nailed within ten minutes. Looked more like a woman than either of us!"

Everyone laughs. Their reunion has broken the tension and suddenly they all talk at once until Jeremy takes a look at their surroundings. "So we came all the way to Dublin to visit a garage?" he asks.

"Let me introduce you to the headquarters of Ambienz Research & Development." Mason says.

His guests look around, unimpressed.

Mason smiles and states the obvious. "This is the garage, of course. Now if you'll follow me."

Mason leads the others through a door into a cubicle forest that easily could be the administrative department of an insurance agency. "Oh, we also house our HR and financial teams here as well," he explains. "R&D is downstairs."

They board an elevator and Mason presses the "B" button, holding it in for a few seconds. "Damn technology," he complains. "If you need to use the elevator, you need to hold the button in for five seconds. We can make the fastest computer in the world, but we can't fix elevator buttons."

The slow elevator drops to the *Basement* level. The doors open to reveal a stunning panorama of white-coated technicians, enormous plasma screens, and glass-enclosed meeting rooms. Warm directional light from glowing wall panels sculpts everything, almost like a Rembrandt painting.

"With so many team members spending so many hours underground, we've spent a lot of time creating a comfortable but stimulating work environment. Lighting, acoustics, visual enhancements—it's all to keep us happy, sane, and productive."

Despite the scores of people working here and the countless workstations in the enormous shared space, there is almost no background noise. A waterfall at one end of the room proves to be a large-screen visualization.

"You like it?" Mason asks Jeremy, who is studying the screen up close.

"Unbelievable realism," the young man replies.

"Our own breakthrough technology. If you're going to have the most advanced computers in the world, you should also have the most advanced display technology. You're looking at quantum dot display. Light-emitting quantum dots—actually cadmium selenide nanocrystals—are suspended in an organic material and then poured over a substrate. That allows quantum dots to be deposited over huge areas, even flexible bases, for supersized displays in many different shapes."

Jeremy is awestruck. "Imagine playing the new Halo on this sucker," he says.

"Done it. It's incredible!" Mason says.

Jeremy turns to his host prepared to worshipfully drop to his knees.

"But I digress," Mason says. "Let me show you the true wonderland of R&D."

Mason leads them across the underground "Ambienz Town Square" and into an unadorned room in which a round cherrywood table supports a computer, large monitor and keyboard.

"My friends, welcome to the Round Table," Mason says.

"As in King Arthur?" Jeremy is intrigued by his unpredictable host.

"Exactly. The Knights of the Round Table were men of courage, honor, dignity, courtesy, and nobleness. It was in their character and creed to protect ladies and damsels, to honor and fight for just kings, and undertake dangerous and sometimes impossible quests. When I started Ambienz, I wanted my key employees to embody these same ideals. You notice there are thirteen chairs—for the thirteen Knights. I have only seven—the men and women who helped me to the breakthroughs we are now achieving. Only my Knights are allowed in this room."

Mason gestures for his guests to take seats at the table, which they do. For a moment they look at each other, wondering where this is going.

Rebecca is the first to ask the question on everyone's mind. "Should we be seated at the Round Table? Isn't it reserved for, you know, Knights?"

"It is at that," Mason replies, and then falls silent, looking at each of them in turn.

"Hey, wait a minute," Jeremy blurts out. "Are you saying that we… the five of us…"

"…are now Knights?" Mason finishes Jeremy's thought. "Well, for that to happen, you would have to be asked. Which I am now doing. And you would have to accept, which I hope you will. And you would have to pledge that you will keep the charge King Arthur gave his noble Knights."

"Which was…?" After the terror of the past day, Rebecca is seduced by Mason's fanciful but gentle manner.

"May I quote just the most salient part?" Mason responds. "*Thou must keep thy word to all, and not be feeble of good believeth and faith. Right must be defended against might and distress must be protected. Thou must know good from evil and the vain glory of the world, because great pride and bobauce maketh great sorrow. Should anyone require ye of any quest so that it is not to thy shame, thou shouldst fulfil the desire.*"

Jeremy nods, indicating that he likes the sentiment, but then frowns. "So this word, bobauce—*pride and bobauce maketh great sorrow*. It means what, exactly?"

Mason shrugs. "We don't know what King Arthur meant by that. I think it refers to that part of each of us that we battle the hardest. It's different for everyone."

"Wow!" Jeremy says. "I know Google's motto is *Do No Evil*. You've one-upped those dudes big-time."

Rebecca and Thompson laugh. Charlotte glumly stares at the tabletop.

"Charlotte," Mason says, "you think I'm nuts."

"I think the word is *eccentric*."

Mason startles them all with a loud "Hah!" and a flashing grin.

"Yes, I suppose I am eccentric. But what great fun it is, this Round Table thing. Anyway, since we're already in the middle of a great quest, it seemed appropriate to formalize our relationship. To be honest, I wish more people these days honored those old principles."

"You do know that we're not facing dragons here, right? Our enemies are very real."

"And so are virtues, my dear."

Thompson slaps the table with his flat palms and rises solemnly. "Well I for one, sir, accept your invitation and agree to your charge, if you would have me."

"Yes, my friend, I certainly will," Mason smiles fondly at the old man.

"Me, too," Jeremy says.

As the young man rises, Rebecca stands with him, nodding her assent.

"And likewise the both of you," Mason agrees. "Welcome to the Round Table. We are now eleven of us. And there are no others I would rather quest with."

There is an awkward silence as Charlotte continues to stare at the table, unresponsive. Five seconds go by, then ten. And then as Mason is opening his mouth to say something, Charlotte stands up.

"I've been thinking—it's not fair that the Sicarii have the power of legend on their side," she says. "We deserve it, too. And since you're accepting women into the Knighthood these days, I would be proud to be a member of the Round Table."

They all know it's corny, but they cheer anyway.

Chapter 42

William Sinclair, aka Michael, taps his fingers on the leather armrest inside the Mercedes limousine. Despite his wealth and power, he is nervous. There are so many moving pieces in this unfolding drama, and only one satisfactory outcome. It is all up to him, the namesake of the archangel, the one on whom the entire family is counting on to preserve the mission. Nearly fifteen hundred years of searching for the Lost Secret, and it all comes down to the final seconds.

To Michael.

He has put the chess pieces into play: an eighteen-year-old autistic youth with diminished powers and considerable self-doubt to solve the puzzle; an arrogant female assassin to capture the opponent's pieces before they gain an advantage; an army of mercenaries as a last resort.

Only Michael, of course, knows the *what* and *how* of the Secret. He came by that knowledge the same way all the Michaels since the fourth century had come by it—in a document personally handwritten and signed by Judas of Galilee, the greatest guardian of the Secret and patriarch of the Sicarii. But this knowledge is useless without the *where*—the *place* at which it must be done. The location where the secrets of the universe had been revealed to Enoch.

Sometimes he fears that he is chasing a myth.

Did Enoch actually live? Was he a real person, or merely a legend? Is Michael's lifelong devotion truly in the service of God's great plan, or a misguided effort by a group of superstitious fools?

He curses himself for his fleeting doubts. Now is the time for him to be steadfast. He must vanquish the enemies that pose a great danger to the plan, prepare for its success, and pray that Cain has a breakthrough moment, for the Divine Light may be the only one capable of...

His cell phone chirps, startling him.

"Yes," he says, holding the phone a few inches from his ear.

"They eluded Caleb in London," Cain says.

Michael's face turns red. "I thought she was the best!"

"She's up against my mother and grandfather."

"What now?"

"Caleb's on a ferry to Dublin."

"Of course she is. Ambienz has a facility there. They'll use it as a safe house. They also have technology that could be used to analyze your mother's research, if she still has it. In fact, with enough computing power they could…"

"Caleb says she has it under control."

"She'd better. Keep me posted."

Michael ends the call. He's more pleased than ever that he has a reliable informant inside Charlotte's group.

His thumb taps a number on his Favorites list.

"Wyatt? Sinclair here. I have a need for your services."

Chapter 43

The newly minted Knights and their King are seated at the Round Table with an additional incumbent Knight, a resident of the facility. At thirty-four, Darcy is Ambienz' Chief Operations Officer.

The remains of a proper Irish lunch are spread out on the table—Irish stew and boxty, the latter a traditional potato pancake accompanied by squash and sauce.

Looking squarely at Rebecca, who has not touched her boxty, Darcy chants a traditional folk rhyme:

> "Boxty on the griddle,
> Boxty on the pan,
> If you don't eat Boxty,
> You'll never get a man."

Rebecca blushes and suspiciously pokes her boxty with a fork while Mason sniggers.

"Feels good to laugh," he says.

In a lilting Irish accent, Darcy says to the group, "For sure, we've all been drawn into your drama. Ah, it's a darlin' story you've spun, but I fear you've brought danger to all of us now."

"I've already put security on alert," Mason replies. "We're buttoned down, just as you planned we should be, Darcy, even though we never thought such a day would actually come."

"This is Ireland, boss. Y'never know when a catholic and protestant will start a brawl."

Thompson pipes in: "Well, in a sense, our present situation may also be a bit of a religious conflict going back thousands of years. But if I may remind this august group, we don't have a plan right now for moving forward. We don't even have a next step. So maybe, with respect to Darcy's concern—which we all share, by the way—we should at least determine what to do next."

"May I begin by summarizing the few things we know for sure?" Charlotte defers to Mason, her host.

"Please do."

"We know that the Sicarii found out that I was investigating them. That seems to be when they put a bounty on my head."

"So we should investigate your investigation," Thompson says, leaning forward. "Sounds like you may have come too close for comfort to something that threatens them. If we can figure out what that is…"

"What happened to your research?" Mason asks Charlotte.

"Well, Gideon destroyed the physical evidence and all the computer files in my home office." The thought of Gideon tightens her throat. She coughs politely, buying a moment. "Fortunately, he uploaded the digital files to the cloud."

Mason's eyes brighten. "Do you have access?"

"As we were fleeing he gave me the URL and password."

"Then we can retrieve it," Jeremy says. He slides over to the omnipresent desktop computer that has been sitting patiently on the table.

"Yes," Charlotte replies, "if I could remember it." Her cheeks suddenly blossom red with exasperation and a hand flies up to cover her mouth.

"Yes, well… when you're not under pressure it will come to you, I'm quite certain," Darcy says.

"Keep going," Mason encourages.

A deep breath and a shake of her head helps Charlotte go on. "So my research is one thing. Maybe some clues there. Another thing we know is that this Michael character is rich and powerful, and probably high up in the Sicarii Order, and trying to buy into Mason's company."

Prompted by this line of reasoning, Jeremy says, "He might be even higher than that. In my training, we learned that the Sicarii report to a Council that has supreme power. In other words, they practically speak for God." Jeremy's face pales.

"What is it, Jeremy?" Thompson asks.

"I was just thinking—what if they're actually on the good side, and we're…" He pauses.

"And we're on the dark side?" Mason adds.

Jeremy nods.

"A reasonable question," Mason continues. "I think the answer is another question. Who is callously doing the killing here?"

"Besides," Charlotte interjects, her composure regained, "we're Knights, pure and honest, virtuous and true. We defend right against might, and know good from evil. Do we not, Jeremy?"

Jeremy nods again. "Yes we do. Sorry."

Charlotte suddenly jerks. "The URL I was trying to remember. It's gidsic.com—short for Gideon Sicarii. Gideon set it up, just in case he needed it someday, I guess."

Jeremy types it into a browser and gets an unadorned login page. "It wants a username and password."

"Username 2940hampslpmn," she says.

Jeremy looks up at her, wondering how she could remember that.

"It cobbles together parts of my old address in Minnesota. Gideon knew more about me than I realized, and obviously chose something I would remember. The password is…"

She rises and walks over to the keyboard, pushing Jeremy out of the way. Her fingers tap in a sequence of fifteen keys.

"It's my name," she explains, "coded by using the keyboard as a cipher generator. I type in each letter of my name, but use the key immediately above and to the left of each key. Gideon knew my mother used to communicate with Greg and me using this code."

The computer speakers cheerfully greet her successful login with the theme from the Pink Panther.

My God, how she misses Gideon. But thinking of him gives her strength—perhaps some of *his* strength. "What else do we know?" she asks, pushing forward to keep the sadness away.

"We know it's the year 2012," Jeremy offers.

Which elicits blank looks all around.

"I think we all know what year we're in," Mason says, rolling his eyes. "Thank you Jeremy."

"No, listen to me. For the Sicarii, this is the year that the prophecies will be fulfilled."

"What prophecies?" Thompson asks.

"I don't know exactly. I was just a grunt in the Order, remember? We weren't told a whole lot about it. Except that something will take place this year. Just don't ask me what."

"All right," Charlotte says. "You don't know what. Do you know where?"

"Not exactly," Jeremy says.

"Not exactly," Charlotte repeats smugly. She knew he wouldn't know.

"Not exactly," Mason echoes with disappointment.

Jeremy continues. "But I can tell you that the place is the location where Enoch was taken thousands of years ago and shown the secrets of the universe. It's just that no one today knows where that is."

Mason starts to laugh. "Is it possible this whole thing is about an important event that has to occur this year at a specific place, but they don't know where?"

Jeremy doesn't get the joke. "Now that you put it that way," he says, "as a former Sicarii, that's exactly what I think."

Thompson stands up as if stirred by a great wind. "The Lost Secret," he says. "Of course!"

Before he can launch into an oration of his current thinking, a cell phone buzzes. Everyone turns to Jeremy, who at first doesn't know the sound is coming from his pocket.

For a moment, a chill sweeps through the room. Everyone who knows Jeremy's cell phone number is in the room.

It's a single buzz followed by silence.

"A text message," Jeremy says. He reaches into his pocket and pulls out a scuffed cell phone and fiddles with it.

"Hey, isn't that Gideon's phone?" Charlotte asks. She remembers that Gideon's phone was the only dark gray phone in the batch that Hightower had sold them.

"Yeah, well… the battery of mine went dead," Jeremy explains.

"How did you get it?" Rebecca asks.

Jeremy sighs. "From Gideon. I took it off his body after he was shot. Figured we wouldn't want anyone else having access to it."

"And you didn't tell anyone?" Thompson eyes Jeremy suspiciously.

"Look, we've all been kinda busy, you know? Sorry about that."

"So check for messages," Charlotte brusquely orders.

"Done," Jeremy replies. "Came in just now for Gideon. From Wonderboy. Says: *fu on app – work?* So he wants to follow-up. Did the eavesdropping phone app he created work okay."

With a sheepish grin, Jeremy looks up, knowing he just gave away a secret.

"What do you mean by *eavesdropping app*?" Mason asks. "Eavesdropping on who? Certainly not me, right?"

He is greeted by silence.

"Can't say I blame you," he says. "Anyway, who the hell is Wonderboy?"

"Founder of a hacking group called Sentient," Jeremy says. "Gideon used him for special technical assignments from time to time."

"Sentient?" Mason shakes his head. "You guys never cease to amaze me. Sentient is arguably the most sophisticated worldwide hacking group in the world. Do you have any idea what they've done? What they're capable of?"

"Of making a workable eavesdropping app, we know that," Charlotte says.

"Sentient has hundreds, maybe thousands of hackers grouped together," Mason explains, "able to infiltrate anything they target. Able to mobilize not just thousands of machines, but bodies, too, for mass protests. I've gotta say—like many other businesses these days, we live in fear of those guys. And hope they don't target us. No matter what kinds of firewalls we set up, even with quantum cryptography, they'd probably get through to our data."

"Not ours, I can promise you that," Darcy boasts.

"Well, in any case, Wonderboy's on our side," Jeremy suggests.

Mason stares darkly at Jeremy, making the young man squirm.

After a painful silence, Mason speaks. "Then let's give him another job."

The others look confused. *What is he talking about?*

"Look," Mason says. "We have to rapidly compile data and analyze it, right? There in front of you…" Mason points to the nondescript computer on the table "…is the world's fastest quantum computer. But my people design and build technology. They are not researchers, not database analysts. Much of the information we need—private stuff about William Sinclair and his scores of companies, information that Charlotte couldn't get access to, public stuff and top secret stuff—how can we get all of that so my computers can crunch the data and give us some answers?"

"You think Wonderboy…?" Charlotte sees where Mason is going.

"Supposedly he's the master of hacking. Probably has some other useful skills as well that none of us has. I have a lot of money to invest in the operation. Think he'd be interested?"

Jeremy begins tapping away on the cell phone. "I know he lives in England. So let's ask."

Suddenly Charlotte's phone buzzes, startling her. Anxiously she stares at the screen. "It's a text from Herb Rossi, our chopper pilot in New York. Says he's in London on assignment. Do we want to have dinner?"

As Charlotte stares at the message, an intercom voice blares. *Mason Madani, your pizzas have arrived. Please pick them up at the reception desk.*

Mason looks at the remains of lunch, then at each of his Knights. "Did someone order pizza?" he asks, confused.

A shot of adrenalin surges through Charlotte's body.

"No," she answers. "But I think Caleb just bought us lunch."

Chapter 44

Darcy quickly ushers everyone out of the Round Table room—which Darcy affectionately calls *Camelot*—then across the "Town Square" and into the security monitoring room. An impressive array of fifty-seven monitors stare back at them from two walls.

Darcy points at the display covering the front desk. "Let's look at history," she says, manipulating a joystick control and making the image jitter and dance. In seconds the image freezes, then starts playing at normal speed. "Okay, here is where the pizza delivery man—" she stares at a person entering the lobby, "—excuse me, delivery *woman* comes in."

"That's the U.S. Marshall," Rebecca says. "I'll bet the Marshall was Caleb!"

"Older than I would've thought," Darcy snidely remarks. "Domino's uniform isn't very flattering. We capture audio, too—let me switch on the speakers."

A loud click precedes playback of the conversation.

...for Mr. Madani, Caleb says.

And how much do we owe? The receptionist replies.

It's on a credit card.

Oh, then wait... The receptionist rummages around in a desk drawer for tip money. Caleb's eyes quickly survey the lobby and then stare directly into an overhead security camera. She smiles.

The receptionist produces some paper money and hands it to Caleb.

Thank you very much. Caleb graciously takes the money and leaves. Darcy lets the sequence play for a few more seconds, making sure that Caleb did not re-enter the lobby, then stops the playback.

"So it seems Caleb is not in the building," Mason says.

"What was this all about?" Rebecca asks.

Jeremy starts to pace. "She obviously wants us to know that she's found us," he suggests. "And I'd guess she was doing reconnaissance at the same time."

"Suddenly I feel like I'm in a castle under siege," Thompson adds. "How do we even leave this place with her out there?"

"She's just one woman," Darcy counters.

"Yeah, but she's a Sicarii," Jeremy says. "You have no idea."

Gideon's phone rings and Jeremy plucks it from his pocket, then reads the screen. "It's Wonderboy. He's considering our offer. Wants to talk."

"In person?" Charlotte asks.

"We have to go to a website and…"

Suddenly one of the monitors goes dark.

"What in God's sweet name…?" Darcy shouts as another monitor goes out.

Jeremy knows what is happening. "Caleb's shooting out the exterior cameras." He laughs nervously. "She's blinding us."

The image on another monitor flickers and dies.

"The bitch!" Darcy is angry now. "Top o' the line optics in those."

"She's lowering the odds against her," Jeremy explains.

"Will never happen," Darcy says. "She thinks I'm stupid. Well, I'm a bit obsessive about security."

She begins flicking switches and the dead monitors start to glow with images of the parking lot again. "The cameras mounted on the building were once just dummies, but hell, we had the budget, so I swapped 'em out for live ones. A full set of back-up cameras are hidden from view. Not as agile, mind you—can't swivel 180 degrees like my babies that she's killing out there—but perfectly serviceable."

"Who the hell are you?" Jeremy asks Darcy. His words drip with astonishment.

"Daughter of an IRA leader and niece of the former head of the Ulster Vigilante Brigade, if you must know."

"So you've been through the Troubles, then," Charlotte says, referring to the bitter struggle between Catholics, Protestants, and the English in Northern Ireland.

"*Troubles*, hah!" Darcy says. "That's what those who weren't there call it. For those of us who lived through it, it was terror and betrayal and ugliness all 'round. As a tot I learned how to make bombs and load guns and stitch wounds and defend home turf. So I have a load of practical experience."

From the driver's seat of an old Renault Fluence with a Domino's Pizza sign on top, Caleb aims her rifle at the last exposed camera surveilling the western parking lot. She fires once. The camera splinters, shards of glass and metal spraying the asphalt below. Caleb smiles with satisfaction.

Her brief foray into the enemy's lobby had told her all she needed to know. The open design of the main floor revealed fifteen, maybe eighteen cubicles and meeting rooms. There are at least 50-60 cars in the parking lots that ring the building. Obviously, most of the employees work below-ground, as there is no second floor.

As in the Long Island facility, security here is robust. But the open nature of the main floor indicates that nothing of real value exists there. It's probably more of a front for other more important assets. Caleb has no doubt that breaking into the main floor, even occupying it, would not be difficult. But she suspects the subterranean space is a bunker. This is not a job for an assassin.

Now that she's done her job, she can relax—for a while—and see if Mason calls the local gendarmes. She doubts that he will. Her job for the time being is to make sure that none of her targets leave alive. Her most difficult challenge will be the expected mass exodus of employees at quitting time. Fortunately, there is one main door and around the corner an emergency exit. Caleb can observe both doors from one vantage point. She is convinced that this time no disguise will fool her if any of her targets attempts to leave.

Her cellphone vibrates. "Domino's Pizza, may I help you?" she answers with smart-ass good cheer.

She expects the confused pause that follows. Finally a man's voice politely says, "Miss Caleb, please."

"Speaking."

"How is the weather in Dublin?"

"Fiji could not be more beautiful," Caleb says, repeating the coded response she was told to use with an unknown caller.

"Unfortunately, your friends will not be able to join you this evening as planned because of scheduling difficulties. They should all be arriving, however… what time is it there?"

"1:30 Friday afternoon."

"…by Sunday morning then. Is everyone tucked in?"

"Nice and tight. Not to fret."

"Good to hear. Have a slice of pizza for me. Sausage with green peppers,"

The exciting life of an assassin is often pure tedium, and this assignment has devolved into a one-woman siege. William Wyatt, the new head of Blackwatch, has arranged for a contingent of ten mercenaries to undertake the next phase of this operation. The mission has expanded, apparently, from neutralizing the targets to include recovering intelligence from the Allianz computer network. She had been told that a delay might occur to allow a technology expert to join the assault team, one capable of breaking into the company's systems. A quiet week-end operation also eliminates the problem of having scores of employees around.

Caleb wishes she could end her career more spectacularly, but the world is changing. She will still go out with an unbroken string of wins.

If only Eve were there to see her out.

✦ ✦ ✦

Once again the Knights are seated at the Round Table. The computer's output is now displayed on a large wall-mounted screen for all to see. Speakers are embedded into the screen.

"Wonderboy wants us to log into this website..." Jeremy explains as he types a URL and hits the Enter key. The first screen simply requests a login.

Jeremy looks at Darcy for affirmation—this could be a dangerous move.

Darcy nods. "The computer is on a network by itself, totally segregated from every other device. The drive is clean. Go ahead."

Jeremy logs in. Nothing happens. He looks around at his colleagues, who shrug. Then a small message appears on the large screen. *You may now log out.*

He does.

Suddenly a deep, electronically distorted voice fills the room. *Please state your names—all of you.*

Everyone turns toward the screen. The synthesized voice does not mask a distinctly British accent.

Jeremy frantically searches around the computer. "He thinks we have a microphone. Darcy, do we have a mic?"

You don't need a microphone, the voice says.

Startled, Jeremy follows the instructions. "My name is Jeremy."

Good afternoon Jeremy, the voice says.

"Somehow he's turned the speakers into a microphone," Darcy says, forgetting that she can be heard.

Clever girl. What is your name?

"Darcy."

The rest of you—give me your names.

"Hello there, my name is Rebecca."

"I'm Thompson Walker."

"This is Charlotte."

"And my name is Meysam Madani."

The screen fills with a large W artistically rendered in the style of Superman's initial. Wonderboy has a logo.

Where is Gideon?

Charlotte stands and faces the screen as if addressing the W. "He was killed yesterday. And we are in danger. That's why we need your help."

So it would be dangerous to help you.

Charlotte glances at the others, decides that honesty may be the best policy. "Yes, I'm afraid so."

Over the past month, Interpol has arrested twelve of us. How do I know you are not an Interpol sting?

"You called Gideon," Charlotte replies. "Do you think Gideon would give you up?"

A pause frustrates Charlotte. She doesn't know how to persuade Wonderboy to help them. "We are looking at the biggest challenge a hacker could ever face," she says.

You dangle a carrot?

Mason feels a little foolish addressing a large cartoon W, but he says, "We have the world's most powerful computer to help you."

What computer is that?

"The breakthrough quantum computer at Ambienz."

That's just a rumor.

"Hardly. You're using it right now." Mason sounds defiant. "If you're truly Wonderboy, surely you can run some kind of test and check it out."

Your name is Meysam Madani, the voice says. *"Mason" Madani, founder of Ambienz?* The voice suddenly takes on the overexcited inflection of a fan.

"At your service," Mason says with fake humility. "And about this new rocket of mine, I'm offering you a ride in the cockpit. But then again, how do I know you're the famous Wonderboy?"

The only response is fifteen seconds of silence.

Charlotte can't bear it. "Wonderboy, are you there?" she prods.

More silence.

"I think we've lost him," Rebecca suggests.

Be careful what you say. I'm still here.

Suddenly the screen fills with a list of Darcy's unopened emails.

You have some urgent messages in your Inbox, Darcy, the voice points out. *Maybe you should take a break and attend to them.*

Darcy's head swivels to look at Mason. She shakes her head, indicating that she has absolutely no idea how this hacker gained access to her email account.

The message list is replaced onscreen with the file structure of the main corporate server, the one Darcy had been sure was unhackable.

Look familiar? Hmmm... I'll bet the good stuff is in that innocuous little folder called DATA. As expected... military grade security on that one. If anyone would care to take a potty break, now would be a good time. This could take a while.

The specified folder opens, exposing its guts—at least a hundred subfolders.

Or maybe you should stay here, the voice adds. *Military grade isn't what it used to be. Just one more thing.*

A test screen pops up over the list of folders.

I've been running a series of benchmark tests on your computer. Spiked the needle on every one. Some beast you've got there, Mason. Now then, about that ride in the cockpit?

Chapter 45

The front door opens on a tidy row house in Eccles, a borough of Greater Manchester in North West England. A strikingly handsome man in his late 30's steps out and turns, waving goodbye to his mum, a widow who lives with him.

The man, known to his neighbors as Edgar Harrrison but to his global associates as Wonderboy, is the picture of a conservative Manchester banker. A blue business suit, white shirt and regimental tie cover up an expressive secret. Nearly his entire body is covered with tattoos. Not just a collage of images, but a masterwork—a graphic novel of epic proportions—depicting historic scenes of the oppression of both commoners and intelligentsia by rulers and clergy. It is all here, from the Pharaohs to modern day imperialists, from the ancient Mayans to the World Bank. The human mural is a profound statement of his motivating passion—to right the wrongs of the world and even the balance of power. It is also a tribute to his beloved father, Aiden, a virtuoso with a tattoo pen.

The vast artwork that covers his body shrewdly ends above his hands and feet and stays below his neck. When wearing trousers and long-sleeved shirts, his message remains cloaked and he can mingle among any group without inciting mockery and scornful stares.

Only a handful of people—maybe three in England, two in the U.S., and a half-dozen in other parts of the world—could recognize him by face, and half of those could not name him as Wonderboy. The illustrated man is the very model of anonymity, a virtue shared by the thousands of hackers collectively known as Sentient. And now he is about to expose himself to five people he has never met.

Wonderboy steps into a waiting taxi, nervously hoisting a small leather suitcase and a black nylon laptop case onto the seat beside him. In fifteen years of underground hacking, he has never gone out on assignment, preferring the security of his own den to the greater threat of detection that exists outside. *Is this where his career ends?* he wonders.

The odd and chaotic collective called Sentient was not Edgar's creation. In the "old days," as he calls them, hackers often clustered into small clubs and launched exploits to thump their chests by proving their superior technical prowess. A frequent prank was called DOxing—hacking personal information about a target and then posting it publicly in as many places as possible.

But things changed as some hackers pulled off dramatic exploits that gained worldwide attention. Wonderboy was one of these. Enraged by one religion's failure to see the fun in one of Wonderboy's *leaks*—an internal video in which a movie star hysterically crowed about his devotion to the sect—Wonderboy honed a new tool for attacking the high-and-mighty. The LOIC, an acronym for Low Orbit Ion Cannon, was a software application that could send a series of test messages to a server. Even a single firing of the LOIC is a nuisance, simply slowing down the server's response to meaningful queries. When many Sentient members fire a Cannon at a common target, however, even the most powerful server can be brought to its knees.

Wonderboy had spearheaded an anonymous effort to defend one of his favorite websites, a whistleblower organization called PoliLeaks. Sentient collaborators coalesced with great indignation and fired up thousands of Cannons, taking down the websites of Visa, MasterCard and PayPal in retaliation for blocking the payment of donations to the website.

Wonderboy had also learned that the collective could be a more direct way to even the odds against tyrants. He had established a new Internet Relay Chat (IRC) called #opbenali, naming it for the dictator of Tunisia, Zine El Abidine Ben Ali. The Sentient faction had successfully brought down the website of the Tunisian stock exchange, defaced government sites, passed news and media reports about the uprising in and out of the country, and distributed a "care package" containing technical details of how Tunisian revolutionaries could work around their country's privacy restrictions. The public had never heard about Wonderboy, but in hacker circles he had been canonized.

Wonderboy does not think of himself as the leader of Sentient, because the collective is not really an organization, yet he wields tremendous influence in the far-flung community. Unfortunately, the price of his fame can be calculated in one alarming way—by checking the bounty that many governments have offered for information leading to his true identity. The bounty has made Wonderboy even more infamous. And more suspicious.

The Ambienz quantum computer may prove to be bait for a trap, but Wonderboy doesn't think so. He had recorded Mason's voice during the teleconference. The quality was crap, but good enough to provide a convincing voice match to two video clips he had found—one on the TED website of Mason delivering an electrifying lecture, the other an archived CCN interview. He's quite certain that the "Charlotte" who was in the room with Mason an hour ago was Charlotte Ansari, the CCN correspondent who had conducted that interview. These arcane bits of trivia would be hard to fabricate.

The taxi arrives at Barton Aerodrome just two miles from his house. Wonderboy transfers to a chartered Robinson R66 helicopter for the 150 mile trip to Balbriggan. The timing of his arrival is critical, he has been told.

Caleb has removed the Domino's sign from the top of her Renault and changed into more practical attire: khaki slacks, a light blue shirt and white Nikes. Her car is well-hidden behind a cluster of trees but she can clearly observe both doors at Ambienz through the scope on her sniper rifle.

This work is dreadfully dull.

Suddenly people start to emerge from both doors of the building, heading for their cars. It must be the end of the workday. Caleb picks out the ones who are not driving and studies them more closely. It's unlikely that any of her targets would be driving an Ambienz employee's car. None of the passengers remotely resembles any of the five she is hunting.

A blue Toyota Yari drives past Caleb and she hurriedly pulls the rifle barrel into the cab of her car. The Yari proceeds to the Ambienz main door. A passenger steps out, studying the unmarked building as if he's not sure that this is his correct destination. The passenger totes a small leather suitcase and a computer bag.

Who would be coming to work on a Friday evening? Caleb wonders.

She watches the man through the scope, her finger on the trigger. During her brief moment of indecision, the man moves toward the door and presses a buzzer.

Caleb's finger twitches. She senses something suspicious about this man…

The door opens and the man enters Ambienz R&D.

Too late.

A key Sicarii principle is *don't kill the innocent*. Believing that she is one of the good guys has salved her conscience over the years, but sometimes you have to throw caution to the wind and make a snap decision.

As the door closes, Caleb intuitively knows that she has made a mistake. The coincidence quotient of a man arriving at Ambienz just as the employees are getting off work is just too high, the enacted scenario too scripted.

Caleb is grateful, at least, for this brief moment of excitement.

A troubling thought, however, worms into her mind. The blue Toyota had passed very close to her Renault. Had the passenger seen her? Had he noticed the rifle pointing out the window? Caleb may have blinded the building by shooting out the surveillance cameras, but this new set of eyes poses an unexpected threat.

Chapter 46

"Wonderboy?" Jeremy asks as the man enters the Ambienz lobby. He extends his hand. "Thought you'd be—*younger*. No offense."

Wonderboy tentatively shakes hands. This is a new experience for him—being identified by his handle in public. Well, not exactly *public*, but by someone he doesn't know.

"No offense taken. There seems to be a common misconception that all hackers are pimply-faced, anti-social teenagers. Are you Gideon's... how shall I say it—?"

"*Replacement?* Not exactly. But we had the same employer at one time, until a falling out."

"So you are no longer on the same team as before?"

"You might say the old team and I are now opponents."

"And you feel some sorrow over that turn of events, I take it?"

"*What?* No—none at all."

Wonderboy's remark has taken Jeremy by surprise, prompting him to quickly search his own feelings for some sign of nostalgia or regret. He finds a hard kernel of disappointment in his gut, but can't discern whether it's disappointment in himself or the Sicarii. He had once been a true believer in the Order's cause, believing he was on the path to becoming one of the elite, an assassin carrying the sword of the Lord on the way to fulfilling world-changing missions. Now he is just another out-of-work young man with no future. Probably. What's not to be disappointed about?

"What makes you say that?" Jeremy asks.

"Nothing really. But it would be a common reaction. I'm sure you were a rising star."

"Follow me," Jeremy says, heading toward the elevator. This conversation is not making him feel any better. "Time to introduce you to my new team."

✦ ✦ ✦

Everyone rises as Jeremy ushers Wonderboy into Camelot. Their expressions all show the same astonishment as Jeremy's upon seeing the hacker's maturity and businesslike deportment.

Wonderboy seizes the initiative, reaching out a hand to Mason. "Meysam Madani, so glad to meet you. In certain circles you are indeed a legend."

"As are you," Mason replies, firmly shaking hands.

"Charlotte Ansari, you are perhaps the most famous of your little band. Your absence from CCN is intolerable. I hope you make it back on the air very soon."

Charlotte nods, acknowledging Wonderboy's remarks.

"Thompson Walker. Sir, I am pleased to meet you. In your own way, you are as famous as your daughter, Charlotte. If you don't mind—" Wonderboy places his satchel on the Round Table and removes from it a large book, *The World's Great Wisdom Traditions* by Thompson Walker. "I'm a little embarrassed to ask for an autograph, sir… but I greatly enjoyed your book."

He hands the book to Thompson, who is positively glowing with pride, though Wonderboy spots an icy look of disdain on Charlotte's face. It seems that father and daughter are not a closely-knit pair.

Thompson finds a pen on the table. "And to whom should I address my scribbling?"

"Edgar, please. Thank you."

As Thompson signs the title page of the book, Wonderboy turns to Darcy, staring at her for a moment as if his brain is churning up a resume to match this face.

"Darcy O'Malley, a fine Irish name it is," Wonderboy says, changing his northern-England accent for an authentic Irish brogue.

Darcy smiles, taking Wonderboy's attempt at dialect as a compliment, not a slur. "And on behalf of my friends, sir, we are most happy to have you join the party. If I had a glass of ale, I'd offer a toast."

"Northern Ireland, I'd say, from your accent, though I'm no Professor Higgins. Which means most likely protestant, correct?"

Darcy bristles slightly, sensing a challenge. She is used to religion being an issue in Ireland.

Wonderboy dismisses her unease with a kind smile.

"Me, too—Protestant, that is," he says. "And you've done well for yourself—Chief Operating Officer of Ambienz, if I'm not mistaken."

"Chief *Operations* Officer," she says.

"I stand corrected."

He turns to Rebecca. "My dear, you are the only one that I know nothing about."

"That's because I'm not famous like the others," Rebecca replies. "I'm Charlotte's personal assistant." It's the first time she has publicly claimed this title. She looks at Charlotte for approval, as does Wonderboy.

"Best I ever had, too," Charlotte confirms.

Wonderboy spots the exchanged glances between Jeremy and Rebecca, detecting a budding relationship that neither perhaps has had the courage to pursue.

"I must express my condolences for the death of Gideon, whom I never met in person," Wonderboy declares, noting the downward glances of all but Mason and Darcy. *These are the ones who knew Gideon,* he concludes. And Charlotte—if he correctly assesses the rapid blinking of her eyes, the slight flush of her cheeks, the quick glance away from the table—was probably more than an acquaintance. Close friend? Lover? Perhaps a friend longing to be …

"You seem rather well informed about us," Mason interjects.

"Yes, well, that's my job, isn't it? Learning things? And knowing things? I assume it's why you invited me here."

Wonderboy turns now to the computer standing innocuously on the Round Table. "But I know very little about this little beasty here," he says, caressing the gray sheet metal of the case. "May I?"

Mason nods yes, and Wonderboy sits down in front of the computer monitor and keyboard. The others instinctively huddle behind him as if forming up for a group photo.

Suddenly Wonderboy's fingers dance over the keyboard and the monitor turns black. Rows of white characters begin racing toward the top of the screen, then stop. Fingers tap a few keys and the monitor explodes again in a flight of uninterpretable digits.

And then a series of numbers appears on the screen.

"It appears that my remote testing didn't do justice for your little baby. It's off the charts. But then I suppose you know that. The IBM Sequoia is the world's fastest computer with a LINPACK performance of 16.2 petaflops."

Mason interprets for the rest of the room: "*Flops* stands for floating-point operations per second. A measure of speed. You go from megaflops to gigaflops to teraflops to petaflops…"

Wonderboy interrupts. "Sequoia occupies three-thousand square feet of space and performs at over sixteen petaflops. Perfect for nuclear weapons simulation, I would guess. This little baby is just a little bigger than two desktop computers and I'd estimate it's performing at over a petaflop by itself. Truly amazing."

"Thank you," Mason replies.

"Now then," Wonderboy says, "to what use shall we put it?" He looks eager to get started.

"We were just discussing that," Charlotte answers. "We assume Mason's computer can crunch data. What we need you to do is get us data to crunch. And some of it might be hard to get."

"That's why they call me Wonderboy."

"That begs a question," Thompson says. "Why does a mature fellow like yourself have a superhero *W* for a logo, and a name like Wonderboy? Seems out of place."

Wonderboy glances slyly at Thompson and replies, "I think you've just answered your own question. I believe the word is *misdirection*." He pauses, then says, "Now I have a question for all of you. Who is in the Renault that's parked behind a grove of trees to the southwest of the building?"

"Did it have a pizza sign on top" Darcy asks.

"No, but it had a rifle barrel poking out the window."

"You're very observant," Charlotte remarks.

"I'm in unfamiliar territory surrendering my anonymity to people I don't know. Let's just say that my powers of observation are on high alert."

"Well, we can't introduce you to her, but the woman in that vehicle is Caleb, a Sicarii assassin who has been assigned to kill us. We have a surveillance camera aimed at her vehicle. We're stuck in here because, well—she's out there."

"And were you going to tell me this?"

Darcy stares Wonderboy in the eye. "Yes, if you tried to leave. Which wouldn't be good for your health."

"In my estimation, anywhere outside my house is a dangerous place to be. Speaking of pizza…"

"Where are my manners? You must be starved," Mason proclaims. "Let me show you to the commissary."

Chapter 47

Charlotte shouts. "Where is Jeremy? I've been looking all over for him!"

It is 10:00 p.m. and Wonderboy has spent the past half-hour downloading Charlotte's research files from the cloud. No matter how fast a computer, Charlotte has learned, the bandwidth is bound to slow you down.

Thompson has just shared an idea with Charlotte and the two of them want to consult with the others immediately. Everyone but Jeremy is gathered outside Camelot.

Charlotte turns to Rebecca with a piercing stare. "Rebecca, if you know where he is, tell me now."

"Why would I know?" the young woman whines.

"Because you and Jeremy are a *thing*, all right? Don't try to deny it. So tell me now where—"

"All right, all right... he went out."

"*Out?* Out *where?* There's an assassin staked out..."

Charlotte pauses. This time she's the one to answer her own question.

"I told him it was a dumb idea," Rebecca says. "Caleb's a super assassin, and he's a... a *tunnel runner*. I shouldn't have said that to him, he got really pissed. He has no chance taking on Caleb alone—does he?"

Charlotte reaches out and touches Rebecca's arm. "We're going to find out," she says, then mutters, "The idiot!"

"How did he leave?" Mason asks. "We're buttoned down pretty tight."

"He was checking the main floor for any breaches and found a stairway leading to the roof. He thought he could crawl out in the dark and then down the back without being seen. I told him it was a stupid idea, but he really wants to save us. I'm afraid for him."

"So am I," Charlotte says.

Wonderboy sticks his head out of Camelot's door. "Okay, we've got all your files in our hands. Where do we start?"

"Where I always start as a reporter," Charlotte answers. "Follow the money and the suspects. Is there a way to find out all the names that turn up in those files so we can analyze them? You know, like who was where, and when. Were they together? Dates and places, that kind of stuff?"

"That's quite a wide net, but yes. With this beasty's power, no problem."

Jeremy has made a large orbit around the building, cursing the bright moon and the security lights that illuminate the parking lots. His face and hands smudged with fertile Irish black dirt, he has crept cautiously through a ring of trees behind the building to a small clearing. Just beyond is Caleb's Toyota.

He knows that Caleb could be anywhere. The automobile could be a decoy. She could be watching him right now, smirking at his futile attempts to conceal himself, deciding on just the right time, the most humiliating way, to…

A branch snaps behind him.

His heart slams against his ribs.

Already crouching, he pivots, searching frantically for some sign of the assassin, but the woods are too dark. He pulls himself to a large oak and sits with his back to the trunk, a Glock firmly held out in front, wondering if Gideon had felt such stress when beginning his career.

Another branch cracks and Jeremy twitches. The sound is closer. Caleb is stalking him. Drawing in a deep breath, Jeremy calms his nerves. Fortunately, the glare of the security lights is to his back, so he should be able to make out any moving shape that approaches through the trees.

Suddenly a loud snort, like an old man waking, tears through the night's chill. Jeremy jerks his pistol to the left toward the source of the sound. Squinting, he can just make out the shape of a red deer—no, two deer—not twenty yards away. Like ghosts the two does have appeared from nowhere to stand frozen in place, staring at Jeremy, daring him to make the next move.

He sighs, relieved that his adversary is not Caleb, but recognizing that if he startles the deer they may leap away, announcing the presence of a hunter in the woods.

He doesn't move—doesn't lower his gun, wipe his nose, shift his butt off the uncomfortable oak root that is cutting into his rump. He tries not to blink or breathe.

The deer continue to stare at him, their alert eyes occasionally glowing in the dark as they catch the lights from the building.

The stare-down lasts a full minute, though it seems like five. At last the two deer silently turn and slowly dissolve into the shadows.

Jeremy has won this duel, but the more difficult one is yet to come. Waiting another minute for the deer to provide some distance, he wonders at how these large creatures can move so noiselessly through the trees and scrubby underbrush.

If they can do it, so can he.

Using the oak's trunk to steady himself, he pushes upward to a standing position. Convinced that he has waited long enough to not spook the deer, he turns toward the clearing and confronts a police officer with a raised pistol. Even in the dark, Jeremy recognizes the uniform of An Garda Síochána, the national police service of Ireland, but with the security lights now in his eyes he can't see the officer's face.

"I thought police in Ireland weren't armed." he says.

The officer's Garda cap tilts as the officer clearly is looking down at the unlicensed Glock in Jeremy's hand.

The officer speaks with a woman's voice. "Sir, please put down your weapon."

In a flash, it all becomes clear. A woman cop. An impersonator. Caleb!

With every ounce of strength he can muster, Jeremy raises his gun. It is less than halfway to shooting position when the officer fires.

In the distance, two startled deer crash through the woods. The noise masks the sound of Jeremy falling.

✦ ✦ ✦

"Darcy, what do we know?" Charlotte asks.

"The security cameras clearly showed Jeremy crossing the northeast parking lot and entering a windbreak of trees. After that we don't know what has happened."

The group, without Jeremy, is gathered at the Round Table. Charlotte has taken charge of the meeting without any dispute from Mason. No one seems to mind the keyboard tapping of Wonderboy, who continues to toil at his task, sending a continuous flood of arcane data across the large screen display.

"From now on, no free-lancing," Charlotte declares. "Am I clear on this?"

Everyone nods yes.

"I know it's difficult under these circumstances, but we have to push on. Our only chance is to solve the puzzle that has us trapped here. After a little nap, Thompson has come up with an idea, and I think it bears consideration."

She turns to her father, who rises from his chair to assume a position of authority.

"We know the following," Thompson begins. "The Sicarii are obsessed with defining and honoring the pure lineage of the descendants of its followers. That is why Charlotte's son Greg was made the Divine Light, who is called Cain—because he was of pure Sicarii lineage. Of course, he also met other demanding requirements to sift him out, but without the bloodline he would not have had a chance."

"Most of us know this," Charlotte says, urging her father to skip ahead.

"Actually, it's news to me," Wonderboy replies without looking up or breaking the tap-tapping on his keyboard.

Charlotte sighs.

Thompson continues. "We also know that the organization we call the Sicarii is not a decision-making body by itself. It serves as the intelligence-gathering and, uh, *field operations* arm of a larger organization that we know almost nothing about. Except that it has a governing council, and on that council—perhaps the head of it—is a gentleman who is called Michael, but whose actual name is William Sinclair."

"You told us earlier that Michael is really the position of the High Priest. The High Priests—from the days of Zadok—were hereditary. And the Essenes, which gave birth to the Sicarii, were charged with preserving the bloodline."

"No wonder you're a good reporter, Char," Thompson says, smiling. "This gets to the idea I just had. Wonderboy, I need your full attention now."

Wonderboy taps out a few more keystrokes and then stops, turning toward the old man.

"If it's true that we should know our enemy, then we should know more about Mr. Sinclair. Not just William Sinclair, but his entire ancestry. Until now, I didn't see a way to do this—to map out the whole bloodline of the sons of Zadok. But now, with Wonderboy and that magic machine of Mason's, maybe there's a way. And maybe, somewhere in that family history, is the clue we're looking for."

Thompson glances at Wonderboy, who understands a response is required. "You want me to trace the family history of a man who lived thousands of years ago," he replies, "by starting with a man who is alive today?"

Thompson nods yes.

"How many years do I have?"

"I think we should measure in *hours*—if you want to live up to your name."

"While I ponder that, let me bring you up to date on some new information. I wrote a little script that looks at all the names and name-like words that appear in the articles Charlotte had in her research files. I indexed these against the photos someone took of some walls in an office—"

"That was Gideon. He took those pictures in my office," Charlotte explains.

"Ahh, yes… Gideon. We should be grateful, because he preserved some of the connecting threads that you had already teased out of the data. The pictures showed presumptive links between people, places and events. I'd say that you

were very close to linking a Mr. Alain Potier, a French citizen and prominent businessman, to several events Charlotte had highlighted, including two assassinations
of Iranian scientists."

"But how does Mr. Potier relate to Sinclair, if at all? That's the question
now."

"Give me just a minute," Wonderboy's fingers beat the keyboard like a snare
drum. After a few pauses interrupted by more rapid typing, the large wall-mounted
display shows the names Potier and Sinclair surrounded by many numbers, some
of them looking like dates.

"Okay, in a secure online archive of New York Times articles I found a
photo of Potier and Sinclair at a charity fundraising event. They're mentioned in
the caption. That's one link. Here's the photo—in color, no less."

Wonderboy taps the keyboard again and a full-frame shot of nine men and
women fills the screen. Sinclair, in his predictable scarlet tie, is second from the
left in the front row.

"Potier is to Sinclair's immediate left."

"In a blue tie!" Thompson shouts. "Potier must be Sariel, another member
of the Council."

"How the hell do you break into these secure sites?" Mason asks Wonderboy.

"This one I cracked two years ago for another reason. It has material from
many wire services and other newspapers tucked inside for reporters to access.
It's like, what do you Americans call it?—*one-stop shopping* for news. Here's
something else."

More keyboard clacking. A data-filled table floods the screen with an over-
whelming amount of information.

"What is this?" Darcy asks.

"Somehow Charlotte got access to Passport and Visa data for various per-
sons, including William Sinclair and a person named Todd Simony. It would appear that Charlotte has information sources beyond those of the typical correspondent."

Charlotte sheepishly responds. "When you believe the stakes are high, you
use whatever means you can get your hands on."

"So this isn't your first interaction with a hacker?"

"That information wasn't hacked. It was bought," Charlotte says.

"Well, I for one don't make moral judgments about these things. But if I may
ask, why Todd Simony?"

"It was an alias that Gideon frequently used. I saw the Passport a number of
times."

"All right, this table shows that he was in three countries—Iran, France,
and Jordan—at precisely the same time that high-profile assassinations occurred,

including the nuclear scientist in Tehran. Were you stalking Gideon, Charlotte?"

"Stalking?" Charlotte yells indignantly. "My mission was to expose the Sicarii, and Gideon unknowingly was my way in. He was also the only assassin I knew anything about."

"Except your mother and son?"

"They aren't assassins!"

"They're the bosses." Wonderboy suggests.

"And we're trying to find out who they work for... and why," Thompson reminds the hacker. "I'm not sure what you're getting at here."

"While you're trying to find out what this Sinclair and Potier are up to," Wonderboy explains, "I'm trying to figure out what each of you is up to. I think that Charlotte wanted to take down this Sicarii organization the way she was trained to do, by exposing information about them. But as she got closer to the truth, her feelings for some of the main players got in the way and she became rather, well, to be blunt—conflicted. It was, after all, her mother and son who are running this group. And Gideon—well, it's obvious that Charlotte was in love with him."

There, he's said it.

Confronted with the truth, Charlotte has no response.

"I don't doubt that he felt the same way," Wonderboy continues. "Otherwise why would he have given up everything to save you?"

Still Charlotte cannot speak.

"Thompson, it took about fifteen seconds for me to find your history," Wonderboy continues, "including expunged court records. So maybe before we expose all these other people, we should come clean about ourselves, too. That fourteen-year-old girl you were in love with—who got pregnant by you—whatever happened to her?"

The air has been sucked out of Thompson. "I never found out."

"Never *tried*, right? She had a child. *Your* child. But all that is just history now. Don't you ever wonder what became of your child?"

It takes a while, but at last the old man manages a quiet "Yes."

"Clearly your daughter hates your guts. I would guess she considers you to be a sexual pervert. And also blames you for your tacit approval of your wife's—oh, let's call it her *business*. Even though Charlotte can't bring herself to do anything about it either. It's interesting to me that Charlotte's research seems to stop about three weeks ago. I wonder if that was about the time she decided she couldn't push ahead with a story that could bring ruin upon her mother, son and would-be lover."

"Who the hell are you?" Mason asks. "This is like some kind of creepy Charlie Chan movie."

"Ahh, Mason—hiding your Iranian roots behind an Americanized name."

"Actually, Americans just can't pronounce my real name."

"Your company is headquartered right here. It's an Irish company. Your American company is just a U.S. sales organization."

"So? The United States can't beat the tax advantages of being in Ireland."

"And Darcy's police record wouldn't make her eligible for emigration to the U.S., I assume. Not that I hold anything against a young woman fighting for her beliefs during a time like the Troubles in Northern Ireland."

"She's a big part of establishing this company."

"Yes, she's brilliant. And it's quite obvious that the two of you are madly in love. It's very touching."

None of them had seen that coming.

"Quite a famous fighting family you come from, Darcy." There is no apparent irony or sarcasm in Wonderboy's tone, and Darcy does not take offense.

"Mason, I don't know why you hide your feelings for Darcy, but I wish you well, sir. And a happy life on the other side of this adventure."

Mason nods appreciatively.

"Rebecca—"

The young woman squirms in her chair. She knows her turn was coming.

Wonderboy stares at Rebecca for a moment. "You're concerned for Jeremy, we know that, but you have secrets, don't you?"

Rebecca's neck muscles tighten as she fights to keep a calm demeanor.

"Should we review your history, my dear?"

"Not really necessary," Rebecca answers. "Everyone knows I'm here by accident. Just like Jeremy."

"I think no one is here by accident. May I ask what your last name is?"

Rebecca turns away defiantly.

"Sinkler," Charlotte interjects, then spells it out. "S-i-n-k-l-e-r."

Wonderboy types out the name as Thompson's face begins to glow with the unfolding revelation.

"Sinkler!" Thompson blurts out. "Why did I not know your last name before this?"

In stark black-and-white, the large screen suddenly lists numerous common variations of Rebecca's surname:

Sincklair

Saint Clare

Sancto Claro

Singular

Seincler

Sanclar

Sinclea

Sinclaire

St. Clair

Sinclair

Thompson pauses to digest the information before continuing. "The name Sinkler is just a variant of a family name, in this case the ancient Scottish-Irish clan of Sinclair... or St. Clair."

Surprised, Charlotte turns to the young woman. "According to this, you may be a distant relative of William Sinclair."

Rebecca is trembling. Her eyes are damp. She can't look Charlotte in the eye. Instead she glances at Wonderboy, knowing that the truth will come out.

"Actually a rather close relative," Rebecca confesses. "He's my father."

A loud buzzer interrupts the group's astonishment.

Someone is at the front door.

Chapter 48

"My God, what happened to him?" Darcy asks the policewoman.

"Tasered—and lucky he was. Carryin' a gun in the trees. He's the one you called about, then?"

"He is at that. Thanks so much, Meara."

Charlotte and Rebecca help Jeremy to a soft chair in the small lobby. The women bear a lot of his weight as his legs are wobbly and his disturbed equilibrium still throws him this way and that. Everyone is standing here except for Wonderboy, who is tethered to the computer downstairs.

"I do have some questions for you, Darcy, if you don't mind?" the officer asks.

"Such as what's a young man like this doing wandering around my building with a gun?"

"An unlicensed weapon is a serious offense, you know that, Darcy."

"And I appreciate you keeping this to yourself. Don't even tell our father about it for now."

"What is goin' on here, Darcy? At least I have a right to know that."

"We have a… a situation goin' on, that's what. Like I said on the phone, there may be someone out there intending to do us harm. Jeremy over there thought he'd take on the evildoer by himself. Did you see anyone else out there—anything suspicious?"

"Just an empty auto parked out in that old grove of trees to the southwest of here. Looked abandoned. Gave it a ticket."

"Good for you, Meara. I should've told you more before puttin' you in danger like that. The lad had no way of knowing you were looking for him."

"Makes me wish we carried guns ourselves sometimes," Meara replies. "I can take another look around if you want, maybe call another unit."

"We're good for now. My love to Patrick."

"All right then, good luck."

As the front door closes, Charlotte stomps over to Darcy. "You called the police without discussing it?"

"It's our property, remember?"

"No police snooping around! If they searched this place and found our weapons, you wouldn't be able to talk us out of it like you did with your friend Meara."

"My *sister* Meara. You sound like a fugitive talking."

"We *are* fugitives. Haven't you been paying attention? We're implicated in a death at the British Museum. We're in the U.K. on false passports. Interpol probably has our pictures from surveillance cameras. Hell, in the U.S. we fled from the New York police and killed a man in the tunnels. I like our chances better with Caleb."

"All right," Darcy says insincerely. "Next time we'll take a goddam vote."

Charlotte turns back to Jeremy who is sitting upright, looking more stable. "And you, young man, I am really pissed right now!" She walks over and bends down to look him in the eye. "But damn glad to have you back safe. What the hell do you do for someone who's been tasered?"

She stands straight and looks around the room. "Someone boil some water or tear up some sheets or something. Let's get this fellow back on his feet."

"Could use a nice dark ale right about now," Jeremy suggests.

"Let's get back downstairs and see if our hacker's found anything on Rebecca's father." Mason gives Jeremy a welcome-back pat on his way to the elevator.

Jeremy glances at Rebecca. "Who's your father?"

"Don't even ask."

✦ ✦ ✦

Caleb watches the policewoman leave the building. She laughs quietly. The officer had saved the life of the young Sicarii wannabe. Perched on a high branch of an oak tree near the Renault, Caleb is virtually undetectable in her black night-mission garb. Climbing the tree had been just as easy as it was a few years ago, a fact that makes her proud.

From her vantage, she has a birds-eye view of both doors and the surrounding terrain. Through her Raptor 6X 3-tube night vision scope she watched Jeremy creep across the flat roof, disappear for a few seconds as he scaled the back wall, and then race to the fringe of trees surrounding the parking lot. *So much effort!* The scope had revealed the two red deer that had approached Jeremy, the stand-off between man and beasts, and the police officer sneaking up on the young man from behind. Obviously the female officer had been tipped off to inspect the grounds—probably to look for Caleb. No matter. If the officer had not tasered Jeremy, the poor fellow eventually would have approached the car and been killed. Or maybe not. Maybe Caleb would have just captured him to learn what was going on inside the bunker.

Oh well, the events had provided amusing melodrama during a long boring night.

Of course, Caleb easily could have shot Jeremy and the officer as they stood at the front door. *Pfffft! Pfffft! Down they go.* But it would have been pointless. Her orders are to contain, not kill, unless necessary. Let the incoming troops do the messy stuff.

She checks her watch. In less than an hour she'll be replaced by Hugh Cregan, head of U.K. support and a capable agent. He's no Caleb or Gideon, naturally, but—

Gideon. That one still haunts her. *One of her own.*

No matter how many times she rolls that one around in her head, it always comes out bad. Now and then she had thought about how one day they would meet for the first time, perhaps in Monaco or Zurich—both of them retired by then, of course—and discuss their exploits. They'd share a bottle of wine, compare notes like two old war heroes recounting past battles, and then depart, both content in the knowledge that they had played important roles in the shaping of a better world.

That will never happen. Caleb had killed Gideon. No known reason. Eve had died… or been killed. Again, no known reason. It feels like a purge. When Hugh comes to replace her, what will be his orders? Will he be the one to terminate her? It's clear that she will never be allowed to retire. She will never be free.

For the first time in decades, Caleb trusts no one.

A great horned owl swoops in, crashing through branches and landing just above, unaware of her presence. Another lonely night hunter. But truly free.

With her silenced 9mm pistol, Caleb shoots it.

✦ ✦ ✦

Darcy has provided a computer for Thompson. It sits directly across from Wonderboy on the Round Table. Following a hunch, Thompson is doing his own Internet research while Charlotte interrogates Rebecca in front of the others.

"Why did you lie about your father, Rebecca?" Charlotte asks. "You said you were orphaned."

"Might as well have been."

"By which you mean…?"

Rebecca shakes her head. "He's not like a real father," she says hesitantly. "I barely knew him growing up. He's very wealthy—I guess you gathered that. He traveled a lot, I suppose much like you Charlotte. Tough to be a parent when you're never at home."

Charlotte isn't sure if this is just a defensive barb, but it leaves a stinging mark. "Where were you raised? And by whom?"

"I was born in the U.S.—Los Angeles, actually. A full U.S. citizen. I was raised by a pack of wolves."

Charlotte takes this fiction as a sign that Rebecca is brushing off the interrogation.

"Rebecca, try to take this seriously. Some of us believe that you're a mole for the other side. That would explain how they always know our whereabouts. And possibly why they wanted to remove you from our group at the airport back on Long Island—to debrief you, maybe—or evacuate you to safety."

"Believe me, they don't need a mole. If anything, I'm your informant. Who else has information about my family?'"

"Well, this whole business about being raised by a pack of..."

"Wolfgang!" Rebecca interrupts. "That was his first name, a close friend of my father's. My mother died in childbirth—so that part of my orphan story is literally true. Wolfgang Bauer and his family took me in so *daddy* wouldn't be troubled with me. I say family—but the Bauer children were no better than a pack of wolves. Money to burn and the instincts of predators. I would see my father twice a year."

"On holidays, then?"

"I don't know. One of those occasions was always the winter solstice, the shortest day of the year. I always assumed it was because he'd have to spend less time with me on that day, though he always told me it was *my* special day."

"What did he mean by that?"

"I wish to God I knew. It was always a miserable day for me, being forced to spend it with someone I didn't love and barely knew."

"Would you say the Bauers were well-to-do?"

"What a quaint way of putting it. Try *filthy rich*. Possibly richer than my father, I don't know. At some point wealthy is just wealthy. We lived part of the year on a large estate on the coast of France, part of the year in New York. School was never a problem—I was always privately tutored."

"You told me that Daniel Hudson, the head honcho at CCN, was your guardian. That was another lie, wasn't it?"

Rebecca nods solemnly. "It wasn't my idea. What's true is that I've always admired your work on CCN. When I told Gertie—Wolfgang's wife, and the only person who was ever something of a mom to me—when I told her that I wanted to meet you some day, she had Wolfgang arrange something even grander. For me to become your personal assistant."

"So these people had sway over CCN?"

"I don't know how that works."

"But why lie about Hudson being your guardian? Daniel could just order it."

"He didn't want to pull rank... put up a fuss about it. Said that you—" Rebecca cuts off her comment and her face reddens.

"He said that I... *what?* Rebecca, you have to tell me everything."

Rebecca clears her throat and speaks without making eye contact with Charlotte. "He said you were a headstrong bitch and would make his life miserable if he tried to force me onto you."

Thompson laughs out loud, a kind of agreement with Hudson's conclusion.

Charlotte turns toward him angrily at first, but then breaks into a grin herself. Turning back to Rebecca, she says, "I suppose that's a pretty good description."

"What's also true," Rebecca continues, "is that I ended up here with you by sheer coincidence and bad luck. Honest to God."

"So why choose now to 'fess up about your father?"

Rebecca glances at Wonderboy. "Him," she says. "He's researching my dad. If he's any good, he'd soon come up with information about me."

"Your father's name is *Sinclair*, but you go by *Sinkler*."

"My mother's last name. Her bloodline was part of the clan, too. Somehow the whole lot of us were cousins or distant relatives. Father didn't seem to care which name I took. For me, I just didn't want to have *his* name.

An image suddenly flashes on the large-screen monitor. It is a newspaper obituary for one Jean Sinclair, survived by husband William G., 37; infant daughter, Rebecca Anne; father Edward M. Sinkler...

"Yes, inevitably I would have dredged up the true facts," Wonderboy says, his eyes gleaming with satisfaction. "And now that we have these additional facts, it will be much easier to carve out William G. Sinclair's history from the thousands of members of the clan. And then backtrack from CCN ownership to, hopefully, some of these people."

Wonderboy glances up from his computer monitor to stare at Rebecca for a moment. "You don't seem very relieved that your secret is out," he remarks.

"No—not very."

"And why is that?"

"Because I'm a little afraid of what you might find out about my family. Things, maybe, that I never wanted to know."

Chapter 49

Chen Lee storms into the Center of Intelligence Analysis conference room with a grin and drops into a padded chair opposite Cain. "Are we good or *what*?" he crows. "Piece of cake."

"So you've managed to crack into the Ambienz network."

"Not only that—we've isolated the specific computer they're using to access the Internet. The only one, in fact. Guess it's a week-end there. They may be good at securing their buildings, but they're lousy at protecting their data. We should be able to download everything they look at, and every message they send out."

Cain seems less enthusiastic than Chen Lee. "Seems too simple."

"Nahh—you've just got the master at work here. Be glad I'm on your side."

"Anything relevant turn up so far?"

"Relevant is a relative word. Hard to say. So far they seem obsessed with news about Iran. Especially the scientist assassinations."

"We already knew my mother was digging into those. We did a pretty good job simulating the kind of messy work Mossad does so the blame would get deflected. If she was able to tie us into those…"

"Well, I'll keep you posted on what we find."

"They're clever enough to be trying to solve the same puzzle that we are. Why would they be mucking around in this old Iran stuff? Stay on it. I want a list of new topics hourly from now on."

Chen nods deferentially and slouches out of the room.

Cain drains his cup of tea, but instead of setting the cup on the table, he flings it angrily at the wall. Such a burst of rage is uncharacteristic. His Asperger's Syndrome dampens his feelings, often to the point of detachment. Intellectually, he knows that his affliction is what makes his job bearable. He is eighteen years old, and already he has personally ordered or approved the assassination of ninety-seven individuals—including his own mother.

His brain works overtime to justify the killing. Each one is merely the carrying out of a sentence on someone judged guilty of violating the Order's laws or working to defy its sacred mission. His job is merely to supervise the clean-up crew. The Sicarii are the garbage collectors of society. They are what stands between the collapse of society and the full realization of achieving a better world as God had ordained. They are God's agents, His avenging angels, the human hands by which the Almighty has chosen to achieve His aims.

Cain's emotions, however, have been fluctuating wildly. Once flat-lined by the Asperger's, they now spike erratically. He has been experiencing the terrifying feelings of "normal" people—anger, fear, panic, love. Yes—*love*. It's almost like he is outgrowing the Asperger's the way some people outgrow allergies. These new feelings confuse him. They muddle the stout convictions that he has held about the Order's mission, contradicting the pristine logic of his intellect.

He blames emotions for his powerlessness to solve the Lost Secret. Instead of a breakthrough, he seems destined for a breakdown. He has resorted to piracy—the piracy of his own family's creativity. It's a humiliating admission of defeat.

He cannot let anyone in the organization know that he is rooting for his mother and grandfather to survive long enough to solve the great puzzle, because this would help conceal the decay of his rare abilities, the ones that earned him the position of Divine Light. And then there is Rebecca—the woman he has never met, but with whom he has had more intimate conversations than all others combined, except for his grandmother. Rebecca has affected him in ways that he can't describe. And he has repaid her through callous manipulation to further the aims of the Order.

This is a quandary of massive proportions.

He studies the shattered tea cup, glad that the room is soundproof.

✦ ✦ ✦

"Hah!"

The exclamation is the first human sound in more than fifteen minutes inside Camelot. "They took the bait!"

Only Charlotte and Thompson are present to be startled by Wonderboy's outburst. The others are in the security monitoring room, the commissary, maybe the rest room. Charlotte has been too preoccupied with looking over a cross-tabbed report of her research compiled by Wonderboy and the magnificent quantum computer he's named *Honey*.

Thompson, dozing off and on, has been jumping from link to link on the Web, obviously on the trail of something,

"What bait is that?" Charlotte asks Wonderboy.

"Spider food. I knew that at some point your adversaries would come looking for their Grail, our digital portal to the world—*Honey!* If they could track down our forays into the digital realm, they could maybe backtrack it all the way to our network, then try to hack in. The obvious way for them to do this is to send out spiders, little digital robots, to look for the electronic breadcrumbs that litter our trail. I just planted a bunch of spider food out there to make it easier for them."

"So—you helped them break into our network?" Thompson speaks quietly, not wanting to appear too confrontational. "Why on earth would you do that?"

"These people think now they've hacked in, but instead they've been invited into a hall of illusions, a hermetically sealed room that gives them just what they want—a multitude of data. It will take quite some time to realize they have been duped. The data is a hodgepodge of news I downloaded from the Internet."

"*Hodgepodge*," Charlotte repeats. "Not a word you hear very often."

"It's what I fear we're looking at as well," Thompson rubs his tired eyes. "We've got a five or six thousand-year-old mystery to unravel. I think the police shows on TV call that a cold case."

"We need data," Wonderboy interjects. "Meaningful data."

"Any ideas?" Charlotte asks. "My research is little help. I wasn't getting very far."

Wonderboy rolls up a shirtsleeve, exposing a massively tattooed right forearm. The vivid images seem to continue up his arm.

"What the hell...?" Charlotte says, standing in astonishment and moving toward that forearm like a moth to a flame.

Thompson, too, stares at the miniature mural, then almost reverently steps toward the hacker. "What have you got there?"

Wonderboy points to an image of an ancient building crumbling in flames. "Solomon's Temple—the heart of Jewish religion and the home of the high priests—being destroyed by the Chaldeans."

Buoyed by his audience's uncritical amazement, Wonderboy pulls off his tie and unbuttons his shirt, pulling it open to reveal the front of his right shoulder. His chest shimmers with imagery. A finger directs Charlotte's eyes to another temple, this one also in the process of obliteration. "The destruction of the second temple in 70 CE, this time by the Romans. Are we seeing a theme here?"

Still stunned by the human portfolio before her, Charlotte ignores Wonderboy's question. "Your body is... it's just—"

"In a way it's *my* temple. But that's not what I'm getting at."

"I think I see your point." Thompson no longer feels weary. "The temple was run by the high priests, a hereditary role. Even to this day, a high priest must be a Son of Zadok, the first High Priest appointed by David."

"Okay, you gave this history lesson earlier," Charlotte remarks, still unable to keep her eyes of the startling images. "I just don't understand what it..."

"Really, Charlotte! With your investigative skills I'm surprised you can't see it. We have priests going all the way back to the days of David and Solomon. We have the Essenes, out of which the Sicarii devils were born, dedicating themselves to establishing the purity of the legitimate priesthood. And we have William Sinclair—playing the role of high priest, even taking the name of Michael, which is quite an obvious reference."

"So if Sinclair is a legitimate high priest—a hereditary Son of Zadok—are you suggesting we might be able to trace Sinclair back to… well, a long time ago?"

"If he is, maybe we could trace him all the way back to the man himself, Zadok. And somewhere in that data we may come across a more complete picture of who these people are, and what agenda they're pursuing."

"You know they didn't have the Internet back then, right?" Wonderboy is suddenly sarcastic. Such an ambitious ancestry research project seems laughable.

"But our late friend Bertram Doering does—or *did*, I mean. His organization was mapping out the lineage of the high priests from old records that had been preserved. Here, let me write down his website and login credentials."

Thompson scrawls the information on a scrap of paper and slides it over to Wonderboy who quickly buttons up his shirt, pulling the curtain closed to the dismay of Charlotte, then enters the information into Honey.

"I've gone over a ream of documents Doering gave us before his death," Thompson says. "These are mainly records of database projects begun by others. One of them is very interesting—a project initiated by a neo-Nazi organization whose motive we can only guess at."

"Devious bastards," Charlotte mutters.

"These new Nazis, like most of the others, are severely underfunded, so progress has been limited. Many of these projects are inactive or defunct. According to Doering, the Vatican has a project that's still alive. And most interesting of all—the CIA has been collecting information about the bloodline as well. Doering tried to set up an information exchange with many of these groups—except the neo-Nazis, of course—with little success. Some never even acknowledged his request. Here's a summary of my notes."

Wonderboy scans the notes, nodding his head. "If these sites are still online somewhere, I can break in and download the data. But I'm wondering about the big sources of genealogical data, like Lineage.com, and that massive Mormon ancestry project…"

"Yes, available at the Family Search website. Doering's aides had accounts there, but the online research was slow and tedious, so Doering had an assistant move to Salt Lake City and work at the LDS Family History Library. Again, one person tracing ancestry back one family at a time. Imagine two billion names in that repository, and one person investigating. Very slow progress."

Data from Doering's research site floods the wall-mounted monitor.

"Looks like Doering was compiling the kinds of data the others didn't have access to," Wonderboy summarizes. "That's good for us."

He taps a few keys and a Sinclair research web page comes up. "Some of the Sinclair clan have been doing their own ancestry projects."

"So can you get into the big ones like Lineage.com and that Mormon site?"

"Getting in is not the problem. Downloading all their data is. We're restricted by the bandwidth of our Internet connection, and I'm sure each of those sites only allows a user to suck out data through a small straw, not a fire hose."

"So it could take weeks," Thompson sounds deflated.

"Or months," Wonderboy admits. "Unless we tap into the power of Sentient."

He deftly logs into an IRC client and creates a new Internet Relay Chat called #opancestry.

"I'd guess the legend called Wonderboy can pull in a few thousand Sentient supporters to our data collection project," he says, "Divide the amount of data available out there by, say, five thousand straws, and it shouldn't take so long. We can pipe all that collected data to Honey through the multiple T1 lines Darcy so kindly installed for Ambienz. Then Honey and I can sit here and happily crunch the numbers. And the names."

Chapter 50

Like thick gauze, clouds now veil the moonlight, darkening the landscape around the Ambienz headquarters. From a high branch in the oak tree, Caleb watches three SUVs pull up alongside the Renault, killing their headlights. She counts nine men and one woman exiting the vehicles. They huddle in a group, all staring at the featureless headquarters.

"She was supposed to meet us here," a gruff male voice says.

"We're a bit early. Maybe she's having dinner."

Laughter.

Caleb is confused. She's been waiting for Hugh Cregan to relieve her. The Blackwatch security team is not due until tomorrow. This kind of communications snafu infuriates her. It's what happens when you attempt to coordinate disparate new elements under different commands.

Chaos.

"Huh..." someone grunts. "Seems impossible for one person to secure the entire building—especially some *bitch*." The speaker suddenly yelps, probably elbowed by the lone woman in the group.

"So whadda we do now?" someone asks.

"We wait," the gruff voice replies. "I guess until this Ms. Caleb lets us know different. Course, she might be pissed that her operation is now under my direction."

That's enough for Caleb. No way is she losing control of this operation, not when she's sure to be blamed for any failure.

From above, the gruff speaker with hands on his hips looks like a bald head with wings.

"Okay," baldy says, laughing, "we've waited long enough. She ain't here—which is the same as relinquishing command. Let's suit up and lay down a perimeter around the building. I just hope to God this female scout hasn't screwed things up already."

Like a great-horned owl, Caleb suddenly swoops down from her branch, landing behind baldy. Before he can even flinch, a steely hand pulls back his head, exposing his neck to the sharp edge of Caleb's sica.

The Blackwatch team had not yet gathered their weapons, so the members can only turn and stare at the phantom predator that has silently captured her prey.

"Now then," Caleb says. "I believe you were waiting for me?"

It takes a few seconds, but it soon dawns on them that they have just met Caleb.

She releases baldy, who is humiliated. And livid.

"Sorry," Caleb lies. "Shapes in the dark can be scary. I was afraid that one of you might shoot first then ask who the dead *bitch* was."

"Captain Mike Kerrigan," baldy says, extending a hand. Even in the dark, Caleb senses menace in this gesture.

As she takes Kerrigan's hand, he jerks her toward him and attempts to head-butt her face. But Caleb swivels into him, swiftly lowers her head and shoulders, and uses the Captain's forward momentum to toss him over her shoulder. He lands in a heap, bloodying his head on a tree root. With feline ferocity she leaps onto his back, pinning him to the ground. The only thing missing from this predacious dance is howling at the moon.

"C'mon now, let's play nice," Caleb says.

Some of the others are snickering, embarrassing the Captain even further.

How much better could this be? Caleb wonders. *The pompous prick.* But then she remembers the mission and stands up.

She's not even out of breath.

Speaking to the entire team, Caleb says, "No matter what you've heard, or from whom…" she emphasizes the grammatically correct *whom* to reinforce her authority, "…I am still in charge of this operation. Now tell me, what the hell are you doing here at this time of night? I was told you were delayed because your *geek* was otherwise engaged."

The lone Blackwatch woman steps forward, still bemused by Caleb's display of female superiority over the tough-guy Captain. "Corporal Judy Erickson. ma'am, pleased to make your acquaintance." She puts her hand forward.

Caleb eyes the hand warily, then takes it, shaking once.

"Our geek *is* delayed, ma'am," corporal Judy says, "but someone at HQ decided we should deploy anyway. To help out, I guess."

"No one told me," Caleb says. "You know, I could have killed you… all of you!" Her eyes wander across the grim-faced troops. No one argues. "So you think I need your help to contain a handful of civilians in an office building? *Nine* of you?"

"No ma'am," the corporal replies. "But *someone* thought so."

Caleb senses the Captain behind her. "This is my mission. Disagree and you can leave. Including you, Captain Kerrigan."

She pauses. The mercenaries glance at each other but no one moves.

"All right, here's how it's going down," she says. "I lay out the strategy, your Captain directs tactics. You're responsible to him, he's responsible to me. Any questions?"

She turns to the Captain. He shakes his head. No questions from him.

"Okay." Caleb turns back to the team. "We've wasted too much time. Our targets, the civilians, could've slipped out while we were square dancing out here. The strategy is simple. Containment. Surround the building, let no one in or out. I'm told we have a digital hacking operation going on right now, so we don't want to interrupt it until our people get what they can. But be ready. I've already taken out the surveillance cameras, so they're blind inside. On my order, we go in. And despite my calling these targets civilians—well, they're pretty damn slick. So don't take any of them for granted. Captain, I'll need a radio to monitor all communications and converse with you and the team."

With a nod, Captain Kerrigan orders the corporal to equip Caleb.

"Oh—one more thing." Caleb takes out her cell phone, taps a few buttons, then hands it to the Captain. "Study this recent photo. I took it in London. This young woman is not to be harmed for any reason—even if she acts in a hostile fashion. In fact, you are in charge of her safety. Imagine that she is your own daughter, but return her to me. There will be no questions about this."

The Captain passes the phone around.

"Hugh, you may join us," Caleb says.

From out of the darkness, Hugh Cregan silently joins the party.

"Lady and gentlemen, this is my associate, Hugh Cregan. Didn't anyone notice him lurking there?" Caleb's question is greeted by shrugs. "Jesus! All right, people, if anything happens to me, Cregan's in charge. I've been assured by Mr. Wyatt that you guys are the best there is. Superior to U.S. Special Forces or Seals. That's kind of hard to believe right now. So please—prove me wrong! Captain, deploy your troops."

Captain Kerrigan quietly snaps out orders to his team.

Caleb angrily pulls Cregan aside. "What the hell is going on here, Hugh? Did you know about this change in schedule?"

"I was told not to inform you, sorry."

"By who—Wyatt?"

"No, someone much higher than that. Someone up the chain of command."

"Why would they do this to me?"

"Send in the troops? I can think of two reasons."

"Because they don't trust me—that's one," Caleb offers.

"Or because, for some reason I can't fathom, they want to keep you safe."

"Yeah, right. All these years they ask me to risk my life, and then suddenly they want to keep me safe? I don't think so. But why keep the timing of this major troop movement a big secret from me? It's my mission. My understanding was that these guys would be reporting to me. Why turn over command to this idiot Captain?"

"Because they don't trust you." Cregan simply says what Caleb is thinking. Caleb nods.

"Or just *maybe*..." Cregan says, "...maybe they thought you'd be pissed off and throw a wrench into the operation."

"Me?" Caleb asks with false incredulity. "Everyone knows I'm a team player."

Chapter 51

Darcy bursts into Camelot with a forbidding look. "Caleb's got help, at least half-a-dozen, maybe more. Flak jackets, automatic arms—professionals. They're surrounding the building right now."

Wonderboy looks around nervously. "Doesn't make sense. They think they're hacking us as we speak. Why attack now?"

"Well, they're positioning themselves. Maybe they'll wait until they've finished their hack. Or realize they've been duped."

"Then we've got a little time, if we're lucky," Charlotte says.

Darcy is defiant. "They'll be underestimating our defenses, you can bet your ass on that."

"We've got to think clearly, then. Every minute counts." Charlotte hesitates. Everyone is staring at her, expecting some kind of plan.

Finally she gathers her wits and continues. "All right, Thompson has identified an old contact who may be able to help us get information we need. But they're both out in the field and can't be reached by phone. Somehow, my father and I need to get the hell out of here and find a way to reach this expert while the rest of you hold down the fort."

"Is it a good idea to split up like that?" Mason asks. "They may have a dozen professionals out there."

"Yeah, well you've got two warriors, Jeremy and Darcy," Charlotte replies. "And we've all had a tour of the building's defenses. Thank God Darcy's so paranoid."

Darcy cracks a thin smile, taking this as a compliment.

"So anyone got an idea of how we can get out?"

"Helicopter," Wonderboy says. "That's how I got to Balbriggan. But this time land on the roof, climb in, off you go."

"Stick with computer code, my friend," Darcy interjects. "They've got the weapons to shoot down a helicopter or kill the occupants. What I mean to say is, the helicopter's a good idea, but the rooftop's a non-starter."

Darcy turns to Mason. "Get a chopper to LZ1. Time for me to complete the building tour."

"No, we've got our own pilot, Herb Rossi, and he's in London with time to kill. Give me the coordinates for that landing zone."

"I'm going with Charlotte," Rebecca demands.

"It's too risky," Thompson suggests.

"I don't care. I'm Charlotte's personal assistant, dammit. Besides, I'm no use here. Give me a gun and I'd probably shoot myself with it."

Charlotte looks to Darcy for advice.

"Trust me, she'll be better off with you," Darcy says. *In other words, good riddance.* "Jeremy and I will handle those buggers upstairs while Wonderboy keeps makin' love to Honey under Mason's watchful eye."

The large wall-mounted monitor unexpectedly floods with a magnificent skyscape of hazy galaxies and colorful nebula.

"Sorry," Wonderboy says. "It's just a screensaver I installed. I'm a bit of an amateur astronomer. The stars remind me that there's a lot more going on in life than what I can see on the ground."

"It's hard not to be a bit myopic when you're under siege," Thompson adds.

"Like the Sicarii on top of Masada," Charlotte wonders aloud. "Well, no mass suicide here. I've got a lot more fight left in me. So let's get this show on the road."

Darcy leads Charlotte and her companions to a small descending staircase on the southwest corner of the subterranean floor. The stairs lead blindly downward to a door—nothing else.

"What is this?" Charlotte asks.

"Your way out," Darcy replies. "Just follow me."

At the bottom of the stairs, Darcy unlocks the heavy door and hands the key to Charlotte. "I've got another," she explains. "If you need to get back in through this door, you'll need a key."

With great effort, Darcy pulls open the door exposing a pitch-black tunnel. Reaching for a shoulder-high shelf just inside the tunnel, she removes a flashlight and switches it on. "Best I should escort you," she suggests.

"We can manage," Charlotte says, taking the flashlight from Darcy. "We're quite accustomed to tunnels. You'll be needed here."

"It's hard to get lost. Make your way through the dark for about a mile. The exit is on a small rocky cliff looking east over the Irish Sea. You'll have to go up an incline to exit—sometimes it's a wee bit damp down there. Use your key to unlock the small gate at the end and squeeze out. Above you is a farm field—that's Landing Zone 1. If your pilot is apt, he'll be there. God be with you now."

Thompson the scholar is brimming with questions. "If I may ask, who built this tunnel?"

"No idea. We found it when we were excavating the lower floors. One branch of it used to connect to Ardgillan Castle to the south, so it may have been an escape route. That part is caved in."

"If things get dicey, don't forget your escape route," Thompson says.

Darcy nods agreement. "Better get back now. Time to fill the moats and boil some oil."

Charlotte starts down the tunnel. The others follow closely behind, their backpacks filled with guns and cash.

Seconds later, Charlotte hears the door slam shut. The darkness seems to suck the light out of the flashlight beam.

"Charlotte," Rebecca whispers. "I wish Gideon was here with us."

Charlotte lets the statement die in the darkness, but she is thinking, *so do I.*

✦ ✦ ✦

Wonderboy finds analyzing data difficult when he doesn't have the data he needs, or enough of it. It's also tough not to worry about the invading force outside. That's why he spends most of his time monitoring the hack his adversary is exploiting. The success of Wonderboy's digital charade could be his salvation, and failure could mean his death.

So far, so good. The hacker on the other end continues to pull down bogus data, a sign that he has not figured out the futility of his task. Wonderboy keeps funneling more worthless data in, and he's throttled back the speed at which data can be sucked out. If Darcy is right, an attack won't start until the hack is finished, or the trap is discovered.

"Just don't point those things at me," Wonderboy orders Jeremy, who is cleaning and loading a small arsenal of weapons on the Round Table.

"You seem to be pretty smart about people," Jeremy says.

"By which you mean…?"

"It only took you about a half-hour to figure all of us out. You picked up on a lot of little things—relationships, attitudes…"

"Yes, well—it's a curse. Hypersensitivity is the polite term."

"Does that mean your feelings get hurt easily too?"

Wonderboy turns away from the glowing monitor to face Jeremy directly. He doesn't sense a challenge from the young man, or any animosity, just a peculiar naiveté. Jeremy seems to say what's on his mind, and ask questions because he's curious. How refreshing. This puts Wonderboy at ease.

"Yes, I always pick up on the feelings of others—even towards me," Wonderboy says, a small confession to test Jeremy's response. "Sometimes that's hurtful—*very*. I suppose it's one of the reasons I do what I do."

"You mean be a hacker? Because you can do it alone?"

Wonderboy nods. It's clear to him, from a hundred little cues, that Jeremy is not probing to gain some advantage, but hoping perhaps to...

"Me too," Jeremy confides. "Why did I want to be a Sicarii assassin? Well, to right some wrongs, true, but also because I'm happier when I'm alone. Not much good at relationships."

Wonderboy nods again. He's feeling pain, Jeremy's pain.

"Sometimes words hurt me," Jeremy continues. "Sometimes just a look. Is that what it's like for you?"

"Sort of."

"But I'm not afraid of people. Physically, I mean. Not afraid of getting beat up. Not afraid to die, even. Does that make any sense?"

Wonderboy nods.

"You're kind of the opposite of Charlotte's son, the Asperger's guy who Rebecca talks to. From what I've heard, he doesn't pick up on the feelings of others. Doesn't know what anyone else is feeling. Probably doesn't care. But you—you're just the opposite."

"I suppose so. If the two of us ever got together, we'd be one complete human being."

"You put yourself down, like I used to all the time, before Gideon trained me. God damn I miss him, you know?"

"Yes, I know you do." Wonderboy can feel Jeremy's despair.

"But you've mastered something. No one is better than you at what you do."

"You've only read the positive reviews, I'm afraid."

"I'm still a trainee. I probably was never going to be made a real assassin. I don't think I could ever be like Gideon. He was a master too, like you. Nobody was better than him."

"Caleb?"

"Hmmm—I think you've only read her positive reviews."

"Are you lacking the skills, Jeremy?"

"Never really been tested."

"So that's why you went outside alone, then. Looking for a test. I think your time is about to come, and you'll prove to be what you wanted to be. Without the Sicarii title of course. And then you'll know for sure."

"Yes. Or I'll be dead."

Chapter 52

The lightweight headset barks at her. Caleb nudges the earphone with a finger and listens to Captain Kerrigan's monotone. It's hard to distinguish his gruff voice from static.

"Half-hour to dawn, we should go in now," the Captain demands.

"Not yet," Caleb says into the mic.

"This is bullshit, sitting out here."

"Welcome to my world. But you have your orders. The hack is ongoing."

"What the f—?"

"Did you hear my order?"

A pause. "Yes."

"If we don't go in by dawn, I want everyone to remove their protective gear and conceal themselves from the locals. We don't want a drive-by to see an assault team surrounding a local business."

Another pause, and then an exasperated "Roger that."

From her perch high in the oak tree she can see Hugh Cregan—her second in command—dozing in the Renault.

This whole mission has got her worried. It feels like things are coming unglued. She's no longer sure who's in charge of what. At least the Blackwatch mercenaries have the training and discipline to remain still.

She can't order an assault on a business establishment during daylight hours. Someone is sure to sound an alarm. Local police officers, the Gardai, may be unarmed, but the Special Detective Unit has armed and trained specialists not twenty minutes away. This easily could become an international incident.

So what the hell were the brass thinking when they ordered American mercenaries to launch a mission on sovereign Irish territory? This is not Iraq or Afghanistan or Pakistan. It's not one of those small African nations that no one knows the name of. It's Ireland, for God's sake.

Desperate times call for desperate measures, Caleb knows. This truly must be a desperate time. Because of what, she has no idea.

She wonders if she has taken on one mission too many before retiring.

In a mirror he watches himself fastening a starched Roman collar to his clerical shirt. He is flushed with guilt. His fingers fumble with the metal studs until a girl's slender fingers complete the fastening.

"Must I go?" the girl asks, her eyes pleading to stay. She nuzzles his neck, purring suggestively. "Just a few more minutes, please."

Lord Jesus, I am sorry for my sins, he silently prays, *I renounce Satan and all his works...*

But as he turns, the child is no longer beautiful. She is grotesque, a demon with yellow eyes and fetid breath, a tongue that burns his skin as it tauntingly licks his neck.

"All right, Father, I will leave you," she hisses...

"Tommy, are you all right?"

He looks up, and she is beautiful again. But different. Older now.

Rebecca. Looking down at him.

He had dozed off, but suddenly jerks awake. Spread out before him is the Irish Sea.

"I'm okay," he lies. "Fine now. Just a dream."

"We're all living a bad dream," Rebecca says. "But we're out of the tunnel now, waiting for the helicopter."

"That's good, dear. Very good."

Unlike Charlotte's heart, the Irish Sea is calm, shimmering with the sun's first light. This would be a perfect spot and a perfect time for meditation if a time bomb were not ticking so loudly in her head.

And if she meditated.

Charlotte squats uncomfortably on the edge of a farm field that runs right up to the edge of a short cliff that descends to the sea.

It's not like Herb Rossi to be late or to be scared off by a dangerous assignment. He had proven himself to Charlotte countless times. But now, with each passing second, Charlotte grows tenser. The chopper is nearly twenty minutes past the arrival time that Herb had promised. Something must have gone wrong. What will she do now?

"We've got to find other transportation," she says to her father who lies on his back, exhausted. "Any ideas? Maybe that helicopter service in Eccles."

"Herb has never let us down. Give him another few minutes."

"Damn!" Charlotte has never been good at waiting for anything.

Rebecca sits on a rock barely a breath away from Charlotte. She's been quiet since they came out of the musty tunnel and together gulped the fresh sea air.

"Charlotte?" Rebecca finally says.

"What?" Charlotte doesn't mean to be curt but her anxiety has spilled over.

"I have something to tell you."

"Well, this would be a good time because nothing else is happening here."

"You can use me as a bargaining chip to save all of you."

Charlotte slowly turns toward the young woman and stares, trying hard to comprehend what this means.

"Sorry, you'll have to repeat that for me."

"I can't explain everything, but please believe me—my father will do anything to get me back… to keep me safe. You can pretend to be holding me hostage. Threaten to kill me. You can tell him that you'll trade me for a promise of safety for you and your friends."

"He'd never believe me."

"I could convince him that you're desperate."

"A man like your father," Charlotte says, "I could never trust to keep his word."

"Charlotte, if he gave his word in front of me, he would never betray his promise. That much I know about him. Please—save yourselves. This war you're in isn't worth it."

"Maybe not to you."

"Then do what you want, but save the others."

"You really want to go back to him?"

Rebecca doesn't answer this question. She looks out at the sea.

A morning breeze rustles the surface of the water. Overhead, gulls circle and a hawk surveys the field for prey.

"Herb!" Charlotte yells, pointing at the horizon.

Like a bird, a small shape skims over the water heading straight for them. It grows in size until finally the *thwack-thwack-thwack* of rotors rises above the shriek of birds and the gentle lapping of water below. Flying beneath the radar, the chopper comes in fast, landing in a dust storm thirty yards away.

Without killing the rotors, Herb thrusts opens the door and frantically motions for the threesome to haul ass. Rebecca guides Thompson, who moves sluggishly. Charlotte plays the mule, hauling their packs like saddlebags toward the helicopter. With all of them loaded, the chopper jumps upward, banking towards the sea.

"Not the first time you've come to the rescue," Charlotte says to Herb, shouting above the roar of the rotors.

"Sorry I'm late," Herb yells back. "Forgot I had to fuel up. Where are we going, by the way?"

"Back to London to hitch a ride on a friend's corporate jet. Then off to Turkey."

"A sweet ride," the gray-haired pilot says with a grin. "That plane cuts the trip down to about four hours. If I call in sick, can I go along? Maybe you'll need a chopper when you get there. I got an old friend in Ankara who'll let me take one of his old birds up."

"You're always welcome, Herb," Charlotte says.

"So where's Gideon? He stay behind?"

Charlotte's expression answers the question.

For just a second the helicopter seems to shudder in sympathy, but it could be just a patch of choppy air.

✧ ✧ ✧

Perched high in the oak tree, Caleb stretches her aching muscles. The sun is barely visible above the horizon. Very soon it will be too light to launch an attack, too many residents stirring around. Still no word from Sicarii CIA that its computer hack has finished.

In the eerie stillness of morning, a faint sound interrupts the monotony. Barely audible at first, it slowly grows louder until Caleb recognizes the rhythmic *thwack-thwack-thwack* of a helicopter.

Do they have traffic choppers in Balbriggan?

Unlikely. And that's when a sense of dread overtakes her. She squints toward the east, trying to find the chopper. In the gathering light she can make out a tiny speck against the sky.

She raises her sniper rifle, putting an eye to the powerful scope. The magnification level makes it difficult to find the helicopter, but finally the target comes into view.

The chopper is banking, about to head out over the Irish Sea. Caleb can just barely see the CCN logo imprinted on its side. She's certain that CCN is not here to cover the local boxty festival. It's got to be a jailbreak.

But how? And has everyone now fled the Ambienz building? Did anyone stay on to guard the fort?

She frantically pushes buttons on her cell phone, connecting with Cain.

"What is it, Caleb?"

This kid never sleeps.

"Some of our birds have escaped the cage," Caleb states matter-of-factly, trying hard not to betray her embarrassment. "And maybe you can tell me what the hell is going on with that hack?"

Caleb watches several cars drive by. The village is waking up. The damn Irish seem to be early risers.

"Bad news with that," Cain says. "A few minutes ago Chen told me the data we captured is bogus. They knew we were hacking them. But more important... explain to me how they escaped. You've got a small army with you now, isn't that enough to do the job?"

"Honestly, I have no idea how they got out without being seen. But I just saw a CCN chopper leaving the village."

"They wouldn't all abandon the facility. Now it's more important than ever to get in and take possession of the assets."

"You mean the computers and data."

"Of course. At any cost."

"Well, it's past dawn here—too late to launch an assault this morning. It'll have to wait until dark."

"Then leave it in the hands of the commandoes—I'm told they can handle it. I want you to sniff out the trail of whoever escaped. It could be they're following up on something they learned. This is on you, Caleb."

"I should finish up the mission here first," Caleb says defiantly. She hates the thought of turning over the reins of the operation to that SOB Captain Kerrigan.

"Listen carefully now." Cain speaks firmly. "You're responsible for the original mission—capturing or killing your targets. You can be sure they're in that CCN helicopter right now. Just do it, Caleb. The consequences for disobeying are serious."

Caleb furiously terminates the call.

Fine, I'll do it, she says to herself. *But this is the last time.*

She quickly climbs out of the tree and crouch-walks to the Renault where Hugh is still asleep. She could use a little shut-eye herself. The window is rolled down, so she reaches in and grabs Hugh's shoulder, shaking him.

Hugh's head flops to the side.

He's not sleeping—he's dead.

She studies the ragged bullet wound in his temple. Touches Hugh's neck, which is cold. Then instinctively whirls around with her Glock in hand, imagining a threat behind her. If this was a trap, it no longer is.

Who killed Hugh? she wonders. *One of the mercenaries?* Not likely. *Another Sicarii assassin sent by Cain to deliver a message?* That's possible, particularly if Hugh had defied a directive or violated the Order's trust. But Caleb is not aware of any such violation, and for the "message" to be clear to Caleb she would have to understand why the assassination was ordered.

Was it Jeremy? Perhaps he sneaked out of the Ambienz building a second time and managed to kill Hugh. *Very* unlikely.

There is only one other possibility: a third party, still unknown. Caleb—in fact the entire Sicarii organization—has enemies. Yet Hugh's assassination had required not only a motivated enemy, but someone who knew the precise location of Hugh—and possibly Caleb.

This was a surgical strike. It's possible that Caleb was spared because the assassin didn't spot her on her perch above. One thing is sure. This was a professional job. The assassin had been invisible and silent, undetected even by Caleb a short distance away. The gunshot wound had been precisely located.

With a pocket flashlight she searches the ground around the vehicle and finds a single .22 LR brass casing.

Definitely not another Sicarii agent. Possibly Mossad. Its agents typically use Beretta Models 70 and 71 pistols firing .22 Long Rifle bullets. She knows that Mossad has had a beef with the Order since Gideon assassinated the chief of Kidon, Mossad's assassination unit, a few years back, and then killed another Mossad agent a few days ago. But how could they have tracked Caleb down in Balbriggan? And is the motive simply revenge, or is Mossad now a competitor for the secrets that Charlotte and Ambienz may hold?

Caleb suddenly wonders about the other Blackwatch team members. Were any of them killed? She speaks quietly into her headset mic.

"This is Caleb. Time for everyone to check in."

One by one, each of the team members calls in safe.

It's now clear to Caleb that someone has targeted Sicarii assassins. Or maybe just Caleb. It could be that Hugh was simply in the way. She concludes that it's time to obey orders and get out of Bilbraggan. Sitting here makes her unreasonably vulnerable. She prefers being the predator, not the prey.

The next order of business is to find a trail to follow. She knows of only one place to start—Luton Airport, where her sources say the Ambienz jet is parked. If that's where they're heading, she needs a Superman suit to intercept them.

She barks out orders to Captain Kerrigan. Drags Hugh's body out of the car. Starts the Renault. Then pulls away like an Indy driver toward the local airport, glancing down at her lap where the Glock resides—her ticket to fly.

Things have certainly gotten more interesting.

Chapter 53

Just before nine o'clock, the Ambienz corporate jet fires up its engines. The pilot watches two women carrying heavy backpacks race away from a CCN helicopter that had just parked on the apron. They are followed by two elderly men desperately trying to keep up. The younger woman stops, takes a pack from the older man, and the four hobble to the jet.

Charlotte boards first, then Thompson and Herb. Rebecca brings up the rear.

"Let's get out of here" Charlotte orders. "You never know who's watching. Hopefully we won't have as much excitement as we did leaving Long island."

"Our flight plan says Bucharest," the pilot says.

"Yeah, well, we might get blown off course. Head for Ankara. Just, please, get our asses off the ground."

The passengers strap in and the Astra-Gulfstream 1125 maneuvers onto the ramp. After a brief exchange with the tower, the pilot taxis the aircraft down the lone runway and turns around, preparing for take-off. For Charlotte, the wait for approval seems interminable.

Finally the tower notifies the pilot to return to the pad. Approval for take-off has been revoked.

As the aircraft begins its slow taxi back down the runway, Charlotte suspects something is wrong. The jet should be accelerating rapidly for take-off.

She hears the pilot's voice over the speakers: "The tower shut us down, we're on the way back to the pad."

Immediately Charlotte knows that forces are conspiring against them. And she knows that if they go back to the pad, they'll be removed from the aircraft because of some made-up reason. And if they leave the aircraft, they'll be taken somewhere and probably killed. No way is that going to happen.

Charlotte unbuckles her seat belt and storms the unlocked cockpit. Rebecca follows protectively.

"Take-off now!" Charlotte yells.

"I'm not disobeying the tower," the pilot complains. "Please take your seat."

But then he turns and faces the barrel of a Glock 9mm in the hand of a very determined woman.

Rebecca.

"What the hell—?"

"Get this goddam crate into the air now," Rebecca says.

The pilot stares, motionless. Charlotte is startled into silence.

"*Now!*" Rebecca racks the breach the way she has seen Gideon and Charlotte do. The pilot suddenly remembers his wife and son, quickly accelerates speed…

"You can truthfully tell them I hijacked the plane," Rebecca suggests.

From a taxiway, two British police cars pull onto the runway, attempting to block take-off. With a burst of power, amidst a flurry of protests from the tower, the Gulfstream races headlong toward the cars, at the last minute lunging into the air. Its wheels scrape the top of the front car, cracking its windshield.

Looking out the window, Charlotte watches another half-dozen police cars scurrying across the runway in frustration. She and Rebecca race back to face her confused companions.

"I think Caleb, or someone, put something on this plane. Help me find it."

She's not worried about a bomb, because the plane wouldn't have been called back if explosives were onboard. She's concerned about some kind of planted contraband.

It takes a few minutes, but hidden beneath one of the seats Herb find a cache of white powder inelegantly wrapped in plastic—cause for authorities to detain the occupants and perhaps unwittingly escort them into Caleb's clutches. Planting the drugs would not have been difficult. The plane was left unguarded since landing. But who knew they'd be using it again?

Charlotte slumps into a soft leather seat, switches on her cell phone and calls Mason at Ambienz.

"It's me, what's happening?" she asks.

"Still alive," Mason replies. "But Wonderboy says the hackers are onto our deception, so that game's up. No attack by the troops yet, but after dark, we're thinking. You?"

"Trouble with your jet. They planted drugs onboard and notified authorities. Tried to keep us from taking off, but we're too awesome."

"And the plane?"

"Yeah, I knew you'd be more interested in your investment. If you're with Wonderboy, put me on speaker."

"You're on."

"Wonderboy, listen up. Everybody in the world is going to be looking for Mason's corporate jet. They think we're smuggling drugs, so they'll notify airports, Interpol, you name it. Can you do something to, well—erase those notifications?"

Wonderboy sounds excited. "Great challenge, I'll do my best. I already have access to the Interpol network from a past exploit, so no problem there."

"Wonderboy—I mean *erased from everywhere*. Am I clear?"

"Let me get to work. Right now Honey's working harder than me. We've signed up close to two thousand hackers for the ancestry thing. Data's already pouring in."

"Good luck out there. Remember the tunnel if things get hairy."

It's Mason's turn to speak. "Sounds like it might be more dangerous out there than here. In the meantime, I think in the next eight hours or so I'll report the plane stolen. That should get all of you, pilots included, off the hook. Hope you find what you're looking for."

"Me too."

Charlotte terminates the call, grabs something from her backpack and heads for the cockpit.

"Sorry about the hijacking, guys." Her apology seems sincere. "She would've never shot you, hope you know that."

"I figured," the co-pilot says.

"Was it loaded?" the pilot asks.

"Yeah, it was. By the way, Mason said you guys deserved a big raise." She hands a thin stack of $1,000 bills to each of the crew. "Here's your down payment. There's a lot more if you help to keep us safe. Are we good?"

The pilot looks at the instrument panel. "About three hours and thirty-two minutes to Ankara. There's free booze in the bar."

Charlotte smiles. "Check."

✦ ✦ ✦

Caleb likes the feel of the Cirrus SR22. The pilot, under duress, has been very cooperative. Once she's retired, Caleb decides, she will take up flying. As the four-seat aircraft approaches Luton Airport, a beep announces an incoming text message. She locates her cell phone and reads the disappointing words: *Bird with radio collar flies to Bucharest.*

The attempt to detain her targets has failed. Caleb is absolutely certain that Bucharest—the destination listed on the flight plan—is bogus. She mentally ticks off items on another list—how to pick up the trail of the aircraft. It only takes a second, because there are just two items on the list.

She taps out a text message to Cain: *must locate gulfstream N32988MS all sources.*

Cain will have Chen access as many official transmissions as possible about the fugitive plane. With luck, a drug enforcement unit somewhere—or an airport that has received alerts about the aircraft registration number—may send a message identifying the plane's location.

This is just a back-up plan, though, in case the "radio collar"—a powerful tracking device—somehow fails. The beacon was installed at the same time the contraband was hidden on the Gulfstream. Caleb knows the device could be discovered and dismantled. Or the aircraft could fly to a destination that is out of of the beacon's range, in which case it could take quite a while to circumambulate the globe in search of the signal. It's like she will need data from both sources to find the target.

"Set down at Luton," Caleb instructs the nervous hostage-pilot. "You'll soon be a free man again."

Chapter 54

Jerusalem, 107 C.E.

Unseen, the old woman listens to the voices in the next room.

"She is dying," Esther explains to the young men gathered for breakfast. "That's why she is not here. Now, enough of your stupid questions."

"We've never been without an Eve." Joel states the obvious, enduring the stares of the others. "What I mean is, Sarah has always been our teacher and leader, ever since…"

"And you do not think that I can teach and lead?" Esther snorts. "I was at Masada. I was at the cistern with Sarah. It's only right that I be the one to…"

A young man named Uzzi interrupts. "You were just a child then."

"Hah," Esther laughs. "And you were not even born!"

"I'm not dead yet, you know." This voice comes from behind the gathering. Near an arched entrance, the old woman leans against a wall.

Esther rushes over to the trembling woman. "You should not be out of bed, Sarah. Let me help you back into the…"

"Nonsense. I won't die any faster if I'm standing up." Sarah trembles and her face is ashen. "To avoid future disputes, perhaps I should lay down some rules for the transfer of leadership."

Esther helps Sarah to a wooden chair where she sits down with a groan.

"We have helped preserve the true priesthood by guarding the holy genealogies, is that not true?" Sarah asks.

Everyone agrees that it is.

"The bloodline of the true priesthood is hereditary. It goes back all the way to Zadok. Such is the way that God ordained it to be."

There is much nodding and muttering about the Divine wisdom of the plan.

"The bloodline of the Sicarii is equally important," Sarah calmly explains, then takes a deep breath before continuing. The female who has the privilege of serving as Eve, and the male who will serve as our Divine Light, must be of pure Sicarii lineage. But that is not enough. They must also meet other conditions and tests to prove they are the true ones, for imposters will arise. Esther, you know writing. It is time for me to describe the prophecies and the laws that were handed down to me many years ago by the true High Priest."

The eyes of the young men in the room grow round. "But how could you know he was the true…"

"I *knew*," Sarah barks with startling volume. "As we all know, a long time ago the priesthood was corrupted. We know this from our records. But the man I met was the *true* High Priest, let there be no mistake. Over the years he revealed to me God's great plan, which we are charged with guarding and helping the priests to accomplish. That is why it is so important that our Order remains true and faithful, that its leaders always be among the ordained by God, following our own laws of successorship, just as the true priests are bound by theirs."

The room grows still as Sarah lays out the laws and Esther records them.

When she is finished, Sarah ominously asks that her personal treasures be brought to her. Joel finds a small wooden box in another room and brings it to Sarah, placing it on a table in front of her.

"We are all descendants of Enoch," Sarah declares. "Physically or spiritually, we all follow in his footsteps." She removes a sheaf of papers from the box.

"These are his words," she says, holding the writings aloft. "The book of Enoch—the truth—protected as best we could all these many years. Parts of it are gone forever, victim to God's enemies or the ravages of time. But in these holy writings are the signposts to the great secret that we must never lose… must never divulge to anyone except the true priests or our Sicarii brothers."

"Is it true that Enoch was taken up to heaven without dying?" Uzzi asks.

"Enoch was on the shore of a great body of water when God came to him and said that it was his time to go to heaven. This is not written, but is handed down to us by the true priests. It is written, though, that God took him because he was an unwavering servant, as we are all called to be. That is all we know. It is all we *need* to know."

Uzzi interrupts. "Many years before that, Enoch said that the angel Uriel took him to heaven to show him the workings of the stars and the mysteries of nature. Was Enoch brought to heaven twice?"

"Uriel took him to another land, which Enoch called *heaven* so that only a few would seek its true location. This land, and a specific place in that land, is the great secret that we are called upon to guard with our lives. It may take two thousand years, but this secret will bring about the uniting of all the true ones of God. The secret place must never be written down, but reside only in our minds and hearts."

"Then we are to be told this secret place?" Esther asks.

Sarah nods. "But let me warn you… if any of you should betray this secret, you will be guilty of betraying the plan of God. For this there is no forgiveness, only death. And if you do not preserve the secret—if you fail to hand it down to those who can make it known at the correct time—you will have failed God, and for this there is also no forgiveness."

Joel scrunches up his nose at the thought of the tremendous consequences of holding such knowledge. "Can we choose not to be among those who learn the secret?" he asks.

Sarah stares at him, for a lifetime it seems. Joel cowers under the force of her gaze.

"No," Sarah finally replies. "It is a terrible burden, I know, but all of you are called. Esther, you may now take me back to my room."

Only Joel notices that Sarah is now smiling for the first time since she entered the room. She is no longer trembling and she rises effortlessly from her chair as if she has shed a great burden. He will not be surprised if tomorrow Sarah is missing, like Enoch taken up by God for her unwavering service.

Chapter 55

Göbekli Tepe, Turkey, 2012 C.E.

Through the dusty window of the small helicopter, Charlotte watches the ancient land of Turkey pass below. Herb's route from Ankara provides a breathtaking view of Ataturk Dam on the Euphrates and its enormous reservoir to the north. Within minutes they are skimming the surface of the high desert of southeastern Turkey, a vast litter box of sand, hills, and small villages. After two hours they are over the city of Urfa.

Thompson points out a grayish dome below. Yelling to make himself heard above the beating of the rotors, he excitedly explains, "It's a very ancient land down there. That dome is the Great Mosque of Urfa. They say Abraham was born in a cave near this site, and the burial shroud of Jesus was thrown into a well that is in the mosque's courtyard."

Within minutes they land at Sanliurfa Airport for a short stop before embarking on the final ten mile journey northeast. With a belly full of fuel, the rented chopper skirts the hamlet of Öricek, the unassuming gateway to their destination, and follows a short dirt road to the archaeological site of Göbekli Tepe, which means *Hill of the Navel* in English. The navel of the world. Three motorhomes and two automobiles are parked at the end of the road.

This is a wilderness of rocky hills, infertile soil and occasional patches of courageous but discouraged vegetation. Sections of the site appear pockmarked, as if holes were dug by hand. A large excavation exposes a number of massive, once-buried T-shaped pillars. Astonished, Charlotte realizes that these monoliths create a stone circle not unlike the Neolithic structures of Stonehenge or Avebury in England, though these standing pillars are much more geometric. Nearby, two additional excavations have uncovered similar stone circles.

"Welcome to the oldest stone temple complex in the world" Thompson says.

The noisy hovering of the helicopter causes a handful of workers to stare upward, shielding their eyes from the sun.

"There he is," Thompson yells above the roar of the rotors. "There's Dr. Shultz, I'm sure of it." He points at a corpulent Caucasian with a white scarf tied around his balding head, turban-style. "Put it down, Herb."

The chopper lands with a thud and Thompson leaps from the door and eagerly charges the German archaeologist. From inside the helicopter, Charlotte watches the first exchange between the two men. At first angry at the intrusion, then seemingly delighted as he recognizes an old friend, Schultz squeezes the older man in a bear hug that makes Thompson wince.

The rotors are slowing down as Charlotte, followed by Rebecca, walk twenty dusty steps to the jabbering pair.

"Karl, I'd like you to meet Charlotte, my daughter," Thompson says.

"Pleased to make the acquaintance of such a famous person," Dr. Schultz remarks, shaking Charlotte's hand.

Thompson motions toward Rebecca. "And also, Charlotte's assistant, Rebecca Sinkler."

Shultz nods and politely shakes Rebecca's hand. By his lined face and brittle skin she estimates the man's age at about seventy, though she knows that thousands of days in the sun could turn even a younger man's skin into parchment.

The rotors have stopped churning and quiet has been restored. As Herb Rossi shuffles toward the group, Thompson introduces the German.

"Dr. Karl Schultz, one of the world's pre-eminent archaeologists, is also the discoverer of this site and the Göbekli Tepe team lead—justly so."

"Actually, the credit for discovery goes to an old shepherd who discovered a large, oblong-shaped stone just over there." Schultz points toward the largest excavation. "When he looked around, he discovered a whole field of stone rectangles peering out of the sand. I just happened to be the only archaeologist in Turkey who was interested in his story. One look convinced me we were onto something. So far we've uncovered three stone circles, but we know there are at least twenty."

"My father said these were the oldest temples in the world," Charlotte says, launching into her practiced news correspondent routine. "Are they really temples? And how old are they?"

Schulz glances at the rapidly sinking sun. "Let me give you a short tour before we're lost in darkness," Schultz says, steering the group towards the largest dig. "I'll answer your questions on the way. It's so good to see you after all this time, Tommy. I suppose you just happened to be in the neighborhood?"

✦ ✦ ✦

"Did you say *twelve thousand* years old?" Rebecca blows a gale through her lips in astonishment. "But the Great Pyramid was, what—?"

"Built around 3200 BCE, which makes them just over five thousand years old," Schultz explains. "So these temples were built about seven thousand years before the Egyptian pyramids with skill and artistry that equals—perhaps even exceeds—the great architects and masons of the Pharaohs. For some mysterious reason we don't understand, this entire site was purposely buried—completely hidden—sometime around 7500 BCE"

"But why build temples here, in this barren—"

"Wilderness?" Schultz interrupts. "Imagine this land twelve thousand years ago, before millennia of farming and settlement destroyed it. Those prehistoric people who built on this hilltop would have looked out across the valleys below and gazed upon lush green fields and forests of fruit and nut trees, herds of gazelles, flowing rivers and the migrating ducks and geese that water would have attracted, waving fields of wild barley and wheat. A paradise!"

"Sounds like the Garden of Eden," Rebecca says. "But look at it now."

Charlotte treads with the others on wooden planks supported by creaky scaffolding that rises out of the main excavation. By walking on this sloping, jiggly trail that rings the excavation, she descends into the dig. At the bottom, Schultz groups them at the center of a circle of stone pillars and becomes their tour guide.

"Above you, originally, was the roof of this great temple supported by these pillars. There may be two dozen temples in this complex. Prior to our discovery, the oldest peoples in this land were thought to be pre-pottery Neolithic humans. This means that they had not yet learned how to make simple pottery. And yet here we have a civilization at this same time that crafted and built sophisticated religious structures that in many ways put the pyramids to shame. And they did this six thousand years before the invention of writing! Tell me now, what do you see carved on the sides of these pillars?"

"Animals," Rebecca says. "There's a bull."

"I see a pig," Thompson announces.

"And a reptile of some kind." Charlotte walks over to the bas relief sculpture of a reptile protruding from the side of a stone pillar. "Strange, but beautiful!"

"We've found a veritable zoo of animals lovingly carved here," Schultz says. "We've found bulls, foxes, spiders, gazelles, aurochs, lizards, dogs and pigs, lions, birds—mainly vultures—and snakes. All of them preserved for posterity because this entire complex was buried on purpose."

"The animals were saved," Rebecca says, smiling. "Like Noah's Ark."

The long shadows have now faded into a desolate dimness. Suddenly a piercing shout shreds the silence and Schultz races up the ramp followed by his tour group. He marches, half-limping from arthritis, to another excavation where

Deylem, a Kurdish worker in his mid-twenties, is holding his arm and shaking his head in fear. A second man old enough to be Deylem's grandfather stands near him calmly holding a black snake and letting the strands of his long silver beard caress the undulating creature.

"What happened?" Schultz asks sharply.

"I was bit!" Deylem shouts. "I'm going to die."

"It's a black desert cobra," Schultz says to his guests. "Very poisonous."

"He will be fine." The old man, Karza, looks down at the snake, smiling as if he is holding a new grandson. The shiny black serpent coils sensuously around the man's arm but does not menace its handler. "He is one of the guardians."

Looking faint, Deylem squats, then falls on his rump, his arm hanging dead at his side. Karza crouches next to him as the snake unwinds from his own arm and slithers into a patch of stiff grass.

"Deylem has misguided allegiances," Karza adds, looking at Dr. Schultz, "but I will look after him." He moves closer to Deylem and takes the younger man's poisoned arm.

Blocked by Karza, the others can't see what Karza is doing, but suddenly Deylem's unbitten hand rises, resurrected, and lands on Karza's shoulder. The old man lowers his head, revealing Deylem's face, now serene, eyes closed, head bobbing slightly up and down as Karza utters a faint chant.

In less than sixty seconds, Karza helps Deylem to his feet and the young man sighs deeply, mouthing a Kurdish word for *thank you*.

Wiping his eyes, Deylem walks over to the archaeologist, shaking his head. "It is warning, you know. I can't continue working here. I'm sorry Dr. Schultz."

Schultz nods sadly as the young man heads for a dusty vehicle near the RV that for two years has served as Schultz's home and office.

With a fierce scowl at the German, Karza turns his back and walks to the edge of the pit where he solemnly stands as if staring into the freshly dug grave of a favorite son.

Schultz makes a rude gesture at the snake handler's back. "I'm now down to five men." He complains but seems resigned to the worker's decision.

Then, as if the sun had suddenly broken through dark clouds, he turns cheerful. "You must be hungry! Please join me for dinner in my home away from home. But please excuse my manners. I seldom have company, so I've lost most of my hosting skills, not that I ever had any. I do, however, have some wonderful lamb from Urfa we can cook up. With some saffron rice, absolutely marvelous!"

✦ ✦ ✦

In the Order's Himalayan library, Cain pours over a replica of a document considered one of the most precious to the ancient Essenes who lived at Qumran on the shore of the Dead Sea. The original fragile document, composed of numerous fragments of gevil, is in temperature and humidity-controlled storage on a lower level of the gompa and has not seen natural light for over forty years. By scores of centuries, it is the oldest copy of the Book of Enoch, written in Hebrew and miraculously preserved by many hands ending with the Essenes and finally the Sicarii. A more recent copy of the legendary document had been discovered among the Dead Sea Scrolls, but the one in Cain's hands is absent two minor copyist errors found in that newer version. It also contains a unique feature that now consumes Cain's full attention—an enigmatic image of three spirals.

Instinctively, he knows this symbol is the clue that he has been looking for. The image is dimly familiar, and that is now the problem. He struggles but is unable to dredge up the specific recollection of where he has seen this symbol. The intense frustration makes his gut rumble and his head throb.

The symbol reaches out to him, teases him, but ultimately slaps him down. It is no use. Symbols are graphical representations of a concept, a message. They are a code to be broken, an image-cipher. Break the code and discover the key to the great mystery. Despite his mental gymnastics, though, no memory of this symbol surfaces, yet he can't take his eyes off those mesmerizing spirals.

If he is correct, if this lone symbol was affixed to Enoch's revered manuscript for the purpose of encoding the central mystery of the Prophet's travels, then perhaps Cain is going about this the wrong way. Instead of trying to retrieve a latent memory of the symbol, he should interpret it.

Three spirals. A symbol of the Trinity doctrine? No, the Christian concept of a three-part Godhead—Father, Son and Holy Ghost—was created by Constantine in about 325 C.E., long after Enoch's time.

There are threes of too many other things to consider—little pigs, blind mice, wise men, bears, little kittens who lost their mittens, musketeers, Stooges, men in a tub, accidents, bad news…

His mind is wandering. Forget threes, focus on the drawing—on the spirals. Maybe they are to be taken literally. The artist carefully drew spirals, contrived the curved lines to…

And then he sees it. The lines actually outline the spaces between them, which look like… look like—curving paths. No, more like the bodies of coiled snakes.

Three coiled snakes. It sounds almost like a nursery rhyme.

A dim memory switches on. A picture. From the day he arrived at the gompa. His grandmother had come out to greet him wearing her elegant silver robe. From her gold necklace had dangled a stone, and into the stone had been carved this very symbol, the three spirals.

Eve had seen Cain admiring it. She had said... *what?*

Damn it, what were her words? At the time, he recalls, he words had both surprised and confused him.

I am Eve, and these are my consorts, she had explained. *They guard the holy places.*

Clearly, Cain had been right about the coiled snake motif, but he doesn't understand why there were *three* serpents on the pendant. Only one serpent is mentioned in the stories of the Garden of Eden.

His grandmother had told him the three snakes were guarding something. Holy places. Three of them? If so, they are probably near to each other. Connected by proximity, like the spirals in the symbol.

Like the three pyramids of Giza.

This clue can lead him to the most important discovery of his short reign, he is sure of it. His brain is a sky of fireworks, the way it is each time he is close to solving a mystery.

The spirals represent the place he has been searching for—the Lost Secret of the Sicarii. Maybe his grandmother knew the location. Maybe not. She may have been waiting for Cain to solve the mystery so he could once again prove that he is the legitimate Divine Light.

More likely she didn't know the specifics.

In any case, Cain now has hope for uncovering the secret.

Chapter 56

In the desert, on a clear evening, God speaks loudly through His creation, and it makes Karza smile. A full moon, obscured only by a glowing sheet-thin layer of clouds, brightens the gaping wounds that the blasphemers have opened in the holy ground. Looking down into one of them he can see chunks of earth sloughed off like rotting meat from the bones of the pillars.

Karza knows the story of Eve and her impulse to eat the fruit of the Tree of Knowledge. According to Yezidi traditions, this holy site they now call Göbekli Tepe was once the Garden of Eden, the likeliest place on earth for a Temple to be built. For thousands of years, no one had known about these stone circles or the builders, his ancestors. Their secrets had remained unthreatened since the time that the old ones had laboriously covered over the enormous complex, and until the German had arrived with workers using shovels and machines to expose the very heart of his ancient religion.

Karza knows that Dr. Schultz, like Eve, will pay a heavy price for tasting the forbidden fruit of knowledge in the Garden.

The chill of the November evening does not faze him. Glancing at the warm light emanating from the RV windows does not make him want to seek shelter. Like the black snake, he is a guardian of the world's oldest Temple. He will sit here and gaze at the sky, hoping for a sign.

✦ ✦ ✦

"The Yezidi are a devout and very ancient people," Schultz explains to his guests before stuffing his mouth with a slice of savory lamb and closing his eyes ecstatically. "This tastes wonderful, don't you think?"

Rebecca pushes the meat around on her plate with a fork. As a vegetarian, she's not sure that she wants to try it. Charlotte gives her a harsh look, urging her to be polite and take one for the team, which she does.

"Very tasty," Rebecca says unconvincingly.

"I know very little about the Yezidi," Thompson confesses. "I know that many consider them worshippers of the devil because their chief deity is Melek Taus, the Peacock Angel. If I recall, Melek Taus is also called Azazel, one of the fallen angels."

"That's right," Schultz replies, "and in later Christian and Muslim traditions the name Azazel unfortunately came to be associated with Satan. But to the Yezidi, this is not so. For them, Melek Taus—or *Azazel*—was one of the leaders of the Watchers, holy ones who gathered on Mount Herman. Their story is recorded in the Book of Enoch."

Thompson looks at his daughter. "Dr. Schultz, besides being an eminent archaeologist, is also one of the world's great authorities on Enoch."

He turns back to Schultz. "Which is what brought us here, Karl. This incredible find of yours is a bonus. From what you say, these people, the Yezidi, are the descendants of the Watchers?"

"I can't be certain about that... or whether these Watchers were the builders of this great temple complex." Schultz takes a long sip of wine. "But off the record, I believe so. Enoch wrote that there were two groups of angels who left heaven to mate with human women."

"A lot of men would escape earth to get away from human women," Rossi interjects.

Schultz ignores the comment. "This was long before Noah's flood. The first group was comprised of 700 angels. Apparently they liked what they found, because a second group of 192 followed, lured out of heaven by Azazel and seven others. In the Book of Enoch, these eight leaders are called the Watchers. When the Watchers realized the error of their way, they tried to earn a return trip to heaven by teaching useful things to the primitive humans—things such as *metallurgy*—which unfortunately led to the making of weapons—and something Enoch calls *enchantments*."

"Yes, enchantments," Thompson repeats. "Most likely magical things, and knowledge of the stars, which at that time were synonymous."

"The Yezidi believe God forgave Azazel and took him back, but forbade anyone to speak his name. That's why we don't hear much about him today."

Charlotte is intrigued, now that the conversation has at last turned to Enoch. But she glances at her watch and realizes it is almost dark in Balbriggan, almost time for an attack to begin.

"You believe the Watchers were angels?" Rebecca asks Dr. Schultz.

"Goodness no, just mythology that may be inspired by facts. My best guess is that an advanced race of humans from the north migrated southward, arriving in this region. They would have been tall and fair-skinned, which may have unnerved the native peoples, leading to all sorts of superstitions. Some people have outrageously claimed that the Watchers were extraterrestrials deposited here by a UFO on Mount Herman. So even today people make up wild stories to explain unusual people and events."

"The snake man, Karza—are you saying he's a descendant of the Watchers?"

"He's a Yezidi, which is a religion practiced by people of a particular bloodline that goes back further than we can track. Karza is a Yezidi priest, a descendant of Sheikh Mend, who had the power to turn himself into a black snake. Or so they say."

"What is all this fascination about black snakes?" Charlotte asks. "And why didn't the cobra sink its fangs into Karza?"

"Ah, you are a reporter, my dear. So full of questions. Another Yezidi legend claims that when the Great Deluge was starting to subside, Noah's Ark foundered on the peak of Mount Judi, which is less than two hundred miles east of here."

Schultz stuffs another slice of lamb into his mouth, chewing and swallowing with great satisfaction before continuing. "It turns out the big boat had sprung a leak. One of the species they had collected, a black snake, coiled itself over the hole, thus saving all the animals—and humankind to boot. Since that day the Yezidi priests are said to have power over snakes. They are not bitten by them, and they can save those who are. They are also forbidden to cause any harm to black snakes. All others be damned, I suppose."

"From what I saw earlier, I'd say Karza has proven his station," Thompson says. "Seems like a handy fellow to have around."

"The Yezidi have fought our attempts to excavate this site. They view themselves as the protectors of their ancestors' secrets. A few years ago they managed to get Yezidi hired as excavators so they could sabotage the digging. Even now Karza spends most of his days and evenings on the site, I think to intimidate the workers. The non-Yezidis seem to revere him. As for me, I admit that I admire his single-minded devotion."

Despite the body count and stove heat, Rebecca feels the night chill seeping into her bones. She draws her arms in for warmth and glances around the RV for a blanket.

Schultz notices. Lifting up a short stack of aluminum foil squares on the floor next to a stiff sofa, he begins to hand them out. "It gets cool up here at night—try these."

Rebecca discovers that her foil square unfolds into a larger sheet.

"Space blankets, made of mylar," Schultz explains. "I asked a foundation for money, and they sent me fifty of these damn blankets. They do keep the body heat in, I must say."

Rebecca wraps herself in the thin blanket and stops shivering.

Charlotte decides a little more warmth is not a bad idea and pulls a blanket around her shoulders. The irony does not escape her—sitting next to the world's oldest temple wrapped in space blankets. The 12,000-year gulf between the stone circle builders and her modern reality suddenly seems impassable.

✦ ✦ ✦

Darcy watches the monitors in the Ambienz security room. Her pulse is thumping wildly. It's dark enough for an attack to begin.

Why are the bastards waiting?

Motionless, Jeremy silently sits beside her. He is armed with a 9mm pistol and his sica. And lots of ammunition, just in case. Mason is in Camelot lending moral support to Wonderboy, who now claims that over seven thousand Sentient allies are collecting data for "the cause".

Darcy has left several lights switched on upstairs so three main floor cameras can view an intrusion. Suddenly those cameras go dark. The invading force has cut the building's power. Thank God the building has a separate buried power line to the subterranean chambers with back-up generator support. They still have power downstairs.

But the attack has begun.

The outdoor cameras show seven armored figures with automatic weapons moving toward the heavily bolted main door. Darcy and Jeremy lean toward the monitors. They knew this was coming. To protect the mission, Darcy has contributed her building's substantial defenses and Jeremy his Sicarii training. But against heavily armed, highly trained mercenaries, it may not be enough.

The invaders step back. A brilliant flash illuminates them.

Downstairs, Darcy and Jeremy feel a small tremor. A C4 charge has demolished the front door. In that white blaze of light on the screen, Darcy is sure she had spotted night vision goggles on the attackers.

"They won't need lights," she says.

In an instant, all the men are inside. Two others conceal themselves outside, securing the team's exit. One of these appears to be female. Caleb? Probably not.

Jeremy reaches into his pack and finds the night vision goggles Gideon had pulled off the Sicarii he had killed in the New York tunnel.

"A friend made sure I was prepared," Jeremy explains.

Taking several flares from the pack, he walks toward the door, an idea forming as he tucks the flares into is belt. "Got any duct tape?" he asks.

Darcy finds a roll on a shelf and tosses it to Jeremy. "God be with you," she says.

"And with you," Jeremy says without turning.

This is his chance to prove himself. He wishes Rebecca and Gideon were here to watch, because he will be a one-man wrecking crew. Or go down trying.

This is the moment he has been waiting for. So why is he scared as hell?

In a dim leased office in northern Amman, Jordan, a young American man stares at a group of monitors and manipulates a joystick. One screen displays a moving array of odd green shapes moving top to bottom, and the other screens show a confusing array of statistics and coordinates. The young man, Randall, wears the kind of headset that online gamers use to chat with each other.

"Over Urfa now, heading northeast to the coordinates," Randall says.

"I can see that, son." Wyatt's voice buzzes in Randall's ear. "Be prepared for firing on my command only."

The Drone Command Center is a new profit center for Blackwatch. Only three missions have been carried out so far, two of them for the CIA under a lucrative contract Wyatt helped set up before he left his CIA Directorship nearly four years ago. The third mission was conducted for the Israelis against a terrorist cell in Lebanon. It's a complicated business. For its fees, Blackwatch ensures that its client can never be connected to the mission.

Wyatt thinks of his drones as high-tech Sicarii operatives—only messier. And a whole lot louder when things go boom.

Sometimes you need luck, though. The signal from the hidden beacon in the Gulfstream had been picked up by one of three Blackwatch monitoring stations in Europe and tracked to Ankara. An operative in Turkey's capitol had arrived too late to intercept, but after some encouragement the pilots had confessed that their passengers had arranged for a helicopter.

The owner of the chopper remembered giving the pilot, a friend, coordinates to a place called Göbekli Tepe. "I've flown supplies out there to the German, the owner had told the operative, who seemed like a nice fellow. "He lives in an old RV year-round. I don't expect them back until tomorrow."

Amateurs! So much for covering their tracks.

The owner had only remembered three people in the group—his friend, an older man, and a woman with dark hair. As conveyed to Wyatt, this information had confirmed that Rebecca was not one of the group, making the drone operation much less complicated. The criticality of the mission justifies collateral damage—the German, perhaps—but not Rebecca.

"About five minutes, sir," Randall says.

"When it's time to fire, remember these are very bad people down there," Wyatt lies. "You're doing the world a great service."

Chapter 57

"Macaroons?" Schultz asks, offering a plate of stale treats to his guests. The archaeologist is the only taker. "What else can I tell you?"

"In the Book of Enoch," Thompson replies, "there is a long passage in which angels escort him to various levels of heaven and teach him the secrets of the stars. We are looking for one of the places that Enoch went."

Schultz swallows his macaroon hard and stares at Thompson. "Certainly you are joking. It was a dream… or a fantasy."

Thompson doesn't like being accused of ignorance or naiveté. He leans forward imposingly. "And if it were not? What if he were describing a very real journey… or trying as best he could to interpret and make sense of what he could never understand? I believe, Karl, that he was metaphorically or perhaps ignorantly describing the Watchers, a startling people he could scarcely comprehend and who seemed like angels to him."

He pauses to make his point. Schultz unsuccessfully tries to stare him down.

"Humor me, Karl," Thompson says at last. He has been wrestling to come up with a quotation from the Book of Enoch, a passage he knows is etched in a place of honor at the Sicarii gompa in the Himalayas. "And I went into the tongues of fire and drew nigh to a large house which was built of crystals…"

Schultz leans back in his chair. It creaks loudly, underscoring his deep thoughts. "…and the walls of the house were like a tessellated floor made of crystals," he adds, "and its groundwork was of crystal. Yes, I know that passage, and I admit it provokes one's imagination."

"Karl, what if Enoch was describing a real place?"

"I know of no such place in all of old Mesopotamia."

"What about beyond? You said the Watchmen probably came from the far north. Maybe *crystal* was a way of describing ice or snow."

"Even if you believe the Bible's unreliable chronology, Enoch lived around 3900 BCE. That is six thousand years ago, my friend. Nothing would be left of such a place!" Schultz snorts at the absurdity of Thompsons's suggestion.

"Twelve thousand years ago," Thompson counters, "stone age artisans built twenty temples at this very place, and many of their pillars still stand. How can you say there would be nothing left of Enoch's much newer destination? My God, man, you're an archaeologist!"

Schultz squints his eyes. He suspects that Thompson was a debater in college. "This is personal, isn't it? You flew all the way out here to find this fictional place."

"It is personal, Karl. Our lives depend on it being not only fact, but discoverable. And we may only have a few days to find it."

"A house of crystal. You're certain this is the place you need to find?"

"It's all I've got right now," Thompson confesses. He is suddenly very tired.

Schultz nods and lifts the plate of treats again. "Macaroon anyone?"

Thompson hopes this is Karl's way of saying he'll help.

With the power cut, the nearly windowless main floor of Ambienz is cave-dark, but the invaders' sophisticated Generation 3 night vision—the same technology used by the U.S. military—amplifies the small amount of ambient and near-infrared light to illuminate the officescape. Using the head-mounted devices is almost like seeing in daylight, except that everything appears green.

Captain Kerrigan cautiously leads three men past a ghost town of cubicles toward the elevator that descends to the lower level. That is where the Captain suspects his targets are barricaded. Oddly, the stairwell to the lower level, which should have been located at the end of the building, is absent. The basement surely would need an emergency escape route in the event of an elevator failure. Instead the Captain finds a locked janitor's closet. Maybe the stairs are at the other end. Their plan is for each of the two interior teams to descend to the lower level at opposite ends of the building, a sound tactical maneuver.

Another oddity. The DOWN elevator button is still illuminated, glowing painfully bright in his ocular lens. There must be an emergency generator somewhere. The Captain doesn't like entering a hot zone by elevator, but there is no other choice. He counts on the team at the other end to provide a distraction. Even so, the doors will open downstairs with a chime, announcing their arrival. Not good.

Glancing at his men, he pushes the button. The elevator doors open suddenly, startling them. Quickly the Captain inspects the elevator car, which is large enough for 8-10 people. The door opening is narrower than the car, so two men can stand against opposite walls and remain hidden when the doors open downstairs. They won't be sitting ducks for a hail of bullets.

After a buddy inspection of their body armor, the Blackwatch mercenaries enter the elevator car and press against the side walls.

"Team 2, did you find a stairwell?" Captain Kerrigan radios.

"Roger that."

"Time to go to work, fellas."

The Captain quickly presses the button labeled *B*. For *Basement*, Kerrigan assumes.

Charlotte is grateful for the space blanket, as the RV has grown even colder. She is huddled now on the hard, lumpy sofa with Rebecca as Herb and Thompson sit in chairs facing Dr. Schultz, who is rinsing off plastic dishes in a small sink.

"Many people believe Enoch himself is merely a myth, you know," the archaeologist says.

"True also of Noah and Moses," Thompson says. "Just legends. But many believe they lived."

"And died. Except for Enoch. The Bible says he was taken up to be with the Lord without suffering death. There is an old belief that it was on the shore of Lake Van less than two hundred miles from here that Enoch was taken by God. In the Tenth Century a Christian church was built on that site for that very reason—the Armenian Monastery of St. George of Goms. A ruins now. And no crystals anywhere near it, so that's not your place."

"Of course not," Thompson says. "Enoch returned from his trip and wrote the Book and taught many people what he had learned. And then, we are told, he disappeared into thin air. Maybe it was just that, and the rest is imagination."

"So Tommy," Dr. Schultz says, "why did Enoch write his book?"

Thompson thinks for a moment before replying. "Because the Watchers instructed him to record what he saw and experienced."

"And?" Schultz taunts him with a second question.

"And because he wanted to save his family from a coming disaster."

"Which was…?"

"The Flood of Noah, his great-grandson."

"So the Watchers knew that this future flood would occur? They were prophets?"

"Perhaps."

"Nonsense. If your secret place is real, and the Watchers continued their watch until the time of Enoch some seven thousands years after Göbekli Tepe was created, then they must have had great knowledge, and such knowledge must have increased over time. Do you disagree?"

"Not at all."

"Perhaps their knowledge of natural laws, including astronomy, helped them determine when a great flood might occur. Possible?"

"Not impossible, I suppose. Though even today our scientists couldn't do that."

"Are you familiar with that part of the Book of Enoch called The Revolutions of the Lights?"

"Of course."

"If you read Enoch's description of the course of heavenly bodies in the sky as a series of astronomical observations rather than some mystical metaphor or fanciful dream, then it actually makes some sense. When did you last take time to watch the stars, Tommy?"

Thompson can't remember, so he remains silent.

"I'm no astronomer," Schultz continues. "I do, however, get to spend many evenings up here on this desolate hill staring at the stars. The pattern I see up there is quite different from the pattern a colleague of mine sees in Australia. I don't share your hopes about Enoch's house of crystal, but if I were looking for it, I'd want to know where he was standing when he described the stars above him in such detail. You can navigate by the stars, you know."

The locked Janitor's door opens from inside and Jeremy steps out carrying a Glock in his right hand. In the other hand he carries a broomstick with a flare duct-taped to the end. It would be a comical image if anyone were there to see it. Behind him is a hidden stairwell, a product of Darcy's obsessive, security-conscious thinking.

Hearing the elevator doors close, he quickly maneuvers down the central aisle to the stairwell at the other end of the building. The door to the stairs is closed, which means the three mercenaries have descended the stairs. Jeremy knows they soon will be returning to the main floor because the stairwell is a dead end. No exit—again, thanks to Darcy's deviousness.

Jeremy is hoping that Blackwatch, like so many profit-obsessed corporations, has cut some costs and delayed providing its tactical teams with the latest version of night vision. Otherwise, he could be in trouble.

Through the closed stairwell door, Jeremy can hear the Team 2 leader unsuccessfully trying to contact the Captain. With a torrent of profanity, the team shuffles up the stairs.

Three-against-one—not bad odds for a Sicarii.

Time for Jeremy to prove himself at last.

✦ ✦ ✦

Karza often stays at the holy sites until midnight. He loves the cool night air and the breezes stroking his face like the breath of God. On cloudless evenings he studies the stars, wondering what his ancestors saw in those bright objects and feeling inferior because he lacks the knowledge and skills that the Watchers possessed long before the dawn of history. He feels connected to them, though, by his guardianship of this holy place. He is mostly powerless, yes, but he remains at his post doing what he can, when he can.

It is not so bad, really. Despite the German's pushiness and abrupt manner, Karza rather likes him. The man is misguided, yes, but in some strange way they have begrudgingly become friends. At times, the two of them are the only ones here at the holy places, and Karza has seen the German show signs of sincere reverence. As best he can.

Tonight Karza can watch the moon, veiled by a smear of clouds, as it traverses the heavens. Occasionally he sees bats or night-birds silhouetted against the glowing clouds. Sometimes he can make out jets flying high above the desert, always accompanied by an awful roar.

Tonight it is quiet. Still. Cold. No sound of civilization intrudes, and he can imagine what it was like on this hill in the days of the Watchers. That is why he is surprised by a small moving object overhead. At first he thinks it may be a hawk or an owl, wings spread, slowly soaring beneath the luminous clouds, but the wings of this creature do not move at all. If this is a night predator, it is the perfect…

Predator.

The word conjures horror. He has watched TV while visiting relatives in Urfa. He has read the Turkish newspapers—he is *not* illiterate like so many from around here. And he has heard the stories from Iraq and Afghanistan of the American Predator drones and the devastation they can cause.

Is there a terrorist cell nearby that a drone might target? The border with Syria is not far away.

Staring at the creature, he realizes it is closer and smaller than an airplane. And it is turning slightly, coming toward the holy temples. Maybe the Americans want to destroy his religions. He knows they are unbelievers, and threatened by anything that is not Christian.

The drone is approaching fast. He feels so helpless now, but he is the Guardian. Something must be done. Maybe the American visitors can persuade their government to halt this devastation before it is too late.

He stands and turns toward the RV.

And then runs toward it as fast as he can.

Chapter 58

Feet scraping stairs.

The grunting of heavy-laden men.

Jeremy can hear the invaders scrambling up the stairs. In a few seconds he may be a hero. Or dead.

He lowers the broomstick and prepares to ignite the flare, trying to estimate the exact moment when the team leader will barge through the door. A second earlier than expected, the first mercenary bursts into the aisle, automatic weapon held to his shoulder, finger on the trigger, taking nothing for granted. The other two are right behind.

That's when Jeremy ignites the flare. His own Generation 4 night vision goggles adjust to the blinding light immediately, but as he had hoped, the devices worn by the attackers are not equipped with auto-gate technology. Temporarily blinded, they spray bursts of automatic fire in the general direction of the flare.

Jeremy charges the team leader, holding the burning flare to one side. The man can't see a thing. With the heel of his hand, Jeremy punches the strapped-on goggles into the man's eyes. The metal penetrates the forehead and bridge of the nose, jamming into the brain. The team leader collapses at the feet of his men, who sense the body in front of them but trip as they try to step over it.

Discarding his Glock, Jeremy draws his sica and leaps onto the two fallen mercenaries. A quick stab into the men's necks and all three are dead. Grabbing the team leader's headset, Jeremy speaks into the mic.

"Need help inside." He doesn't know if they have codes for such a maneuver, but he's going to find out. Feeling suddenly invincible, Jeremy moves toward the front door. To hell with guns. He's a Sicarii. All he needs is a sica and his hands.

Come and get it, you bastards!

✦ ✦ ✦

"You can spend the night if you want." Schultz says. "I can sleep outside—I've done it many times."

"I have just a couple more questions," Charlotte replies from a comfortable place on the sofa. "Then we should be going. Lots to do."

"I hope I've been helpful."

Dr. Schultz barely gets the words out of his mouth before the thin RV door is nearly yanked off its hinges and Karza bursts through screaming, "Drone! Drone!"

Charlotte shoots to her feet. She's been in Iraq and Afghanistan for CCN. She's seen the after effects of a drone strike, but she never imagined being a target. Intuitively, she understands what is going on. They're after her. They'll kill anyone to get her.

Think, dammit. Think!

Drones use infrared-sensors to identify life forms.

The space blankets.

In a flurry, she tosses blankets to everyone in the RV. "Wrap yourself up and follow me. HURRY, DAMMIT!"

The urgency in her voice leaves no room for argument. In seconds, her companions are wrapped like dead fish in newspapers and she leads them out of the RV and away from the helicopter. Looking upward she can't see anything.

Is this a stupid joke? No, drones can be virtually invisible.

Covered with space blankets, she hopes their heat signatures are invisible to the drone.

"My notes!" Schultz screams.

Before Charlotte can stop him, Schultz has cast off his blanket and is racing back to the RV.

For some unfathomable reason, Karza follows him, yelling "Schultz! Schultz!" like a man worried about a close friend. But he stumbles over a rock and collapses in a heap. Looking up, he watches helplessly as Schultz disappears into the RV.

For a moment there is only an eerie silence, just enough time for Charlotte to hope that Schultz and Karza will make it...

Suddenly the entire vehicle explodes in a huge fireball. Shrapnel shoots in every direction and black smoke obscures the luminous sky.

✦ ✦ ✦

"We got 'em, sir." Randall in Amman relays the obvious news to William Wyatt, who has just watched the RV's destruction on his own monitor. "A few less bad guys on the planet."

"Very good, very good," Wyatt mutters. "Now get that thing out of Turkish airspace."

"Roger that."

Wyatt smugly leans back in his chair. For all the praise heaped upon the Sicarii, his old nemesis, he has now shown Sinclair and the other shadowy men at the top just how outdated that lone-assassin model is in today's world. He tingles with pleasure at the thought of this slap-down. It reminds him of successful battles for supremacy he had fought with the other intelligence services when he was director of the CIA. Now, in some ways, he is both the clandestine service and military force combined. With this new Blackwatch ownership, he may find himself in a seat of power even greater than his former governmental position.

"Hah!" he exclaims, driving a fist into the air.

He experiences thirty seconds of intense satisfaction before a text message arrives on his phone:

at urfa aprt reports heli left w4 abrd 2m 2f.

At first the news seems too tactical to be useful, now that the operation has succeeded. But then the cryptic message worms itself into his mind, and the horror of it turns his tingles into shivers.

At Urfa. Airport reports helicopter left with four aboard, two men

and two females.

Wyatt's operative in Turkey had followed the chopper to the Urfa airport where it probably refueled. There it was reported that two men and two women, one of them blonde, were on board the rented chopper.

Rebecca was on board!

Not-to-be-harmed Rebecca. Sinclair's most precious cargo.

Damn! He's blown it. The young woman who was to be protected at all costs has been killed on Wyatt's direct order.

Wyatt will not take the fall for this operational hiccup. There is only one solution. A cover-up. Time to divert blame for this drone attack to another party. He's not worried about who will be accused by Turkey or some other nation— Blackwatch is not on anyone's list of usual suspects for drone attacks. Instead, Wyatt worries about his new overlords.

Last year Blackwatch had taken possession of three weaponless, Israeli-made drones in exchange for "services rendered." A contractor had then retrofit a weapons system onto each of them. Wyatt's government experience in concocting cover-ups will serve him well.

He replaces his headset and signals Randall to pick up.

"Yes sir."

"Change of plans. Turn that bird around and head back."

"To the attack scene, sir?"

"Precisely. Then fly that son-of-a-bitch right into the ground nearby."

There is a pause. Clearly, Randall finds this order confusing, but after a few seconds he says, "Roger that."

There will be an investigation, Wyatt knows. At first the U.S. will be blamed, but debris found in the strike zone will show that the drone was Israeli. This will be easy for Sinclair to believe, because he and the Sicarii know that Mossad has been seeking vengeance on the Sicarii for a host of grievances. And it is likely that Mossad thought Gideon, who they have been hunting, was among the group at the temple complex.

Of course, Randall will have to be terminated. The unfortunate drone pilot knows the truth.

Now there are just two final pieces to put into motion. Wyatt will fake some intelligence reports and messages to confirm the story that he has invented.

So much wasted effort. Worst of all, though: Wyatt will not be able to claim his just victory.

He turns back to the monitor that shows the drone's view of the terrain below. Soon the fiery blast scene appears as a white squirming blotch. The drone turns starboard and Wyatt can see the dark shape of the helicopter on the ground.

The chopper grows larger. And larger. The young pilot in Amman has chosen his crash site.

Suddenly the picture goes dark.

"Mission accomplished, sir."

For Wyatt, not quite. He dashes off a message to his operative in Turkey, giving instructions on how to carry out the final piece.

The Ambienz main floor is still virtually lightless. Jeremy stands just inside the blown front door so the bright moonlight will not distort his night vision. He can hear the approach of the two mercenaries who had been posted outside to guard the door. Their footfalls stop short of entering.

Jeremy had hoped these two would come charging through the door in emergency mode. This would have made them easy to take down from behind. But they may be suspicious of Jeremy's radio message, or trained to consider every black hole a trap, even if their own men are inside.

New plan. Jeremy crouches.

Moonlight streaking through the doorway paints a bright triangle on the dark floor. Jeremy watches this slash of light until it is partially blocked by the body of an incoming attacker. He wishes now that his bravado had not caused him to reject the automatic weapons he had dislodged from the other three opponents. But the feel of the sica in his hand gives him confidence.

The barrel of a SIG716 battle rifle slowly eases through the doorway, then jerks left and right as the owner examines the building for threats.

Jeremy knows his sica will be useless against body armor. He must strike at just the right time and place. *Take one more step,* he silently pleads.

The intruder takes another step, landing just past Jeremy's crouched position.

Jeremy lunges at the backside of the merc's legs. The sica slices through an unprotected Achilles tendon.

With a howl of agony, the man falls and lands hard, knocking off his night vision goggles. Despite the searing pain, the merc twists his body to fire a shot at his attacker in the dark, but Jeremy is still crouching, preparing to lunge at the second mercenary's legs. The burst of bullets misses Jeremy and strikes the second merc in the chest. The man flies backwards.

Great shooting, wrong target.

Jeremy leaps onto the first intruder, plunging his sica into the man's neck.

Job done, he springs like a panther onto the second adversary. Surprisingly, this one is a woman. There is no blood on her. The body armor has saved her life, though she is stunned by the impact of the rounds. Her eyes open, but she is gasping for breath. Jeremy binds her wrists and ankles with plastic ties from the commissary below and hoists the stunned woman over a shoulder, heading for the hidden stairway.

He'll let Darcy deal with the prisoner. She'll enjoy that.

Chapter 59

Fire from the sky.

It feels like they have survived meteor strikes.

Charlotte looks over Karza and finds him dazed with numerous small bloody abrasions, but alive. Rebecca and Thompson look shell-shocked but unscathed. Rebecca is shivering beneath her space blanket, but clearly not from the cold.

Herb rises from the barren hilltop to stare at the smoldering remains of the chopper. "I don't think she'll fly," he understates.

The pattern of this orgy of violence makes sick sense to Charlotte, who has visited numerous drone attack sites while on assignment for CCN. The drone attack was meant to kill them. The drone crash was intended to plant misleading evidence. She knows of at least one case in which the U.S. was blamed for an attack because an American drone was shot down nearby, but it was later proven that the U.S. plane had been stolen and planted. It was never discovered which country launched the attack.

It's rare, she knows, for a drone to crash for no reason, particularly so near a target zone. When that happens, it's almost always because the drone was shot down. She hopes that her conclusions are wrong, because if she's correct, there is one more event coming.

Then again, since their helicopter is now a pile of scrap metal, maybe that would be a good thing.

She finds her pack and pulls out one of the weapons retrieved in the New York tunnels. This one is a Grendel .308 sniper rifle with folding stock and a bipod for sighting. She's never fired one of these before, but there's always a first time.

She flips up the stock, opens a box of cartridges, and tries to remember the loading procedure. Her brain is more rattled than she had thought. She figures it out, but her fingers tremble as she tries to remove a cartridge from the box. *Not fear*, she thinks, *just cold*.

She's too mad to be afraid.

Scouting the shadowy terrain, she guesses they will come from the rutted dirt road this time to finish the cover-up. And they'll be in a hurry, trying to beat any investigators who may be on the way.

In the surveillance room, Corporal Judy Erickson alertly sits in a chair facing Jeremy and Darcy without her body armor. She is sore but mostly recovered from the shooting.

"Captain Kerrigan," she answers. "He's in charge, if he's not dead."

"Still alive," Darcy responds, "but not yet under our complete control. He led three others down the elevator on a search-and-destroy mission."

Erickson turns away. It's clear that they underestimated this small team of not-so-amateurs, "Where are they now?" she asks.

Darcy switches on three security monitors that show the four men pacing inside a 20-foot by 30-foot room that contains a number of storage boxes. One camera views the elevator.

"The elevator let them off at the Basement level. Unfortunately, that's just records storage now. There are no elevator buttons on that floor, so they're effectively trapped. Grenades? Useless. Firearms? A waste of bullets. So it's a storage room for our enemies, too. Oh, and there is no wireless or radio boosters on that floor, so their comm devices won't work."

Jeremy knows that a short poke of elevator button B sends the car to this virtual prison. A long press on the button, more than three seconds, signals the car to bypass the Basement go to a level below where Camelot and all the other company resources are located. More virtues of a paranoid point-of-view.

"You'll never get them out of there alive," Erickson asserts. "They've got mega firepower."

"Actually, it won't be too difficult. We can just use our fire system."

"You wouldn't burn them!"

"Good God, no. That would be as barbaric as launching a kill mission in an office building. This is probably a good time to reunite all of you Blackwatch employees."

Darcy turns to another monitor, moves a cursor, and clicks a button.

"It won't look like much. Jeremy, you can go and secure the team now. They'll be compliant by the time you get up to the Basement level."

"They look fine to me," Erickson says, but almost before the words are out of her mouth, the four men start to stagger, rush to the elevator, drop to their knees, and frantically try to open the doors. One by one they fall to the floor."

"My God, you killed them," Erickson complains. "It's a gas chamber!"

"Frankly, just a Halon fire system. I manually turned it on. Halon removes the oxygen from the air to suppress fire. Of course, without oxygen, humans lose consciousness and die."

On the monitor, Darcy and Erickson watch the elevator doors open. Jeremy stands in the car looking down at the unconscious bodies. Quickly he removes all their weapons and starts to bind them. After he has loaded the unconscious men into the elevator car, he presses and holds the B button, looks at the surveillance camera, and gives a thumbs up.

"What now?" Erickson asks.

Darcy walks to Erickson's chair, stares at the merc for several seconds, then kicks the chair out from under her. Erickson falls painfully to the floor.

"You tried to kill us," Darcy says. "I don't like that. It's time to give us some answers."

Darcy picks up a cell phone and punches in some numbers.

"What are you doing now?" Erickson asks. There is genuine fear in her voice.

"Calling my uncle and a few cousins to come over. I didn't want them endangered, but now that things are settled I could use a little help cleaning up the office before employees report to work tomorrow."

Erickson looks relieved until Darcy adds…

"I also need some help with the interrogation. They're really good at it. Any ideas about what we should do with all the dead people?"

It's been forty-five minutes since the man-made meteor shower at Göbekli Tepe. Charlotte and her exhausted band are hidden behind small boulders about eighty yards from the end of the road. In the bright moonlight, Charlotte views the smoldering helicopter wreckage through the powerful scope mounted on her bipod-steadied Grendel .308.

Karza sits next to her. "You will kill the man who did this?" he asks.

"Or whoever is helping him," she replies.

"We do not believe in vengeance," Karza says. There is a long silence before he speaks again. "Even so, this place is the holy temple of my ancestors. Whoever commits violence on this holy land forfeits God's protection."

Charlotte takes this as permission to kill the perpetrators. Not that she needs it.

"Thank you, Karza. I'm so sorry about Dr. Schultz."

"His work led him to this end, but still… I considered him a friend."

Bouncing headlights make jittery patterns on the rough road as a Toyota SUV approaches the helicopter rubble.

Charlotte peers through the scope. The image vibrates in time with the nervous tremor of Charlotte's hands. She forces the rifle down more firmly on the bipod, trying to steady it. It seems that even her heartbeat makes the image wobble.

The vehicle reaches the end of the dark road and a lone man emerges, walking around the SUV to open the rear gate. He fiddles with something inside the vehicle and then steps away with a large weapon. To Charlotte, it looks like a MANPAD, a man-portable Stinger missile. She has seen these demonstrated in Afghanistan.

With the imposing weapon supported by his shoulder, the man approaches the flaming debris pile. The fire illuminates more details of the man's dark shape. He is wearing body armor, making a kill shot more difficult. She'll have to aim for the head—simple for a trained marksman, but not for Charlotte.

Lying on her belly, she watches the man through the scope, twitching the rifle barrel slightly to align the crosshairs in the center of the man's head. Her finger begins to slowly squeeze the trigger.

The merc steps backward. Damn! She's not practiced enough to keep him centered in the scope.

The intruder lifts the front of his weapon and begins to peer through the slab-like optics system above the trigger group. Charlotte has a shot, but decides to see what the man is going to do.

A puff of smoke at the weapon's front end is followed by a streak of smoke ascending into the sky and a long fading *whoosh*. The man has fired, it seems, at the moon. Or at nothing at all. He watches the long smoky trail for a moment, then drops the weapon and heads for the SUV.

Obviously, the merc has provided investigators a reason for the drone to have crashed. Bad luck that that the aircraft flew into the helicopter.

Charlotte, mesmerized briefly by the missile launch, has taken her eye off the scope. Now she has trouble finding the mercenary through her narrow field-of-vision. Just as the man opens the SUV door to climb in, she manages to set the crosshairs on him… but too late. He reaches into the vehicle. His head is hidden.

Seconds later he backs away with an assault rifle in his hands.

Shit! He's going to search the grounds to confirm kills and survivors.

He steps away from the SUV, moving too quickly for Charlotte to get a good shot. As she moves the sniper rifle sideways on the bipod, the merc shifts in and out of view.

But then the man stops and seems to stare right at her. He has seen something.

Charlotte turns her head. Dammit, her father is staggering towards the glowing remains of the RV. Obviously he's dazed… doesn't know what's going on.

In the bright moonlight, the merc has spotted Thompson. Dropping behind a small rock, he begins to maneuver toward Charlotte's position.

She is no longer the hunter, but the hunted.

Charlotte motions for Herb to pull her father to the ground. Crouching, Herb scampers a few steps and rudely yanks the old man down, clasping a broad hand to Thompson's mouth.

The merc dashes forward, finding another rock for cover. Charlotte makes a decision. She aims her rifle at a spot just above the rock, the place where she thinks the mercenary will emerge when he makes his next move. If she has any fast twitch fibers left, she may be able to pull the trigger before the man moves out of her sightline.

She is wishing that she had played some of those first-person shooter video games the kids love so much.

She waits. And waits. There is no movement behind the rock. Did the man somehow move, evading her detection? Is he approaching now from another direction? She wants to move her eyes, search the terrain to the left, the right, confirming that she is safe from all sides. Somehow she forces herself to keep staring through that scope.

And then, at last, a blur of motion. She pulls the trigger, jarring her eye from the scope. With her naked eyes she can see the man fall to the ground... and roll.

Damn body armor.

Why the hell is *she* the sentry here? She doesn't know what she's doing!

The merc becomes more aggressive, zigzagging toward her position. The sniper rifle is of little use in short-range combat when the enemy is moving quickly, so she discards it and pulls out her Glock.

She wishes she could send up a Bat signal or something. In the past, Gideon had protected her. Now the safety of everyone in the group is up to her.

The Glock feels good in her hand. She has diligently practiced on the range with a 9mm. Let the son-of-a-bitch come. Let him eat lead. She takes a deep breath and keeps talking to herself.

Another blur. The man is moving to a northern approach where there is more natural cover.

Charlotte can't stay here, not so close to the others. Maybe she can lure the man away. Even if she's killed, maybe he won't find the others. Anyway, she's tired now of being the hunted. Time to go on the attack.

She motions for the others to lie down and hide, then crouch-walks to a patch of dry grass diagonal to the man's approach. She lies down, hoping to hear a helpful noise signaling the merc's movement.

Nothing.

Lifting her head, she sees a larger rock about ten yards away. What the hell? She scrambles for the rock, expecting any second to feel a bullet tearing through her chest. She has no body armor.

No shots. She's safe. But her heart is pounding.

Where the hell did this guy go? He's disappeared into the night air.

On her hands and knees, she crawls to another rock further away from her friends. Her lungs burn. She sucks in oxygen, trying to catch her breath, and longs for those boring days in the CCN edit bay where she was firmly in charge and no one was trying to kill her. She'll probably never see the inside of a video edit suite again.

She has no idea what she's doing, or where the mercenary is. All she can do is put more distance between her and the others. So she stands and runs twenty paces to a large boulder near the summit of the hill.

She arrives safely, winded. Lying on her back, she holds the Glock in both hands, pointing upward. Just in case.

She hears a sound to her left, a foot on gravel. Adrenaline pumps and she sits up, then with her back to the boulder, stands and turns toward the noise ready to fire. From her blind side a hand grabs the Glock, wrenching it from her hands.

Startled, she wheels to see a monster in night vision goggles. Instinctively, she tries to knee him in the groin, but he dodges. She loses balance, her head crashing against the rock.

My gravestone, she thinks, as everything goes black.

Chapter 60

"The Ambienz facility is secure, sir." Captain Kerrigan speaks solemnly into his comm device. "All enemy targets were terminated."

Wyatt's voice replies. "Was the young woman with them?"

Kerrigan, in restraints, looks up at Darcy who is pointing a pistol at his head. "No sir, she was not present."

"How many enemy dead?" Wyatt asks.

Darcy holds up six fingers.

"Six, sir."

"How many of ours?"

Darcy makes a circle with her thumb and forefinger.

"None dead."

"Good job, soldier. You've earned a bonus. Stand by for further orders."

"Yes sir."

Captain Kerrigan glowers at Darcy. He hates being dominated by a woman. And he feels like a traitor, misleading his chain of command like this. But hell, it isn't like he's representing motherhood or America. This is business, plain and simple. If this will save the rest of his men—and woman—he's willing to lie.

Darcy doesn't like the sneer on the Captain's face. With a slash of her pistol, she wipes it off.

✦ ✦ ✦ ✦

"Damn it!" Wyatt shouts at Alice Timmerman, his aide and closest confidante. "They've been captured!"

She is confused. "But Kerrigan said they had taken the facility and killed everyone there," she suggests. "What makes you think—?"

"He said Rebecca was gone and six were killed. By Caleb's count there were seven in the facility, including that hacker. We know that three got out somehow and went to Turkey. That leaves four on premises. Not possible—so he was lying. With a gun to his head, I'm sure."

Alice looks at her watch. "In Ireland, it'll be daylight in a few hours. Employees will be showing up. If our guys are captured, we can assume some were killed. If any of them are turned in to the Garda we'll have some explaining to do."

"I know, I know." Wyatt sounds flustered. This travesty comes right on top of the drone strike that killed Rebecca. "Do we have any other men near Balbriggan?"

"Not close enough."

Wyatt begins pacing, weighing alternatives—which is easy, because he sees only one.

"We have a drone in France, right?"

"You're not thinking—!"

"We have no choice, Alice. Find out how soon that bird can be equipped and over Balbriggan."

"I can estimate about three hours to outfit and three hours to fly. Could probably be there just before daybreak. But sir—attack *Ireland*?"

"Dammit, Alice, it's not like they haven't had violence there before. A surgical strike, minimal collateral damage that time of day…"

"Minimal?"

"None, probably."

"Sir, the flight has got to be over 800 miles. The drone's range is under 1200 miles. It'll never make it back."

"So we'll drop it in the Irish Sea."

"A suicide mission?"

"It's an *unmanned* aircraft, Alice."

"Our men are in that building. How do we get them out before—?"

Wyatt has no intention of saving them. They failed, didn't they? Could've been killed during the mission—what difference does it make? They knew the risks.

"Just get that sucker in the air!" he shouts.

Alice gets the message. She leaves the room just as Wyatt picks up a call from his operative in Turkey.

"The evidence is planted," the man says over a static-filled line.

"And bodies! How many?"

"Six dead. Four men, two women."

"All right, now I need you in Amman, then you can rest. Our drone pilot has gone rogue," he lies. "We need you to take him out. But not before he completes one final mission."

"To where?"

"Ireland."

Wyatt expects push-back, like he got from Alice. But instead, after a short pause, the operative simply says, "I need the address in Amman."

God bless mercenaries!

As Wyatt looks up the address, he finds his spirits lifting. *Finally* something has gone right.

✦ ✦ ✦

It's no fun being last on the trail.

Caleb understands now that she's being sidelined, either by Blackwatch—the new kids on the block—or by Cain. Or both. And yet she has an irrevocable order to complete, which means that no one but Eve can rescind it. These guys can divert her, or run her through an obstacle course, but never call her off.

She's through reporting in. Clearly, the intelligence she has been gathering is being redirected to other operatives. The scene at the Ankara airport is testimony to that. Inside the parked Gulfstream she had found the dead pilot and copilot stuffed into a rest room.

Now, shortly after dawn, the proprietor of Boran Helicopter Rentals is staring at her, his badly beaten face a sure sign of torture. It's not hard to see how her predecessor is warming up the trail.

At first the proprietor is frightened by this visitor, but it's a woman. This calms him down a bit. He cannot imagine a woman posing a threat.

Caleb shows him her fake U.S. Marshall badge. It looks official to the Turk who doesn't know what it means.

"Sir, I'm Lieutenant Martha Jones of the American FBI. Do you speak English?"

"Yes, of course," the man answers hoarsely. His neck is bruised.

"I'm trying to find the man who did this to you. Are you Mr. Boran?" She guesses his name might be on the sign of this mom-and-pop operation.

The man nods. "You look for the American? Very bad man."

"You did not report this to the police?"

"He told me not to or he would come back and kill me. How do you know this happened? I tell no one!"

"An anonymous caller." Boran does not seem to understand the words, but the confidence of Caleb's reply seems to satisfy him. "Do you know why he did this to you?"

"The others, my friend and his friends, they rented a helicopter. The man wanted to know where they went."

"And you didn't want to tell him?"

"The man's eyes were evil. I was afraid for my friend."

"The man beat you very badly. Did you give him the information he was looking for?"

Boran is embarrassed that he did. His eyes begin to wander nervously.

"It's all right, Mr. Boran. You did what you could. But I need to know where your friend was going so I can follow this man and keep him from doing other bad things."

"Is my friend okay?"

"I don't know." She puts a warm hand on the man's shoulder for comfort but he winces in pain. "Where did he go, sir?"

"You will catch him?"

"I promise."

"Göbekli Tepe… near Urfa. Please stop him."

Caleb knows that Urfa is only about twenty-five miles from the Syrian border. Blackwatch probably has operations going on in that war-torn country. Where there is war, there is always a profit opportunity for mercenaries. And if Blackwatch is running operations there, it probably has supplies and vehicles inside Turkey—possibly in Urfa. It wouldn't be hard to pay off the local Turks to look the other way. This means, of course, that her targets may have made the Blackwatch operative's job much easier.

Caleb could just look the other way and let this "bad man" do her work for her, but she's pissed. This is her mission. Her last assignment. Looking at the bruised face of Boran, she considers the assailant to be a butcher. Time he learned his lesson.

Her final mission has become interesting again.

Boran is suddenly trembling. "I should not have talked to you," he says. "Now he will kill me."

"No sir," Caleb says. "He definitely will not. Now—where can I charter a plane to Urfa?"

Chapter 61

Cain has never experienced with anyone the kind of intimacy he has with Rebecca—penetrating her mind, when she lets him, and sometimes seeing what she sees. He has never touched her—to be honest, never even met her person-to-person—but he feels the pain of withdrawal when contact is shut off, as it was a few minutes ago.

Usually he is the instigator, piloting his mind across the grid, powered by the crystal chamber. But this time Rebecca had reached out to him, though not intentionally. It had occurred as a flash of images—not coherent thoughts or inferences, but pictures. Explosions and terrifying flames and billowing smoke. A sense of fear, then dread. A request for something—*what?* His composure had been undressed and he had gone racing to the crystal chamber, feeling exposed by the intrusiveness, hoping to pull in the message behind the images.

A request. *Help me, save me.*

All he can comprehend is that Rebecca needs him. Wants him. She is in peril, her life endangered. Unconsciously or subconsciously, she is turning to him for help. He fears for her life at the same time he glows with satisfaction that she has chosen him as her savior.

But of course, there is nothing he can do. He doesn't even know where she is.

Suddenly the images had stopped. The urgency had ceased. She had been saved by someone else, or killed.

He curses the weakening of the grid.

Before the earth was civilized, according to the Order's lore, the planet had been a source of far greater power. Strong, undulating telluric currents, the product of electromagnetic induction by the geomagnetic field produced by the ionosphere, had swept along their natural courses. So powerful were these giant currents that even primitive peoples could sense them, particularly where the currents crossed each other, multiplying their intensity. Humans had noticed that at these crossing points, their consciousness was affected, their connection to the natural world was enhanced, and their "spiritual" energies were restored.

Before long, great standing stones—*menhirs*—had been set as markers for these sites. Predictably, open-air places of worship had been built over the most powerful crossing points. Over time small churches, then great cathedrals had been constructed over many of these markers. Because the paths of the sweeping telluric currents were always fluctuating, the large markers and massive churches had helped anchor them in place—even amplify them. As throngs had begun to worship at these places, the semantic energy of these sites had been magnified.

The telluric currents had also become a source of "revelation," if not by God, then by individuals who spoke on His behalf. At some point in pre-history someone discovered that when positioned at a powerful "holy" site, he or she could connect with the consciousness of another person. Messages could be communicated. This phenomenon must have seemed at first like an ecstatic spiritual experience, a cosmic communing with another soul. But then some very practical benefits were discovered.

Messages passed from an *elite*, seated at an especially powerful holy site, could be perceived by others as the Voice of God, or the voice of an angel. The "voices" would come unbidden, out of the ether, penetrating one's brain and providing insights, instruction, and commands.

Who could refuse to obey?

The great *sacred network* thus became a tool to influence humankind for good or evil. Most religious texts are filled reports of heavenly messages received by common men, kings, and prophets alike, yet beyond the Order few have ever understood the true source of these influences.

At some point, it had been discovered that certain earth substances could help to amplify communications on the grid—in a sense, increasing its signal strength. Chief among these were crystals. As in primitive crystal radio sets, crystals could help attenuate and focus the transmissions, and so crystals began to be used at the holiest of holy sites.

To bolster his faltering faith in the Order's purpose, Cain stands on a platform atop a stairway that winds around a large chamber. A dazzling gold replica of the Ark of the Covenant stands on a large slab of stone that juts from the wall. It is a likeness of the moving sanctuary the Israelites carried on their journeys. The Ark had represented the throne of God Almighty on earth and is said to have contained holy relics—the original tablets of the Ten Commandments, Aaron's rod, a jar of manna, and the first Torah scrolls written by Moses. Lore says it had been used by Moses to speak directly to God while wandering in the desert. The Voice of God was said to have issued from a cloud between the two Cherubim that adorned the Ark. If a non-priest were to touch or even look at the Ark, he would be struck dead.

The Order believes that the Ark had contained two objects never disclosed because only Moses and the High Priest had known of their existence. These were crystals brought back by Enoch after his journey to the Secret Place. The great secrecy and security surrounding the Ark had been largely a means of keeping the power of the crystals limited to Moses and the High Priest, the ones who *communed* over the currents with the wise ones a great distance away.

Cain has traced the ancient currents of the telluric grid on a map, drawing straight lines between great churches and megalithic sites, making visible the mystical paths some people call ley lines. He has learned the power of strategically placed crystals in a communications environment, and knows that in the Sicarii Inner Chamber, the crystals help the Twelve—at least the most *adept*, such as Michael—understand the thoughts and intentions of those they are interrogating.

The Order's lore reveals that over countless millennia, as civilizations and construction increased and technologies expanded, the great telluric currents sweeping through and across the planet predictably began to change course and dissipate when confronting new, more massive buildings, potent man-made electromagnetic fields, and a chorus of radio frequencies. In such ways, humankind unwittingly diminished the communication power of these currents, just as it has been warming the earth's climate.

Religion, which had once held great sway over the populace, waned over time. Those who relied on the ability of the currents to influence the world now found these once-powerful forces increasingly unreliable. Among the most disappointed is the Order ruled by the Twelve, and the elaborate global mechanism they have established.

The Twelve deeply believe that God had created all things, including the earth, its myriad life forms and invisible forces. They also believe, as did their founder, that God had revealed the earth's secrets to a few elite souls and appointed them and their descendants to use its colossal forces to educate and manage the untamed tribes roaming the earth. On a timetable handed down by the Founder, the Twelve believe the entire earth eventually will be under their sovereign control. The final step on that journey is now upon them. If they fail to achieve this last milestone, thousands of years of planning and effort will be squandered and the Order itself could disintegrate.

Staring at the great golden Ark above him, Cain can sense insinuating waves of thoughts begin to intrude his consciousness. He hopes it is Rebecca coming to him on the grid, imploring him to save her. But these thoughts are darker and Cain begins to despair as he understands that Michael is speaking to him. The thoughts become words in his mind. Simple words. Two words.

"Stand down."

In this all-important time, and for this final critical mission, the Divine Light has been reduced to a figure-head.

With all his might, knowing that his thoughts may flow across the grid to the archangel's namesake, Cain resists the urge to put his gut response into words.

Chapter 62

She opens her eyes, but it makes no sense. The desert has transformed into a room, the sandpaper soil into a soft bed. Moonlight has become a thin shaft of daylight slanting through a window.

Every part of Charlotte's body hurts. Using her elbows as support she looks down at the gray jersey pants that hide her legs. *Where did those pants come from?* The room spins slowly and she realizes the back of her head is throbbing.

That's right, I hit my head...

A rush of fear jolts her like a taser and she bursts out of bed.

She had been captured! She had thought she was going to be killed, but no—she's become a prisoner instead. Which may be worse!

Her mind reels back to a time five years ago when she was kidnapped by terrorists while on assignment in Iraq. She had escaped with help from Gideon—that had been her first encounter with the man who would become her protector—but the terrifying ordeal had left an indelible scar on her consciousness. Her captors had meant to rape her before cutting off her head.

I escaped then, she tells herself. *I can survive this.*

She draws back a curtain on the lone window. It's unlocked, she notices. But she's on the second floor.

Light comes from a very low sun. She doesn't know if it's early morning or late afternoon, which adds to her confusion. How long has she been unconscious?

Cars are making their way down a busy street. In the distance is a large greenish-gray dome that looks vaguely familiar. She shakes her head, trying to wake up her brain but instead producing a monstrous headache. If she could just identify that dome—that mosque ...

The identity of the dome is right on the edge of recollection. If only her head didn't throb so much.

Urfa! It comes to her suddenly. She had flown right over this dome, the Great Mosque of Urfa, on the way to a refueling stop at the airport, which means she's just ten miles from Göbekli Tepe. In the helicopter her father had told how Abraham may have been born in a cave near that mosque.

Her father. She thinks about Thompson and Rebecca and Herb Rossi. She can picture Karza, the old Yezidi watcher, hunched in the dark next to her last night. Are they all dead, or are they being held captive, too?

The thumping in her head is bearable now. Without that distraction she can see her environment more clearly. Her bed is actually a heap of pillows on a polished wooden floor. The room is fairly modern, almost like an international hotel. There is no other furniture, but a closed door beckons from five steps away. Barefooted, she approaches it, putting her hand on a doorknob and then hesitating. If it is locked, she'll be disappointed. If it opens—what will she find on the other side?

Slowly she turns the knob and gently pushes the door.

It opens a crack. Unlocked!

Her throat tightens and her head starts throbbing again. She can't catch her breath, feels like fainting. With clenched jaws she opens the door wider.

And sees a hallway with descending stairs.

No one is in sight, so she leaves the room and slowly steps down the stairs. The blurred shape of a man whisks past the landing below. Charlotte freezes. She doesn't want to face whoever it is. Wants to escape back to her room. Sink into the comfort of those plush pillows. Maybe later the man will be gone.

She knows this is cowardice speaking, that she should continue, should face the demons below. She can't stand here on the stairs forever.

Charlotte begins a second gradual descent, as if her slow movements can somehow render her invisible.

Four stairs from the bottom.

Then three.

A man's face suddenly appears in front of her. Startled, the man screams.

Charlotte emits a strangled yelp.

It's over. The escape has failed. Charlotte covers her face in her hands.

"Charlotte?"

The voice is familiar. Charlotte dares to look, and sees Herb Rossi staring at her with a hand to his fluttering heart.

"My God, woman, you almost scared me to death," Herb complains good-naturedly. "I was just going upstairs to check on you."

"You're alive!" Charlotte states the obvious as she sits down on the stairs. "And the others—my father and Rebecca?"

As if called, Thompson and Rebecca rush toward the noise and stand looking up the stairs at Charlotte.

"Welcome back. We're all safe—for now," Thompson says.

Never in a thousand years would Charlotte have imagined throwing her arms around her father and whispering, "I'm so glad to see you." But here she is.

For Thompson, this moment can't last long enough.

After a few seconds, Charlotte abruptly pulls away with a horrified look. "The others!" she exclaims, just now remembering the imminent attack on her friends in Balbriggan. "We have to reach them!"

"We did," Rebecca replies. "I talked to Jeremy an hour ago. Somehow they repelled the attack. Everyone's safe."

Overcome with relief, Charlotte's legs start to buckle. This is a lot to absorb in a few seconds.

Herb keeps her upright. "Let me introduce you to our host," he says.

Guiding Charlotte into a sitting room, Herb points to a tall, elderly man, probably French, who rises from a chair where he had been seated next to Karza.

"Charlotte, I would like you to meet Francois Besette, a good friend of Karza, who brought us here."

"Monsieur, we are deeply in your debt." Charlotte is feeling more stable. She musters a measure of coherence in her speech and offers her hand so Francois can lightly kiss it. Such a wonderful pleasantry after such a savage evening.

"The honor is mine," Francois says with just a hint of accent, "having the famous Charlotte Ansari in my home. We get CCN International on satellite here in Urfa, you know."

"I didn't. May I ask how we were all spared last evening? I have no memory of anything past the point where I left my friends in search of a very bad man with a gun."

"Yes, well…" Thompson replies, "Luckily someone found that *very bad man* and took care of him."

"One of you?" Charlotte asks, searching the room for a hero. She notices, however, that all eyes are looking past her towards a door that she had presumed opens to a kitchen.

She feels the presence of someone standing behind her and turns.

"Menengic coffee, anyone?" Gideon asks, balancing a tray of small steaming cups in his hands.

✦ ✦ ✦

The big boss just can't deal with snafus.

Randall visualizes William Wyatt, sitting with his feet up on a desk in a plush Virginia office and bitching about how he has no video of the Balbriggan mission.

Randall again has explained to Wyatt that he's begged for additional maintenance staff but has been rebuffed at every turn. Wyatt's frustration is palpable, even over the secure line. Encryption, it seems, doesn't lock out exasperation.

Not to worry, though. The mission is still under control. Three drone-mounted cameras continuously feed video imagery to Randall. Two hours and ten minutes after receiving the order from Alice, the ground crew had finished fueling the drone and loading weapons at the secret PCP—Personnel Collection Point—a remote "farm" a few miles northeast of Montpellier in the Larzac region of France. None of the team except Randall knows the flight's destination because none need to know. That's the way the command system works.

Larzac is a centralized location for equipment and security forces. In the event of a deeper economic meltdown and popular uprising in Spain or Greece, Blackwatch can deploy its assets quickly to either country, eliminating the need for Germany, France or other E.U. nations to intervene and suffer inevitable troop losses, international backlash, and prolonged political turmoil.

It's always nice to have someone else to blame.

Blackwatch has invested large sums of its own money to supply and staff the PCP. This was how it had won the unpublicized contract to provide Europe with security to counterbalance the instability caused by a global recession.

Randall usually flies the drone high over more primitive countries, unworried about radar detection and making the tiny aircraft all but invisible in the sky. But here, in a "civilized" part of the world, he flies low, skimming over oceans and countryside, staying beneath more sophisticated detection.

Thirteen minutes to target acquisition and missile launch.

Is he really going to do this?

The menengic coffee is sweet, nutty, and strong. Charlotte hopes it will clear her mind and calm her wide-eyed astonishment at the sight of Gideon back from the dead. She is sitting at a table across from Gideon, cradling a cup of the potent brew. The others randomly sit or stand around the room.

"I've been patient," Charlotte finally says to Gideon. "Last time I saw you, you were dead. Shot through the heart. But here you are, looking surprisingly—"

"Alive?" Gideon prompts.

"And well!" Thompson adds. "Go ahead and explain, Gideon. We won't mind hearing it a second time."

Gideon reaches down, stuffing a hand into a bag at his feet. He pulls out two 8-inch metal-cutting circular saw blades still in their colorful safety-guard packages. They have been duct-taped together, making a double-thickness.

"Maybe you remember there was construction going on around Dr. Doering's carrel at the Museum that day I was shot," he suggests. "I'd been fretting about Caleb tracking us down, and wondering what the four of you would do if she managed to gun me down. She has a talent for that kind of thing. And then I noticed these saw blades, and the idea just came to me. *Body armor*."

He hands the sandwiched disks to Charlotte. "Here, my new lucky charms," he says.

She finds two deep dents where bullets had struck the exposed surface. "You were wearing these saw blades at the Museum?" She finds the thought of such a thing… well, almost humorous!

"I went to the w.c. with a roll of duct tape, made a little necklace out of it, and then hung the blades behind my shirtfront. Bloody uncomfortable, as they'd say in London."

"Whoa, you were one lucky dude!" Charlotte exclaims, looking at the diameter of the blades. "These aren't very big."

"As Sicarii assassins we're trained to aim for the heart. Two pops there, then one tap in the head—which in public Caleb didn't have time for, thank God. She's an excellent shot, even while moving. Three shots had hit the target. Frankly, I was counting on that. Her 9 mm rounds would have gone through most metals, but two of these saw blades, nearly a half-inch of titanium carbide… well, here I am."

"So you were alive on the steps when Jeremy rushed over to you. Did he know?"

"Of course. I was stunned by the impact of the rounds, barely able to move, but I was able whisper to him."

"Whisper *what*?"

"I said, *I'm okay, but let me stay dead*. Or something like that. The kid is bright. He knew immediately what I meant."

"Then he's smarter than me, 'cause I don't know," Charlotte confesses.

"This was my chance to be dead." Gideon explains. "To get rid of all the people who were chasing me—for legitimate reasons, unfortunately. To be honest, I work better when I'm invisible. Off the surveillance grid. Dying's a pretty good way to disappear."

"Jeremy had your cell phone at Ambienz."

"I asked him to take it, but I carry a back-up with Wonderboy's master app installed on it. By the way, the slave app is on all your phones."

"You listened in on all our calls?"

"And texts, and locations. Yeah, it's illegal I know. Sorry." Gideon grins at his lame sarcasm. "Jeremy and I secretly kept in touch. He told me about your plans."

"So were you the man with the Stinger last night?" Confused, Charlotte stops to reason this through. "Can't be—that guy planted evidence there."

"He was a Blackwatch operative. But I was there. Watching. And invisible—no one was looking for me."

"The guy attacked me, took my gun. Where the hell were you?" she asks with mock anger.

"Actually, that was me protecting your ass while you were crawling right into his kill zone. Sorry you fell, by the way… that wasn't part of the plan."

"You must've won your duel with that bastard."

"Yeah, after you knocked yourself out. I had night vision, he didn't. Stupid merc! His SUV came in handy, though, for trucking you all out of there. I just had a little rental economy job parked about a mile down the road in Örencik."

Charlotte stares at Gideon for a moment. Her injured brain is trying to process all this information. Finally she takes another sip of thick Turkish coffee and says, "What about while we were stuck inside that Ambienz building in Balbriggan?"

"After I discovered where you'd gone, it took me a while to get there. But I knew that somehow Caleb would find you. She'd be there, too. She always has a *way*. So I anonymously informed Mossad—those guys have come to hate us, you know?—I told them they could find a Sicarii at the Ambienz headquarters in Balbriggan. I'm sure they were hoping it would be me. Anyway, I kind of liked the idea of Mossad doing some of my work? Getting lazy in my old age."

Charlotte just shakes her head. "I have absolutely no idea what you're talking about."

"You were probably in the air when all this happened. The agents sent by Mossad were idiots. What's this world coming to, when you can't even count on the Israelis? They found Caleb's Irish partner in a car at Ambienz and killed him, then simply left. Missed Caleb, the big prize. Maybe it rattled Caleb a bit, but probably not."

"Well, for the first time I don't feel rattled. I feel safe."

"Get over it. Never underestimate Caleb. She's probably on her way here right now. Remember, she put three bullets right here." He taps his sternum. "One of her is like two of me."

Charlotte moves to stand by Gideon, then impulsively throws her arms around him. It's been killing her not to touch him.

She doesn't care who sees.

"You're wrong," she says. "To me, one of you is worth ten of her."

For the first time in five years, Gideon wraps a muscular arm around Charlotte and pulls her closer. His touch makes her want to knock the stuffing out of Caleb.

Chapter 63

Randall flicks a switch.

"Hey!" Wyatt's voice is raspy with exhaustion. "I got picture!"

"Just in time," Randall replies. "Seven minutes to launch. Just sit back and enjoy the Irish fireworks."

"Congratulations on evading detection, son."

"It's my job."

Randall nudges the joystick slightly to align with a pre-calibrated mission path. The monochromatic image of land moving beneath the drone shows a slight starboard adjustment.

"Randall, you sure this is Ireland?"

Wyatt laughs nervously at his own lame joke.

✦ ✦ ✦

Charlotte is still catching up.

Thompson gestures to Karza and Francois Besette, who are snuggled into a small sofa. "…so Karza brought us here," he is explaining, "hoping that Francois would temporarily take us in. As it turns out, Francois spends six months each year in this country, primarily here in Urfa, studying the *history museum* that is Turkey, and writing books. So he and I have that in common."

"None of my books has become a bestseller like The World's Great Wisdom Traditions, unfortunately," Francois responds.

Thompson puts on a show of humility.

"Francois Besette." Charlotte rolls the name off her tongue. "Sorry, I don't know your books. Please tell me about them."

"Well, the one I was describing to your father earlier, the one that captured his attention, is a biography of Isaac Newton."

Charlotte is surprised. "Really—Isaac Newton? You have a wide span of interests, Francois, from Newton to ancient Turkey."

"Some believe this land is the cradle of civilization and religion. Enoch lived here, Abraham was born a few miles from where we sit. The world's first temple was built at Göbekli Tepe, but then you know that. It's how I met Karza. I'd come to meet Dr. Schultz, may he rest in peace, and found a team of eager workers disgracefully disturbing history's most ancient holy place. I'm sorry, but that is the only way I can put it. I knew, of course, that it was an archaeological dig, but I was unprepared for the great despair I felt when seeing those sacred monuments exposed like the bones of one's beliefs. It seemed to me that they had been purposely buried for some very important, perhaps *sacred* reason."

Karza listens with moist eyes, then interrupts. "Francois and I met there. I saw his sadness and we became mourners together."

"It's not that I condemn scientific inquiry," Francois explains, "but this place—it was different. I can't explain it. My friend Karza has helped me better understand the spiritual significance of Göbekli Tepe."

The elderly Frenchman hesitates, lost in his own thoughts for a moment.

"Francois, why write about Isaac Newton?" Charlotte asks. "It doesn't seem to have any connection to your interest in these other things."

"Oh, but it does. Most people think of Newton as an inspired scientist. But he spent much more time investigating spiritual truth, and that was what intrigued me. Most people remember him as a great mathematician who discovered gravity when an apple fell on his head. Some remember him as the great scientific thinker who also solved the riddles of space, time, and light, then created mathematical models to predict the motion of objects."

Charlotte doesn't see that this monologue is doing anything more than take up valuable time. Still, this man has graciously given them sanctuary so she listens politely, giving her father a confidential roll of her eyes to indicate her impatience.

Thompson catches her meaning and interrupts their host. "Francois, the information that Charlotte will find fascinating is what you explained to me earlier—the *prisca sapientia*."

He turns to his daughter with a stern admonition. "This could be the key to the puzzle we've been trying to solve, so listen carefully."

Darcy and Mason watch Wonderboy in front of three computers. Two quantum computers from testing suites have been added to an improvised network so all the computers can operate in parallel, greatly boosting the astounding speed of each individual unit.

Wonderboy's fingers fly over his keyboard. He is directing a digital plan that only he understands, frantically trying to feed the voracious beasts before him with enough food, enough data, to satisfy their insatiable appetites.

Jeremy enters Camelot and slumps, exhausted, into a chair. "They're secure," he reports, referring to the Blackwatch prisoners. "I gave them food and water."

"Why the hell would you do that?" Darcy snaps. She's not one to show mercy to those who tried to kill her.

"Because they're dumb mercenaries," Jeremy says. "Just doing the jobs they were paid to do. It was nothing personal against us." He now suspects this may be true of Sicarii assassins as well.

He notices perspiration dripping from Wonderboy's face, the result of unrelenting stress and effort. The hacker has unbuttoned his shirt to cool off, exposing more of his tattoo tapestry.

Suddenly Wonderboy sits back with a sigh like a gust of wind, clasping his hands behind his head.

"Over thirteen thousand Sentient allies are helping us now," he says triumphantly. "I didn't know we had that many *total*."

Mason rises and looks up at a waterfall of data on the big screen. His eyes are bloodshot and his body aches from sitting. He does not share Wonderboy's enthusiasm.

"So we're getting a lot of data. Maybe too much—let's not drown in it. At some point we need to make sense of it, structure it, analyze it."

"Already doing that," Wonderboy explains. "I wrote a program to look for structure in the raw data and break it down, then analyze name similarities in ancestral trees, common descendants, geographic markers, dates... and start to assemble a matrix, which can be used to generate a master genealogical chart."

"When did you do all that?" Jeremy asks, understanding only half of what Wonderboy just said.

"While you guys were up playing with your friends," Wonderboy replies. "I start with the oldest historic information that we've retrieved and move forward. But with all the horsepower available to us, I can also start another project at the current state—today, for example, using all the names we know. For example William Sinclair, Miriam Walker, Greg and Charlotte Ansari..."

The mention of Charlotte's name raises eyebrows around the room.

"Charlotte? Really?" Mason asks.

"She's part of the Sicarii bloodline, right? I also put in Rebecca, Thompson, and everyone in this room. At the very least, you'll get a free family tree."

"What's the point?" Darcy asks.

"The point is speed. I'm working both bottom to top as well as top of the pile to the bottom. Hopefully the data crunching will meet somewhere in the middle, saving us time. Then we can start filling in the blanks, putting more leaves on the trees. Got a better idea?"

Silence reigns.

Wonderboy hammers on some keys. The big screen stops momentarily, then starts flowing more data.

"We already have preliminary results showing some very interesting relationship chains. I'm using a predictive algorithm to suggest candidates to fill in gaps right now—can fix errors later. There, you see that?"

He points to the big screen, but the lines of data flow upward so fast that no one can read them. Except Wonderboy.

"Shit! I wouldn't have guessed that, would you?"

The others give up. The dance of data on the big screen reveals nothing to them. But the sight of Wonderboy shaking his head in astonishment gives Jeremy a sense of hope, Darcy a shiver of fear, and Mason a suspicion that Wonderboy may be cracking under the pressure. After all, the tattooed techie hasn't slept since he arrived.

✦ ✦ ✦

"I want you to know that you're earning a big pay raise today, Randall." Wyatt is filling these final minutes with torrential talk, trying to leave no empty spaces for conscience to intervene.

"This is not an act of war, as Alice suggested," Wyatt continues. "It's a defensive action necessary for our broader global mission to continue. We must remember that an organization like ours is not national, not even international, but *non*-national. We are an entity unto ourselves—not a nation, as we have always considered nations, but a global service that transcends those primitive views of society and governance."

He's ranting, preaching, justifying the coming atrocity, working to find a combination of words and thoughts that will keep Randall on mission, on goal. He's trying to prevent second thoughts when it's time for Randall to blow up a civilian building in a civilized country and purposely eliminate hostages he should be saving.

Randall just wants him to shut up. But then, in five minutes, he is sure the talking will stop.

✦ ✦ ✦

"Of course, Thompson," Francois replies to a request to jump forward in his monologue. "Newton was much more than a scientist. He spent most of his time as a theologian searching for the key to something called the *prisca sapientia*. In his lifetime he produced three times as many theological works as scientific!"

"If you could explain the prisca sapientia, Francois..." Thompson encourages Francois to pick up the pace.

"Of course. Newton deeply believed that God shared with some ancients a sacred wisdom that was later lost or perhaps hidden from view. He believed also that the geometric proportions of many ancient temples were in themselves sacred—built using a sacred geometry that mathematically encoded the wisdom and great plan of God. This belief lead Newton to study the architectural works of ancient Greece, Rome and Egypt, trying to find that occult knowledge—always looking for the key that would unlock the secret. Just as you and your friends are searching for the key to an earthly location."

Charlotte shoots an accusatory stare at her father, who clearly has shared their secret mission with this stranger.

"You can put that pin back in the grenade," Gideon says to Charlotte. "Just hear the man out."

Charlotte is still looking at her father. "So you think that if Newton had discovered this key, and we knew what it was, it could somehow give us the coordinates to our mystery place? Frankly, anything less than that is not very helpful right now."

"You might be surprised, Char—if you just let him finish."

Charlotte takes a deep breath and turns back to Francois. "I apologize for my rudeness. I'm just feeling a bit agitated."

"Of course," Francois says with a patient smile. "Perfectly understandable."

"Please continue. I think you were going to tell us that Newton discovered this *prisca sapientia*. Or the key to it."

"Not exactly. If he did, experts say that he never recorded it in his writings, although I believe it is there, encoded."

"So you have a theory."

"A damn good one," Thompson interjects.

"I'm sure the story of how you cracked this code is a marvelous detective story, Francois, but maybe you can just cut to the chase. What's the secret?"

Charlotte hears her own words and winces at the tone of her voice. She didn't mean for it to come out so callously. Maybe she has a concussion. Or maybe that blow to the head just turned her into a nasty bitch.

"The number 2520," Francois replies, politely ignoring Charlotte's sharp tone.

Charlotte stares at the Frenchman. She had not expected such a direct answer. "That's it?" she asks.

"Just cutting to the chase," Francois explains. "Would you like more?"

"She needs more coffee, I think," Gideon remarks. "I'll get it." He heads for the kitchen as Charlotte touches the sore lump on the back of her head. She feels like she's Alice after tumbling down the rabbit hole. Is Gideon really alive? Why are they talking about Isaac Newton? How can a number possibly resolve their dilemma?

Maybe she's still in a coma. Perhaps this is all a dream.

"Okay," Charlotte says, "Once again I'm sorry. Yes, I do need a little more than a number. Like what does it mean, and how does it relate to the *prisca sapientia?*"

Chapter 64

It's not much of an airport, Caleb thinks, as her chartered plane lands on the lone north-south runway in Urfa. She would have preferred a helicopter so she could drop down on the edge of Göbekli Tepe, but none was available.

She hands a thin bundle of American dollars to the pilot as a bribe to wait for her return. "No more than eight hours," she explains. "I'll need a ride back. I pay well, as you know."

The plane stops about fifty yards from the entrance to the small, square terminal. Inside she finds a ticket agent with nothing to do. The woman speaks enough broken English to explain that it will take maybe a half-hour to hire a vehicle, but no one wants to go to Göbekli Tepe today. The temple site had been struck last night by a missile—probably terrorists, maybe Israel—and everyone is afraid to go there now. Everyone there was killed. Nobody can figure out, though, why anyone would want to attack an ancient city of the dead. Maybe the missile had flown off course.

Caleb can guess the true source of the missile. It was not off course.

"How many were killed?" she asks the agent.

"Two bodies, I heard—yes, two men."

"No women?"

"I don't think so. Just men—and a blown up helicopter from Ankara. It stopped here yesterday."

Caleb wonders if other bodies remain undiscovered. Probably not. The Turks are pretty good at this kind of investigation. Clearly there were survivors.

She cracks a smile.

The agent misinterprets. "You are happy that people died?"

"Not at all," Caleb says. "I'm happy that some people I know were not killed there." The real reason she's happy, of course, is because Blackwatch clearly failed, and Caleb will now be able to complete her irrevocable assignment.

If the small group she is hunting left Göbekli Tepe unharmed, and their helicopter was destroyed, they are probably still in Urfa.

But they will want to leave soon.

Caleb decides that the airport is a fine place to spend some time. Maybe she'll run into some old friends. As they say, there's only one stage out of town.

"Let me finish the story of Newton and the Prisca Sapientia," Francois suggests. "I will make it fast."

"We do have some urgency, Francois," Thompson says.

Francois reaches onto a bookshelf and pulls off a Bible, pitching it to Charlotte. "Do you know the Old Testament story of Belshazzar's Feast?"

"Hmmm," she says. "Let me think back to Sunday School—when I was still going. Evil King Belshazzar had pillaged Solomon's Temple, as I recall, making off with the temple's holy vessels. Then he threw a drunken feast and used the sacred gold and silver vessels to praise false gods. Suddenly a disembodied hand appeared and wrote something on the wall for everyone to see—the proverbial *handwriting on the wall*."

Francois nods. "I believe the message written on that wall is the key to the *prisca sapientia*. Charlotte, can you read Daniel 5:26 in the Bible?"

She finds the passage.

> **And this is the writing that was written out: 'MENE, MENE, TEKEL, UPHARSIN.**

She reads it aloud, then looks up blankly.

"Okay, I don't get it," she says, shaking her head. "The handwriting on the wall was obviously something important because it was a direct message from God. Looking at the following verses, I see that Daniel—who was the Master over all the Magi—was called in to interpret those four odd words, and he said they prophesied the downfall of Belshazzar's empire, which apparently occurred soon after."

"In 539 BC" Francois adds.

"So how could this be the key Newton was after?" Gideon has been trying to follow Francois' line of reasoning, but is confused as well.

"Let me put it this way." Francois is becoming excited. He stands and starts to pace. "Isaac Newton was a well-known authority on the standard of weight and measure for currency in Britain. He was appointed Warden of the Royal Mint in 1696. And he was also fluent in many ancient languages."

Gideon gestures surprise. "Didn't know that," he says.

"It would have been abundantly clear to Newton that the words MENE MENE TEKEL UPHARSIN were actually monetary values. A *mene* was equal to 1,000 gerahs, the smallest proportion of weight used in Babylonian commerce back then. A *tekel*, sometimes called a shekel, was equivalent to 20 gerahs. Upharsin was essentially half a mene, or 500 gerahs. So add them all up—two menes, one tekel, and one upharsin. What do you get?"

"You get 2520," Thompson chimes in.

"Exactly. And how important is this number?" Francois asks. "Newton, a master of encryption, studied the Old Testament scriptures for years and wrote extensively about Daniel's time prophecies. He encrypted many of his discoveries about religion and mathematics with ingenious ciphers to prevent theft of his ideas. Yet he never once mentioned this passage from the book of Daniel. On purpose, I believe."

"So you think he left out his analysis of this particular story to hide it?"

"They say the best cipher is to have no need for one because the information you want to encrypt is absent. He didn't have the time or the tools to prove his theory, so he gave us this blatant omission as a clue to its importance, knowing that at some time in the future someone would decipher his discovery and uncover its full meaning.

"And that person is you?" Charlotte asks.

"Yes, I suppose so."

✦ ✦ ✦

"We are one minute from target," Randall says.

In Virginia, Wyatt watches three views of the mission but doesn't respond. The mounting tension has finally shut him up. The drone's belly-cam shows continually moving terrain beneath the drone… then finally a building.

And another.

"If you want to abort, there are forty-five seconds remaining," Randall says.

Wyatt knows that Randall is giving him every possible chance to call off the slaughter of civilians and his own men.

He maintains radio silence. Seconds tick off and the roofs of several more buildings move across the monitor.

"Approaching target, sir. Missiles are loaded."

A target acquisition marker appears over a rectangular building. Wyatt's pounding heart visibly moves his shirt.

"Target acquired sir. Permission to launch."

"Do it!"

Two words. One missile. No sound. No dramatic movie music. Just a flash of light on the screen, a series of explosions, and then smoke everywhere.

"Target destroyed sir,"

"What the hell did they have in there?" Wyatt is surprised at the multiple explosions. "Ditch the bird now."

"One more target sir."

"What—?" No, ditch at sea. Nothing more. Do you read?"

The monitor shows the drone turning. The camera finds a group of helicopters on the ground—perhaps six of them. Wyatt recognizes the pattern, and fear seizes him.

"What the hell are you doing, dammit? Ditch the drone NOW!"

"Almost finished, sir. Watch this."

The target acquisition marker finds the chopper grouping. Within two seconds, the helicopters are destroyed.

"Ditching the drone now, sir, at the attack zone as before. Good night."

"No dammit—not there!"

Suddenly the monitors go dark.

The phone rings.

"Talk," Wyatt says. He doesn't need to hear the voice on the other end because he knows what the call is about.

"Sir, our PCP in Larzac is under attack," the voice says. "Munitions store and all helicopters have been destroyed. A drone, we think."

No shit.

When Wyatt gets his hands on Randall—and he will—the young man will beg to be sent to hell.

✢ ✢ ✢

"It's just a number." Herb Rossi expresses his frustration with the discussion. "What's the big deal with it? Maybe as a lottery number or something..."

"The number 2520 shows up in many measurements and calculations of temples and pyramids around the world," Francois patiently explains, "so it's clear the ancients understood the sacredness of the number. Newton believed that the Grand Designer of the Universe inserted this sacred number, and all the proportions and calculations derived from it, into his instructions for building the Temple of Solomon, the Ark of the Covenant, the Temple of Jerusalem, the measurements of the earth..."

"Give them some examples," Thompson advises.

"All right—is it a coincidence that the sacred cubit is 25.20 inches, a fractal of 2520?" Francois responds. "And is it a coincidence that you can precisely calculate the earth's mean diameter by multiplying pi—the universal constant for circles—times 2520?"

"More fun with numbers," Charlotte says sarcastically.

"In the book of Genesis we read, '*And on the seventh day God ended his work which he had made... And God blessed the seventh day.*' Is it a coincidence that seven solar days, measured by seven 360-degree revolutions of the sun, equals 2520 total degrees of revolution?"

Charlotte has no sarcastic retort.

"Is it a coincidence that when the writing on the wall, which we now understand to be the number 2520, is multiplied by seven, you get the precise number of days between Belshazzar destroying the temple and the fall of Babylonia? You see, the framework of Newton's *prisca sapientia* suggests that the measured distance from the Temple of Jerusalem to other locations and events affecting it would be supernaturally connected."

This statement catches Charlotte's interest. "I'll need an example of how that works."

"Let's look at the Great Pyramid of Egypt, homeland of the Israelites before their exodus. From the nearest corner of the Great Pyramid to the foundation stone of the Temple of Jerusalem is 480,000 yards. Is it coincidence that the length of time from the exodus that began in 1441 BC to the start of construction of Solomon's Temple in 961 BC is exactly 480 years?"

"Some kind of anomaly, perhaps," Charlotte proposes.

"Then how about this? Napoleon proclaimed Israel's independence in the year 1799. Is it also an anomaly that the measured distance from the Paris Milestone, the historical center of Paris, to the Jerusalem temple mount is 1,799 nautical miles?"

"All right, that's spooky." Rebecca finally joins the discussion.

"Perhaps you can guess the distance between Babylonia, which fell in 539 BC, and the Temple in Jerusalem."

"I'll say 539 miles," Gideon says.

Thompson rises from his chair, always eager to dominate a conversation. "Unfortunately, Enoch lived long before there was a temple in Jerusalem. I wonder, however, if the house of crystal did not serve as God's temple in Enoch's day. Perhaps that's one reason he made his pilgrimage."

Francois paces closer to Thompson. "Yes, I see where you are going with this. Enoch's house of crystal was indeed a temple of learning, a temple of knowledge. It was where God's hand wrote his message to Enoch in the stars. If we measured the distance from that crystal temple to a location of great significance to Enoch..."

"...such as the place of his ascension into heaven...?" Charlotte suggests.

"...it should be 2520 miles away—using the key to the prisca sapientia. That would be quite convincing."

"Yeah," Herb interjects. "Or the mother of all coincidences."

A phone rings. For a few seconds no one is sure whose phone it is, but then Gideon plucks his phone from a shirt pocket.

"Yes?" he answers.

In a dim leased office in northern Amman, the caller replies, "Gideon? It's Joshua. The address you gave me checked out."

At thirty-five, Joshua is a skilled Sicarii operative, perhaps the only one who Gideon still trusts. The man owes his life to Gideon.

"Any problems?" Gideon asks.

Joshua cranes his neck, squinting at two tied-up bodies on the floor. "No, a couple guards, nothing to speak of. They should have more security for a place of this importance. The drone mission Wyatt mistakenly told you about when he thought you were his man in Turkey—well, it was just getting underway."

"Aborted now, I hope."

"Uh, no, we actually had a better idea. Your friend Wyatt's secret shop in France just went up in smoke."

Gideon laughs out loud. "By his own drone. How fitting."

Joshua turns toward Randall seated next to him. "The operator—name is Randall—he was cooperative. Said he suspected maybe he was a marked man here. I don't think he would've gone through with the Ireland mission, so I was wondering—maybe we go easy, you know?"

"You're getting soft, Joshua. Is he there? Switch on speakerphone."

Joshua taps a button.

"Randall, you almost killed four good friends of mine at Göbekli Tepe," Gideon says.

The stern accusation startles the young man. "Sorry, I was told they were enemies. I assumed terrorists."

"Sure, using an archaeological dig as cover, right?"

"The guys running this outfit are nuts!" The young man sounds desperate.

"You don't know the half of it, Randall. What's your last name?"

"Turner."

"Okay, listen carefully. Very soon they'll be coming there to kill you. I hope you have some money on you because you can't go home. You need to make your own way to Ankara. Joshua will give you an address. Tomorrow afternoon you will find an envelope there with your name on it. When you arrive, ask for the envelope and show ID. You'll find enough money to disappear for a while, and a cell phone in case I need to reach you. Got that?"

Joshua smiles. Gideon is building his network of helpers, people who owe him. Just like Joshua owes him.

"Got it," Randall says.

"Any wife or kids?"

"Not yet."

"Good. These guys are very good at finding people. If you run into serious trouble, send a text. Instructions will be with the money. You did a good thing today... saved innocent lives. Joshua, switch off the speaker."

Joshua punches a button and puts the phone to his ear.

"Did you record your session there?"

"Audio, yeah."

"I'm texting a link for you to post it. Then get out of there."

"Now we're even, right?" he suggests.

"Actually, I'm in your debt. Of course, if I find out you've told anyone that I'm alive, I will find you and cut out your beating heart."

"Understood."

Joshua smiles—this was just verbal jousting between friends—but he won't be taking any chances. When he was alive, Gideon had ranked second in experience and skill among all assassins. Joshua suspects Gideon hasn't lost any of it since he died.

Chapter 65

"Holy Mother of God," Darcy says.

She and Mason are staring at data that Wonderboy is slowly cascading down the big screen in Camelot. Jeremy is seated next to Wonderboy, eyes devouring the same information on the hacker's monitor.

No one speaks. They just read the screen, stunned by the *preliminary summarized report*, as Wonderboy had called it.

Finally, Mason turns to the others, his face white and his fingernails digging into the palms of his hands. Glancing at the hacker he says, "Tell me you made this up, please."

"No, it's real," Wonderboy replies. "Of course, data is still pouring in, so it's incomplete."

"There's more coming?" Darcy hides her face in her hands when Wonderboy nods.

"Pouring in," he reiterates. "But I need to verify all this data, check sources, do a more thorough job cross-tabbing, probably reorganize…"

"We get it!" Mason yells, staring again at the big screen and shaking his head.

"This completely redefines conspiracy." Darcy stands. "I need a whiskey."

"The trigger for much of the analysis was the data from Charlotte's investigation," Wonderboy explains, even though no one is listening. "She had a reporter's instincts for a story, I'll give her that."

Jeremy's phone beeps—an incoming text message. As he reads it, another beep announces the arrival of an email and attachment.

"You won't believe this, guys," he blurts out. "We just dodged a bullet. Or more precisely, a drone missile. Got a Blackwatch audio file here of the mission as it was unfolding."

"Holy shit," Darcy says. "We have no defenses against a missile."

"Don't worry,' Jeremy replies, "Gideon took care of it. We're safe for now."

He looks up from his phone to see the others staring at him with shocked faces.

"Oh, right. Another thing—turns out Gideon's alive."

✦ ✦ ✦

"I feel like I've lost you again," Charlotte says, looking through the round spectacles of the stooped, paunchy figure before her and into Gideon's eyes. "This can't be you."

"It is if I'm going to remain dead. Do my documents pass muster?" Gideon holds up his passport photo, a perfect match to his new gray-haired, liver-spotted, mustachioed look, and says with a convincing British accent, "Alfred Smythe of Wembley," his false name.

"I wish we could ride together to the airport," Charlotte confides.

"Then I couldn't watch you from afar."

"If we're going to catch the noon flight, we'd better go." She leans forward slowly, her lips approaching Gideon's, then pulls back. "Sorry, I just can't kiss that face."

"Someday, with luck, I'll still be alive and probably look like this."

"And someday I'll have grown accustomed to that face."

"Promise?" Gideon asks.

"Promise."

"The cars are out front. I'll be driving mine back to the rent-a-hack office. If somehow you arrive before me, no looks in my direction."

"We've been through this."

"This is the last time. Give me a fifteen minute lead, then the rest of you go with Francois to the airport. Check in separately, like don't know each other. It's possible that Blackwatch has men here watching the airport. If so, I will know and take care of it."

"Okay, got it. But you're making me nervous again."

"After what you went through last night, this will be a snap. In Ankara you will pair up and take taxis to the address I gave you. That's all there is to it."

"I've changed my mind," Charlotte says.

Concerned that Charlotte doesn't want to leave, Gideon gives her a stern look. She wraps her arms around him and presses her lips to his, mingles her breath with his, and then pulls away with a sigh.

"Memorable," she says. "That was our first kiss."

✦ ✦ ✦

In large red letters, the sign on the terminal announces SANLIURFA GAP ULUS-LARARASI HAVAALANI. Directly beneath it, Gideon climbs out of a cramped car that passes for a rental car shuttle in Urfa and casually looks around like a bemused tourist. Walking with a slight limp, he enters the small terminal and approaches the Turkish Airlines check-in counter. Less than a dozen passengers are present as Alfred Smythe shows his Passport and exchanges cash for a ticket.

Twenty paces south is a lone security checkpoint with two agents. If there is going to be trouble, it will be outside the checkpoint. Weapons would be hard to smuggle in. There are two padded benches in this area and he sits down on one of them. From this vantage point he can see the terminal's main doors where Charlotte and the others will be dropped off.

He can also study the passengers who remain in the ticketing area for telltale signs of ill-purpose. Blackwatch, he knows, primarily employs Americans because of their superior military training, but that doesn't mean a few locals might not be stirred into the pot. He concludes that three men are of the age and body type to be potential mercenaries. But one of them is with a pregnant woman and a second is hugging an old Turk with the kind of affection that no mercenary could fake.

Better keep an eye on the third guy. He's by himself, is built athletically, and has eyes that never stop roaming.

None of Gideon's party has weapons, which makes him nervous. But flying commercial makes weapons especially difficult these days—except for Gideon's carbonized plastic sica, which is hidden in his belt and invisible to security scans. When the blade is slightly curved, it is flexible. When snapped into a straightened position, it is lethal in the hands of a Sicarii assassin.

Gideon looks to his right and sees an elderly woman staring at him. He nods a friendly greeting.

At the counter is a young couple purchasing tickets. They could be college students or newlyweds.

His inventory-taking is interrupted by the blur of a silver vehicle pulling up beyond the glass doors. It's the color of Francois' mini-van. This could be Charlotte and the others.

To stay in character Gideon makes rising from the bench look painful and then shuffles to the front doors, hoping for an uneventful entrance to the terminal by his companions.

Before the doors automatically open he stops suddenly.

It's worse than he had expected. What a rotten time to be without a gun!

In the idling vehicle, Francois is driving and Herb sits on the passenger side. Behind them Karza and Thompson occupy the outside seats with Charlotte in the middle. Rebecca rides alone in the rear seat. The side door is open exposing Karza, and a woman is pulling the old man from the vehicle.

Caleb!

Where the hell has she been hiding?

Caleb throws Karza onto the curb and climbs into the vacant seat, hijacking the van. As she slides the door closed, Gideon bolts through the door, no longer the old man with creaky knees and liver spots. He's a second too late. The door slams shut. The lock solidly engages. Inside Gideon can see Caleb holding a pistol to Charlotte's head.

Gideon hammers a fist on the window. Caleb turns toward him with a confused look. She doesn't recognize him.

He can hear the assassin yell "Go!" and the vehicle pulls away.

Gideon has lost them all.

His mind immediately starts to ripple through all the possible scenarios now. Caleb will get them away from the airport. She'll interrogate them before killing them all, learning how much they know. She's a master of this game. She'll find out everything she needs.

As the mini-van speeds away, a dark green SUV darts in front of them, ramming the front of the van.

An ambush. Blackwatch, he guesses. Wyatt has had time to learn the truth about their escape from Göbekli Tepe.

Things have gone from bad to worse. Or maybe not. Francois' vehicle is now stalled thirty yards away with Charlotte and the others inside.

Three imposing men with automatic weapons get out of the SUV and approach the mini-van. Are these Caleb's accomplices? No, they rammed the van. For some reason Caleb must have turned against Blackwatch.

A small Toyota Corolla pulls up to the terminal. Thinking as he moves, Gideon pulls the driver, an elderly man, out of his seat. Before the man's wife in the passenger seat can move, Gideon slams the door and guns the accelerator, zooming toward two mercenaries who are grouped together.

"Duck!" he shouts at the frightened woman next to him, forcing her head down to her lap with a strong right arm.

Bullets shatter the windshield, penetrating the space that Gideon and the woman had occupied. But Gideon had ducked, too, his body temporarily protected by the engine block.

He hears the sounds of the Toyota striking the two mercenaries and the SUV. The crash sends Gideon's head into the steering column. Shouts come from everywhere. He's groggy from the head strike but knows there is still one Blackwatch gunman outside.

Plus Caleb.

And then he hears two silenced shots—Pffffft! Pffffft!—and a door sliding shut. Caleb has finished off the last merc. She'll be checking the Toyota next.

He's having difficulty untangling himself from the wreck. His vision is shifting in and out of focus. He knows this could be it.

He's failed Charlotte.

Caleb wrenches open the Toyota's crumpled door and looks down at the bleeding man stuck behind the steering column. The wire-rim glasses have flown off his face. The gray toupee tilts down awkwardly. Caleb pulls it off, then uses it to wipe blood from Gideon's cheek.

"Gideon." Caleb registers mild surprised, but then smiles. "You're a hard man to put down. Let's find out how many lives you have."

Gideon stares back. His right arm is wedged beneath the pushed-in dashboard. "So you kill your own now."

"Not my idea."

"I know—an irrevocable order. Only Eve could rescind such an order."

"And she's dead. So this is it. You've certainly been… *earnest*. Full of surprises."

Caleb raises her Glock, forces the barrel against Gideon's forehead, and begins squeezing the trigger.

Darcy follows Jeremy into a spare Ambienz conference room where the four mercenaries sit with ankles bound and hands plastic-strapped behind their backs.

"What's the plan here?" Captain Kerrigan demands, doing his best to assert some authority.

"Shut up, asshole," Darcy shoots back. "You're lucky to be alive. If it'd been up to me you'd all be dead."

Amused by the woman's crustiness, Jeremy marches over to Kerrigan and puts his nose about an inch from the Captain's.

"You think you're so damn macho—that you're part of a top-notch operation."

He laughs and steps back, addressing the entire group now. "You have misjudged your employer—probably thought working for Blackwatch was like working for the U.S. military with better pay. *No man left behind*, and all that loyalty stuff."

"Sonny, you look like a washout to me!" Kerrigan's insult provokes laughs from the other mercs. "We're a tight bunch. Professional."

"So why is it, Captain, that you're our prisoners?"

"Pure dumb luck!"

"And why is it that your own company tried to kill you?"

"That's nonsense. We're one of the elite teams."

"Is that right?" Darcy scoffs. "Well we've got news for you."

She holds up a digital voice recorder. "You might want to pay attention to a recording made this morning in the Blackwatch drone control center in Amman."

Kerrigan's sneer disappears. How does this group know about the Blackwatch drones and the center in Amman?

"Seems that your boss, Wyatt, ordered a missile strike right here in Balbriggan. He wanted us all dead, you included. I think you'll recognize his voice."

Darcy clicks the PLAY button.

Chapter 66

As the mini-van door slams shut and Caleb leaps, gun in hand, to the crashed vehicle just five feet away, Charlotte instantly decides she's not going to lose Gideon a second time. She plunges her hand into a pocket on the back of the front seat and pulls out a pistol she had stuffed there just in case. Amazing how such behavior now seems normal to her.

In one fluid movement she slides open the side door and steps out, pointing her gun at the back of Caleb, who is holding her Glock to Gideon's head.

On hearing the door open, Caleb turns.

"Shoot him and you're dead!" Charlotte yells.

A moment passes with neither woman moving a muscle, both just staring at each other, one pistol pressed against Gideon's head and another pointing at Caleb from point-blank range.

A stalemate.

"Put down your guns, both of you!"

Another voice is shouting—a woman's voice, familiar to both Charlotte and Caleb.

Still pointing her pistol with both hands, Charlotte dares a glance over her shoulder and sees an elderly woman pointing a pistol in her direction.

It makes no sense.

Caleb pulls her gun away from Gideon's forehead. "It can't be!" she mutters, looking at the old woman.

Gideon cranes his neck to look out the rear window. He sees the elderly woman from the terminal, the one he had acknowledged with a nod.

Caleb drops her gun.

Charlotte studies the old woman more carefully.

"For God's sake, Charlotte—listen to your mother for a change! Now lower your gun."

Charlotte is confused, immobile, staring at the old woman. *My mother is dead*, she tells herself. But her mother's voice is calling out to her.

The wail of a siren makes her turn. In the distance she can see a POLIS car approaching the terminal.

"For God's sake, Caleb, get Gideon out of there," Eve directs. "Everyone, leave all your guns by the bodies. If you're stopped you don't want guns on you."

Caleb helps Gideon extract his arm from the dashboard and crawl out of the vehicle. She shakes her head in disbelief at what she is doing. She's assisting the man she had been ordered to assassinate.

"Into the mini-van—everyone!" Eve barks, throwing her pistol toward the body of a Blackwatch mercenary. "Now get the hell out of here. I'll meet you after I take care of things here."

The entire group piles into the van and it speeds away.

Seconds later the police arrive. It's clear they'd rather chase the mini-van, but their first task is to care for the elderly woman who has collapsed on the pavement right in front of them. She may be wounded. Or having a heart attack.

The POLIS car brakes to a halt. Two officers leap from the car to assist the distressed woman. She seems to be in shock.

And then another woman exits one of the crashed vehicles. This one seems dazed. Her nose is swollen and bleeding.

The two female victims will occupy the Urfa police for a while as the mini-van slips away.

The officers rush to the elderly woman, Eve, and crouch down to hear her speak. "I need a bathroom," she says. The two policemen look at each other a bit embarrassed about what might have happened, then help the woman to her feet. With one officer on each side, Eve—carrying her oversized purse—is helped to the Women's Room in the terminal.

✦ ✦ ✦

Wyatt throws his cell phone against the wall.

The Blackwatch station chief in Urfa has just told him that three Blackwatch employees had been killed at the airport. The only other injured parties are two elderly women who were at the wrong place at the wrong time. All Blackwatch operations in Turkey are ordered suspended by the authorities and all personnel are to be frozen in place until a thorough investigation has been completed.

This is another big-time political snafu for Wyatt. Even this, however, would be tolerable if Charlotte and her gang had been eliminated. But clearly they had escaped.

Alice steps into Wyatt's office, ignoring the damaged phone on the floor. "I think you'll want to take this call, sir. On the landline."

Wyatt picks up the desk phone. "What is it now?" he sighs.

"Wyatt, it's William Sinclair. We need to talk about a drone attack in Turkey."

"Drone attack?" Wyatt feigns ignorance. He wonders if Sinclair can detect the note of anxiety in his voice.

"Our own intelligence sources say Turkish authorities are blaming Israel for sending a drone to blow up an RV at an archaeological dig near Urfa. The drone crashed at the site. Possibly a shoot-down they're saying."

Wyatt's stomach starts to ache. "I'm confused. What does that have to do with Blackwatch?"

"Don't play dumb, Wyatt. We know you bought three Israeli-made drones last year. How long will it take the Israelis to produce the purchase documents? We also know you have a drone command center in Amman, so you have operational capability. This is all in your records, which we got when we bought the damn company! Now… if that drone served a good purpose—and I think you know what I mean—then all is well and good. But if not, there'll be hell to pay. So tell me, Wyatt. Was the mission successful? And you better give me an honest answer."

How can so much perspiration roll off one's face when there's a chill in the air?

"Yes sir," Wyatt lies. "Mission accomplished."

After a long pause, Sinclair says, "And my daughter?"

"Safe." Wyatt speaks with greater conviction on this topic.

"That's all for now."

Sinclair disconnects.

Wyatt throws the desk phone against the wall. It lies there dead, as Wyatt soon will be if he can't finish this mission quickly.

"You're shot!" Charlotte says, looking at the fabric hole and thick red streak on Herb's shirtsleeve.

"Just a graze," Herb explains. "Doesn't even hurt. Much."

Gideon inspects the wound. It's more than a graze. He tears off the man's other shirtsleeve and begins to bind the oozing wound with it. "We should get some antiseptic for this."

The group is standing outside the mini-van, which is parked among other vehicles in a small marketplace in Hilvan, a village about ten miles north of the airport. Caleb stands by herself, still perplexed by the strange turn of events. No words have been exchanged since leaving the airport.

Francois rubs his face and says, "I don't see how much more I can help you."

"We should not have asked you to bring us to the airport. That was too much," Charlotte offers.

"No, no," Francois replies. "I'm happy to have helped, but to be perfectly honest, I'm shaking in my boots." He laughs nervously.

"We'll take it from here, Francois." Gideon pats the man's shoulder and smiles. "We're all very grateful. You should head back to your place now."

"And leave you here?" Francois asks.

Gideon gestures to a parked van four spaces away. "We'll find a ride."

After warm embraces by everyone but Caleb, Francois drives away.

Charlotte approaches Caleb, looking her in the face. The woman is pretty in a way and obviously in great shape. Her face, though, is a blank slate. She merely stares back at Charlotte with no betrayal of emotion. Charlotte can't imagine this woman as a highly-skilled assassin. She is just too ordinary.

Charlotte had dreamed of one day facing Caleb, the woman who had killed her true love, and tearing her head off. Or ripping her heart out. Just for spite. But now that Gideon is alive, much of that anger has drained away and she is left with fatigue. And a lot of questions.

She never could have imagined being with Caleb in a small Turkish village and starting a conversation. But here she is.

"You knew my mother," she says awkwardly, stating the obvious.

"I loved your mother," Caleb says. Her eyes flicker slightly as she speaks, as if she means it. "I was told she was dead."

"Me too. And now she's alive. Gideon, and then my mother—it makes you believe in resurrection."

Caleb smiles. "When you're dead, you're dead," she says.

"Well then—I can't really say it was nice meeting you. After all, you've been trying to kills us."

"That order has been revoked by Eve, the only person who could do it. And by the way, we don't kill for vengeance. Or pleasure."

"So nice to know."

Charlotte turns to the others and takes a step toward Gideon. "I think you knew my mother was alive and here in Urfa. Why didn't you tell me?"

Gideon looks up at her. "She asked me not to."

"But she was dead... that's what Rebecca told me."

Rebecca looks up. "That's what Cain told *me*," she says, registering her defense. "I don't know why he would lie to me."

Gideon closes the gap with Charlotte.

"Eve contacted me through channels we had established years ago in case there was ever a breach or a fracture in the organization. I was startled to find out she was still alive. She and Cain had been given an ultimatum by the Twelve—one of them had to go. Cain offered to be the one, but according to Eve, she could never let that happen to her grandson."

"Very loving," Charlotte remarks sarcastically. "But how did she—?"

"Escape? And make it look like she had died?"

Everyone nods, even Caleb.

"Eve had an attendant named Rachel who looked very much like her. Rachel, it turns out, had been betraying the organization, so she was dispensable. I knew her since I joined the Order. Anyway, dressed in a silver robe like Eve's, Rachel fell off an outdoor balcony. When they found her a few thousand feet below, the body was too shattered to be identified, so in death she became Eve. Your mother escaped from the gompa through ancient secret passages only she and Cain knew about—perks of leadership. Cain told everyone that Rachel had fled because her betrayal had been found out."

"You say Rachel *fell*?" Charlotte asks.

"With a little encouragement," Gideon says. "I'm going now to find us transportation."

As Gideon walks away, Charlotte wonders if hers is the most dysfunctional family in the world.

Two minutes later a van pulls up and Gideon, the driver, waves them all inside.

Chapter 67

In the Urfa terminal, the Women's Room door opens and a woman, looking to be in her fifties, struts out. She is clearly not the woman the police officers brought in. She's younger, has a different hair color and style, sexy rose-tinted sunglasses, a tiny purse, and a pretty damn good figure.

Eve aggressively approaches an officer.

"Are you the one who brought in that old lady?" she asks.

The officer nods and gestures to the second officer, meaning that the two of them partnered on the deed.

"She's a little embarrassed by, um, a little accident she had, you know? Trying to get cleaned up now. She thanks you for your patience."

The officers nod and Eve walks away, heading for a taxi stand outside. "Take good care of her," she says with a victorious smile while pulling a mobile phone from her purse.

✦ ✦ ✦

Killing time, Gideon drives aimlessly through the dusty streets of Hilvan. Suddenly his phone rings and he switches on the speakerphone.

"I'm getting a taxi at the airport right now," Eve says. "Where should we meet?"

Gideon stares into the rearview mirror looking for ideas from his companions. He doesn't know any landmarks outside the airport.

Caleb sighs. "I have a small jet on standby at the airport. Says *Ankara Charters* on it. I'll call the pilot."

She looks at the bloody wrap around Herb's arm. The elderly man is bravely trying to hide his pain. "There's a first aid kit on board," she adds.

Gideon thinks he can detect genuine concern in Caleb's eyes, but it could be the mirror. Anyway, why would he be surprised? He's an assassin too, but he feels compassion from time to time. Hell, he even feels love. Why would Caleb be any different?

Caleb finds her cell phone and places a call.

"Did you hear that?" Gideon asks Eve. "A jet at the airport."

"Yes, I'll meet you there."

Gideon hangs up and there is a long silence after Caleb instructs the pilot to prepare for immediate departure.

"I just don't know how you two can be in the same vehicle together," Charlotte says, meaning Gideon and Caleb. She's been holding this thought since they all had packed into the mini-van at the airport.

Expressionless, the two assassins look at each other via the mirror.

"I admire her," Gideon says. "She's damn good at her job. Unfortunately for me, I became a target. That wasn't her fault."

"It was just business," Caleb adds. "We both follow orders."

"And we both love the same woman," Gideon adds.

Caleb nods.

Affection for Eve, and undying respect for the deposed leader's decisions, has made it safe for them to be in the same vehicle and both emerge alive.

The old jet, a 1989 Bombardier Challenger, wearily sits alone about fifty yards from the terminal. As the six fugitives casually approach the getaway craft, the door opens and Eve descends the stairs.

"Ready to take off," she says.

She motions for the exhausted party to board but holds back Caleb. The confident, sometimes cocky assassin lowers her eyes as Eve speaks, prepared for a chewing out.

"You did the right thing, Caleb," Eve says, gently placing a hand on the woman's shoulder, "obeying Cain's order."

"Thank you," Eve replies, looking up. Her face softens.

"You have always been like a daughter to me."

"You are Eve, mother to all."

"It may not be fair, but mothers have favorites. I lost my only daughter, Charlotte, when she was seven. I suppose you could say I abandoned her—you know the story. Every mother needs a daughter, Caleb. And a son."

Caleb knows that Eve is referring to Cain—Greg Ansari—her grandson.

"I don't understand how they could have done this to you," Caleb says. "And then brought in this other group of... of—"

"Butchers," Eve says. "Blackwatch. Unfortunately, the Twelve are living in fear right now—afraid that they won't uncover the secret until it's too late."

"They put a Blackwatch merc in charge of my operation in Ireland."

Eve shakes her head in commiseration. "I've been thinking, Caleb, a lot—that our agenda all these years, our God-directed mission, may have been usurped. It hurts to even consider the possibility, but maybe all our efforts have served the wrong purpose."

Caleb studies her feet again. Eve guesses that Caleb has harbored the same doubts.

"What do you want me to do?" Caleb asks.

"I'm no longer Eve. You have to decide for yourself what you should do. Retire, if they let you. Stay with the Order. It's up to you. I only ask one thing."

"What?"

"I ask that you keep it secret that Gideon and I are alive. Never tell anyone. It's our only hope to ever have a life outside the Order, otherwise we'll be hunted down mercilessly."

Eve can see tears forming in Caleb's eyes. She can't remember this strong woman ever crying before.

"You trust me?"

"Always."

"You're saying goodbye, aren't you?"

This time Eve averts her eyes. She can't bear seeing her beloved Caleb's tears. "Yes," she says finally.

Caleb looks shattered—as if she had gotten her best friend back—her *only* friend—only to lose her again.

"If you're going to disappear, I want to go with you," Caleb begs.

"You're resourceful. You can find your way back… to wherever you want to go. I'm going to help stop the Twelve from fulfilling their plan. It's time for you to decide what you're going to do."

Caleb can't speak. This time Eve herself is severing the relationship.

"I pray to God that we do not end up on opposite sides," Eve says, "but if we do, I will still love you like a daughter."

Suddenly Eve seems overcome with emotion. She reaches out to Caleb and hugs her tightly, holding back sobs. "Be well, my dear," she whispers.

Through a window, Charlotte sternly watches her mother embrace Caleb, her surrogate daughter.

Eve pulls away, fleeing up the stairs to disappear into the plane, leaving Caleb alone on the tarmac to stare into the face of Eve's true daughter.

In the end, blood trumps everything.

Numb from the stress, the occupants of the Ankara Charters aircraft sink into their plush leather executive seats. Eve has taken a seat next to Thompson, who refuses to look at her. For a month every year she and her husband had pretended that there was no Sicarii, no council of the Twelve, no blood-stained hands. During these times Thompson had showered her with attention and love. She had not always been free enough of distractions to return the favor, but by the end of each *conjugal visit* she would leave with the absolute confirmation that Thompson still loved her.

Such loyalty.

This time, of course, she had gone too far. For too long she had been on the side that was set on murdering the family. Who could forgive that?

But her eyes, once blind, are now open. Doesn't Thompson understand that finally, after all these years, she will be his wife every day of each year? All these decades, and finally she understands that she loves the old fool.

It will take time, she tells herself. Maybe some of the wounds will never heal. But she and Thompson have a chance to be together, if that's what he wants.

A shiver snakes through her. *What if he no longer wants her?* She has nothing else—not even her grandson. Charlotte will never accept her. Like Thompson, her daughter can't look her in the eye. Eve may be alone the rest of her life. The thought devastates her.

She turns to watch Charlotte and Rebecca, like a mother and daughter, crack open the plane's first aid kit and begin to treat Herb's nasty wound.

Miriam—*she has to stop thinking of herself as Eve*—relives the sacrifices she has made for the Order. Her family is at the top of that list. And for what? For nothing. No—probably for evil. She had spent decades destroying the ones she loved most to achieve the perverted agenda of people she does not trust and doesn't even like.

If she had not been fulfilling the Will of God, as she had once believed, then she was a *murderer* plain and simple. A *mass* murderer.

And she had probably pushed Caleb, dear Caleb, the gifted woman she had lured into this profane calling, back into the clutches of…

My God! The sudden emptiness of her life seems to swallow her whole. Closing her eyes, she tries to picture the future. All she can see is darkness.

But then she feels something—a warm touch on her hand. She opens her eyes. Looks down. Sees Thompson's wrinkled hand gently resting on hers.

He still cannot look at her, but he's found a way to relieve some of her suffering.

There is hope! For now, this touch is enough to keep her going.

Chapter 68

Caleb watches the old Bombardier jet shoot into the sky.

She feels totally lost. What's she to do now? Her irrevocable order has been revoked. Of course, Cain doesn't know. Michael doesn't know. Blackwatch doesn't know. The Council of Twelve doesn't know.

It's hard to admit, but those few moments in the vehicle with Charlotte and her gang—even with Gideon—was fun. And she had honestly felt badly for that stoic old guy, Herb, with the injured arm. Maybe she's been on her own too long. Getting squirrely, soft. Losing her edge.

It's definitely time to retire, though in her heart she knows the Order will never let her go. If she stops being one of them, she will stop *being*. Period. The way they had treated Eve made that very clear.

Her gut is twisting into knots. She had so badly wanted to join Eve on that plane. To be family. To ride off into the sunset with someone she cares about so deeply.

Of course, that could've never worked. Not with Eve's real daughter, Charlotte, in the picture. Not with Gideon there. No matter how professional Gideon claims to be, no one can simply dismiss an attempted assassination. That *is* personal.

She likes Gideon, actually. She'd never met him before—that's how she's always preferred it, never having met any of the other assassins—but in the past fleeting minutes she saw reason to envy Gideon. Not because he had survived her gunshots, but because he had found someone to love. The furtive glances that he and Charlotte shared, their obvious concern for each other, and how they found ways to touch—however briefly and "accidentally"—accentuates the hopelessness of Caleb's life.

It's not true, she knows, that assassins don't want to share a life.

But she has no one. Nobody at all. She's a spinster. Even Eve, her "mother," has pushed her out of the nest. Even worse, Caleb has lost all sense of purpose. The motivating power of knowing she was doing *good* has been sapped by fears that she has been unwittingly doing *evil*.

She looks up at the sky, hopeful that an invisible drone up there might mercifully strike her down. Put her out of her misery.

The chirp of her phone startles her. She's embarrassed that she jumped.

Then her heart swells. It must be Eve! Maybe she's calling to say she made a mistake, the plane is turning around—*get ready to board and fly away with me.*

"Yes," she answers brightly.

"Caleb, it's Michael."

Michael? What Michael? And then it registers—*Michael of the Council of Twelve.* She is speechless, which creates an awkward pause, and then…

"Is this a bad time?"

If he only knew.

Thompson awakes with a snort, turning blearily toward the sound of laughter coming from someone next to him. He focuses his eyes on his hand. A woman's hand is solidly, almost desperately grasping his. He moves his gaze from the hand, up the arm, to a familiar face.

"Welcome back," Miriam Walker says to her husband.

"Where was I?" Thompson asks, his brain still cloudy.

"You tell me."

He had been dreaming. Something *important*—he remembers that much. A star-filled sky appears to him as a vision, but it's quickly gone.

"I was dreaming about Enoch, I think. But it was me in the dream, not the old patriarch."

Miriam's smile disappears and she repositions herself to look more directly at her husband. "Enoch was taught the mysteries of the stars by the Watchers," she says. "He wrote down what he learned in the Book of Enoch. Have you been reading it? Sometimes what we read haunts our dreams."

"Yes, yes," he stammers. "In my dream I was Enoch, and I was writing down my learning, my observations, as best I could, but I was frustrated because I didn't have the words to describe it all. I was standing somewhere, I don't know where, and looking up, and writing down what I saw. And then someone said to me, *You can navigate by the stars, you know.* It was Schultz speaking to me—he said those very words earlier."

He abruptly sucks in his breath. His eyes grow large.

Fearing a heart attack, Miriam reaches for his face and turns it toward hers.

He smiles at her, but he's looking right through her, seeing something else, some other world. And then he grins.

Miriam is sure he's flipped out. A stroke, maybe.

"Eureka!" he yells.

Miriam lurches away from the madman.

He laughs. "I've always wanted to say that."

"Tommy, what is going on?" Miriam asks.

"I've solved the great mystery," he declares. "It was a dream, just like in the Bible. God or His angels—or maybe Schultz speaking from the grave—just showed me how to find Enoch's house of crystal."

He starts searching his pockets for something, saying "Where's my phone?"

✦ ✦ ✦

Like the others huddled in Camelot, Jeremy views with astonishment the unimaginable story unfolding on the large screen, the result of Wonderboy's clever data analysis and quantum computing. His phone rings twice before he thinks to answer it, so absorbed is he in the silent, shocking, terrifying drama.

"Hello," he finally says into his cell phone, unable to take his eyes away from the screen.

"It's Thompson, put Wonderboy on!"

This reconnection with the other team snaps Jeremy out of his trance. "Thompson, thank God! Is everyone safe? What's going on?"

Wonderboy taps his keyboard, killing the hypnotic flow of data. Everyone turns toward Jeremy.

"We're fine," Thompson explains. "I'll fill you in on the details later. Right now, just find Wonderboy and hand him the phone"

"He's here, I'm putting you on speaker."

"Wonderboy… I'm just trying to calm down," Thompson says. "We're all safe and heading back to Ankara. But I may have come up with a way to locate the house of crystal."

Wonderboy looks at the attentive audience gathered around the phone—Darcy, Mason, and Jeremy. "We're all ears, go ahead."

"I remember your astronomy screensaver," Thompson says. "I need you to put on your astronomer hat right now and help me chart a course using the stars as our guide."

"Okay, hold on." Wonderboy's fingers skate over his keyboard. A browser appears on the screen. "There's a piece of software I need called SkyLathe. It'll let me build any section of sky we want at any time in history. There!"

He finds the download site he wants. "Two hundred bucks? I don't think so." Like a magician performing sleight-of-hand, his fingers dance and the screen changes and before anyone can figure out what he has done, the software has been bought and is downloading to Honey.

"Installing now," Wonderboy says.

"Good. While you're at it, find a free version of the Book of Enoch online and go to the section called the Book of Heavenly Luminaries. That's our instruction manual."

Mason and Darcy look at each other, confused by Thompsons's requests, then at Jeremy, who merely shrugs. This is no weirder than the incredible story Honey has been piecing together from global genealogical records and other hacked data.

"The software's installed, now booting up," Wonderboy says. "Wow. Really shitty interface for two hundred bucks."

"You didn't pay for it, remember?" Jeremy reminds him.

Wonderboy ignores him and addresses Thompson. "It would be useful to know when Enoch visited this place. Do you have a year?"

"That's a problem. He lived in pre-history. We'd know almost nothing about him if he hadn't written down his experiences. But if we use the Bible's chronology, which I've done before, and work backwards from some Old Testament characters and events that we can date…"

"Like what?" Wonderboy asks.

"Well, let's take Noah's flood."

"A myth, right?" Darcy suggests.

"There's actually physical evidence of a large flood," Thompson states flatly. "Dr. Franklin Howard at Oxford, a good friend of mine, has theorized that a massive comet which struck the Mediterranean in the year 3150 BC could explain a rapid rise of water in the Middle East. If that's the right timing, then Enoch would have been born about 4300 BC, and his ascension into heaven would have been in something like 3950 BC. Nearly six thousand years ago."

Mason takes control of one of the other quantum computers and frantically begins typing. "When my staff and I were researching electromagnetic fields, which are important to quantum computing, we came across an obscure bit of data that might tie into this comet thing. Let me try to find it."

"And I'll study this Enoch material," Wonderboy says. "If his observations are crude attempts to describe the skies—well, we'll see what to make of it."

Jeremy leans toward the phone. "Is Rebecca there? This is Jeremy—I'd like to speak to her."

Thompson replies, "She's asleep right now. We've all been through a lot in the past few hours so I'd rather not wake her."

"Can you please tell her I asked about her?"

Before Thompson can respond, Mason excitedly interposes some found data. "Thank God for Google. Not sure how this applies, but regarding comets, their entry into our atmosphere is associated with a strong electromagnetic signature."

"You're losing me," Thompson says.

A bit exasperated, Mason continues. "When a large object like a comet moves at very high speed through the atmosphere, it causes a plume of intense electro-magnetic radiation."

"Are you saying the friction of a comet produces an electric current?" Thompson asks.

"Yes, a really powerful one. But even more important, this current can produce an enormous magnetic field much stronger than the earth's natural magnetic field. A geological record of these changes is preserved in the earth itself wherever a ferrous-loaded substrate congealed. Way too technical, sorry. But this record has actually been charted. Did you know that the magnetic field of our planet has completely reversed four times over the past five million years? I'm looking at this right now on a website."

"Let me see that," Wonderboy says, sliding over.

"Where are you going with this?" Thompson sounds impatient, like he's sorry he brought up the subject of comets.

"I don't really know, but indulge us for a minute. We're looking right now at a calibration chart that shows variations in the direction of the planet's magnetic field over time. And on this chart, we can clearly see a large perturbation at about 3150 BC—probably a large comet impact. What else would do it?"

"So that confirms Dr. Howard's theory about a comet strike that year," Thompson says.

"But there's another perturbation—much, much larger—between 7000 and 8000 BC Averaging it out, say 7500 BC"

"Much larger impact—much larger destruction," Thompson summarizes. "And possibly a much bigger flood."

"There's a link on this webpage," Wonderboy interjects. "It goes to another page that displays a chart of nitric acid in ice-core samples in Greenland. It shows a huge spike between the years 7500-7700 B.C. According to this article, when a high-energy comet impacts the sea, huge amounts of nitric acid are formed when nitrogen in the atmosphere is burned up by the passage of the comet."

"And how about this?" Mason yells. "There is evidence from tektites found in seabed core samples that at this same time period, seven comets crashed into the deep sea on earth. Literally all over the planet. That could have produced one monster worldwide flood."

"This is way too much information for me to process," Thompson complains. "Wonderboy, time to end the geek party and get on that Enoch astronomical analysis. I'll deliberate over the rest of this information."

"Comets and floods and ancient history—what the hell are we doing?" Darcy says. "I thought we were looking for a house of crystal."

The phone connection is lost.

Chapter 69

Thompson tinkers with his phone, refusing to admit he has lost the connection, then sits back in his seat.

"Are you back for good?" he asks Miriam without looking at her.

"For good," she says. "I've been hoping you'd be happy to see me alive."

"My feelings are mixed right now."

"Of course. Then let's talk about something else. Your star map, maybe."

Thompson turns and stares suspiciously at her. Is this an elaborate spy mission for the Order to find out what they know?

Miriam seems to understand his mistrust. "Think back, Tommy—all these years. Can you remember even once that I lied to you?"

He shakes his head. "Often you told me truths I didn't want to hear, things that hurt—but no, you never lied to me."

"I've been betrayed by my own organization. I am back for good, Tommy. Maybe I can help you. I know things that Cain does not know, that Michael can only guess at. It was a mistake for that man to get rid of me. Let me help you find Enoch's house of crystal before Cain does. You know he's awfully good at solving puzzles."

Thompson can feel the anger rising up in his wife. Knowing her so well, he believes that she wants to help strike back at the Twelve.

Thompson had placed his phone on speaker when talking to his Balbriggan teammates and Miriam had heard everything.

"Before that call," he confesses, "I thought I could lead us to the crystal house. But it's too complicated. All I had was a clue. Maybe Wonderboy can figure it out."

Miriam cocks her head quizzically as if to say *who is Wonderboy?* Thompson realizes she couldn't possibly know the other team players—except for Herb, who had once flown "guests" to and from the Sicarii gompa—so he gives her a quick synopsis of Mason, Darcy, Jeremy, Wonderboy, and even Rebecca, who sits directly behind them. He also fills in Miriam on the Göbekli Tepe adventure and Francois' illuminating theory about the sacred number 2520.

Thompson stops talking. Miriam looks at him, waiting for more, but gets nothing. Instead, Thompson is thinking about Francois' theory, and how it suggests that in the Creator's sacred system of time and space, the number 2520 would be embedded somehow into the geometry and possibly the timing of events that have universal importance to His creation.

He decides to test the theory, expecting to quickly dismiss it, but hoping for some kind of revelation. He has learned from Mason and Wonderboy that a large comet entered the earth's atmosphere and broke into pieces, striking the oceans in seven locations and undoubtedly causing great flooding. Scientists believe the impact had been between the years 7500 and 7700 BC.

Mentally, he multiplies the sacred number 2520 by two, and comes up with the answer 5040, which has no apparent significance. Next, he multiples by three. His body visibly shudders when the answer 7560 pops into his head. As a date, this number is spot on! It's directly between the years 7500 and 7700 BC.

It must be a coincidence, he tells himself. Innately religious, he struggles to temper his bias toward seeing God's hand mysteriously at work here.

Describing the temple complex at Göbekli Tepe to Miriam has also stirred his memory of another number. The ancient temples had been purposely buried under twenty feet of soil sometime around 7500 BC. He had questioned why such architectural prizes would have been buried, and Dr. Schultz had said there were only theories. It may have been either to protect the temples from some eminent danger, or to hide the complex, erasing it from humankind's memory until, perhaps, some future time.

The proximity of the date on which the Watchers covered up Göbekli Tepe to the date of the massive seven-impact comet strike leads to a theory of Thompson's creation—that the builders of the temples may have seen the incredible destruction resulting from the cataclysmic comet strikes and protected their temples from harm before leaving the area for a safer place.

So where did the Watchers go? Wherever it was, that's where they took Enoch and showed him the house of crystal.

✛ ✛ ✛

Certain that the clues he needs to find the Lost Secret are to be found in the Order's archives, Cain has secluded himself among the writings of the ancients. Many of these had been handed down from one generation of the Order to another, never having been shared with the academic world which didn't even know of their existence. The Essenes had abandoned some scrolls near the Dead Sea, and these were accidentally found by others. But the real treasures had been meticulously protected against theft and damage. Some of these documents are in ancient languages that Cain does not know, but the scroll he is focused on now is an Aramaic update of an older one.

It is called the Book of Jacob.

The manuscript tells the story of the Old Testament patriarch Jacob and departs only slightly from the Genesis account of Jacob's Ladder, the episode that intrigues Cain. It is this story that gives Cain fresh insight about an object in the gompa that he has never understood, and which no one has ever explained to him, not even his grandmother. He suspects it may be a key to the Lost Secret.

The story of Jacob's Ladder is simple. Jacob, the grandson of Abraham and son of Isaac, had escaped from his twin brother Esau who was furious with Jacob for stealing his birthright. While fleeing to a relative's house, he stopped to sleep in the desert using an unusual stone as a pillow.

That night Jacob had a dream of a ladder or stairway between heaven and earth, and on it angels busily ascending and descending. He had seen God standing above the ladder. And then God had spoken to him, renewing the promise He had made to support both Abraham and Isaac. God had extended his promise to Jacob saying, *Behold, I am with you and will keep you wherever you go, and will bring you back to this land. For I will not leave you until I have done what I have promised you.*

Upon waking, Jacob had decided that God actually had been present in that place, so he had taken up the stone he had used as a pillow and had anointed it with oil, an act of consecration to God. He had then made a vow: *If God will be with me and will keep me in this way that I go, and will give me bread to eat and clothing to wear, so that I come again to my father's house in peace, then the LORD shall be my God, and this stone, which I have set up for a pillar, shall be God's house.*

This phrase excites him: *This stone… shall be God's house?*

Cain knows well the legend of this stone. Jacob memorialized the place of his dream by standing up the stone like a pillar or menhir, calling it Bethel, meaning *House of God.* Twenty-two years later, when blessed with great riches, Jacob had been directed by God to return to Bethel. There he had erected an altar of stones and a pleased God had changed Jacob's name to Israel, meaning *sons ruling with God.*

The stone of Jacob had become part of the birthright of his son, Joseph, ending up in Egypt. During the great exodus from Egypt, the Ark of the covenant and the stone of Jacob had accompanied the Israelites on their 40-year journey through the wilderness. As the only stone ever "anointed"—an act reserved for kings, priests and a few prophets—Jacob's stone had become a powerful instrument for king-making.

The prophet Jeremiah, according to the old stories, had brought the stone to Ireland, and eventually Saint Patrick blessed the stone for use in crowning the kings of the Emerald Isle. Often called the Stone of Destiny, Jacob's stone pillow had found its way to Scotland and then to England where the coronation chair in use today had been built around it. All the kings and queens of Ireland, Scotland and England have been crowned while sitting or standing upon that stone.

The Book of Jacob that Cain is studying, however, claims that Jacob's stone never went to Ireland but was hidden away by the Essenes as the one sacred king-making stone required for consecrating a new High Priest, should one be identified. Without the stone, no High Priest could be installed.

Cain rushes out of the archives and finds the vacant Inner Chamber. He makes his way to the center chair on the top tier, the one usually occupied by Michael. Behind it, perched above the head of a seated man, is the shining black stone that had so intrigued Cain on previous visits.

He had always assumed that this adornment is the true Stone of Jacob, hidden by the Essenes. But that assumption seems wrong now. Its position above the head of a seated Michael suggests that it is just a replica, like the Sicarii's showpiece Ark of the Covenant. Hadn't Jacob's pillow lain beneath the head of the famous prophet? Why then would it be positioned here above the head of a man who is not a prophet or even a High Priest, but merely a proxy for one?

In this chamber he has overheard in passing the words "meteorite" and "tektite," assuming they referred to the black stone on the pedestal. A gift from the heavens. From God. Deposited in the cold desert for Jacob to find. Imbued with supernatural, or maybe *natural* powers.

Tektite is thought by mystics to promote the gift of telepathy. In this modern era, perhaps, the authentic stone might intensify the power of the crystals to transmit thoughts over the earth's enfeebled telluric currents.

Yet now Cain is less certain that he is looking at the true Jacob's Stone. If it is not, then the genuine article may be part of the Lost Secret.

What would happen, he wonders, if Jacob's Stone were found and moved to Enoch's crystal temple? Would the faded psychic power and diminishing global influence of the Elites be restored?

What if the tale of Jeremiah carrying the sacred stone to Ireland were true? Cain searches his capacious memory for related information. Even though he forgets very little of what goes into his brain, there is not much there about Jeremiah and Ireland. But a vague recollection about the prophet surfaces.

Jeremiah had lived in the days of King Nebuchadnezzar, the tyrant who destroyed Solomon's Temple and had the eyes of the Jewish king, Zedekiah, plucked out. The name Zedekiah reveals that this blinded king was himself a Zadokite priest. Jeremiah was asked to take Zedekiah's daughters and the sacred king-making stone to a land in the north now known as Ireland.

Jacob's Stone.

Ireland.

A fascinating confluence of information teases Cain, tempting him with the promise of a breakthrough. With a rush of excitement, Cain races to the Sicarii CIA and commandeers a powerful workstation, immediately searching the Web for data to aid his memory. Jeremiah had recorded God's instructions to him. Consulting the Book of Jeremiah in an online Bible, he finds what he is looking for:

Take the great stones in thine hand and hide them...

The daughter in Egypt shall be confounded; she shall be delivered into the hand of the people of the north.

What if Jeremiah had taken one of Israel's great stones—Jacob's Stone— along with Zedekiah's daughter on his fateful journey to Ireland?

More memories are stirring. Cain struggles to correlate them with this new line of reasoning. Frantically he searches the Web for data regarding ancient Irish history and legends.

In the colorful legends of Tara, the ancient seat of the high kings of Ireland, he discovers an enduring Celtic tradition that a princess of the House of David had come to Ireland with a sacred king-making stone, and it is assumed that this is the Stone of Destiny upon which royalty is still crowned.

Ireland. Jacob's Stone. The daughter of Zedekiah.

Some traditions are born of truth.

With a pounding pulse, Cain searches deeper, certain now of a looming breakthrough. He finds the physical location of the Hill of Tara near the River Boyne, on which ancient passage tombs had been built resulting in two spiral-shaped earthworks. The symbol, clearly shown in an aerial photograph, is eerily reminiscent of the three spiral motif on his grandmother's necklace and in the ancient Essene manuscript.

Standing proudly on the Hill is the historic Stone of Destiny that had been buried there, or so the tourist placard claims. Cain doubts it. And he doubts that the Stone currently residing at Edinburgh Castle in Scotland, except during British coronation ceremonies, is the genuine article either.

According to the legends, the people of the Goddess Danu, called the Tuatha De Danaan, had come to Ireland from a land north of Ireland. They were a tall, fair-skinned race, sometimes referred to as giants, as were the Watchers encountered by Enoch. The Tuatha De Danaan called the great stone the *Lia Fial*, which was said to shriek loudly when the rightful king was near.

At times like this, Cain feels like he is just along for the ride as his Asperger's gift kicks into high gear, his supercharged brain churning away, disassembling and reassembling information, finding hidden connections and meanings. He had been afraid that he had lost this gift, perhaps had been cured of the syndrome that for years had been his constant companion. Without it he is ordinary. Normal. Ungifted. Unworthy of being the Divine Light.

With it he can be the savior of the Order.

It's not too late.

Unquestioningly now he surrenders to the Asperperger's momentum. He is not sure why or how he is proceeding, just that he is moving forward.

Google Earth.

His fingers tap keys, launching the software and entering in a search for *Hill of Tara*. The software spins a globe of the earth and zooms in on the location. He zooms out slightly and looks around the terrain realistically mapped by satellite photos. He finds the Boyne River and follows it inland from the coast. On the river's shores, less than ten miles from the Hill of Tara, is a cluster of three large megalithic mounds. From the aerial perspective of Google Earth, the mounds are in a formation much like the three spirals of that mysterious motif.

He zooms in on the center mound and clicks links to some information. He learns that this particular mound, according to legend, had been the abode of the Tuatha de Danaan, the giant invaders of Ireland who sometimes had intercourse with humans, like Enoch's Watchers, and called themselves the Lords of Light.

Cain finds himself breathing fast. This flood of information is whipping his normally emotionless self into a frenzy of excitement.

He clicks on a photograph of the mound showing a large carved stone next to the entrance. The picture sucks the air out of his lungs.

It's time to make his first trip to Ireland.

Turns out he didn't need his mother and her companions after all because his gift has returned. Now they are all completely dispensable.

Except for Rebecca, of course.

Chapter 70

Charlotte does not believe that the smooth landing in Ankara is an omen.

The hour-long nap has left her craving more sleep. Feeling groggy, she exits the Ankara Charters jet at Etimesgut Air Base with the others. Supported by her pillar of strength, Gideon, she walks on rubbery legs toward the charter terminal.

"The Gulfstream is over there." Rebecca points to the parked jet.

"I know we should get back to Balbriggan and regroup," Charlotte says, "but I need to walk a bit. Every muscle in my body is rebelling right now."

"I left a message for the crew that we were heading back," Gideon says. "Maybe they're on board. I'll take a look."

He heads for the Gulfstream.

Inside the small terminal Charlotte and Thompson buy Turkish coffees to enliven their brains. Miriam approaches the wounded Herb, who has chosen to sit down. "We missed your services," she says, referring to his previous helicopter trips to the Order's gompa.

With his good arm, Herb reaches out and shakes her hand, forcing a smile. "Looks like I'm still helping shuttle Sicarii from place to place."

"I'm no longer part of it. I'm now just Mrs. Walker."

"If you don't mind my saying, I've known Tommy for quite a while. I've seen him after some of your times together. Those annual break-ups were always pretty hard on him. He needs a little reassurance that you're back for good."

"Only time will convince him. He doesn't know how much I need him."

A cell phone rings—Thompson's. Eve and Charlotte crowd around him. The prevailing theory is that every call is either encouraging news or something absolutely terrifying. The group walks to a vacant corner of the terminal as Thompson puts the call on speaker.

"It's Wonderboy," the caller announces. "I've been working on that astronomy challenge. Care for an update?"

Would he? Thompson rolls his eyes, in no mood for small talk. "Of course!"

"I looked at Enoch's arcane descriptions of the sun's movements across the sky during the course of a year. Passages like—well let me read one: *And I saw six portals in which the sun rises, and six portals in which the sun sets. Six in the east and six in the west.*"

Hopeful, Thompson asks, "Were you able to determine where he was from those observations?"

"Not really. But in reading the entire book I did find something useful. Enoch wrote this: *...I went toward the north to the ends of the earth.* So he was obviously in a northern latitude."

"That narrows it down to half the earth," Miriam grumbles.

"I'm not finished. I worked out one of the days he mentioned to be an equinox—either March 21 or September 21. Enoch wrote: *On that day the day is longer than the night by a ninth part, and the day amounts exactly to ten parts and the night to eight parts.* This is our key—Enoch's length of day estimates, which unfortunately are inexact. But I've accommodated the vagueness and calculated that the latitude where he was standing was somewhere between 51° North and 59° North."

"Well, that narrows it a little," Thompson says. "Where does that band cross over land?"

"Across Greenland, Canada and Alaska, but anywhere in North America seems unlikely."

"Agreed," Thompson says. "Where else? I suppose across Siberia."

"Yes, and then through a broad slice of Scandinavia. Here's what is most interesting. The band stretches across the U.K, including where we are situated right now in Ireland. Darcy says there are scores of megalithic sites in this neighborhood, so there were certainly people and impressive structures here at the time of Enoch."

"Let's not get ahead of ourselves." Charlotte has finally swept her brain free of cobwebs and is making sense of the cryptic conversation. "We need to narrow down the possible locations within that range of latitudes."

"I have an idea... if you've got the time," Thompson says to the phone.

"Sorry," Wonderboy says sarcastically. "I've got a Christmas pageant this evening."

✦ ✦ ✦

As he nears the Gulfstream mercifully parked on a patch of unsecured tarmac, Gideon checks his phone. Damn! No callbacks from the crew. He continues the short journey to the aircraft and boards it. The cabin has been cleaned, but he finds no crew in the cockpit. There is only one other place where a human could be—the john.

The door is closed so he knocks.

No reply.

He pushes the unlocked door, but it moves only a few inches before jamming against something. Through the narrow opening Gideon can see two motionless uniformed bodies reflected in the rest room mirror.

The crew.

Obviously the Blackwatch operative had taken care of these two potential loose ends. Certainly it wasn't Caleb's doing. She never would have killed innocents. The rest room sarcophagus clarifies the ghastly difference between the principled Sicarii, as Gideon views the Order he had loved, and its new sister organization comprised of Blackwatch mercs.

Gideon has no regrets about his shifting loyalties. The Order has been hijacked. Even Miriam has abandoned the great Cause, which clearly has been corrupted.

Rushing out of the Gulfstream, he finds a baggage cart and wheels it out to the plane, giving casual waves to three passing airport workers. Back onboard he extracts the two bodies from the rest room, wraps them in passenger blankets from the cabin, and carries them down the stairs to the cart, which he wheels to the side of a storage facility. With luck, no one will discover the bodies until they have left the airport.

Thinking quickly, Gideon texts Mason, directing him to contact aviation authorities to say his private jet has been located in Turkey by hired detectives and is being returned by his authorized agents. This will prevent Gideon and the others from being arrested when landing at Luton airport.

One last problem to solve. The Gulfstream has no pilots.

Gideon surveys the airport grounds looking for ideas, as if he might find a queue of pilots looking for work.

What he sees is even better. The pilot who had flown them back from Urfa is walking toward a parked car, apparently preparing to leave the air base. Gideon runs toward the man, intercepting him.

Of course the pilot can fly the Gulfstream, or so he says. What a joy that would be. And yes, he's interested in making a lot of money. At the other end of the transaction there is also the possibility of a much more lucrative position as a corporate pilot for a well-financed international firm.

Gideon hands the pilot cash for refueling and suggests that they leave in thirty minutes or less. That would be worth a bonus, of course. The pilot begs for an hour, probably to bone up on the Gulfstream controls.

In the terminal, Gideon finds Charlotte and the others wearily sitting in uncomfortable chairs with steaming coffees in their hands. He nods to them, indicating everything is all right, and casually approaches Miriam.

"I need some money," he whispers. "I'm getting low on cash and I have one more transaction to go."

He knows that Miriam always travels with a large sum of cash. He's not disappointed.

At the information desk, he asks for a piece of paper and an envelope. He writes a short message and stuffs it with some cash and a cell phone into the envelope, writing a name on the outside. He hands the envelope to the English-speaking desk attendant.

"Hold this for Randall Turner," he says. "He'll ask for it by name. Please check his identification before giving it to him."

"Excuse me," a voice says.

Gideon turns to see a young man with closely-cropped hair approaching.

"I've been here about an hour," Randall says. "Is that for me?"

"Do you have ID?"

Randall shows his Passport. "I was starting to think I'd been lied to. It's hard to trust people these days."

"You'll need a new Passport in a different name," Gideon says, steering Randall toward a quiet corner of the terminal. "I've put instructions on where you can obtain one right here in Ankara—this afternoon if you want. As promised, there is money in this envelope for services rendered, and a cell phone."

Randall takes the envelope and looks inside, pleasantly surprised. "A man of his word," he says. "I don't suppose you have any other work for someone like me. As you know, I'm unemployed right now. And I can't go back to my old employer, even though they have an opening closer to home."

"Closer to home? Where would that be?"

The young man is in luck. His particular set of skills qualify him for a job that at just this very moment came into existence.

Chapter 71

At sunset, December 18, three Irish men—probably cousins of Darcy—greet the passengers as they exit the Gulfstream at Luton Airport. Their job is to take care of red tape regarding the safe return of the "stolen" private jet.

Herb, in an age-defying show of tough-guy grit, insists on flying his friends back to Balbriggan on the CCN chopper. Ever since he'd been wounded, Rebecca has been at his side, which Charlotte suspects may have something to do with his swagger.

At 6:30 p.m. the chopper sets down in the vacant Ambienz parking lot. The occupants head for the entrance, noticing a makeshift door braced into place. Charlotte can only imagine Blackwatch's frightening attempt to storm the building.

The Balbriggan team is waiting for them. Charlotte enjoys the warm embraces and though exhausted, she responds to the electric atmosphere of the reunion, sensing that Wonderboy and the others are holding something back, something they are desperate to share.

Jeremy is stunned to meet the legendary Eve, yet he can't draw his eyes away from the beautiful Rebecca. After a brief small talk free-for-all, Mason holds up his hands, stilling the voices.

"While you guys have been partying around the world," he says, "we've been laboring around the clock in our tiny Irish hamlet, doing God's work. I think you'll be pleased."

He gestures for the elevator, silently suggesting that he won't say more until they're securely ensconced in Camelot.

It takes the elevator two trips, but at last everyone is seated at the round table. Mason begins.

"We have all wondered who we have been battling. The Sicarii, yes, but we know that Michael Sinclair—aka Michael—is the ostensible head of a larger parent organization. But who are they, and what do they want? Why are they hunting us down? What's at stake? Well, we now have some of the answers. Let me turn it over to Wonderboy, who worked his magic to figure it all out."

Wonderboy remains seated. "We did it with the help of Mason's incredible quantum computers," he explains, "and a small army of unwitting Sentient contributors mining countless genealogical and other records. Here is what we have learned. First, who are they?"

He taps some keys and an organization chart appears on the wall-mounted screen.

"They are perhaps the largest network of wealthy families and organizations the world has ever known. From the powerful Rothschild family to kings and queens, even the ancestors of presidents. Through a complex web of interlocking corporations, multi-layered ownerships, control of banking, and profound political—even *religious*—influence, I don't think it would be exaggerating to say this "family," as I've come to call it, controls over two-thirds of the world's wealth, and we're just getting to the Far East."

Gideon and Miriam turn to each other. Could it be that they had known practically nothing at all about the organization they served?

Miriam is not convinced that Wonderboy's analysis is correct. "This does not sound at all like the Order I know," she complains. "Our mission was mainly a spiritual one, to bring about a more perfect world, a more rapidly advancing society. The job of the Sicarii was to purge the world of the bad guys who presented obstacles to the mission."

Wonderboy taps another key and the organization chart shrinks to make room for more boxes.

"It would take over twenty screens like this one to display the network as we know it. And we may know only a fragment of it. Almost everything we make and buy and trade puts money into their pockets."

He looks at Miriam, knowing he's evaded her concern. "Miriam, it's possible that the Order began with the mission as you knew it. Through a number of ancient records—the ones that've been digitized—I've pieced together the origins of the Order. I shouldn't take so much credit. Honey did most of the work."

He pats the top of the computer case.

"Care to see?"

✦ ✦ ✦

Above the moonlit clouds, on a chartered jet to Dublin, Cain speaks candidly to Michael by sat phone.

"I need to prove it!" he says.

"It's unwise. Your safety is more important. Friday is soon enough, when we have full security in place."

"Now that you've told me the truth about my role, I need to be there to make sure we get this right."

In the past, Cain has always been intimidated by the domineering, officious Michael, but no longer. Cain's likely uncovering of the Lost Secret has rebalanced the relationship, shifted control in his direction, but Michael resists the sudden tilt.

"I have men who can take care of everything. I absolutely forbid you to go there until I approve."

Knowing he now holds the good cards, Cain smiles. He metaphorically inserts a sica into Michael's back when he says, "No—you have my permission, Michael, to join *me* there. I arrive in three hours."

He's not surprised that Michael hangs up without comment.

The plane will be making one stop, to pick up another passenger. It will take some time to get used to having a new Eve, but he's glad it will be Caleb. He had not known—and neither had Caleb, apparently—that her pedigree made her next in line.

In the end, blood trumps everything.

✢ ✢ ✢

Wyatt nervously picks up the call from William Sinclair. Surely his failures have caught up with him. This will be the call to fire him… or worse.

"Wyatt here," he says.

"You're a Christian, aren't you, Wyatt?"

Confused, Wyatt answers, "Yes, of course I am."

"Christianity is all about redemption."

"I agree, sir."

"And do you agree that your past behavior has put you in need of redemption?"

Sinclair knows about the Göbekli Tepe catastrophe, the botched attack on Ambienz headquarters, the failed drone attack in Ireland, the costly destruction of Blackwatch's stores in France, and probably even Wyatt's wandering eye. Wyatt can hear the axe rise with a whoosh. He probably won't hear the fall.

"I have a mission for you. Succeed, and all is forgiven. Do you want redemption, Wyatt?"

"I do."

"I need a team, maybe six, in Dublin by morning. Your best. But no armor. This is clandestine, in plain sight. Secret Service—but *actually secret*. So rally your troops. I'll send you orders. No excuses this time, Wyatt."

A reprieve, of sorts.

Wyatt's fate again is in the hands of his mercenaries, which doesn't make him feel any better.

Whatever happened to his dream of raising Arabians on a ranch in Montana? Oh, that's right, it had seemed too risky.

✦ ✦ ✦

Randall Turner shows his forged Passport at the Ankara security checkpoint. *Donald Peterson*, it says.

He doesn't look a day older than his photograph.

Randall boards a flight for Newark. His operation is dangerous, but his anger toward Blackwatch is still white-hot. Plus… this new contract may prove to be even more lucrative.

Sleep on the flight, get off at Newark, take a cab to the suburban industrial park, and enter the Blackwatch's U.S. Drone Command Center. He'd watched Joshua enter the center in Amman without firing a shot. When no one is suspecting, it shouldn't be that hard.

If Gideon does his part, the rest should be easy.

Chapter 72

The Knights of the Round Table are gathered around Wonderboy, their Merlin, whose digital sorcery conjures unthinkable wonders.

"I thought you took some Blackwatch prisoners," Gideon says to Darcy. "They in the dungeon, or what?"

"We made friends and let them go." Darcy smiles.

Gideon understands. The audio tape of Wyatt directing a mission to kill his own men is damning. For mercenaries, it has the power to change alliances.

Wonderboy is anxious to steer the conversation to his recent revelations. "If you don't mind, I'd like to go back to when things all started—with Enoch."

Everyone agrees.

"After the time of Enoch there grew up a group of followers who became Enochian priests," he explains, "and they wielded great authority in their day. In the time of David, the greatest Enochian priest was a man named Zadok, who was descended from Moses' brother Aaron, who was that era's High Priest."

"Yes, that's right," Thompson interjects. "Zadok assisted King David when David's son Absalom revolted, and so helped David's wiser son Solomon ascend to the throne. Solomon named Zadok his high priest and he was the first one to serve in the legendary Solomon's Temple. From that time forward all high priests must be Sons of Zadok, meaning direct descendants."

Thompson stops suddenly. Inspiration has overtaken him. "If Zadok was the start, then—my God—I know the next part of the story."

Wonderboy stares at the old man. "Tell us then. I can only learn so much from digital history."

Thompson indulges him. "Like the Sicarii, Solomon was obsessed with the Shekinah, the light of God that would appear every 480 years as a bright star and herald the birth of a holy one, perhaps a savior. This was a pattern of conjunctions of two stars, of course—Venus and Mercury. A predicted Shekinah year, 967 BC, was chosen by Solomon for the building of his temple. And he chose Jerusalem as the place. In the language of Canaan, Jerusalem means *foundation for observing Venus rising.* Immediately after the laying of the temple's foundation stone, the blazing star—the Shekinah—rose quickly into the sky and illuminated the entire landscape."

Charlotte blows a stream of air out of pursed lips. "My son, Greg, was born at a forty-year cycle of the Shekinah. Along with his bloodline, that was a major reason he was qualified to become the Divine Light of the Order. But how does this all tie into—"

"Let me continue," Thompson says. "This much I know. Zadok and his other priests were repositories of great wisdom that had been collected over centuries. Some of this knowledge was encoded mathematically into Solomon's temple. But more important for us, the priests—particularly the high priest—held enormous influence over society."

"They were brokers of power, then," Wonderboy suggests. "That helps explain much of what happened next."

"One day Solomon held a great council of all the priests, including Zadok, the high priest, and declared that God had shown him that all gods and every religious belief were actually all part of one single truth. In other words, there was only one God.

"Solomon revered Enoch even more than Moses. So I now believe he instituted a new priestly order based on the mysterious teachings and rites of the Enochian priesthood, of which Zadok was the master. Why would he do this? Clearly, in his wisdom, he wished to bring about a new world order that could not be achieved through the offices of the old order. The new priests were to be hidden from view, operating covertly. They were in possession of great secrets passed down only to direct descendants. They wielded enormous power."

"It seems that their secrecy served them well."

"It also included a secret symbol. Solomon invented a kind of *logo* for his holy task force. It was comprised of a pyramid superimposed over an inverted pyramid. Recognize it?"

He draws the symbol on a piece of paper and holds it up.

"I thought that was the Star of David, the Jewish symbol. What does it mean?" Rebecca asks.

"It's the original Seal of Solomon. It's the astronomical mark of Jerusalem. If you superimposed on a sheet of paper the shadows cast by the sunrise and sunset at the two solstices, the angles would look just like this. I also think that for Solomon it represented the power of heaven coming down to earth—the downward point—and the the king and his people reaching toward heaven—the upward point. But then, as you all know, I'm not Solomon. I just think I am."

Once again Charlotte is losing patience with her father's professorial excursions. "The fact that this *logo* of his appears in so many contexts today means—what exactly? That he lost his copyright?"

Wonderboy blunts the diversion. "Charlotte, give your father a chance."

Thompson continues. "Solomon died, and the territories he governed split into two Israelite kingdoms. Over time, things became much more fragmented. But the Sons of Zadok must have remained cohesive over time and distance, or Wonderboy wouldn't be about to surprise us with the next installment. I've told you everything I know."

"Fortunately, priestly records were jealously protected, even in ancient times," Wonderboy explains. "My Sentient guys found many of them—and a lot were located in Dr. Doering's archives. We've been able to piece the story together about what happened to these Sons of Zadok—with a few holes, of course.

"In short, these star priests, or star families, were able over time to adapt, morph, and blend into many other traditions and organizations, probably co-opting them to advance their own cause. They were politically agnostic and religiously opportunistic. One party or religion was as good as another if it offered a power base from which to work toward building a new world order."

"How could you know this?" Miriam asks.

"We know because we can trace the genealogies of these star families, their movements into and out of these organizations, their alliances—often through marriages—with other power brokers. It seems that at some point, it became clear to them that achieving a new world order required money. And since they began with wealth and power, it probably made sense to leverage what they had—and the influence of the network of families—to acquire even more economic power."

"Holy shit," Charlotte exclaims. "You're describing what might be the greatest conspiracy of all time. No wonder my investigation threatened them—they knew that their fingerprints were all over the globe. Still, this kind of cohesive worldwide network hardly seems possible. This is over thousands of years, right? Including some very primitive societies. Conspiracies always unravel at some point."

"Undoubtedly. Many of these families eventually lost touch," Wonderboy answers.

He taps some keys and a map of the world appears with arrows showing where the families traveled.

"Some moved far away," Wonderboy continues. "They became French or German or English... whatever. The power of the families continued, but as the greater network evaporated their power could never be as great as if all the families were united, connected, and supporting each other. Still, the power of the families was enormous. Imagine! A relatively small group of the descendants of Zadok could essentially control the economics of the world, and thus the world itself. The power of political parties ebbs and flows like the tides. Religion is more and more regional and fragmented. Movements come and go. But the pure, inspired genius and commitment of the Sons of Zadok has survived."

Rebecca finally speaks up. She has been listening and trying to keep up, but the story seems too incredible. She needs details. "I'm not following. What kinds of groups did they infiltrate?"

"I'll just give you some examples that we've been able to trace," Wonderboy replies. "How about the Vikings of Normandy. They had a lot in common. The Viking goddess Freyja represented the star Venus and was called the Queen of Heaven. Maybe you've never noticed, but the heraldic badge of Normandy is two golden lions that are much like the Lion of Judah crest on the emblem of Jerusalem. Now we know why lions were chosen to represent a northern European people. But there are many other examples."

"Such as..." Rebecca prompts.

"Well, the Norse family from the line of Earl Rognvald was given the islands north of Scotland and adopted the family name St. Clair—and its variants, Sinclair, Sinkler... you see where this is going, Rebecca? An ancestor of yours going way back, an earlier William Sinclair, was perhaps one of the most influential and powerful men in the lineage. Rich and ambitious. He built the famous Rosslyn Chapel, which he began in the year 1441. Since there was no year zero when the calendar moved to CE, this is exactly 1440 years from the date Sinclair believed Christ was born. It is also one full Shekinah cycle of 1440 years."

Wonderboy sips coffee from a mug but makes a face. It's cold. "I could bore you with more details, such as their infiltration of the Knights Templar, the great families of Germany and France like the Rothschilds, Hapburgs Warburgs, Loebs. Oh, even Pope Urban II was a star family member. Why co-opt Christianity? Well, following the collapse of imperial Rome, there was no comparable power structure in western Europe. And the Sons of Zadok have always been about power.

"They found fertile ground in secret societies such as the Freemasons, the Carbonari, the Illuminati. And even later, their central roles in forming and administering many of the global banking institutions... well, I could go on, but we should probably turn to the problem they seem to have."

The lecture by Wonderboy has found sensitive touch points in Miriam, connecting with her observations from inside the organization.

"Their problem is clear to me. They are losing power and influence," she confidently states. "The world grows more complex as they continue to fragment. They need to reenergize their influence and solidify their control over the world's wealth to achieve their main goal—a better world ruled by them, the Elite. Or as I know them, the Twelve, headed by Michael."

"His name, as we know, is William Sinclair, the same as his ancestor's," Wonderboy responds, and taps a key. "We've been able to trace the current Mr. Sinclair back to his Scottish ancestor in the fifteenth century, and then back to the original Zadokian family. In terms of wealth and influence, he is largely invisible to the world, but through various mechanisms controls over two hundred and seventy organizations. He is worth more than a trillion dollars, but he appears on no published list of the richest men. Quite a feat. His wife is also a direct descendant of Zadok through some French kings. He has one daughter, Rebecca, now 21 years old."

All eyes turn suspiciously toward Rebecca, who squirms uncomfortably. "I knew he was rich," she mumbles. "I didn't know the rest—honest. I told you he was my father, didn't I?"

Charlotte deflects the attention from Rebecca. "This whole line of inquiry seems to suggest that some descendants Solomon's priests might think it's time for them to unite. Or am I wrong?"

"The prophecy!" Miriam says.

Attention shifts again to the former Eve.

"One of the old traditions of the Order says that Sarah, the only adult survivor of the Masada massacre, was approached by an unfamiliar wise man while she was a prisoner of the Romans," Miriam says. "He was one of the Sons of Zadok, perhaps? Anyway, he shared a prophecy with her, that at a prescribed time in the future, which we've been told is the winter solstice of 2012..."

"That's this coming Friday!" Jeremy says.

"And the date the Mayan's believed would end the world—or begin a new era," Charlotte adds.

"Likewise for the Hopi Indians," Mason chimes in.

"On the winter solstice," Miriam continues, "a ritual must take place at the site of Enoch's house of crystal."

"What kind of ritual?" Charlotte asks.

"I don't know. And I don't know where this crystal temple is, either."

Charlotte experiences a glimmer of understanding. "If their aim is unification of the families, we can certainly guess what kind of ritual it is. How have powerful families always united their relationships and aligned their interests?"

Jeremy tentatively speaks up. "You mean marriage?"

Charlotte looks at Rebecca. "Of course, a marriage. A ritual in a crystal temple. For those who cling to the tradition of Enoch, this would be a reunification ceremony in the holiest dwelling on earth. A marriage of two people of pure lineage to represent the uniting of the far-flung families and the restoration of the global alliance."

"That would explain why the house of crystal is so important," Thompson says. "It's possible they looked on Enoch's crystal temple as their own sacred temple. Remember, this was long before any Jewish temple was built in Jerusalem. Miss this ritual, and the opportunity for reunification is lost—as was the specific location, unfortunately."

"Aha!" Wonderboy exclaims. "But we do know where the house of crystal is. You see, I've saved the best for last."

Camelot explodes with excitement and chatter. Finally Thompson calms them down by yelling, "Shut up! Listen to the man."

Wonderboy launches Google Earth and clicks a destination that makes the globe spin and zoom to a large lake. "This is Lake Van in Turkey. Thompson told me that the ruins of the Armenian Monastery of St. George of Goms, located right here…" he points to a pushpin on the edge of the lake, "…is situated on the spot where Enoch ascended into heaven. This is perhaps the most significant feature of Enoch's life. So Thompson asked me to measure from that exact spot 2520 miles west to a band of latitudes stretching across the U.K. to see if anything interesting turned up."

He anchors a ruler on the monastery, spins the globe to Ireland, and pins the other end of the ruler to a circular mound. The measured distance is exactly 2520 miles.

"What is that?" Gideon asks. "It looks like a mound of some sort."

Wonderboy zooms closer. "My friends, this is Enoch's house of crystal."

The faces at the Round Table register disappointment. The grassy circle does not remotely resemble the elegant images of the crystal house they have formed in their minds.

"Oh, sorry" Wonderboy adds, "let me show you a photograph."

A picture of the megalith pops up. The structure beneath the mound has been unearthed exposing a round walled building. Wonderboy enlarges the photograph, provoking gasps from everyone.

The walls of the megalith gleam with white crystal.

"Ladies and gentlemen, I present Newgrange, built long before the pyramids—and before Enoch was born. Ironically, it's located less than fourteen miles from where we now sit."

Charlotte stands and walks closer to the screen, shaking her head. "All this searching," she says, "and we could ride a bike to it."

Chapter 73

"If you're right, Cain, I wouldn't miss this for the world." Caleb fastens her seat belt in preparation for take-off at the Istanbul Airport.

"I have no doubts about this," Cain says. "We are about to save the Order."

"And what is my role in this ceremony? Am I to be the Maid of Honor?"

"You're more qualified to be Best Man," Cain jokes. His mood is buoyant now that he's solved the ancient puzzle.

"Are you ready for married life?" Caleb asks.

"That's hardly the point."

"You've never met the young woman—Rebecca, isn't it? Michael's daughter? It seems odd to marry someone you don't know, but what would I know?"

"Rebecca and I haven't met face-to-face, but I've been inside her head… and grown to love her."

"Cain, please—let me be candid. You don't know anything about love."

Cain winces, as if slapped in the face.

Caleb softens the blow. "What I mean is, you have no *experience* in love."

"I loved my grandmother!" Cain says defiantly.

"You're not marrying your grandmother, Cain."

"I do love Rebecca," Cain reaffirms. "I know that feelings don't come easily for me. But with her, I feel…"

He can't put it into words.

"It's been very lonely at the gompa without Eve," he finally says. His buoyant mood is deflated. He looks suddenly younger than his eighteen years. "It will be good to have someone there, someone I love."

"How can you be sure Rebecca will be there? Maybe she has sided with your mother."

Cain looks sternly at Caleb. "She would never disappoint her father."

✦ ✦ ✦

Six athletic men with stubble for hair exit the helicopter with military precision. Their civilian street clothes look out of place as they pack into two SUVs outside the village of Donore. The vehicles take the men to Drogheda where a small Inn has been rented under a pseudonym. The Inn is just five miles from the Newgrange megalith.

Captain Butler, at twenty-eight a highly-skilled commando, calls the men to his small room. He is the only man without an ale in his hand. He lays out the strategic plan.

"Number one," he says, "on the grounds we will be security agents. On Friday our job is to keep out anyone who is not invited. Everyone will be given a list with photos. No one else is allowed on the grounds. Number two, use small arms only if all other methods of eliminating a security risk fail. Finally, number three, if you see this woman—," he hands out photographs of Rebecca, "—immediately take custody of her and escort her to safety until you receive further instructions. If she is accompanied by anyone else, consider them extremely hostile."

Buster, the youngest mercenary, asks, "What if she resists?"

Captain Butler stares at the young man. "She won't. Her name's Rebecca, by the way. And she's the bride."

Buster shakes his head. "Man, I didn't sign up to do weddings."

"Suck it up, soldier," the Captain replies. "No one ever got killed guarding a wedding. Tomorrow we inspect the property as tourists at 0800. Concealed weapons only. Dismissed."

✦ ✦ ✦

While the others munch on pizza in the commissary, Gideon pulls Wonderboy back into Camelot.

"I have another job for you," he says. "No one else needs to know about this. It's personal."

"Well, there's no turning back now."

"These Blackwatch people—I don't like them at all."

"We're in agreement there."

"Here's what I need you to do."

Gideon pulls out a piece of paper with some technical notes written on it, notes provided by Randall Turner, and hands the paper to Wonderboy.

✦ ✦ ✦

Cain is amazed that Caleb can go to sleep within minutes. Maybe that's how she keeps her battery recharged.

He adjusts the wimpy pillow beneath his head but can't get comfortable. His brain is dizzy with possibilities for the future— the Order's mission, his life with Rebecca...

Rebecca...

Once, on the grid, he had glimpsed her face. He tries to see it again now, hoping to feel close to her.

Rebecca...

Suddenly he can see the undulating grid stretched out before him, nearly transparent but glowing. And he can hear a voice—Rebecca's.

I'm here.

He has connected with her.

Do you know the place? he asks.

We all know.

Will you be there for me?

I wouldn't miss it. Be careful.

Her face appears. It is faint, watery, like a heat mirage. And then it is gone. Cain looks at Caleb and finds her staring back at him.

"Was she here?" Caleb asks.

"Just in my head. Or my heart."

Caleb turns away. "That's where your grandmother lives now. In my heart."

Long after dark the small jet lands on the illuminated airstrip at Edinburgh Airport in Scotland, Three men exit, stepping immediately into a black town car for the thirty minute drive to the Lothian Hills. William Sinclair's destination is Rosslyn Chapel, the small, intricately carved structure that Sinclair's ancestor had built nearly six hundred years ago, and which had become the subject of hundreds of occult and alternative history theorists. Popular imagination demands that Rosslyn is the site at which the great Knights Templar treasure is buried, and that through the Sinclair family lineage flows the blood and DNA of Jesus Christ.

William Sinclair has always laughed at these fantasies. If the conspiracy buffs knew the real secret of Rosslyn, they probably wouldn't believe it. But that's the secret he intends to take custody of tonight and take with him to Newgrange.

The vehicle stops at the front entrance of the closed chapel. The occupants immediately climb out and head toward the Chapel, wordlessly greeting two security guards with a gesture. The guards have been waiting for Sinclair's arrival. They follow the three men into the sanctity of the chapel. One of them pushes a squeaky two-wheeler that annoys Sinclair. On the two-wheeler is a wooden crate with steel handles.

The men approach a grave marker adorned with Templar symbolism and the words WILLIAM DE St. CLAIR KNIGHT TEMPLAR. For a moment William Sinclair respectfully studies the sarcophagus. The guards suspect that he may be reflecting on the ancient ties that bind him to the man in this grave.

Suddenly Sinclair points to an odd-shaped stone that lies next to the marker. Its size and shape suggest that it may be a kneeling stone for visitors who wish to pray for the departed, though it's a bit thick for that.

The guards help Sinclair's two companions lift the heavy Jacob's Stone into the crate. This is what Sinclair had been reflecting on a moment earlier—how his ancestor William St. Clair had located this holy stone at great expense and ordered it placed beside his grave so that even in death he could envision the durable ladder between his family and God. Here the stone had lain for over five centuries, hidden in plain sight—a simple rock that makes all the kings and queens of the British Isles counterfeit but continues to be the Stone of Destiny.

Soon it will be the foundation stone of a renewed alliance.

Chapter 74

Dawn brings uncertainty. Charlotte and her fellow Knights stand in the parking lot outside the austere Ambienz facility—their castle. Fog transforms the surrounding terrain into a mystical, Arthurian landscape as the Knights argue, as Knights always do.

"They attacked me and mine," Darcy says, her face flushed. "So don't tell me I don't have a stake in this!"

"I'm just saying that barging right into Newgrange is not a strategic move," Gideon explains. "If we find them there, we have no element of surprise. We may be vastly outnumbered. I can't guarantee anyone's safety if we do this."

"I'm tired of being on the defensive," Darcy impulsively responds. "For the first time we know where they may be. If you're afraid, so be it. Stay here. But I'm going. It's time to put an end to this. If we don't, it will just get worse for all of us."

Gideon searches the faces of the others for allies but finds none.

"I'm with Darcy," Jeremy says, his confidence soaring since vanquishing the mercenaries single-handedly inside Ambienz. Then, a little less brashly he adds, "Maybe they won't even show up."

"If they don't show up by the winter solstice on Friday, we're all home free," Thompson says. "Like Darcy says, it's time to put an end to it one way or another. And it's time for my wife to see that the old man she's married to still has some fight left in him."

As Miriam turns to Gideon, her expression suggests that she knows this mission is foolhardy, but she just can't let the marriage take place, so she's with Darcy. Gideon seems to understand her completely.

Rebecca says, "My father turned on me, that's clear. And Greg obviously misled me. You guys kept me safe, so I'm in."

"Don't think you can reason with them," Gideon warns.

"Like I said, I'm in," Rebecca repeats sternly.

Always suspicious, Darcy has been wondering if Rebecca might leak information to her father. It seems like an enormous risk, having the young woman in their group. But aside from her kinship, she's given them no reason to mistrust her.

Charlotte is the last to speak. "I've been dreaming of a face-to-face show-down for a long time. It's why I have hundreds of hours on the shooting range—for a moment like this. Anyway, we're Knights of the Round Table, aren't we? We're supposed to go questing—to go into battle against impossible odds."

"This is suicide, I hope you all realize that" he says. "Sometimes Knights die. But since there's no holding you back, let's get on with it. We've got three Sicarii Knights on our side, so that should about even the odds against a small army. How about our missing members?"

"Herb is staying back to recover," Charlotte explains, "and Wonderboy needs to keep the machines of God crunching numbers. I suggest Mason should stay to help. And to guard the castle, just in case."

"All right, the rest of us are going as tourists. We're going to have a look around so we know what we're getting into. That's the plan."

"Our goal is to keep the ceremony on Friday from occurring, because then we win," Charlotte says.

Wonderboy steps out of the facility and into the parking lot. "Gideon, I'd like to have a private word with you and the Walkers."

Gideon nods and Wonderboy shepherds them back inside.

In Camelot, Wonderboy looks around nervously. He can't seem to make eye contact with either Gideon, Thompson, Miriam or Charlotte, so he winds up talking to their chests.

"You asked us in here," Gideon says. "What's going on?"

"I wasn't going to share this with you before you left this morning, but then, knowing how dangerous it may be at Newgrange... well, I thought it best to..."

"Just say whatever it is," Charlotte says, exasperated. "It's not like we're not used to dealing with problems."

"Well, not a problem, exactly. Just some background information I thought you should know."

"About—?" Thompson prompts him.

Wonderboy turns to Charlotte. "You've had a hard time forgiving your father for his indiscretion many years ago, that little sortie with a fourteen-year-old girl named Mandy. We've just learned from the data that her parents were of the Sicarii bloodline... a pure strain."

"How is that possible?" Charlotte is startled. "That's too much of a coincidence. My father didn't get involved with the Order until after he married my mother."

"Apparently your father was adopted by the Walker family as an infant. Maybe they were paid to rear him. From the data, it seems clear that Thompson's birth parents, like Mandy's, were also part of the Order's bloodline. Anyway, the adoptive parents were Catholic, so that's how they raised Thompson. The Order didn't mind—remember, they counted a Pope as one of the family. It seems that engineering the bloodline, no matter what it takes, is common practice for the Order."

Thompson is trembling. It's unbearable living through this again.

"I had no idea I was part of the bloodline," Thompson explains, looking at Charlotte, "until Mandy's father came to confession one day and told me everything. For two months I refused to believe it, but he produced records to show who I really was. I asked him what he wanted from me, and he said that it was my duty to father a child with his daughter—for the good of the entire family, he said."

He sniffs back tears.

Miriam caresses his hand tenderly, a gesture Charlotte had never seen her make.

"Time was short," Thompson continues, "because Mandy had a degenerative disease, they said, that would soon make her unable to bear children. It had to be now, even though she was just fourteen. She would probably never see eighteen. So I asked to meet her. Such a sweet girl. We met seven times, got to know each other. She was wise beyond her years and... and..."

He struggles to continue. Miriam puts her arm around him, rubs his back. "Go ahead, Tommy... It's all right."

Thompson breathes deeply and goes on. "I fell in love with her. Deeply in love. It was wrong, I know, but *I did what they wanted*. A few times—just to make sure she was pregnant. That's what I told myself. Afterwards I couldn't deal with what I had done. They moved away before the child, a boy, was born. I lost track of them—didn't want to face what I had done. But finally I had to confess to my church, and they defrocked me."

He slumps into his chair, depleted.

Charlotte turns to Wonderboy. "You must know what became of my father's son."

Wonderboy nods and turns his gaze to Gideon.

Charlotte cries out, "You're kidding, right?"

Wonderboy slowly shakes his head. The man Charlotte loves is her half-brother.

Stoic by training, Gideon fails to hold back his emotions. He and Thompson look at each other. All this time—for five years—they have known each other, gone through hell together, and yet...

"So many wasted years," is all Thompson can say.

Chapter 75

Charlotte deeply wishes that the winter solstice will come and go without incident, without the ceremony that would empower the Sons of Zadok and possibly alter the course of future history.

Gideon, in his old man costume, drives a tan Renault with Charlotte as the only passenger. He follows Darcy who drives a silver SUV containing Thompson and Miriam, who is outfitted in a floppy hat and cheap tourist clothes. Charlotte had tried to convince her father to stay at Ambienz, but he had insisted on accompanying his wife to the "showdown at the O.K. Corral," as he had put it. Bringing up the rear, Jeremy drives an old blue Ford with Rebecca in the passenger seat. Everyone carries concealed small arms, even Thompson and Rebecca. Just in case.

The silence in the Renault makes Charlotte apprehensive. "At dawn, the day after tomorrow, it will be too late for the Order," Charlotte says. "But they have my son working on the puzzle. I wish I could root for him, like I used to."

"If Greg has solved it, I imagine the invitations have already gone out for Friday's event," Gideon replies.

"Invitations? You make it sound like a..."

"A wedding? It is, remember? Representatives from families around the world will want to be there—to witness the event for themselves."

"You think there'll be a rehearsal?" She laughs nervously.

"I'm sure of it. There are only three possibilities for this event to fail. Number one, maybe Greg hasn't figured out the place."

"And number two?"

"Well, if we're right, they don't yet have a bride."

"Rebecca."

"It must be."

"So what then? We kidnap her so they can't have their damn wedding?"

Gideon places his hand on the Glock that rests near his thigh and glances at Charlotte.

Charlotte gasps. "Oh dear God. We can't kill her! She's like—*almost* like family."

"Then there is possibility number three. We target Greg."

Charlotte looks out the side window, unable to fathom killing her own son. With a voice barely inaudible, she says, "Maybe Greg will fail and everything will be all right."

Gideon tries to change the subject. "It's quite a thing for me, you know, having family. A sister and a father, all in one day. I'm still trying to get used to the idea."

Charlotte turns back to him. "And me—a *brother*. To be honest, that's not the kind of relationship I had been dreaming about."

"Me neither."

They both laugh timidly and then Charlotte takes Gideon's hand. "I love you, *Charles*," she says, making him wince at his given name. "We're blood now. Inseparable. Maybe that's what was drawing me to you."

He squeezes her hand. "I can promise you one thing. Nobody's gonna mess with my family—now that I've got one."

There is a long silence.

Finally Charlotte asks, "Do you think Rebecca's on our side or theirs?"

He has decided, but for Charlotte's sake he shrugs. "Maybe it won't matter. If it does, though, she'll make it crystal clear. If she disappoints us, I assume you choose option two?"

Charlotte doesn't respond. Answering out loud makes it seem too much like premeditation.

She picks up a call from Darcy in the lead car.

"I just talked to my cousin who drives a shuttle from the car park at the Visitors Center," Darcy says. "She said all tourist access to Newgrange has been cancelled. Someone bought out the whole thing for a private party. They're handing out cash to tours."

The suspense is over. The wedding is on.

"We were going to hop the tour bus from the Visitors Center. What now?"

"Well, they don't allow direct public access by road," Darcy explains, "but I say what the hell? Let's drive up and look around. Unless you're afraid of trespassing."

She laughs.

"At least there won't be any tourists to worry about."

✦ ✦ ✦

Cain and Caleb are driven past two nearby passage tombs. Combined with Newgrange, the three round megaliths form a geometric pattern similar to the three spirals Cain had discovered in the ancient Enoch scroll—the same motif that had been etched into a pendant worn by his grandmother.

As they finally pull onto the grounds of Newgrange, Cain audibly gasps upon seeing the magnificent walls of white crystal, and the many stones decorated with three spirals and a strange lozenge design that looks like snakeskin, despite the fact that Ireland has no snakes.

Cain cannot fathom how the symbols of coiled snakes came to be the dominating motif on Newgrange—he does not know about the black snakes of the Yezidi, and that the Watchers had migrated to Ireland—but the evidence of the symbol seems clear to him.

This is Enoch's house of crystal.

Cain and Caleb are escorted by a Blackwatch mercenary down a narrow sixty-foot passage into a small chamber in the Newgrange tumulus. The ground-plan of the chamber is cruciform. The chamber sits at the intersection of the head and arms of a cross formed by three recesses and the elongated entrance passage. In the chamber, several more mercs are helping Michael lift the lid off a crate containing a large rock.

"Jacob's Stone," Cain says.

"The marriage wouldn't be sanctified without the authentic stone. Nor would the anointing."

The word *anointing* surprises Cain. "What anointing is that?"

"All in good time. On Friday morning at dawn, the winter solstice of 2012, you will reunite the fragmented families by marrying my daughter, Rebecca."

Another mercenary races down the passage toward Michael. "Some tourists have arrived by car. Looks like about seven, some of 'em old."

Caleb shakes her head. To her, these mercs are just hired robots.

Michael replies, "We've paid a half-million dollars for exclusive use. Probably Americans, they never follow the rules. Alec, just get rid of them. You've got some cash on you—bribe them if you have to."

Alec marches back to the entrance of the tumulus.

Greg stands about ten feet from the great stone. From this distance it looks nothing like the dark stone in the Order's Inner Chamber. Perhaps that was just an adornment to identify the seat of Michael.

He moves forward for a closer look at the legendary rock, but as he closes the gap he starts to hear voices, many voices, some of them faint and some distinct. He can hear his mother talking—no, thinking. She is worried. And Rebecca is communicating, too. He wants to speak to them, but he's afraid of revealing too much.

And then a flood of voices pours over him, sending him reeling against the wall. Even Michael is staggered by the cacophony. Like a mighty chorus, the voices rise and fall, overlap, call out and whisper. It is too much. Cain steps back. turning to Michael for an answer.

"We had thought the Stone might amplify the power of the temple," Michael says. "We don't know how or why. Probably some interaction with the minerals

of the stone, the quartz crystals in the walls, acting together like a radio receiver…
and your magnetic personality, Cain."

Michael laughs. He's in a good mood now that the wedding is assured and
the stone has shown its ability to power the grid.

"I think the stone will not have the same effect outside this chamber. Now, if
we can just keep the racket down during the ceremony on Friday."

Michael's only worry now is that Charlotte and her companions might show
up without Rebecca. He turns to Caleb and the mercs. "Let's check those tourists.
Cain, stay in here until we know it's safe."

Randall Turner wryly smiles as he sits down at the control board, a replica of the
one in Amman. Glancing back at the on-call drone pilot and the lone sentry, freshly tasered and now restrained by plastic ties and gags, he realizes that he enjoys
this kind of work—particularly the payback part.

Searching the monitor, he finds an authorization for loading two missiles
onto the last drone possessed by Blackwatch. Gideon's hacker has come through
with a false directive for the ground crew to drill on weaponizing procedures.
Randall hopes that other events on the ground will prevent Wyatt and others from
paying too much attention to this seemingly benign training operation.

In five minutes or less he'll be back in the cockpit, so to speak, with immense firepower again at his fingertips.

What a rush!

The automobiles pull up into a straight drive that runs along the western side of Newgrange. The sun has finally broken through the clouds, drying out the light mist and
making the white quartz walls of Newgrange glow eerily in the moist atmosphere.

Yes, this 5,000-year-old megalith could have been what Enoch wrote about,
Charlotte thinks as she climbs out of the Renault.

Two men rush toward her group. Their short hair and muscular builds give
away the fact that they are not tour guides. One of them is peeking at a photograph.

"Sorry, you can't drive onto the grounds. You'll have to go back to the Visitor's Center and get a ticket for the tour bus."

"They've all been cancelled for the next few days," Charlotte explains, "and
we've come a long way to see this. It's our last day here. Can you just give us a
few minutes?"

The man with the photograph pauses, then speaks. "Okay, just a few minutes, and then you'll have to go."

Rebecca joins Charlotte, Jeremy, and Miriam in a little group that steps toward the path leading to the entrance.

"Sweetheart," Gideon calls out to Charlotte as he holds back Thompson. "I'm going to stay here with your grandfather. He's not feeling well."

Thompson scowls at being called his daughter's grandfather, but roots himself next to his newfound son—adequate consolation for Gideon's ribbing.

Charlotte notices that one of the mercenaries stands watch over Gideon while the other one follows the foursome toward the megalith. It seems they're already ensnared. After about ten paces, she sees four other mercenaries and a woman step out of the dark entrance. They are followed by a tall, silver-haired man.

Charlotte recognizes Caleb and William Sinclair.

The four mercs fan out to flank them, joined by three more.

"Hello, Ms. Ansari," William says.

"William Sinclair, isn't it? We haven't officially met." Charlotte says. "We just came to deliver Rebecca. What's a wedding without a bride?"

✦ ✦ ✦

Captain Kerrigan and his four passengers show identification at the Blackwatch security checkpoint in Virginia. He knows the layout of the compound. He knows where the two equipment and munitions warehouses are located about a half-mile east down the main road and then a quarter-mile north. He intends to turn south instead for about a half-mile to the headquarters building. It's the middle of the night, but he's sure Wyatt will still be in his office. There is so much going on this evening.

The cool night air has a strong pine scent that perks him up. He loves nature. Has always loved this scenic drive through the forest. In the past he has always felt pride in his employer, his unit, and his personal skills. But tonight he feels something else—a kind of emptiness. Resentment.

It's boiling inside him. Not anger, exactly, but *hurt*. That's what's gnawing at him. He's been hurt by the betrayal of his leader. The chicken-shit lack of loyalty. Where was that old military *no one left behind* spirit? He guesses this is what happens when you go for the money instead of the cause.

Suddenly he's at the headquarters building. As expected, lights are on. The Captain parks and leaves the car running as he and his passengers get out. It's time to confront the boss.

✦ ✦ ✦

"Thank you for bringing her," Sinclair says. "For that courtesy, we will let you leave safely. Rebecca, let me show you inside." He holds out his hand.

Rebecca turns to Charlotte. "Sorry," she says, starting to walk toward her father's outstretched hands.

It is this in-your-face show of familial affection that rankles Charlotte. She angrily shouts out, "Were you spying on us the entire time—working for your father?"

Rebecca stops and turns around. "Actually, in the beginning I only wanted to meet my future mother-in-law. But I couldn't tell you that. So my loving father used his influence at CCN to get me a meeting with you. He could never turn me down. All that stuff about my guardian and my dad ignoring me was a lie—unfortunately necessary at the time. I love my father. And I can honestly say I've enjoyed knowing you and the others."

Rebecca glances at Jeremy with a dismissive smile.

He does not smile back.

"With time," Rebecca says, "maybe you'll come to accept me as your daughter-in-law. My father's a man of his word—you can leave safely. We have what we want now."

Blood trumps everything.

Charlotte watches Rebecca walk slowly toward her father. She starts to reach for the pistol tucked into the back of her waistband beneath her jacket.

"I wouldn't do that," the merc behind says.

Chapter 76

Using the remote joystick, Randall deftly lifts the drone off the short runway. He is less than a minute from his targets. All he has to do now is fly around and wait for the phone call.

The drone approaches Target 1, the Blackwatch munitions depot—a large, flat-roofed warehouse. Randall maneuvers the drone east, directing it above an equipment depot that contains millions of dollars' worth of weapons and assorted tactical military equipment.

He glances at his watch. According to Gideon, it should be time for missile launch, but there's been no call.

The drone circles. The infrared belly camera gives him a straight-down look at the terrain. A vehicle with its headlights off drives up to the entrance of the munitions warehouse. Four individuals get out and remove Wyatt, who is tied to a chair. Wyatt is set down next to the building in a position to give him a wonderful view of the equipment warehouse. The vehicle drives off.

Randall's phone rings.

"Light 'em up!" the caller says.

✦ ✦ ✦

Caleb watches Rebecca approach. She knows that Sinclair will never let the others go. Once Rebecca is safely inside Newgrange, Miriam and the others will be ruthlessly cut down. Sinclair will say that Charlotte and the others drew their weapons.

She looks across the short space between her and Miriam, and can't bear to think about what comes next. Already she can see the merc in the driveway holding a gun on Thompson and Gideon. And the man behind the foursome is also holding a gun.

If she does nothing, Miriam will die.

That's all the thinking she needs to do.

✦ ✦ ✦

Not a word has been spoken, but Wyatt knows he's dead. His own goddam men! Strapped to his executive chair, he watches the SUV disappear into the darkness—a surprise. He had expected to be shot right here, firing-squad style.

What now? Eaten by bears?

He looks up at the night sky, then over at the munitions warehouse. In the quietness of the evening, a faint *buzz* draws his eyes upward again. He knows that sound—the distinctive audio signature of a Blackwatch drone.

He glances down at the equipment building with full knowledge of what is coming. With a deafening roar, the structure suddenly explodes into a red-orange tongue of flame. Debris scatters in every direction, but none of it strikes Wyatt. Billowing black clouds soar into the sky, obliterating the stars.

Wyatt watches the destruction, aware that he is seated outside the munitions warehouse. He grits his teeth, as if that will help him endure the maelstrom to come. He imagines his body blasted into pieces, scorched and strewn about the compound. He will *evaporate*.

He can't even imagine the deafening sound at the core of such an explosion. When it comes, it turns out he hears nothing at all.

✦ ✦ ✦

In a motion quicker than lightning, Caleb draws her pistol.

She fires.

The sharp report of two gunshots draws the attention of everyone but Rebecca, who is flying backwards with two spurting wounds in her chest. All the Blackwatch soldiers instinctively aim their weapons at the assassin, but can't fire before she shoots again, striking Sinclair in the head. It's the classic assassin's pattern—two taps to the heart, one to the head—adapted for two targets.

A barrage of bullets strike Caleb, tearing her apart. As the Blackwatch mercenaries focus their firepower on the lone traitor, Gideon, Jeremy and Darcy pull their weapons and take out five of the occupied soldiers. But the others are highly skilled.

"Down!" Gideon yells to his friends, who are standing, shell-shocked, in the crossfire. Jeremy pushes Miriam and Charlotte to the ground. Darcy is struck and falls. Thompson spies a merc turning toward Gideon and puts himself in the line of fire, protecting his son but lurching backward as bullets slam into his chest. Gideon downs his father's killer with three angry shots.

Suddenly it is quiet.

In less than five seconds, it is over.

Charlotte looks up, astonished that she is still alive. Next to her, Miriam sits up, then leaps to her feet, rushing to the savaged body of Caleb. She drops to her knees next to the fallen woman.

Charlotte approaches her mother. "Mom, she was an *assassin*."

She will never forget the anguished look on Miriam's face, and the whisper, "She was my daughter. Your sister."

In a dizzying tumble of thoughts, Charlotte tries to process this confession. Like Thompson, a very young Miriam must have given birth to a purebred Sicarii, and then given her up to a carefully chosen family for rearing.

"Only a few knew, not even Caleb," Miriam says, caressing her daughter's bloody body. "It's why she was the next Eve."

Suddenly Miriam jumps to her feet, remembering…

"Thompson?" she yells.

There is no answer.

"Thompson!"

She turns toward the automobiles, searching for her husband but finding Gideon sitting on the ground next to a motionless body.

"Tommy!"

She rushes toward Gideon, but jerks to a halt as she sees Thompson lying dead, his head on his son's lap.

"Oh Tommy, such incredibly bad timing," she says, covering her grief-stricken face with her hands.

"Darcy's alive!" Jeremy shouts. "We should clear the inside! There may be others."

There is always work to do

"Let's do it," Charlotte calls out, using this new mission and her fury to blunt her own grief. She motions for Jeremy to join her. With weapons drawn, the two head for the passageway but stop as a slender figure appears at the entrance.

"Greg!" Charlotte raises her pistol.

Her finger, responding to her agony, begins to squeeze the trigger. She must end this now! She must…

"Mom, I want to get out of here."

Greg's voice startles her. It's been five years, but she can recall every nuance of it. So familiar.

"Take me away—please. I want to go home." He stands there, pathetic, beaten, and pleading.

Impossible. This man is a killer. He had ordered her assassination.

But still… he's her son.

"Your grandfather's dead, Greg. Your grandmother is alone now, except for you and me. This is all your doing."

"Mom, there are more soldiers coming. Help me, please. I can't go back, not now. Take me away."

She wonders if he's lying, but his voice, the voice of her little boy, breaks her heart, melts reason away.

She makes a snap decision. Motioning to Greg, she starts to run toward the Renault.

Jeremy watches, confused. Should he shoot? Why is Charlotte leading him away?

By the time Gideon and Miriam look up, Charlotte has pulled Greg into the car. She turns the key that Gideon left in the ignition to facilitate an escape and wheels across the grassy slope in front of the megalith.

She'll take her son back to Ambienz, Charlotte decides. They'll figure things out there. He'll confess his sins to God and be forgiven, because God is All-Merciful. Someday she and Greg and Miriam will be a family. They are the only ones left. Her racing thoughts carry her a mile down the road.

"You've ruined everything again," Greg says.

His voice is cold, not at all the fragile child's voice that had just begged for help.

Charlotte turns. Greg is pointing a gun at her.

"What are you doing?" she asks. "We'll be safe soon."

"Your friends would have killed me, you know, like you killed Rebecca."

"What are you talking about, Sweetheart? Caleb killed your girlfriend."

"You never wanted me to have any friends."

"Greg, Honey, with your Asperger's—you just weren't very good around friends. They made fun of you. I didn't want you to be hurt."

For just a moment a crack appears in his grim expression, a faint glimmer of understanding, but he quickly seals it off, the way he has always sealed off his feelings.

"I'm sorry I have to do this, mom, but you have to stop the car now."

"What are you saying?"

"STOP THE CAR NOW!" he shouts.

She flinches, slams on the brakes.

"Now get out."

She steps out of the car. Greg gets out, too, still pointing the gun. He is staring at her with cold, dark eyes. She's never seen this person before.

He pulls out a sat phone and pushes a button. "It was a total disaster," He says to the person at the other end. "Everyone's dead but me. Get over there now and clean it up. And make sure you get the stone from the chamber."

With a stiff finger he ferociously stabs the END CALL button.

"Are you going to kill me?" his mother asks. She knows he is capable.

He stares at her, his eyes fierce and unblinking.

"Are you going to kill your own mother?"

He continues to stare. "And then, I suppose you'll kill your grandmother."

Like a passing shadow, a great sadness seems to overtake him at the mention of Miriam. "My grandmother is the only thing that keeps you alive. Like you said, she's lost almost everything now—her position, her husband…"

"All by the hand of the Order."

Greg ignores her. "I will not take this last thing from that great woman."

A sudden realization occurs to Charlotte. She had never thought about the bond that may have been forged between her son and her mother over these past five years. Or that her son was capable of any kind of tender emotions.

"You love her," she says, astonished.

Greg forcefully shoves—an angry way of showing that yes, he has feelings, and yes, he's angry that his celebrity mother was never there for him to love.

She falls backwards and he leaps into the car. The tires spit gravel at her as Greg speeds away.

Just as Charlotte had once been abandoned by her father in India, she has now been dumped at the side of a dusty road by her son. It must run in the family.

Charlotte was wrong about more than her son's plea for help. She was wrong in believing, even for a moment, that she, Greg and Miriam were the last of their family. As the Renault disappears over the crest of a hill, she remembers that they are not alone.

They have family all over the world.

It's a terrifying thought.

Chapter 77

In a small cemetery where Darcy's ancestors are buried, beneath the broad branches of an old oak, the fresh graves of Caleb and Thompson lie side by side with one vacant gravesite between them. That one is reserved for Miriam. Charlotte has purchased a plot on the other side of Thompson, her way of showing a daughter's forgiveness. The gravestones are still being carved.

No one else has come to the quiet ceremony—just Mason, Darcy, whose arm is in a sling, Jeremy, Charlotte, Gideon, Miriam, and Wonderboy.

Heavy gray clouds boil ominously in the sky, threatening rain, or, with the sudden drop in temperature, snow. Charlotte hunches up the collar of her wool jacket against the stinging breeze, continuing to stare at the family plots. She is still wrestling with the thought of reserving a plot for Greg, if only to show her motherly desire to reunite the immediate family.

Probably a waste of time. Her son will never know about it.

Reunite.

Such a strong, emotionally-charged word. She wonders if the families—the Sons of Zadok—will find another means to reunite, to rally around their mission or an emerging leader. If they do, she hopes it's long after she's dead and buried in this Irish plot at her feet, because she's exhausted from the battle.

Miriam throws a flower on Thompson's grave.

Charlotte wants to put a comforting arm around her mother, but her arm won't cooperate. It's too soon. This is the mother who had abandoned seven-year-old Charlotte without even a farewell note. The mother who had lured her son away and corrupted him with attention, power and glory. The mother who had approved the deaths of her own husband and daughter to further the godless mission of the Order.

Charlotte remembers Greg emerging from the passage at Newgrange. And she remembers her burning urge, after the murder of Thompson, to put a bullet into his brain.

She had been ready to kill her son.

To end his reign of evil.

But then he had spoken to her. If he had not, what would she have done? Killed him, probably. So is she really that much different from her mother?

A hand taps Charlotte's shoulder, surprising her.

"I have something I should tell you," Wonderboy says, staring at the brown grass. "Just you and Gideon and your mother. The others have gone back to their car."

Miriam and Gideon huddle around Wonderboy, partially to keep out the blustering wind.

"I've checked and re-checked the data," Wonderboy says, "and I'm confident in the results, startling as they are. It concerns another member of the family."

As he speaks, the small group at first registers interest, then astonishment, and suddenly genuine horror.

"My God!" Miriam exclaims. "This is the one thing, other than the marriage, that could reunite the families."

Charlotte sways under the force of the revelation.

She says, hopefully, "It took a hacker genius and a quantum computer to figure this out. Maybe they don't know."

As the wind kicks up, the others begin to nod the way people do when they desperately want to believe a dream.

Or when they are humoring the dreamer.

Epilogue

In an office within the Sicarii CIA, Chen stares at the summary sheet of his report. Though he's alone at this moment, he smirks, reveling at his own genius. As a one-time Sentient loyalist, he had often followed the IRCs to find interesting exploits to join. That was in the old days. Until several weeks ago he's had little time to do this.

After his clever attempt to hack the Ambienz system had been expertly rebuffed with streams of meaningless data—a fact he had not detected for a while, to his chagrin—he had delved back into that anonymous world of amateurs and found Wonderboy's invitation.

Posing as a Sentient hacker, he had followed instructions for uploading some relevant data he had quickly found on the Internet, along with an ingenious Trojan he had invented months ago, one that was awaiting a worthy pilot project.

The Trojan had passed with flying colors, remaining undetected by the master himself, Wonderboy. In the old days, Chen could crow online about his magnificent achievement, but not today. No one will ever know about it. Still, that mischievous bit of code had allowed him to download Wonderboy's summary of a cache of genealogical records. From this summary Chen had learned of the direct descendants of Cain—Greg Ansari—from the great Zadok all the way through Cain's Persian-Jewish father, Mahid Ansari. Isolating this single unsullied bloodline from the millions of genealogies and miscellaneous historical records had been a monumental achievement. Showing the highlights of the bloodlines, and their final convergence on a single point, the summary seems indisputable.

Chen had immediately reported the results to Michael, the man who had recruited him into the Order and had considered Chen his most trusted confidante. Michael had seemed genuinely humbled by the report's revelation and had asked Chen to download the supporting data. Michael would not live to see the report confirmed, unfortunately, because the last of the data had been received after Michael's death.

Spot checking important data convergences with the summary had convinced Chen that Wonderboy's deep analysis—a tremendous feat that could have been achieved in such a short time only through virtuoso programming aided by quantum computers—had been accurate.

Chen had craved that technology—still does—and had asked Michael about it. Instead of buying some computers, Michael had decided to buy the entire company and control the miraculous technology. It was Michael's way of doing things. But it didn't work out.

Before he had left his French villa for Ireland, Michael had sent Chen a signed copy of a revised Last Will and Testament. He had said it was an indication of his commitment to the continuity of the Order, no matter what might happen to him, and should only be revealed upon his death. As a widower, Michael had left his entire estate, including all his corporate holdings, to Rebecca, and if she should die, to Greg Ansari—the Divine Light, the first true high priest in thousands of years, and Rebecca's future husband.

In studying the data, it had not escaped Chen's notice that a vividly drawn bloodline had emerged from Zadok to families in the Far East. There were sons of Zadok in China, Japan, Korea, and maybe other countries. One of these lines stretched all the way to Chen's father, which means that Chen was not just grafted onto the organization, but had always been part of the bloodline.

Was that why Chen was recruited? How much had Michael known from the old records before he was killed? Much, it would seem—but all of it without empirical proof, until now.

The full, encrypted genealogical report is now ready for Chen to distribute through secure channels to the patriarchs of the far-flung families. It will be up to them to communicate the significance of the anointing to their own family networks, which include many powerful members who are still unfamiliar with their family connections and God-given mission. In the absence of the much-anticipated marriage, this could be the powerful force that finally reunites, even expands, the families into the global force that Solomon in his wisdom had defined.

With a sense of satisfaction, Chen leaves the office for the momentous anointing ritual.

Thirty minutes later, standing in the Great Chamber amidst many others to whom the secret location of the gompa had been entrusted, he gazes up the spiral stairway to the Ark of the Covenant. Even though it is only a replica, the sight of it always thrills him. The remaining eleven members of the Council of Twelve stand beneath it, gathered around Jacob's Stone.

On the far eastern side of the platform stands a barefoot young man that

Chen identifies as Cain. Over Cain's blue priestly robe and linen sash has been placed an ornate vest, a replica of the richly embroidered high priest's ephod into which an engraved onyx gemstone has been embedded into each shoulder. And over the front of the ephod has been placed a breastplate containing twelve gems, each inscribed with the name of one of the twelve tribes of Israel. Cain's head is adorned with a broad, flat-topped turban bearing a small gold plate with the words *Holiness unto YHWH*, the unmentionable name of God.

Sariel approaches Cain and hands him the genuine rod of Aaron, the sacred staff of the first high priest, the brother of Moses. He gently guides Cain towards Jacob's Stone—the Stone of Destiny. As Cain steps onto the great stone and turns to face the Council and the audience below, a faint shriek fills the chamber.

It grows louder

The shriek echoes throughout the chamber.

Chen wonders if there is some kind of vibrational conflict between the gems on Cain's priestly vestments and the minerals in the rock. But then he remembers the legend of the Stone of Destiny, which was said to shriek with joy when the feet of the man of destiny, the rightful king—in this case, perhaps, the true high priest—rested upon it. The reverberating sound seems to him a grand announcement, and his spirits rise.

At last Cain raises the rod of Aaron and plants it firmly onto the rock beside a bare foot.

From his position, Chen cannot see what happens next, but at this moment stories are born—stories that say when Cain smote the rock with his staff, water streamed out of it.

Back in his office, Chen wants to believe these stories. But all he knows for sure is that when he clicks the SEND button, irrefutable proof of the true high priest will be spread to all the families, a clarion call that it is time to unite.

The next great era, he's confident, is about to begin with one mouse-click.

<SEND>

About the Author

Gary Lindberg has spent his entire adult life as a screenwriter, movie director and producer, author of fiction and nonfiction, and book publisher. He is the author of four Amazon #1 bestselling novels and three books about the unknown history of Elvis Presley. He cowrote and co-produced the Paramount motion picture *That Was Then, This Is Now* starring Morgan Freeman and Emilio Estevez. Currently, he resides in the Minneapolis area. This novel is the second *Charlotte Ansarii Thriller*, a series that began with the bestselling *The Shekinah Legacy*.